The Gray Ghost
and The White Skulls

TWO CLASSIC ADVENTURES OF

by Walter B. Gibson
writing as Maxwell Grant

plus The Red Room
a radio classic by Sidney Slon

Foreword by
Everett Raymond Kinstler

with New Historical Essays by
Will Murray and Anthony Tollin

SANCTUM BOOKS

This Sanctum Books edition is an unabridged republication of the text and
illustrations of two stories from *The Shadow Magazine,* as originally published by Street & Smith Publications, Inc., N.Y.: *The Gray Ghost* from the May
1, 1936 issue, and *The White Skulls* from the November 1945 issue. "The
Red Room" was broadcast September 27, 1942 on *The Shadow* radio series.
Typographical errors have been tacitly corrected in this edition. These stories
are works of their time. Consequently, the text is reprinted intact in its original
historical form, including occasional out-of-date ethnic and cultural stereotyping.

International Standard Book Numbers:
ISBN: 0-9822033-3-0   13 digit: 978-0-9822033-3-0

First printing: January 2009

Series editor/publisher: Anthony Tollin
sanctumotr@earthlink.net

Consulting editor: Will Murray

Copy editor: Joseph Wrzos

Cover and photo restoration: Michael Piper

The editor gratefully acknowledges the assistance of Jim Vadeboncoeur, Jr.,
Everett Raymond Kinstler, Rory Feldman (ThurstonMasterMagician.com),
William V. Rauscher and Dwight Fuhro in the preparation of this volume.

Published by Sanctum Books
P.O. Box 761474, San Antonio, TX 78245-1474

Visit The Shadow at www.shadowsanctum.com..

Volume 25

CONTENTS

Two Complete Novels From The Shadow's Private Annals As told to Maxwell Grant

Thrilling Tales and Features

Cover art by George Rozen and Modest Stein

Interior illustrations by Tom Lovell and Everett Raymond Kinstler

FOREWORD by *Everett Raymond Kinstler*

Growing up in the 1930's, I was exposed to art in the pages of books and magazines—and comic strips. I would pore over the illustrations of Howard Pyle and N. C. Wyeth, the magazine reproductions by Norman Rockwell, James Montgomery Flagg, Dean Cornwell, and the comic strips by Alex Raymond *(Flash Gordon),* Hal Foster *(Tarzan* and *Prince Valiant)* and Milton Caniff *(Terry and the Pirates)*...a diversified and brilliant group of artists who inspired me. Motion pictures—serials and double features, then solely black & white—added to my desire to be an artist. The world of imagery and imagination, storytelling through art, impacted me deeply.

A New York City kid, I attended public school, played baseball and engaged in all the things kids do...but most of all I drew. Midway through my second year at the famous High School of Music and Art, I decided I was in the wrong school, as my interest in realistic drawing and illustration was being discouraged. I transferred to the High School of Industrial Art, a no-nonsense school that focused on learning the disciplines and art techniques that I felt I needed. A classmate of mine was Anthony Benedetto, who later changed his name to Tony Bennett.

Just before my sixteenth birthday, I made a decision that was to shape the rest of my life. I decided to leave school and enter the professional art world. Looking back, I realize I was consumed with the desire to make my life and living as an artist. I answered a comic book publisher's ad for "an apprentice inker" at a salary of eighteen dollars for a six-day week. Mine was a grueling routine but it provided invaluable training for an aspiring young artist. I was called upon to draw hundreds of faces, figures, animals, objects, and to create backgrounds as well. I learned how to tell a story with pictures that would capture a reader's attention.

After a year of holding down a six-day-a-week job, I began looking for freelance assignments for the pulp magazines. At the time there were over a hundred pulp magazines, dealing with subjects as diversified as Westerns and detective stories, romance, aviation, horror, and science fiction. The cover of each magazine was in vivid and often garish color.

But I hadn't left the comics behind. While illustrating for the pulps I continued to create and draw my own comic books that ranged from adventure strips to war stories. At that time I also felt the need to learn more about my craft and I enrolled in the Art Students League, a legendary NYC art school.

Everett Raymond Kinstler and his friend Tony Bennett in the artist's New York studio.

Here my life took an important new turn. I elected to spend my afternoons studying painting and drawing from life with Frank V. DuMond, a former illustrator whose students included Rockwell, Flagg, Georgia O'Keefe, and other major American artists. DuMond was both my teacher and my friend, and his influence on me was profound. The most important thing he said to me was, "I won't teach you to paint, but to observe."

To support my studies at the League, I continued to freelance, working far into the evenings, often round the clock with cigarettes and coffee to meet constant deadlines. I went to see art directors weekly in search of assignments. In 1945 I visited Street & Smith, one of the prominent publishers of pulp magazines. Among their publications were *The Shadow* and *Doc Savage,* both prominent and successful magazines. At one time the superb actor Orson Welles played The Shadow in the popular radio series. His announcer, Ken Roberts, became a friend of mine forty years later!

I was a dedicated listener of the weekly radio drama *The Shadow*... and later a reader of the pulp magazine named for the hawk-nosed man of mystery. The image and personality of The Shadow stimulated my imagination and appealed to my visual senses as an artist. I wish I'd had other opportunities to depict this iconic figure in American popular culture.

The Street & Smith art director assigned me a Shadow story, *The White Skulls,* to illustrate. The year was 1945, I was eighteen years old, and the country was still at war. Almost all the illustrators were in the service, including Tom Lovell, who was in the U.S. Marine Corps. Tom had spent many years illustrating *The Shadow,* and had progressed to illustrating stories for many leading magazines.

I had enormous admiration for Lovell, and he was a major influence on my early illustrations. Tom's Shadow illustrations were superb... a masterful contrast of black & white, complemented with good draftsmanship, and always with simplicity and a sense of drama. Decades later, Tom became a good friend, and I often visited him in his handsome Santa Fe home. He had deservedly become a prominent painter recreating the story of the American West. His early illustrations had given him the background and skills that made him the fine artist he was. During one of our visits, Tom referred to a volume on his bookshelf titled *The Shadow Scrapbook.* The edition reproduced many of his wonderful dry brush and ink illustrations, and included a page on me that showed my double-page illustration for *The White Skulls.* Tom was extremely complimentary about my work. I just nodded in agreement and replied, "They *were* pretty good, weren't they?"

Kinstler's portrait of artist Tom Lovell

My reaction surprised him and he repeated his praise: "No, I mean they were wonderfully composed and very dynamic." I eventually confessed to him that the only reason they were so good was that I had "swiped my illustration" from a couple of Tom's 1930s Shadow drawings to study his approach and make certain that I had the character right. All the points that he found noteworthy in my drawings were because of Tom Lovell, not Everett Kinstler.

In 1984, The Players, a legendary theatrical club in NYC, honored Walter Gibson, the writer of the Shadow novels. The club, of which I am a member, had many of my oil portraits of actors on their walls.

I was introduced to Mr. Gibson and told him that as a young man I had illustrated one of his Shadow stories. He replied right away, "Yes, it was *The White Skulls*...November 1945." He had remembered specifically forty years later!

Everett Raymond Kinstler is widely recognized as one of the world's foremost portrait artists, and has painted more than 1500 well-known personalities. "The only high school dropout with a life membership in the Yale Club" has painted six U.S. Presidents from life, including the official White House portraits of Presidents Gerald Ford and Ronald Reagan. His pulp, comic book art and paperback illustrations are chronicled in Everett Raymond Kinstler: The Artist's Journey Through Popular Culture 1942-63 *by Jim Vadeboncoeur, Jr. (Underwood Books, 2005), while his portrait art is collected in* Everett Raymond Kinstler: My Brush with History *(International Artist, 2005). More of his art can be viewed at www.everettraymondkinstler.com.*

THE GRAY GHOST

A Complete Book-length Novel from the Private Annals of
The Shadow, as told to

Maxwell Grant

CHAPTER I
THE RAIDER IN GRAY

"THEY call him the Gray Ghost, sir."

It was a solemn-faced butler who made the statement. He was facing a group of four young people, who were seated, smiling, in the mellow lamp glow that lighted an enclosed porch.

Opened windows gained a wafted breeze; the tang of the air, the distant blasts of steamship whistles, betokened that the house was near Long Island Sound.

"Yes, Mr. Gilden." Solemnly, the butler nodded to the tuxedoed young man who formed the center of the group. "The Gray Ghost is what they call him."

"The Gray Ghost," chuckled Gilden. "Come, Furbison! Don't tell me that you believe in spooks!"

"There are those who do, sir. Butlers, housemaids, chauffeurs—here on Long Island. They have seen the Gray Ghost prowling about—"

Gilden stopped the butler with a laugh. The young man turned to the other persons beside him. One was a young man his own age; the other two were girls who looked like sisters, both in their early twenties.

"Fancy it," chuckled Gilden. "We are living in the twentieth century. Here am I, Pierce Gilden; and you"—he gestured toward the other man—"Alan Reeth, both of us imbued with the realism of

the modern age. We come to the home of Martin Debrossler, a wealthy banker."

Pausing, Gilden swept his hand about to indicate the surroundings.

"We are chatting with the banker's beautiful daughters," continued Gilden, with a bow toward each of the girls. "On my right, Jane Debrossler; on my left, her sister, Louise. The scene is one of modern romance, until it is disturbed by a man who believes in ghosts and sprites. A superstitious

The most formidable foe The Shadow had ever encountered —for bullets couldn't harm him, nor water drown him! But the Arch-foe of Crime penetrated his weakness!

person who should have lived in the Middle Ages, when they had ghouls and werewolves, warlocks and witches—"

GILDEN stopped short, laughing; the others had joined in his mirth. They were looking at the butler, whose face had reddened, whose manner was apologetic. Gilden straightened his face.

"I mean you, Furbison!" he accused, in a tone of mock seriousness. "You tell us of the Gray Ghost— a fabulous, impossible creature! You expect us to believe—"

"Really, sir," interposed Furbison. "I meant no ill. I hope that I have not disturbed you—"

"Mr. Gilden is joking," interrupted Jane, the younger of the sisters. "He is merely having fun at your expense, Furbison. We know that you don't believe in ghosts."

"Quite right, miss," nodded Furbison, relieved. "I was merely repeating the remarks that had been told me."

"We understand," smiled Jane, "and it was my fault, Furbison, for starting the talk. I am sorry. You may go now, Furbison."

"Thank you, miss."

Furbison departed. Jane turned to Gilden.

"Really, Pierce," declared the girl, "this matter is becoming quite serious. All the domestics believe that there is a Gray Ghost."

"And they hold him responsible for recent robberies?"

"Yes. It may seem outlandish; nevertheless, the robberies have occurred!"

It was Louise who added the next remark.

"The robberies have been alarming," declared the elder sister. "Somehow, they don't seem to be the work of an ordinary human."

Gilden nodded.

"I know," he said. "Mrs. Tyndale's pearls, for instance."

"Yes," agreed Louise. "She is positive that none of the servants knew where they were hidden. Yet they were stolen, and there was talk that the Gray Ghost was seen that night."

"And the Trelawney paintings," added Jane. "They were spirited away in the middle of the night!"

"From an empty house," objected Gilden. "That was not remarkable."

"There were two caretakers, Pierce."

"Both were probably asleep. They didn't talk about the Gray Ghost, did they?"

"No. But others did, according to Furbison—"

Jane stopped as two elderly men appeared at the door of the sun porch. Gilden and Reeth arose. Jane smiled and spoke to the first of the two who entered.

"Hello, father," said the girl. "You know Pierce Gilden. And this is Alan Reeth."

Martin Debrossler shook hands with the young men. He introduced the man who was with him as James Pennybrook, his attorney. While they were chatting, a horn honked from the front of the house. It was Debrossler's limousine, ready to take the young people into the city. The four went from the sun porch, leaving Debrossler and Pennybrook alone.

"MORE talk about the Gray Ghost," remarked Debrossler, as he and Pennybrook heard the car pull away with its merry party. "The girls love to bait Furbison."

"Your butler believes that there is a ghost?"

"I think he does. It annoys me, Pennybrook."

"Why should it?"

"Because Furbison has more sense than an ordinary servant. He should not listen to such fables."

Pennybrook shook his head.

"I am not so sure that it is a fable," he declared. "There have been robberies. Someone has accomplished them."

"Not a ghost!"

"Of course not. But a person, perhaps, who has been mistaken for one. Your must remember, Debrossler, that they call this person the Gray Ghost."

"What does that signify?"

"That he must present a definite appearance. We must picture him always in some grayish garb. Otherwise, all the reports would not conform."

"I believe that you are right, Pennybrook."

Debrossler sat nodding. His eyes were keen; they sparkled beneath his shocky gray hair. Pennybrook watched him rather stolidly. The lawyer, owlish-faced and almost bald, formed a distinct contrast to his companion.

"You are right, Pennybrook," repeated Debrossler, "and that fact troubles me. The Gray Ghost is a cunning thief, whoever he may be. He is a menace, here on Long Island."

"Not to those who keep their business secret," objected Pennybrook, "and that certainly applies to you, Debrossler."

"Of course. Even my daughters know nothing of my business. They have callers—such as young Gilden and this chap Reeth, who is from somewhere in the Middle West—but none of the visitors know anything about my affairs."

"Unless someone comes here to talk business—"

"That never happens, Pennybrook, except on evenings when I know that Jane and Louise will not be at home. Take tonight, for instance. I knew the girls were going to the theater. I ordered the chauffeur to be here with the car. Jane and Louise have gone; the young men are with them. I shall not be disturbed when Hiram Windler calls."

Debrossler paused to consult his watch.

"Nearly half past eight," he remarked. "Windler should be here in a few minutes. Let us go upstairs to my study."

"Why not talk with him down here?" inquired Pennybrook, rising with Debrossler. "You say that we shall not be disturbed."

"I have the money in my study," stated Debrossler, in a cautious tone. "One hundred thousand dollars."

"What?" queried Pennybrook, stopping short. "You brought cash from the bank?"

"Of course! Windler is a hoarder—you know that, Pennybrook."

"But he must have a bank account."

"Apparently not. He said that he wanted cash for his properties; that he would not sign the papers unless I produced the entire sum. Go and get your briefcase, Pennybrook, and meet me in the study."

THE lawyer stopped in a hallway vestibule while Debrossler ascended gloomy stairs to the second floor. At the top, Debrossler paused in a dim side passage, while he produced a key to unlock a heavy door. He paused a moment, waiting for Pennybrook. Deciding that the lawyer had mislaid his briefcase, Debrossler unlocked the door.

The barrier swung inward; Debrossler stopped on the threshold in profound amazement. The study was lighted; that fact startled him immediately. His eyes looked toward the center of the room, instinctively seeking the desk where he had placed his money.

There Debrossler saw the sight that made him gape. Standing beyond the desk was a half-crouched figure, clad in a jerseylike suit of mottled gray. The man was masked by a hood that projected downward from a rounded cap, all a part of his odd garb. Glaring eyes shone through slits in the cloth.

In his right hand, which was covered by a glove that formed part of the sleeved jersey, the intruder held a gleaming revolver. His left hand, also covered with finger pieces of gray, was half drawn from an opened drawer of the desk.

The gun was covering the door at which Debrossler stood. The other hand was clutching a thick batch of crisp green currency. The intruder had found the money that Debrossler had brought home from the bank.

One hundred bills, each of thousand dollar denomination; money intended for payment to a visitor named Hiram Windler—such was the swag that the gray-garbed thief had gained. Martin Debrossler, horrified, was watching his own wealth as it was plucked from before his very eyes.

But it was not the vicious daring of the theft that riveted the banker; nor was it the menace of the pointed revolver. Stark fear, the facing of the incredible, was the emotion that made Debrossler incapable of action. Debrossler had rejected the impossible; yet it stood before him. He knew the identity of the man whom he saw.

The intruder answered vague descriptions that Debrossler had heard. He tallied with the mental pictures that the banker had formed of a person whose existence he had ridiculed.

The hooded, jersey-clad robber was the Gray Ghost!

CHAPTER II
CRIME COMPLETE

A SNARL came from the covered lips of the Gray Ghost. The utterance proved a fact that Debrossler had recognized; that the intruder was a human being, not a wraith.

The lighted study showed the jerseyed form too well to make it appear deceptive. Yet Debrossler was gripped by the thought that this prowler, seen in duller illumination, could easily be accepted as a ghost, if viewed by superstitious persons.

The rumors voiced by servants were thus established. That knowledge, however, did not bring comfort to Debrossler. The banker would have preferred to face a specter, rather than this human vandal who had come to pilfer cash. The revolver, clutched by a human hand, was a physical menace that made Debrossler quail.

Satisfied that his victim would make no move, the Gray Ghost bounded from behind the desk. Thrusting the sheaves of currency beneath a broad fold of his jersey, the thief sidled toward the window, all the while holding Debrossler motionless with the gun.

The window was open; that proved how the crook had entered, for Debrossler kept the window locked. Quick work with the jimmy was evidently one of the Gray Ghost's specialties.

To reach the window, the Gray Ghost was forced to pass close to Debrossler. With another snarl, the robber warned the banker to stand his ground. Debrossler would have done so, but for an interruption that both he and the Gray Ghost heard.

Footsteps from the stairway.

Debrossler took the sounds as an indication of Pennybrook's approach. He saw the Gray Ghost hesitate and glance toward the door. For a moment, the revolver no longer covered the banker. Debrossler gained sudden alarm; he foresaw death for Pennybrook should the lawyer make too rapid an entry. With that dread for another man, Debrossler spied opportunity for himself.

With a sharp cry, the banker hurled himself upon the Gray Ghost. He grabbed for the crook's gun arm.

THE Gray Ghost swung viciously with his revolver. His blow was hasty, for he was half wrestling his wrist from Debrossler's grasp. The banker stopped the blow and clutched the Gray Ghost's throat. With a hard twist, the crook flayed his left arm sidewise and delivered a forearm uppercut to Debrossler's chin. The banker did a diving sprawl across the floor.

The Gray Ghost leaped for the door and pressed the light switch. As he did, another man entered.

Gasping, looking up from the darkness, Debrossler saw a struggle just within the door.

"Hold him, Pennybrook!" cried the banker. "Hold him—"

The shout was too late. Something thudded in the darkness. There was a groan; a figure slumped to the floor. The Gray Ghost leaped away from the man whom he had slugged with the revolver. He grabbed the door and slammed it shut. Debrossler, on his feet, made another dive for the intruder.

Again, the Gray Ghost sent the banker sprawling. This time, Debrossler rolled over and thumped against the desk. His head spun; dizzily, he heard a clamber at the window. He tried to rise; but slumped.

Someone was pounding at the door. Debrossler heard an anxious voice. It was Furbison. The butler was unable to unlock the door. It had latched with the Gray Ghost's slam.

"Outside!" gasped Debrossler. "Summon aid! At once, Furbison!"

A muffled clatter told that the butler was running downstairs. Debrossler hoped that he would not encounter the Gray Ghost. Furbison, alone, would be no match for the desperado.

In the darkness, Debrossler managed to find his feet. He steadied himself against the desk; then stumbled toward the door. Halfway, he tripped over a prone, unconscious body. Sprawled, Debrossler found new trouble in rising. He crawled to the door, pulled himself up in rickety fashion and found the light switch. He clicked it.

Looking toward the floor, Debrossler saw Pennybrook. The lawyer had received a hard slug from the revolver. His bald head showed a lump as large as a bantam's egg. Debrossler approached the lawyer but found himself unable to lift Pennybrook's dead weight. While he struggled with the task, there were new footsteps outside the door. Debrossler dropped Pennybrook and opened the door.

On the threshold stood a stocky man, with swarthy, square-set countenance; behind him was Furbison, anxious-eyed. The man at the doorway flashed a badge.

"You're—you're a detective?"

Debrossler gasped the query. The stocky man nodded.

"Acting Inspector Cardona," he replied. "Driving out here from headquarters. You're Martin Debrossler?"

Debrossler nodded.

"Your butler stopped my car," explained Cardona. "Told me he thought there was murder going on inside. Who's this man?"

He indicated Pennybrook. Debrossler gave the lawyer's name and explained how he had entered the fray. Furbison brought in Pennybrook's briefcase, which had been dropped at the head of the stairs. Cardona, meanwhile, had lifted the lawyer to a couch in the corner of the room.

"He'll come around in a few minutes," decided the acting inspector. "That bump looks like a surface one. We'd better send for a physician, though."

CARDONA picked up the telephone on Debrossler's desk. The line was dead.

"Cut wires," grunted Cardona. Then, after a glance toward the window, he queried: "Who was the fellow who made the getaway? Could you identify him?"

"He was masked," replied Debrossler. "His face hooded. He was dressed in a tight-fitting suit of gray."

A gasp from Furbison: "The Gray Ghost!"

Cardona swung about and eyed the butler. Slowly, he began to nod.

"I've heard those rumors," announced Cardona. "It's the Gray Ghost, all right. But he's no ghost."

There was a groan from the couch. Pennybrook was rising, rubbing his sore head. The lawyer stared at Debrossler; then questioned weakly:

"The money?"

"Gone," replied Debrossler. "The Gray Ghost stole it."

Then, rousing himself to a pitch of excitement, the banker turned to Cardona.

"Look!" Debrossler pointed to the desk. "There is the drawer he rifled! The Gray Ghost ripped it open, lock and all! He seized my money! We must overtake him!"

For the first time, Cardona realized that a robbery had been completed. Swinging to Furbison, he ordered:

"Get over to the next house. Call the local precinct. Tell them to put the patrol cars on the hunt. Describe the Gray Ghost."

Furbison scurried away. Cardona put another question to Debrossler:

"How much did the Gray Ghost get?"

"One hundred thousand dollars," answered the banker. "All in currency."

Cardona stared. He had supposed that the crook had netted nothing more than spare cash.

"One hundred thousand dollars," repeated Debrossler, grimly, "and only one man knew that I had the money here. Find him, Inspector, and you will have a clue. Perhaps he is even working with the crook."

"Who is he?"

"A man who lives only a mile from here. He had business with me. He insisted that I bring one hundred thousand dollars here, to my home."

"What is his name?"

Cardona showed impatience. Debrossler nodded willingly.

"The man," declared the banker, "is Hiram Windler. He is—"

Debrossler stopped. Cardona had raised an interrupting hand.

"Tell me," demanded the acting inspector. "What time was Windler due here?"

"At half past eight," replied Debrossler. "That is why I came up here to the study. Why do you ask?"

"Because," returned Cardona, "I was on my way to Windler's when your butler stopped me. It was on account of Windler that I came to Long Island."

"Windler summoned you?"

"No. Unfortunately, he was unable to do so."

Debrossler stared, puzzled; so did Pennybrook, half slumped upon the couch.

"Windler could not summon you?" queried Debrossler. "What do you mean by that, Inspector?"

"I mean," replied Cardona, solemnly, "that Hiram Windler is dead."

Then, as the listeners stared in total silence, the acting inspector added:

"He was murdered at eight o'clock tonight."

CHAPTER III
THE LAW'S TRAIL

IT was ten o'clock when a coupé pulled up in front of a squatty house near Long Island Sound. A tall driver alighted; he was immediately challenged by a uniformed policeman, who put the query:

"What do you want here, sir?"

"My name is Lamont Cranston," spoke the arrival, in a leisurely tone. "I have come to see Police Commissioner Weston. I am a friend of the commissioner's; I observed his car in the driveway."

The policeman hesitated; then decided to admit the visitor. Cranston was attired in evening clothes. He looked like a friend of the fashionable commissioner.

Inside the house, the tall arrival ran into Acting Inspector Cardona. The stocky man gave immediate greeting. Lamont Cranston was known to Joe Cardona.

Dim hall light showed a slight smile upon the hawklike features of the arrival. Cranston followed Cardona to a parlor, where he was greeted by a man of military appearance: Commissioner Ralph Weston. The commissioner tugged at the tips of his pointed mustache.

"How did you happen to come here, Cranston?"

"I was driving out on Long Island," replied the visitor, quietly. "Coming into the city, I took this route through Holmwood. I saw your car; I chanced to remember that Holmwood is within the New York City limits."

"So you scented crime. You were right, Cranston. There was murder here tonight. The owner of this house was slain. His name was Hiram Windler."

"And the murderer?"

"Appears to have been a rogue who styles himself the Gray Ghost. Be seated, Cranston, and you can listen to the summary which we are just beginning."

To Commissioner Weston, Lamont Cranston was simply a friend who had shown some interest in the solution of criminal cases. Actually, this personage who posed as Cranston was The Shadow. He was a master sleuth who moved by night, bringing disaster to men of crime.

TALK of the Gray Ghost had brought The Shadow to Long Island. But he had traveled farther than Holmwood, in his quest for signs of the phantom crook. Passing through Holmwood on his return journey, The Shadow had stopped in a store. He had heard discussion of Windler's murder, for the news had already spread.

These were matters that The Shadow did not mention to his friend the commissioner.

Weston had motioned to Cardona. The acting inspector brought two persons into the room. Both appeared to be servants. One was a Chinese cook; the other a Swedish housemaid. The Shadow recognized that they had already been quizzed.

"Hiram Windler had no family," summarized Weston. "These are the only other occupants of the house: Lee Wan, the cook; Lempe, the maid. However, until a week ago, Windler had a secretary, a young man named Culden.

"Windler owned property. It was Culden's task to classify those holdings and to arrange matters pertaining to their sale. Culden finished the work six days ago. Tonight, for some unknown reason, he returned."

"I bane see heem," announced Lempe, nodding. "Ya, I bane see Mr. Culden in room right here. I tank he come for dinner."

"That was at six-thirty," stated Weston. "Lempe was the only one of the two servants who saw Culden."

"Me cookee flied lice," chimed in Lee Wan. "Busy in kitchee. No see Mr. Culden halfee past six."

Weston silenced the cook with an impatient gesture. Continuing, the commissioner stated:

"Windler remained downstairs after dinner. At eight o'clock, he went upstairs to his bedroom, since he always rested at that hour. Lee Wan had opened the door of the back stairs. He heard a shot; accompanied by Lempe, he found Windler dead.

"The local precinct was notified by these servants. The investigation showed an opened window; the murderer had evidently jumped to the ground. The earth in a flower bed is scuffed; but bears no trace of footprints.

"Inasmuch as Windler often retired at eight o'clock, the investigation was confined to these grounds, despite the fact that Windler's hat and overcoat were in the bedroom. It was not until later that we learned of Windler's intention to go out this evening. He had an appointment with Martin Debrossler, a banker who lives about a mile from here. Cardona can tell us what occurred at Debrossler's."

Cardona nodded. He added a brief statement to Weston's.

"I was coming past Debrossler's at twenty minutes of nine," declared Joe. "A butler stopped my car. He was Furbison, who works for Debrossler. Trouble in the house; I entered and found Debrossler and his lawyer, Pennybrook.

"Both were in the second floor study. They'd been bowled over by a robber who answered the description of the Gray Ghost. The fellow had gone out the window with a hundred thousand dollars intended for Windler.

"No footprints there. We've searched all the roads between this house and Debrossler's. Patrol cars have covered highways, stopping cars leaving this area. The crook was too fast for us. He made a getaway."

THERE was a pause following Cardona's statement. Then Weston continued the summary.

"Police boats have also patrolled the Sound," declared the commissioner. "We have given them a fair description of Culden; but the details are meager. Lempe and Lee Wan class him as of medium height, slender build, dark complexion and with brown eyes and dark hair. That, however, could fit any number of persons.

"Since Lempe did not see Culden leave the house, there is a chance that he remained here. We suspect him of being the murderer; also of having played the part of the Gray Ghost. Having lived on Long Island for several months, Culden could be the man responsible for previous robberies.

"There was time for him to murder Windler; then go to Debrossler's on foot; therefore, he may have had no car. To leave Holmwood, without an automobile or a boat, Culden would have had to take the train. Cardona, give me the report of your visit to the railroad station."

Cardona produced a wadded paper and a local timetable.

"A train went into the city at seven twenty-six," stated Joe. "The next was at eight twenty-six. Culden couldn't have taken either of them. He was here at eight o'clock and at Debrossler's at eight-thirty."

"Precisely," approved Weston. "Proceed, Cardona."

"There was a train at nine twenty-six," continued Cardona, "but Culden wasn't on it. The station agent was out on the platform; only three people went aboard and he knew all of them. There's another train at ten twenty-six; a last one at eleven twenty-six. I've posted men to watch both of them."

"Culden will not be on either train," predicted Weston. "He would have been a fool to leave here by railroad. We can count upon it that he will not appear at the station tonight. Nevertheless, we shall leave the men on duty.

"Come. Let us go to Debrossler's. You may accompany us, Cranston."

DRIVING his own car, The Shadow followed the commissioner to Debrossler's. The course led away from the direction of the railroad station, in a rather roundabout circuit. Both houses were one street back from the Sound; but there was no road that followed the shoreline.

This meant that the cars were forced to go a few blocks inland, to a wide, tree-lined avenue. Halfway to Debrossler's, a single street went out to the Sound; passing that thoroughfare, The Shadow saw lights in the distance. From previous knowledge of this district, he knew that the street led to the Holmwood Beach Club, which had a private clubhouse near its pier on Long Island Sound.

At Debrossler's, another street made a dead end when it neared the Sound. Debrossler's house was lighted; The Shadow pulled in alongside Weston's car. There was a question that needed explanation; namely, why Cardona had happened to be coming past Debrossler's house.

The question was answered shortly after The Shadow had been introduced—as Cranston—to Debrossler and Pennybrook. Cardona mentioned that he had taken the wrong road to Holmwood. He had come into town from a road that passed beyond Holmwood.

Debrossler and Pennybrook were seated in the enclosed porch. The banker was grumbly; the lawyer, moody. Both attitudes were explainable: Debrossler's by his loss of a hundred thousand dollars; Pennybrook's by the blow that he had taken on the head. Debrossler heard Weston's theory concerning Culden and agreed with it.

"Confound it!" expressed Debrossler. "I knew that Windler had a secretary; but I never saw the fellow, nor did I know his name."

"Could Windler have told him about this transaction?" queried Weston.

"Certainly," assured Debrossler. "I talked with Windler more than a week ago. That was when we made this appointment."

PIERCE GILDEN—guest at the Debrossler mansion preceeding the robbery

"Then Culden did not need to visit Windler tonight."

"Except to find out if the appointment had been postponed. There was a chance that I might have gone from town and therefore have put it off until a later date."

Weston nodded wisely.

"Culden is the man we must find," he decided— "unless there is someone else who could have known your plans to have the money here. Who was at this house tonight, Mr. Debrossler?"

"My daughters," replied the banker, "and two young men. One man was Pierce Gilden, whom we know quite well. The other was Alan Reeth, from out of town. But none of them knew that I had an appointment with Windler, nor that I had brought the money home with me."

"When did they go out?"

"At least ten minutes before the Gray Ghost entered my study."

"They went to the city?"

"Yes. In my big car. Towden, the chauffeur, was driving. We called Towden from another house, a short while ago. I talked to him at the Manhattan garage where he always parks the car."

"What did he have to say?"

"Simply that he had driven straight into the city and reached the theater before nine o'clock. He delivered all four passengers in time for a late movie."

"I see. What time did the young men arrive here?"

"At seven o'clock, for dinner. They were here until half past eight. My daughters can vouch for that, Commissioner."

THERE was an unpleasant pause. Debrossler seemed piqued because Weston had quizzed him concerning persons who could not have had a part in either crime. It was The Shadow who ended the pause; he delivered a remark in the quiet tone of Cranston.

"One point is evident, Commissioner," he stated. "Anyone who left Holmwood and went directly to the city would have a perfect alibi covering a period of at least one hour."

"It only takes thirty minutes to drive into town," objected Weston.

"And thirty to return," added The Shadow. "Of course"—he paused, speculatively—"if one went by train, the period would be longer. Let me see that timetable, Cardona."

The Shadow secured the train schedule.

"Yes, I am right. The railroad trip requires forty minutes. In by train, out by automobile, at least seventy-five minutes. One hour and a quarter—"

"That has nothing to do with the matter, Cranston," interrupted Weston, testily. "Your calculations are unnecessary. Why concern yourself with the time element?"

The Shadow smiled. In Cranston's fashion, he glanced at his watch.

"It is nearly eleven," he remarked. "I wish to be in New York before midnight. Hence I must leave you, Commissioner. May I use your telephone, Mr. Debrossler?"

Then, before the banker could reply, The Shadow corrected himself.

"Ah, I had forgotten. Your wire has been cut. Very well, I shall call the club from a store in Holmwood."

THE SHADOW departed. Weston reviewed his summary for the benefit of Debrossler and Pennybrook. The commissioner made his exit with Cardona. They started toward the town of Holmwood. Not far past the street to Windler's, they heard the tinkling of a grade crossing bell. Cardona pointed to flashing lights.

"That's the eleven twenty-six," said Cardona. "Just starting into town. We can stop and tell the two men to go off duty, Commissioner."

Weston agreed. The chauffeur swung the car into a driveway beside the old-fashioned station that marked the terminus of the Holmwood branch. Cardona leaned from the window and beckoned to two men who stood near the lights of the station platform. They approached and shook their heads.

"Two women went in on the last train," reported

one. "Nobody got aboard this rattler. There it goes—pulling out."

Weston and Cardona watched the two-car train slide from the platform. When the red cars had gone, they saw the station agent walk into the waiting room to close up for the night. Weston ordered the two watchers to board his automobile. The commissioner's machine pulled away.

The rumble of the electric train had faded in the distance. All was silent about the platform where small lights, spaced apart, made but a pitiful glow against the blanket of surrounding night.

It was then that a figure stepped into view. The solitary arrival appeared tall and conspicuous upon the deserted platform. Commissioner Weston would have been perplexed, had he remained to witness the approach of this lone personage. The commissioner would have recognized his friend, Lamont Cranston.

The law, sure that it had identified the Gray Ghost as Culden, had been content to depart with that one clue.

The Shadow had decided to remain in Holmwood.

CHAPTER IV
THE SHADOW'S TRAIL

"WAS that the last train to the city?"

The station agent looked through the wicket as he heard the query. Closing the office for the night, he had not detected footsteps in the waiting room. Peering, the station agent nodded as he viewed the features of Lamont Cranston.

"Too bad, sir," he said. "You'll have to take a cab down by the restaurant. It's a couple of miles over to another line, where you can board a midnight train."

The Shadow nodded. He paused to light a cigarette.

"Not many late passengers use this station, I suppose."

"That's right, sir. Not going into the city, anyway. There'll be some out, though, on the train that arrives here at eleven-fifty."

"You close the office before that train arrives?"

"Yes, sir. Nobody buys tickets at the end of a trip."

The Shadow gave a quiet chuckle at the man's logic. The station agent began to consider himself a wit. Affably, he leaned on the ledge inside the wicket and began to talk of the most important news that had come to Holmwood.

"Did you hear about the murder, sir?" he queried, in an awed tone. "Some killer got old Hiram Windler. They say it was the Gray Ghost!"

"The Gray Ghost?"

"Sure! Everybody's been talking about him for the last few weeks. He's been robbing houses right and left, at lots of places along the Sound. This is his first murder, though."

"Do the police know his identity?"

The station agent leaned closer, in the manner of a man who possessed inside information.

"There were detectives posted here tonight," he undertoned. "Looking for a fellow named Culden. Thought maybe he'd gone in on the nine twenty-six."

"Would you know Culden if you saw him?"

The station agent shook his head.

"Not unless I was told who he was. Kind of medium build, the detectives said, with dark complexion. There was a fellow looked like him on the seven twenty-six; but that couldn't have been Culden."

The Shadow looked unconvinced. The station agent explained:

"Don't you see how it was, sir? The murder wasn't until eight o'clock; and there was a robbery at half past eight. If a man had gone in on the seven twenty-six, he wouldn't have reached the Pennsylvania Station until eight-twelve."

"What if he had stopped off along the line?"

"This fellow didn't. He went all the way into New York. The baggage man told me about it when he came back on the next trip."

"The baggage man?"

"Sure. This fellow had a dog with him, so he had to ride into New York on the baggage car. It wasn't much more than a pup. The baggage man said the pooch howled all the way into Pennsy Station. When he got there, the fellow had to check the hound somewhere South. Yes, sir, I'll bet he had a rare time with that pooch. Nice hound, though. Looked like a bird dog."

"I suppose you told the detectives about the dog."

"Yeah. But they weren't interested. They were looking for Culden. This inspector fellow, Cardona, said that any guy carrying a dog with him wouldn't have been Culden."

REMEMBERING that his hours were ended, the station agent moved back into the ticket office. The Shadow strolled out to the platform and entered his coupé, which was parked beyond a line of high bushes. Soon the ticket agent came from the station and locked the door behind him. He let the platform lights remain illuminated because of the train due at ten minutes of twelve.

Within the darkness of the coupé, The Shadow delivered a whispered laugh. His visit to the station had brought results. It fitted with a theory of his own, one at variance with Weston's.

The Shadow had placed Culden.

It was plain that Windler's secretary was connected with crime; but in a minor capacity that could not be proved against him. The law would have a difficult time breaking down Culden's denials of complicity, should the missing secretary be captured.

Culden had come to Holmwood to find out if Hiram Windler intended to keep his appointment with Martin Debrossler. That fact learned, Culden had left Windler's house with promptitude. He had contacted another person, the real criminal, who intended to masquerade as the Gray Ghost.

Then Culden had set out to establish an alibi. The Gray Ghost did not intend to murder Windler until after the victim had dined. Culden's job, therefore, was to be aboard the seven twenty-six, riding into New York at the time of the murder.

Robbery was the Gray Ghost's next step—requiring a prompt visit to Debrossler's, following the murder of Windler. Culden's alibi would be good almost until nine o'clock. But the alibi itself was a tricky proposition. To be sure that it would hold, Culden needed two things to back it.

First: an excuse for having come to Long Island, to make the visit at Windler's seem innocuous. Second: witnesses who would positively remember that he traveled all the way into the Pennsylvania Station on the local train.

The dog served both purposes.

Culden had stopped somewhere to obtain the dog during the hour between his departure from Windler's and train time. He could say, if questioned later, that he had come to Long Island to get the dog.

Because of the dog, he had found an excuse to ride into New York in the baggage car. He had rendered himself so conspicuous that the baggage man and other members of the train crew would remember him, if called upon to identify him later. At the same time, Culden had not found it necessary to mention his name to the men in the baggage car.

That proved much to The Shadow.

It showed that Culden had wanted to avoid questioning, if possible. There were reasons why he held such preference. Though his alibi was solid, Culden was probably squeamish about explaining himself to the law; it would be better to dodge that ordeal, if possible. Moreover, since he was working for the Gray Ghost, he was doing a service for the murderer by his policy aboard the baggage car.

Since the train crew did not know that they had carried Culden, the police had naturally picked the secretary as the man they wanted. Weston and Cardona had chosen a blind trail. They were after the wrong man.

Real clues to the Gray Ghost might still be found at Holmwood. That was why The Shadow had remained.

MINUTES passed. A train slithered into the station. Several persons alighted and walked away. The conductor extinguished the platform lights. Soon a man approached The Shadow's coupé. The Shadow spoke in a whisper; the man stepped aboard the car.

The arrival was Harry Vincent, an agent of The Shadow's. He had caught the last train from New York, in response to a telephone call that The Shadow had made immediately after leaving Debrossler's. Harry had arrived at eleven-fifty. A distant clock was at present chiming midnight.

The coupé purred softly, as The Shadow drove out to the road. In even tones, The Shadow briefly divulged developments to Harry. A short ride brought them to the vicinity of Windler's residence. The Shadow parked the car in darkness; he instructed Harry to be ready at the wheel. That order given, The Shadow stepped from the coupé.

While awaiting Harry, The Shadow had donned garb of black. A shrouded figure in the darkness, he moved invisibly to the walls of Windler's house. Police had ended their vigil; nevertheless, The Shadow was cautious as he utilized a tiny flashlight. Rays fell only upon spots of The Shadow's choosing; the light, itself was muffled in the folds of his cloak. Harry, back in the car, could not observe the blinks.

Windler's grounds had been well scoured. The Shadow, however, had a purpose of his own. Beginning below the window through which the Gray Ghost had escaped, he examined the flower bed. The earth was soft and uneven; it bore no footprints.

The Shadow knew that the Gray Ghost had not lingered after his flight from Windler's. Therefore, The Shadow sought evidence of some prearrangement. His flashlight showed wide-spaced streaks in the dirt. The Shadow saw a probability.

The murderer had prepared for his swift exit by placing some soft covering upon the flower bed. Landing upon it, he had made no definite footprints. A simple dragging process, accomplished with removal of the covering, had enabled him to avoid leaving a clue.

The ground about Windler's was hard. The police had found no traces of the Gray Ghost's path. Since the killer had headed for Debrossler's, the law had naturally searched in the direction of the road. The Shadow tried the opposite procedure. He moved across the lawn in the direction of the Sound.

THE SHADOW came to a high stone wall, which formed an extension of a hedge on the Sound side of the house. The police had been thorough enough to examine the thick hedge. Finding no breaks in it, they had gone elsewhere. They had entirely neglected the wall; for it was the most difficult route by which anyone could have departed.

With a springing leap, The Shadow clutched the top of the wall, a good eight feet above the ground. He scaled the barrier, poised upon a broad ledge and used the flashlight. The wall was of stone; the top cracks were filled with mortar. The Shadow found crumbled patches of stone; against a roughened, mica-tinted edge, he discovered a strand of gray.

It was a thread from the Gray Ghost's jersey.

Leaning over the far edge of the wall, The Shadow shone the flashlight downward. The glare showed dust, streaked like the dirt of the flower bed. The Gray Ghost had dropped his blanketing cloth from the top of the wall. Leaping off, he had again avoided footprints.

Dropping from the wall, The Shadow used his flashlight along rough, tufted ground that produced a tiny path leading toward the Sound. He knew that he was following directly upon the Gray Ghost's trail, even though no new clues marked the path.

The Shadow's opinion was well-founded. He had seen through the murderer's game.

Leaving Windler's, the Gray Ghost had held two desires. One was to cover his trail; the other was to reach Debrossler's. He had, therefore, chosen a course that would serve both purposes.

By taking to the wall, he had left searchers baffled. By reaching the Sound, he had gained access to a water route, a much safer course than any he could have taken by land.

At the shore, The Shadow found a decrepit pier that had probably been built by a former owner of Windler's house. The old recluse had abandoned the landing place. Its paint had become a faded gray. The Shadow streaked the flashlight along the broken-down pilings, which were flimsy, for the pier had never been a strong one. The glow showed what The Shadow hoped: a dab of white against one post.

The Gray Ghost had docked a rowboat at Windler's old pier. The side of the craft had scraped a piling. Judging from the height of the white paint above the water, and allowing for the tide, The Shadow could calculate the approximate size of the boat. He knew that the Gray Ghost would have preferred a rowboat to a small motor craft. Oars could be handled with a degree of silence; the *put-put* of a motor would have been difficult to cover.

RETURNING to the coupé, The Shadow ordered Harry to drive toward Debrossler's. As they reached the road that led down to the Holmwood Beach Club, The Shadow gave another order. Harry took the road to the club.

Lights glowed; music was audible as the coupé neared the Sound. The club's pier was a large one, wide enough for cars to park. There was also a broad driveway to the left. The clubhouse stood beyond that space. Fully a dozen cars were parked in the drive.

A dance was in progress at the club. Guests had therefore parked their cars in the drive. Some had already left; but the space looked ample for at least fifty cars. It followed that no one had parked upon the pier. That space was used only when persons came to the beach to swim.

The Shadow whispered to Harry. The agent drove the car out to the end of the pier, swung crosswise and extinguished the lights. Total darkness covered the coupé. The Shadow stepped to the pier.

Following the side of the pier most distant from the clubhouse drive, The Shadow moved inshore. Turning his flashlight toward the water's edge, he saw a stretch of hard sandy beach. Situated below the pier, on the right side when one faced the Sound, that strip of beach was completely isolated. No one could have viewed it from the clubhouse; which was several hundred feet away.

There were boats drawn up to the inner edge of the beach. The Shadow took to the sand; he approached the boats and used the flashlight. He found a white rowboat, its sides dripping wet. Running the flashlight along the sand, he saw the scraped line along which the boat had been drawn from the water.

There were no traces of footprints. The Shadow sought the answer in the boat itself. He found the clue he wanted.

A broad, thick piece of canvas was wedged beneath the bow. Folded hurriedly, it formed a crumpled mass. The Shadow pulled out the canvas and spread it across the boat. He flicked his flashlight.

Dirt, dust, wet sand.

All were conspicuous upon the canvas. They showed the Gray Ghost's trail.

Not only had the canvas served the murderer at the flower bed and beyond the stone wall; he had utilized it finally when he had drawn the boat up from the water. Tossing it, outspread, from the bow of the boat, the Gray Ghost had stepped upon the canvas to draw the boat after him. Thus he had gained rocky soil, where footprints would not show.

He had also shaken the canvas well before wadding it into the rowboat. There were no footprints upon the canvas. To an extent, the Gray Ghost had nullified his trail. Nevertheless, The Shadow could easily picture the killer's course.

A guest at the club dance, the Gray Ghost had left. He had taken the rowboat and made a trip to Windler's. Following his action there, the murderer had rowed back along the shore of the Sound. But he had not stopped at the beach. He had kept on to Debrossler's.

After perpetrating robbery as his second crime, the Gray Ghost had rowed back to the club beach. Oiled oarlocks, noted by The Shadow, proved that the trip had been made in speedy silence.

The Gray Ghost had returned to the dance at the clubhouse. He might be there yet. Possibly he had left with departing guests. One thing certain, the Gray Ghost's identity could be better established if more clues could be obtained.

A whispered laugh sounded in the darkness, as The Shadow returned toward the coupé. Before he sought the Gray Ghost in person, The Shadow intended to search a spot where other evidence might lie.

The Shadow planned an immediate visit to the home of Martin Debrossler.

CHAPTER V
MISTAKEN IDENTITY

HARRY VINCENT stopped the coupé some fifty yards from Debrossler's house.

The place was ablaze with light. Cars were parked outside. Moving figures could be seen at the illuminated windows of the enclosed porch.

The police had left Debrossler's; but evidently the people there were still concerned about the Gray Ghost's daring crime.

Harry had, of course, extinguished the lights promptly. He heard a whisper; he guessed that the coupé's door was opening, even though he could not hear it. Harry conjectured that The Shadow intended a new investigation, despite the fact that people were about at Debrossler's.

Harry was correct.

A stealthy shape was gliding through the darkness of Debrossler's ample lawn. Silent and unseen, The Shadow reached the house wall directly below the window of the banker's study. A flashlight glimmered; then went out.

Certain factors were apparent to The Shadow, as he stood beside the looming house wall. The Gray Ghost had taken an easier leap from Debrossler's window than from Windler's. The tilt of the ground made that evident. Windler's bedroom had been above the lower side of the lawn, where the ground sloped downward. Debrossler's was on the upper side. Here, the crook had taken little hazard in dropping to hard ground.

Offsetting this was the matter of entry.

At Windler's, the Gray Ghost must have entered with ease. Culden had probably told him of unlocked doors, or windows on the ground floor. The murderer had found no difficulty in reaching the upstairs bedroom through the house itself.

At Debrossler's, however, the Gray Ghost had been forced to find means of entering a locked room on the second floor. His only course had been to jimmy the window of the study. To reach that point, he had necessarily scaled the wall.

Unquestionably, the man who had played the Gray Ghost was both powerful and athletic. The fact that he had deliberately leaped the wall beside Windler's hedge was proof that no ordinary physical hazard bothered him. His reliance upon the rowboat as a means of speedy and effective transit also marked him as an athlete.

Added to these was present proof. The Gray Ghost had used no ladder to enter Debrossler's study. He could not have carried one away with him; and the police had found no ladder on the grounds. Through sheer physical ability, the Gray Ghost had clambered up to the study window.

THE SHADOW had a simple test whereby he could learn the difficulty of that task. His flashlight stowed beneath his cloak, he began to scale the wall himself. Gripping projecting stones with his gloved fingers, he dug the soft-toed points of his shoes into spots below. Beetlelike, The Shadow ascended to the study window.

Carefully muffled, the flashlight glimmered while The Shadow clung to a projecting stone. A new strand of gray appeared in the light. It was a bit of cloth attached to the pointed prong of an iron shutter catch, at the wall to the left of the window.

Extinguishing his light, The Shadow felt for the catch. It wabbled as he gripped it. The Shadow swung his free arm across and found the catch on the opposite side of the window. He gripped it, released all other hold and remained suspended.

The evidence told The Shadow that the Gray

Ghost had grabbed the shutter catch at the left. It had come loose under the strain. The inference, therefore, was that the venturer had been of heavy build, his weight greater than The Shadow's. For The Shadow himself was gaining support from the remaining shutter catch.

How had the Gray Ghost gained a sufficient hold?

The Shadow's light glimmered upward. It showed the shutter above the broken catch. The shutter was of metal; its hinges heavy. With the catch broken, the Gray Ghost had managed to support himself upon the window ledge; he had grabbed the shutter to use it as a new support.

Trying this, The Shadow found the process simple. The shutter hinges were rusty. Swung outward from the wall, the shutter remained in fixed position. The Gray Ghost could have sought no better support while he used his right hand to jimmy the study window.

The window itself had been closed after the police investigation. It was unlocked; The Shadow raised the sash and entered. He used the flashlight to examine the broken lock. The Gray Ghost had splintered wood with the jimmy. An easy process; yet one which bore out The Shadow's previous findings. The Gray Ghost had been a man of unusual physique. It had taken a powerful wrist to accomplish the jimmy work so capably.

Suddenly, The Shadow's flashlight became black. At the opened window, The Shadow had heard an approach below. Leaning out into the darkness, he listened. He caught mumbled voices below the wall.

"I saw it, Towden," came a trembling tone. "I tell you, there was a light at the study window!"

"There's no light there now, Furbison."

"It wasn't the study light. It was like a little flashlight. We must inform the master!"

"A good idea! Get inside, Furbison. I'll watch here."

In examining the jimmied window, The Shadow had allowed an unguarded blink. It had been spotted by two men roaming the lawn: Furbison, the butler and Towden, the chauffeur. Towden evidently had returned from the city with the moviegoers.

Evidently, Debrossler had instructed his servants to look about the grounds. Faring forth, they had arrived too late to surprise The Shadow making entry. But Furbison had spotted the flashlight, and was going in to inform Debrossler.

THE SHADOW'S only course was departure. An easy route would be the window. A surprise drop upon Towden would be effective. But it would also betray the fact that there had actually been someone in the study. The Shadow preferred to have

Debrossler think that Furbison's observation of a blinking flashlight had been a product of the butler's imagination.

Therefore, The Shadow chose the door leading from the study.

Beetlelike, The Shadow ascended to the study window.

Opening the door from the inside, he stepped into the gloomy upstairs hall. He closed the door behind him and moved to the stairs. Halfway down, he paused. Furbison had entered. The Shadow waited while the butler passed through a living room to the enclosed porch.

Descending to the lower hall, The Shadow heard voices. The living room was darkened; he entered it. With gliding course, The Shadow reached a pitch-black spot behind a door that was opened inward from the porch. This was one section of a French window; it had a drawn shade. A trickle of light, through the crack of the door, was insufficient to disturb the darkness of The Shadow's hiding place.

From this vantage point, The Shadow could hear and see the persons on the porch.

Furbison was speaking to Debrossler.

"Pardon, sir," said the butler, "but I have just left Towden—"

"Do not interrupt us," broke in Debrossler. "I know that you've left Towden; otherwise he would be here with you."

"But he is outside, sir—"

"Where he belongs. No interruption, Furbison."

"Very well, sir."

Patiently, the butler stood by, while Debrossler resumed his conversation with others present. The group was clustered; through the crack of the doorway, The Shadow could see everyone.

Pennybrook was present. The lawyer had recovered from his moodiness. Apparently, his headache was ended. Debrossler's two daughters were also on the porch; with them was a young man, tall, but of slender build. His face was pleasant; but serious. His complexion was light, like his hair. His air was polite; he was faultlessly attired in a tuxedo. The Shadow knew that this must be Pierce Gilden or Alan Reeth. The man proved to be the former.

"That's how the Gray Ghost made his getaway," declaimed Debrossler, "and if you're anything of a detective, Gilden, perhaps you can furnish us with some clues."

"The police have found none?" inquired Gilden.

"They have attributed the crime to Windler's secretary," replied Debrossler. "But no one seems to know much about the fellow, except that his name is Culden."

"Culden," mused Gilden. "I never heard of him. I don't like the name, though." He paused to deliver a wry smile. "It sounds too much like Gilden."

"That's so," put in Pennybrook, with a laugh. "It wouldn't be past those police investigators to get the names mixed. Don't worry, Pierce. If they arrest you, we can vouch for you."

"Of course," laughed Louise Debrossler. "You were not out of our sight, Pierce, from seven o'clock until midnight. Jane and I will supply your alibi."

"Excellent!" decided Gilden. "I am glad that we went out together tonight. I am sorry, though, that Reeth did not come back from the show with us."

"He stopped off at his hotel," explained Jane. "Alan is going out of town tomorrow."

"LET us get back to the matter of the Gray Ghost," decided Debrossler. "Let us try to decide who he might be. The Gray Ghost is acquainted with this part of Long Island. He knew of affairs tonight.

"He cannot be myself, nor Pennybrook. Nor could he have been you, Gilden; nor Reeth. Windler was murdered; he was not the Gray Ghost. We come logically to Culden. The police are right. Culden is the Gray Ghost."

"I agree with that," asserted Pennybrook. "But what good does it do us? Where is Culden?"

"Or where will he be?" queried Gilden. "What places should be searched for him?"

Debrossler shook his head; then suddenly paused.

"I wonder," he remarked, "if there is anything to the old theory that a murderer returns to the scene of a crime."

"Nothing to it," put in Pennybrook. "You won't find Culden coming back to Windler's."

"Or here," added Gilden. "That theory is fiction, Mr. Debrossler."

Debrossler was stroking his chin. There was a momentary pause. Furbison, tense and quivering, put in a remark.

"Pardon me again, sir," inserted the butler, "but you were just speaking of something that I came to tell you. I think that you are right, sir."

"About a criminal returning?" queried Debrossler, suddenly interested. "Do you support the theory, Furbison?"

"I do, sir. I am sure that the Gray Ghost has already returned."

"To Windler's?"

"No. To this house, sir!"

"You have seen him?"

"Not exactly, sir. It was a flashlight that I saw, blinking in your study."

"What!" roared Debrossler. "And you stood here like a dead log? What folly, Furbison! By this time, the scoundrel must be gone!"

"Hardly, sir," returned Furbison. "Towden is outside, watching the study window."

Men were on their feet. Debrossler took command.

"Come with me, Pennybrook; and you, Gilden. Furbison, join Towden."

The banker pulled keys from his pocket.

"We have no revolvers," he declared, ruefully. "Bah! I should have had the police commissioner leave a weapon with a temporary permit. But we have canes, in the hallway rack. Stout ones. Arm yourselves with them. Let us deal with the Gray Ghost."

The girls delivered alarmed cries. Debrossler silenced them, and Pennybrook added his challenge.

"Let me meet the Gray Ghost," announced the lawyer. "I have a score to settle with him."

"We shall all deal with him," declared Debrossler. "Come! We have no time to lose."

The three men hurried through the living room, leaving Furbison, anxious-eyed, upon the threshold of the porch. The butler was shaky. He did not relish the idea of joining Towden in the darkness. As he started to advance, he heard a call from Debrossler.

"I believe we'll need another cane, Furbison—"

"There's one here, sir," replied the butler. "Behind this door to the porch."

Two things happened at once. Debrossler, at the door from the hallway, pressed the light switch. Furbison, at the threshold of the porch, swung the door behind which The Shadow stood. The butler, wild-eyed, saw the cloaked figure. He gulped the only identity that came to his mind:

"The Gray Ghost!"

FURBISON was between Debrossler and The Shadow. The banker did not catch full view of the shape against the wall. He saw Furbison totter back in fear. Thereupon Debrossler sprang forward, game for battle.

Like a living whirlwind, The Shadow hurtled outward into the room. He was upon Debrossler instantly; he spun the banker about and sent him floundering against a table. The Shadow reached the hallway. There, he was blocked by Pennybrook.

The lawyer was swinging a heavy cane, apparently anxious to deal with the Gray Ghost. He bashed a stroke at The Shadow; the black-clad invader stopped Pennybrook's arm with an up-swinging fist.

Plucking the cane from Pennybrook's grasp, The Shadow swung it on a wide sweep to the floor. As Pennybrook tried to grapple, The Shadow thrust the cane between the lawyer's ankles. Wrenching away, he applied a twist. Pennybrook sprawled.

The Shadow had released the cane. He was driving toward the front door. Gilden was picking a cane from the rack; the young man dropped it in his haste and leaped, bare-handed, upon The Shadow. Fiercely, Gilden tried to grip The Shadow's throat. Gilden's strength proved puny.

The Shadow wrenched away the grasping hands. Gaining a jujutsu hold upon Gilden, he swung him about toward the inner end of the hall. Pennybrook had regained his feet and was ready for a new drive. With a heave of his shoulders, The Shadow

propelled Gilden's light form squarely against the lawyer. Gilden and Pennybrook fell in a huddle.

The Shadow gained the door.

Debrossler's daughters were screaming the alarm from the windows of the porch. Towden had heard them. The chauffeur was rounding the house when The Shadow encountered him.

Another grapple in the darkness. Towden never had the slightest advantage. The Shadow had expected him. With a huge swing, he sent the chauffeur headlong into a clump of shrubbery. Making for the street, The Shadow gained his car.

Harry was ready at the wheel. The coupé roared away. At The Shadow's order, Harry performed a circuit, skirting the town of Holmwood. Near the end of the roundabout course, they heard the wail of distant sirens. The alarm had gone out; police would soon be covering roads. The Shadow gave another order; Harry swung the car to the left. They came out upon a traveled highway.

The coupé had cleared the danger zone. Police would regard it simply as another car coming from some Long Island town more distant than Holmwood. The Shadow's keen choice of a route had enabled him to elude any closing mesh.

Back in Holmwood, a new search would be on. The law would gain the report that the Gray Ghost had returned. The Shadow's investigation had been ended for tonight; but he had profited by the brief episode at Debrossler's.

The false report of The Gray Ghost's return might well produce advantages. The Shadow could foresee unusual developments from this case of mistaken identity.

CHAPTER VI
HARRY REPORTS

THE next afternoon found Harry Vincent at the Holmwood Beach Club. He was seated on the veranda, watching events upon the pier. Bathers were diving from the springboard; others were swimming near the beach.

Harry had gained an introduction at the club. He had driven out from New York at noon, armed with a letter from an investment broker named Rutledge Mann. The letter had given him entrée. Mann knew the manager of the Holmwood Beach Club.

The club had accommodations for overnight guests, but few persons availed themselves of the privilege. Harry had found no difficulty in obtaining a room; he had also had a chance to study the club register and note the names of those who had stayed there the night before. There were only half a dozen on the list.

Idling on the veranda, Harry considered a mental picture which he had long since formed. It was one

in the populated vicinity of the Holmwood Beach Club unless he had possessed good reason for being there.

So far, Harry had learned only one matter of consequence. The rowboat that the Gray Ghost had used was the property of the club. Thus it gave no clue to the Gray Ghost's identity; but it did substantiate The Shadow's belief that the man had been a guest at the club. Otherwise, he might have had difficulty in learning about the boat's ownership.

While he lounged on the veranda, Harry realized that his choice of suspects must be one of elimination. Even if he found a man who fitted the description given, that person might be someone other than the Gray Ghost. The result might be that Harry would find several persons to watch.

that The Shadow had given him—a description of the man who could have played the Gray Ghost. Detail by detail, The Shadow had listed the wanted man's qualifications.

The man, should Harry find him, would be at least six feet tall and one hundred and eighty pounds in weight. He would have brawny arms, for he was a capable oarsman. Chances were that he would prove to be an excellent swimmer; also a sportsman. The murderer of Hiram Windler had relied upon a single shot with a revolver. He would be good with a gun.

The man would have social status. The fact that he had been a guest at last night's dance indicated that point. The Shadow had come to the conclusion that the Gray Ghost would not have taken a chance

Like a living whirlwind, The Shadow ...spun the banker about and sent him floundering against a table.

TALK was rife concerning the Gray Ghost. Persons who stopped on the club veranda gave their versions of the crimes that had taken place last night. The Gray Ghost's depredations had produced one important result: Residents of Long Island were arming for the future.

Influential residents of Holmwood had applied for gun permits. They had been granted the privilege. Towns farther out along the Sound were copying the example of Holmwood. Though superstitious servants might regard the Gray Ghost as a phantom murderer, landowners certainly considered him to be a human being. Last night's robbery had marked the largest endeavor in a series of successful thefts. Long Island intended to gun for the Gray Ghost.

Yet there was rumor that the Gray Ghost was superhuman. People were ready to believe it; skeptical laughs were half-hearted when the subject was mentioned. The facts were that the Gray Ghost had vanished after each crime. Then there was the matter of his supposed return.

There were many versions of The Shadow's flight from Debrossler's. All of them accepted the testimony that the fugitive had been the Gray Ghost, back again. Some of the stories had the Gray Ghost vanishing like a will-o'-the-wisp from a circle of thwarted captors.

While he listened to such chatter, Harry watched all who came to the clubhouse or the pier. Not one man whom he had seen, tallied with the requirements. Some were tall, but lacked weight. Others were husky but only of medium height. One man who might have tallied proved himself a dub when he entered a canoe, nearly tipping it. Harry doubted that he could be the Gray Ghost.

Watching the pier, Harry heard someone on the veranda whisper:

"Here come the Debrossler girls. Pierce Gilden is with them."

A sporty roadster had wheeled into the drive. Harry saw a young man alight and help two girls from the car. Thinking of the Gray Ghost, Harry studied Gilden. He noted that the young man, though tall, was of slight build. The notation, of course, was nonessential. Pierce Gilden, of all persons, could not have been the Gray Ghost last night.

THE group approached the veranda, to be surrounded by eager questioners. Harry heard calls for exact descriptions of what had happened with the Gray Ghost's return. The girls began a wild story. They had been almost hysterical; they were ready to credit the Gray Ghost with a complete evanishment. Gilden was called upon to support their testimony.

"Maybe he is a spook," declared the young man, solemnly. "But I'd have to be shown. When he hit me in the hallway, he bowled me over like a ten-pin!"

Someone inquired if Gilden had actually grabbed the Gray Ghost. Gilden nodded.

"I had hold of him," he asserted, "but he was as slippery as an eel. An electric eel would be better. The jolt that hit me was as hard as an electric current!"

"That's what you said before, Pierce," insisted Louise Debrossler, "and that's why I think the Gray Ghost is really a ghost. Human beings cannot deliver an electric current."

"I said that I was jolted," repeated Gilden, "just as badly as if I had grabbed a live wire. But I didn't get a shock."

"You would not have described it as you did, Pierce," declared Jane, "unless you had really experienced something uncanny when you seized the ghost."

"Let's drop it," expressed Gilden, impatiently. "I'm fed up with all this talk. Call the Gray Ghost whatever you want. If I'd had a gun, he would have stayed where he was. Ghost or no ghost, a bullet would stop him. I'll have a gun later. This permit business is a good idea."

The trio went toward the pier, followed by questioners. Harry watched the departure; then chanced to turn toward the clubhouse door. He stared at a man who had just stepped out on the veranda.

Tall, heavy-built, this newcomer was a young man with a rugged, square-jawed face. His profile was choppy; Harry noted the glint of eyes that stared from beneath straight-lined brows. The man looked like an athlete. His sleeves were rolled to his elbows; Harry saw forearms that would have suited a crack oarsman.

The newcomer fulfilled the description of the Gray Ghost.

The club manager was at the doorway. He spoke to the husky man on the veranda.

"What do you think of this Gray Ghost, Mr. Renright?"

"Not much," replied Renright, gruffly. "People hereabouts seem gifted with imaginations. By the way, I'm going uptown. If there are any calls for me, I'll be back in an hour."

Renright strode away. Harry saw him enter a parked coupé and drive toward Holmwood. Remembering the club register of overnight guests, Harry recalled the name of Colin Renright. Approaching the door, Harry spoke to the manager.

"That chap who just came out here," remarked Harry—"was he Colin Renright?"

"Yes," replied the manager. "You know him?"

"I have met him. I didn't know that he lived in Holmwood."

"He doesn't. He lives out at Narrowneck. He used to be a member of this club. He stops overnight, occasionally."

"Quite an athlete, I understand."

"Renright is. A sportsman, too."

"Will he be back later?"

"In an hour or so."

"I'll say hello to him when he returns."

Entering the clubhouse, Harry went to a telephone. He put in a call to Rutledge Mann, and made a report. Mann promised to have facts concerning Renright within the next hour. He then proceeded to give Harry special instructions.

LEAVING the club, Harry went to his own coupe. He drove away on a new mission. Mann had informed him that facts had been learned regarding the dog that Culden had taken into New York. The dog had been shipped South; the shipper's name was P.T. Yenner, whose address was a Holmwood residence. It was Harry's temporary job to visit Yenner's and make inquiry.

Rutledge Mann, as contact agent for The Shadow, had many sources of information. His capacity of investment broker gave him wide acquaintance. Mann had been cooperating effectively today.

Harry found the Yenner residence. It was only a few blocks from the railway station. The place was closed; but a gardener was clipping hedges. Harry drove up and accosted the man.

The hunting dog that furnished an important clue to The Shadow.

"Mr. Yenner is away?"

The gardener nodded; then added: "In Europe."

"Too bad," observed Harry. "I understand he had a hunting dog for sale."

The gardener shook his head.

"'Twasn't for sale, that hound," he declared. "Mr. Yenner had him sent to the hunting lodge in Carolina."

"Then the dog was shipped some time ago?"

"No. He only went last night."

"But you said Mr. Yenner was in Europe."

The gardener became voluble.

"'Twasn't Mr. Yenner as shipped him," he explained. "The hound was too young; that's why I was a-keeping him here. Last night, the man as was to ship him called here."

"And took the dog?"

"O' course. He was a friend of Mr. Yenner's."

Harry nodded, as if he understood.

"I probably know the man who called here," he remarked. "I know most of Mr. Yenner's friends. What was the name of the chap who took the dog?"

"Can't answer that one," replied the gardener. "His face was a new one to me. But 'twasn't anybody but a friend of Mr. Yenner that would ha' knowed about the hound. Like yourself, sir. That's why I give him the dog."

Harry drove away. He had gained new proof of Culden's subtle tactics in framing an alibi and producing a false trail. Culden must have known Yenner as an acquaintance. He had arranged to ship the dog some time ago. Knowing that Yenner would be in Europe, Culden was sure that the dog incident would not be brought to light.

REACHING the club, Harry put in a call to Mann. He reported on the Yenner matter; then received information that concerned Renright. Harry was to contact the athlete; to claim friendship with a Californian named James Dinsey, whom Renright knew. Mann gave Harry concise facts concerning Dinsey.

He was on the veranda studying these memos when Renright drove up. Pocketing his notebook, Harry arose and greeted the husky when he reached the porch. Renright looked blank when Harry introduced himself.

"You ought to remember me," laughed Harry. "I was at the bachelor's party they gave Jim Dinsey, that night at the Waldorf."

Renright delivered an exclamation, as he thrust forth his hand. Harry received a powerful grip.

"You're a friend of Jim's?" queried Renright. "One of the California crowd I met that night?"

"I've just come East," returned Harry. "Jim told me to look you up. I called the Merrimac Club; they told me you were a member here."

"I used to be; but I'm seldom around Holmwood any longer. I'm living out at Narrowneck. I belong to a club out there. How would you like to go along with me, Vincent? They're holding a shindig tonight. You can stop over at the club."

"Great! I'm on a vacation. I've been aching to find somebody who knew Jim Dinsey. All of his friends seem to be out of town."

"Come along with me, then. I'll show you a good time. Wait until I check out of here."

Harry followed Renright into the club. At the desk, Renright obtained his key and spoke to the manager.

"I just applied for a gun permit," laughed Renright. "I think I'll join the ghost hunt. It's a break for me; I've always wanted to have a revolver for target practice. This Gray Ghost business makes it easy to get one."

As soon as Renright was gone; Harry told the manager that he would check out later. He remarked that he was going to Narrowneck with Renright; that if he did not return, he would send someone for his luggage and his car. To make sure of no complications, Harry paid his bill.

When Renright returned, Harry met him. They strolled out together. Renright gained no inkling that Harry had registered as a guest at the Holmwood Beach Club. Nor did he suppose that the coupé near his own belonged to Harry.

They entered Renright's car and drove away. Heading toward Narrowneck, Renright began to chat about Jim Dinsey. Posted regarding their supposedly mutual friend, Harry kept up the conversation. Matters were working as he wanted them.

Of all persons who might be the Gray Ghost, Renright was the most eligible. From now on, Harry's lone task would be to keep close beside the suspect.

CHAPTER VII
A BROKEN TRAIL

IT was dusk in Manhattan. City lights twinkled beneath increasing gloom. But in one secluded spot, complete darkness already persisted.

That was The Shadow's sanctum. A hidden abode somewhere in Manhattan, it was a place of utter blackness; except when its master was present. Thick, Stygian gloom pervaded this mysterious room. It ended with the sound of a *click*.

A bluish light appeared suddenly, to shine its shaded beams upon a polished desk. Beneath those rays appeared long, white hands. The Shadow was in his sanctum.

Report sheets fluttered to the desk. Keen eyes began a study. Agents had done their work. Day was ended; The Shadow's turn had come.

Besides contacting Harry Vincent, Rutledge Mann had held negotiations with Clyde Burke, another of The Shadow's agents. Clyde was a newspaper reporter; he was an excellent man at making queries. Clyde was the agent who had visited the Pennsylvania Station, to learn about Culden's shipments of the dog.

The man at the baggage room had supposed that Culden was Yenner. In course of conversation he had given Clyde a lead. Culden had sent a porter to the parcel room to obtain a checked package. When Culden had left, the porter was following him; lugging a heavy; unwieldy bundle.

Word of this had been relayed to The Shadow previously. He had ordered Clyde to another duty: inquiries at taxi offices. Claiming to have lost a bundle like Culden's, Clyde had visited every cab company in the city. He had gained a result.

One taxi driver had turned in a report. He had taken a passenger from the Pennsylvania Station to an address just off Eighth Avenue. Driving away, the cabby had seen a large package in his cab. He had returned to the house and left it there.

The cab company was concerned about the matter, since it was possible that the package might be Clyde's. They were willing to make inquiry at the address.

Clyde had forestalled it by stating that he would prefer to go there himself and identify the package, if it proved to be his own. Clyde, of course, expressed the possibility that the package might have remained in the cab during several trips; and hence might be his mythical bundle.

The Shadow was not surprised to learn of the package episode. The report concerning Culden had indicated something quite definite. Before going out to Long Island, Culden had checked the package, intending to pick it up after he shipped the dog. He had also planned to leave the package in the taxicab, that the driver might return it to him.

Culden had extended his alibi. He had one more witness, should the pinch come; namely, the taxi driver. The incident of the package had been important enough for the cabby to remember.

THE SHADOW finished with the reports. He clicked off the sanctum light. His present mission was to take up the work where Clyde had left off. The Shadow was going to the house where Culden's cab trip had ended.

Settled darkness hid the path which The Shadow followed. An interval had passed when he appeared upon a thronged sidewalk near Times Square. The Shadow was in the guise of Lamont Cranston. With leisurely stroll, he approached a hack stand and entered a parked taxi. He gave a low-toned order to the shrewd-faced driver.

The cab wheeled away, bound for Culden's address. The man at the wheel was Moe Shrevnitz, one of the speediest cab drivers in Manhattan. Moe's cab was an independent, uncontrolled by any company. Actually, it was owned by The Shadow, who called the taxi into service on occasions such as this.

Moe sped northward on Eighth Avenue; he reached the designated street and turned left. He stopped abruptly, a dozen houses from the corner. He was close to the required address. The Shadow alighted and made a pretense of paying fare. Moe drove away, along the westbound street.

The Shadow observed the houses. They formed a row of old-fashioned residences that had known a better past. Some had shuttered windows that betrayed their emptiness. Others were dwellings above basement storefronts. A few had been turned into cheap apartment houses.

The one which The Shadow sought had lighted windows. From its appearance, The Shadow decided that it served as a boarding house. It did not look like an apartment building; there were too many lighted windows for it to be an ordinary residence.

Ascending a short flight of stone steps, The Shadow rang the doorbell. Soon the door opened; a bulky, pleasant-faced woman nodded a greeting at sight of the well-dressed visitor.

"Good evening," remarked The Shadow, in the quiet tone of Cranston. "I have called to see a gentleman named Mr. Culden. I understand that he is living here."

"Ah, yes, sir," replied the woman. "It's the new lodger you'd like to see. I had almost forgot his name, until you mentioned it. There's so many of them comes and goes."

The Shadow was not surprised that Culden had given his right name. Probably he had counted upon the landlady forgetting it. The woman was the type who would spend much time in housework, with little opportunity to read the daily newspapers. It was policy for Culden to avoid an alias. He had evidently gambled on the chance that the landlady would not connect his name with the one mentioned in the reports of murder on Long Island.

"A gentlemanly young man he is," asserted the woman, "and it's no surprise to me to find that he has friends of the same sort. He's been in the house most always since he came here, excepting last night."

The Shadow made no interruption. The information might prove valuable.

"'Twas then he went out for the first time," continued the woman. "He went away in the afternoon; but he came in last night, sir, at quarter to nine sharp. It's nice to have a boarder that keeps early hours."

SHE paused. The Shadow questioned:

"Mr. Culden is in his room at present?"

The woman shook her head.

"It was a half hour ago he went out," she declared. "'Twas a respectable young man who called and asked for him. Not such a gentleman as yourself, sir, but a man who spoke pleasantlike, though he had his coat collar up like this."

The landlady gestured, as if raising coat lapels about her chin.

"'Twas odd to see him wearing a coat," she continued, "with the weather mild as it is tonight. He talked with Mr. Culden, quietlike. 'Twas then that Mr. Culden said he would go out. He had nary hat nor overcoat; but out he went, saying he'd be back again soon."

"I see." The Shadow nodded slowly. "Regarding this visitor—he held his coat collar with his left hand; his right was in his pocket."

The Shadow indicated the pose. The woman gazed, amazed.

"Right you are, sir!" she exclaimed. "'Twas that very way he stood! Ah, I understand. He is a friend of yours, like Mr. Culden."

"Not exactly," returned The Shadow, with a slight smile. Dropping his hands, he added: "When Mr. Culden returns, tell him that he had a caller. He may expect to see me later."

"The name, sir?"

"It is not necessary."

The Shadow stepped away from the door. The woman gawked, puzzled; then closed the door and went back into the house. The Shadow paused at the foot of the stone steps. Deliberately he lighted a cigarette and flicked the match, still burning, to the curb.

The Shadow had correctly classed Culden's "respectable" visitor.

Culden had received a summons from the underworld. The caller had been a hoodlum, one of better appearance than his pals, clever enough to put up a "front" that would bluff the landlady. He had come for Culden. Unsuspecting, the secretary had walked into a trap.

The muffling coat collar had been the man's move to cover his face against later recognition. The hand in the pocket had held a gun. Culden had gone out with his supposed friend rather than receive a dose of bullets.

The Shadow could picture an automobile waiting farther down the street, ready to take Culden for a ride. The secretary had known that he was "on the spot"; that the ride might be a one-way trip. Nevertheless, he had acted as did many others under such threatening pressure. He had gone quietly.

WHILE The Shadow lingered, a taxi wheeled up from Eighth Avenue. It was Moe's cab; the driver had rounded the block and had parked at the corner. He had seen The Shadow's match-flare signal.

As The Shadow boarded the cab, he glanced along the street toward a parked touring car. He saw a man moving beside the automobile.

There were men in that car. A cover-up crew, posted to watch for other visitors. Some slinker had sneaked up while The Shadow was talking to the landlady. The woman's voice had been shrill enough to carry to the sidewalk. The slinker had gone back to the touring car. It would be The Shadow's turn to be on the spot, once he rode in Moe's cab.

Calmly, The Shadow spoke to the taxi driver. He toned instructions from the interior of the cab, while opening a briefcase that had been beneath the seat. Folds of black cloth settled over The Shadow's shoulders. A slouch hat came next; then gloves and automatics, which clicked ominously in the gloom. The Shadow gave a final order.

Moe started westward. He passed the parked touring car at high speed, riding in second gear. Whizzing for the corner of Ninth Avenue, Moe gave every indication that he expected pursuit.

For a moment, the occupants of the touring car were caught unaware; then growls sounded, as the gang-manned car sped to the chase.

Moe jammed the brakes as he swung right at the corner. A door swung open; The Shadow dropped to the curb as the cab made momentary halt. Then Moe was off again, speeding away with his empty cab. From the side street, the touring car came roaring in pursuit.

Whirling out from between parked cars, a black-cloaked figure blocked the path of the oncoming machine. Headlights showed the weird shape, a living being who brandished a pair of heavy automatics. Like a form conjured from nowhere, The Shadow was challenging the passage of the crooks.

A harsh shout, as the driver jabbed the brake pedal; then changed his tactics and pressed the accelerator instead. The touring car jolted, skidded, then seemed to leap forward like an unleashed Juggernaut. The hoodlum at the wheel was ready to overhaul The Shadow. He had recognized the arch-enemy of crime.

Almost beneath the headlights, The Shadow wheeled across the street. He took the direction that the driver did not expect. With that move, he misled others also.

Again the car skidded, as the driver tried to stop it short. Snarling crooks yanked at a machine gun which they had thrust from the right side.

The thugs were too late.

As one man fired wildly with a revolver, The Shadow tongued automatic jabs from the curb. One bullet clipped the aiming thug's wrist; a second

clanged the machine gun; then a third zipped a hand that was grabbing for the rapid-fire weapon. The far door of the touring car ripped open. Howling crooks went bowling to the street.

The driver had dropped sidewise. A bullet sizzled past his shoulder and splintered the windshield. Undaunted, the driver clung to the wheel and gave the car the gas. Not quite stalled, the automobile responded. It rocketed out into the traffic of the avenue.

The Shadow fired a final bullet. He found the left rear tire of the touring car. Careening, the car skidded to the left, missed a stopping truck and sped away in flight. Its wheels were equipped with new safety tires. The Shadow's single bullet had failed to ruin the inner tube.

Two crooks had scurried off between parked cars. It was The Shadow's turn to give pursuit. He swept across the street and reached the parked line on the right. The crooks had already commandeered a taxi on the avenue and had boarded it to make a lucky dash for safety.

Police whistles were shrilling; distant sirens soon would raise their wail. The Shadow had crippled his foemen; but he had no chance to pursue them farther. The Shadow's laugh, however, carried triumph as it whispered in the darkness.

The crooks had not guessed that he was the man in Moe's taxi. Their opinion would be that The Shadow had been in ambush, awaiting their arrival. Such was the report that they would carry to the person who held Culden prisoner.

For The Shadow knew that the missing man still lived. Had he been slain, no cover-up crew would have made such vicious effort. Culden was a link in crime, needed by some crook who had become his captor.

New angles had developed in the case of the Gray Ghost.

CHAPTER VIII
NEWS TO THE SHADOW

IT was late the next afternoon. Headlines had screamed the word of new crimes. The Gray Ghost had become a front-page figure. His case was one that brought mystery.

Last night, the police had gained a lead to Thomas Culden. They had gained the secretary's full name; they had learned that he had been living at a boarding house near Eighth Avenue. But he had made a mysterious departure before the police uncovered the facts.

There had been battle in the street where Culden lived. That, too, had brought perplexity; although it had started the investigation that had produced inquiry at the boarding house. Finally, there had been new robbery on Long Island. An empty house had been entered; whether or not the crooks had made a haul was a question, for the owners were in Europe.

Reports told simply that the house had been left in disarray; the crime, itself, had been attributed to the ever-present Gray Ghost.

Crime, as a rule, caused no talk at the exclusive Cobalt Club, which boasted the most conservative membership of any Manhattan group. Quiet usually persisted at the Cobalt Club; loud or excited discussions were taboo. But on this particular day, the rule had been broken. Distinguished-looking men were gathered in little groups; their faces were long and troubled, their conversation heated.

Many of the club members were residents of Long Island. All were wealthy, otherwise they would not have belonged to the Cobalt Club. They were persons who feared future raids by the Gray Ghost.

Police Commissioner Weston was a member of the Cobalt Club. He had arranged for gun permits for those who lived on Long Island, including the ones outside the city limits. More than that, he had come to the club in person to chat with members and allay their fears of death and burglary.

Word-weary, Weston managed at last to break away from the final group. Tartly, he requested that no one disturb him for the next half hour. That courtesy conceded, Weston entered the grillroom to indulge in a light meal. He saw a lone diner seated at a table and smiled in relief as he recognized Lamont Cranston. Weston joined his friend at the table.

"JOVE, Cranston!" began the commissioner. "My head is in a whirl! It is great to meet someone who will not bother me with incessant questions."

"You made a mistake in coming here," remarked The Shadow. "You should have known that you would be deluged with questions about the Gray Ghost."

"It was policy to come. The members of the Cobalt Club are influential. I had to reassure them."

"Even though you yourself are perplexed."

Weston smiled; then shook his head.

"This Gray Ghost business is not quite so complicated as you think, Cranston," declared the commissioner. "We have begun to get at matters. Meanwhile, we have allowed the newspapers to speculate as much as they desire."

The Shadow made no comment. Silence was the best encouragement for the commissioner. Weston was in no mood to answer questions; but he was willing to talk uninterrupted.

"Regarding Culden," stated Weston, wisely. "He may not be the man we seek. We made inquiries at his boarding house. We learned that he arrived there, two nights ago, at quarter of nine. I remember your statements, Cranston, regarding the time element. If Culden reached the city at quarter of nine, he could not have been at Debrossler's at half past eight.

"Of course, he could have murdered Windler. But so could the raider who entered Debrossler's. Therefore, we have come to the conclusion that the capture of Culden may not mark the end of our quest. We feel quite sure that the man knows something; his disappearance indicates it. Nevertheless, he may simply be a tool; not the Gray Ghost himself."

The Shadow preserved silence. Weston wagged a finger.

"I know your thoughts," declared the commissioner. "You are wondering about last night's events on Long Island, where a closed house was entered. You are thinking that Culden might have been responsible for that entry. Perhaps he was; but not in the capacity of the Gray Ghost.

"Inspector Cardona has brought in a complete report. Apparently, several burglars were in the game last night. Moreover, it seems that they drew a blank. Simply a stab in the dark; a band of criminals trying to emulate the Gray Ghost's tactics.

"We have a clue." Weston leaned across the table. "It is a good one. A man was seen on Long Island yesterday afternoon; from the description given of him, he was ugly faced and could have been a certain thug known as Shanty Uhving.

"Working on this clue, Cardona was prepared. He found fingerprints on a window pane at the Long Island house. Those prints have been identified; they belong to Shanty Uhving. Our theory, therefore, is that a criminal band has moved into the Gray Ghost's preserves. Culden may be the head of that crew.

"All this is confidential, Cranston. I merely thought that it would interest you; and enable you to realize how well our investigations are progressing."

THE SHADOW had finished his meal. He left the commissioner and strolled from the grillroom. Passing through the lobby, he considered the statements that Weston had made.

The Shadow knew that Culden could not be the leader of any criminal band. The man had been forced to leave his boarding house under threat. Culden was simply a tool who had served the Gray Ghost. Some criminal, muscling in on the Gray Ghost's game, had snatched Culden and was holding him a prisoner, hoping to gain information that would help in future jobs.

Last night, the Gray Ghost had been idle. Weston was correct on that point. Today, The Shadow had received a report from Harry Vincent. The agent had been with Renright at Narrowneck, all during the preceding evening. Assuming that Renright was the Gray Ghost, this proved that the elusive lone wolf could not have been at large.

The Shadow wanted to find Culden. Unquestionably, Windler's secretary could tell facts. Thanks to one point that Weston had divulged, The Shadow had a lead through which Culden could be found. The lead was "Shanty" Uhving. Through that underling, The Shadow could uncover the new crook who had begun to compete with the Gray Ghost. Once the Gray Ghost's rival was found, Culden could also be discovered.

The Shadow knew that Weston would proceed with a search for Shanty Uhving. The police would call upon stool pigeons; they would use every effort to nail Shanty in a quiet way. That failing, they would stage a roundup; probably tomorrow night. It would be The Shadow's task to move more rapidly than the law.

Stopping in a telephone booth, The Shadow made a call. A quiet voice responded; it was that of Burbank, who served as a quick contact with active agents. The Shadow gave instructions. A search was to begin, with Shanty Uhving as the quarry. With this order, The Shadow gave a definite lead.

He had heard of Shanty Uhving in the past. The fellow was a small-fry hoodlum who had dropped from sight. In the past, Shanty had palled with another crook of his own caliber. That thug's name was "Bump" Pannard. The law had never connected the two.

Shanty Uhving would be in some hideout, if news had leaked that he was wanted. Bump Pannard, however, would be at large in the criminal badlands. He could be located by a search through gangdom's domain. Bump would probably produce a trail to Shanty; to the big shot whom Shanty served; then, finally, to Culden.

A long trail, but one that would develop quickly if followed wisely. Thus The Shadow's search for Shanty involved Bump as the first move. Capable agents would be on the job. Supporting them, The Shadow would himself join the campaign. Harry was still with Renright at Narrowneck. The Shadow was free to press the search for lesser crooks who were in Manhattan. Harry was capable of covering the supposed Gray Ghost.

DUSK had arrived; Manhattan was aglow. In certain quarters, however, gloominess persisted. Skulkers were abroad.

The grapevine, invisible telegraph of the underworld, had not yet substantiated rumors of a possible roundup. Small-fry thugs felt at liberty to prowl the confines of the underworld. They numbered hundreds, those shifty hoodlums. One among them was Bump Pannard.

COLIN RENRIGHT—young sportsman with whom Harry Vincent makes friends

Among these denizens of scumland, there were others of a different ilk. They were agents of The Shadow—a chosen few who camouflaged themselves as rowdies and thereby roved at will. One was Cliff Marsland, a square-jawed, hard-fisted chap whom the underworld regarded as a man at odds with the law. There was "Hawkeye," a crafty, shifty prowler who could pick up the most difficult trails.

Moe Shrevnitz was present also. He was covering the fringes of the badlands—cruising in his cab, parking and making visits to lesser dives frequented by hoodlums. All the while, Moe saw to it that he reached certain contact points on schedule.

For there was another searcher in the underworld tonight: The Shadow.

Sometimes garbed in black; sometimes disguised as a sweatered hoodlum, the master sleuth was penetrating deep into the realm where crooks gathered. The Shadow was covering a huge area on his own. He changed his disguise at the times when he contacted Moe's cab. The Shadow was speeding the search for Bump Pannard.

ALL during these hours of early evening, another agent was on duty elsewhere. Harry Vincent was lounging about the premises of the Narrowneck Club, out on Long Island. He was the guest of Colin Renright. Harry and the athlete had become chums.

In his study of Renright, Harry had found the fellow to be a dynamic sort. Renright had many friends at the Narrowneck Club; and they regarded him as a good fellow. Renright was a man of reserve; that was the chief reason why he was likable. Yet Harry could not drop the conviction that beneath the surface, Renright might possess a flaring disposition. Harry was of the opinion that Renright would prove dangerous if crossed.

Today's news of crime on Long Island had perplexed Harry. He still suspected that Renright might be the Gray Ghost. After dinner, Harry had received a telephone call from Burbank, with the information that last night's crime had not been the work of the Gray Ghost. Thus Harry's original conjecture was supported. The fact that he had watched Renright last night and found the man guiltless did not prove anything to Renright's credit.

Tonight, Renright had suggested a trip into Holmwood, to look up some friends. When Harry joined Renright beside the latter's car, he noticed a bulge in the man's overcoat pocket. Harry guessed that Renright's application for a gun permit had gone through, for the bulge indicated a revolver. Harry was carrying an automatic of his own; but he did not mention the fact to Renright.

They drove into Holmwood. When they reached the club, Renright inquired after several friends. Gaining information, he turned to Harry with a laugh.

"That's odd," asserted Renright. "They've all gone out to Narrowneck. We'll have to travel back there."

"They'll be at the club?" asked Harry.

"No," replied Renright. "They've gone to a stag party at Tom Forbel's. A great chap, Forbel. He has plenty of money and doesn't mind spending it. He has a flare for rare gems; we'll probably see some of them."

"We're going to Forbel's?"

"Certainly. He keeps open house. I know him well; he'll be glad to see both of us."

Two persons entered the club as Harry and Renright were leaving. One was Pierce Gilden; the other was Jane Debrossler. Harry caught their conversation.

"Thanks, Pierce," he heard Jane say. "Awfully nice of you to take me into New York. Louise took one car and father has the other. They thought the train was good enough for me."

"It isn't," laughed Gilden. "Therefore, my car is at your disposal. But don't expect me to go to the concert with you. I hate music in the raw."

Renright had noticed Harry, when he eyed the couple. Outside, Renright asked:

"Friends of yours?"

"No," replied Harry, "but I know who they are. The girl is Jane Debrossler."

"The banker's daughter?"

"Yes."

"Was the chap Pierce Gilden?"

"Yes."

"So he's the fellow I heard about!" laughed Renright. "The one who tried to stop the Gray Ghost. I'd like to have that opportunity, Vincent."

"Perhaps you will, Renright. The Gray Ghost is still at large."

"Rummaging through empty houses, according to the newspapers. No, Vincent, we can't count upon meeting the Gray Ghost. Whoever he is, he's lost his nerve. Too many people gunning for him."

Renright tapped his pocket as he spoke, making it plain that he had a revolver there. Harry smiled, as they stepped aboard the coupé. He agreed with Renright; there would be little chance of a meeting with the Gray Ghost. But he did not believe that the daring crook was finished with open crime.

When they reached Forbel's, Harry decided, he would call Burbank; then proceed to keep a steady eye on Renright. That settled, there would be no Gray Ghost at large.

Though he did not foresee it, Harry was due for a huge surprise. But before that amazement would take place, action in the case of the Gray Ghost would open up in the underworld of New York, where The Shadow's agents were prowling.

CHAPTER IX
THE NEEDED LINK

"CLIFF!"

The hoarse whisper came from the gloom of a darkened alleyway. It was Hawkeye who spoke. Cliff Marsland's low-toned response announced his identity. Cliff questioned:

"Any news, Hawkeye?"

"I've spotted Bump!" exclaimed Hawkeye. "Saw him in Doughboy Raddin's poolroom! You know the gang in there, don't you?"

"Sure! I know Bump, too. Leave it to me, Hawkeye. Tip off Moe to cover."

The agents parted. Cliff headed for the pool room, which was not far from the Bowery. He lost no time in getting there; for he knew that Bump's sojourn might be brief.

In fact, Cliff was lucky. When he entered the front door of the poolroom, he was just in time to encounter Bump on the way out. Bump was a hard-faced customer, whose jaw looked as solid as a rock. His eyes were beady, sullen; they darted quickly as Bump heard Cliff utter a greeting. Then Bump recognized the entrant. He responded:

"H'lo, Cliff."

"In a hurry?"

"Kind of."

Despite his noncommittal statement, Bump Pannard paused to find out what Cliff wanted. With a nudge of his thumb, Cliff drew Bump to a corner away from the door.

"I'm getting a crew together," Cliff confided. "Maybe I could use a guy like you, Bump, and a couple of others if you know they're right."

"What's the lay, Cliff?"

"Nothing—just yet. But there'll be something doing after I'm all set. There's lots of ways to use a bunch of gorillas."

"Big dough?"

"Maybe. If I can find a big shot who can use the crew. But the way it stands right now, I'd take anything. I've been getting stale, Bump."

"The bulls ain't after you?"

"No. That's one thing I don't have to worry about. But what good is it, if I'm doing nothing?"

Bump nodded. He was thinking about something. Cliff hoped for a reference to Shanty Uhving. He had paved the way for Bump to mention a pal. But when Bump spoke, he brought a new twist to the conversation.

"How'd you like to step into something, Cliff?" queried the hard-faced thug. "Easier than what you got in mind?"

"I'm listening, Bump."

"It won't be big dough; but it'll come soft—"

"Pipe it."

"There's another guy who'll have to do the talking. All I'm asking is, will you come in?"

Cliff shrugged his shoulders; then queried:

"You say it's good?"

"Red hot, Cliff!"

"O.K. I'll take a gamble."

BUMP nudged toward the door; Cliff followed him. They reached the sidewalk. Bump signaled across the street. A touring car, top raised, pulled from the opposite curb. There were two men in the front seat. Bump opened the rear door.

"Slide in, Cliff," he said. "We got business."

Cliff showed no hesitation. He entered the touring car with Bump. They pulled away. Cliff glanced through the rear window, in the direction of the Bowery.

"Good dope, Cliff," approved Bump. He gave a glance of his own. "Yeah, I always take a squint to see if anybody's tailing us. Say—where'd that taxi come from?"

"Just swung in off the Bowery," returned Cliff. "It isn't following us."

It was Moe's cab. Cliff knew that the smart cabby had arrived in time to see him enter the touring car.

But Cliff's comment lulled Bump. The hoodlum gave no further thought to the trailing cab.

The course of the touring car was northwest. After a fifteen-minute trip, the driver reached a side street that showed little traffic. He found a parking space. Bump nudged Cliff and they alighted from the car. The other men followed them. Bump led the way to the front of a small apartment building that was wedged between two rows of houses.

Inside the small lobby, Bump picked a button on the name board. Cliff noted the apartment number: it was D-3; but there was no name in the space beside it. This space was one of many vacancies. Cliff slipped his hand into his coat pocket. He performed a quick, but simple, operation while the hand remained in the pocket.

Cliff was carrying a pack of cigarette papers; also the stub of a soft-lead pencil. On the top sheet of the cigarette papers, he marked "D-3"; then quickly twisted the paper into a little wad. He brought out the pack of cigarette papers; also a bag of tobacco. Starting to roll a cigarette, he let the tiny wad of paper fall to the floor.

The door of the apartment house was buzzing. Bump clicked it open. Cliff and the others followed Bump.

They reached an automatic elevator, entered. Bump pressed the button for the third floor. Cliff was continuing his action of rolling a cigarette. Just as he completed it, Bump remarked:

"Got any idea who we're going to see?"

Cliff shook his head.

"I'll tell you who," informed Bump, with a grin. "Dude Cottran!"

The name brought a real stare of surprise from Cliff.

"Didn't guess it, did you?" laughed Bump. "You thought Dude was sticking to that flossy nightclub of his. Well, he's still handling it as a sideline; but he's got something bigger. You'll hear about it, Cliff."

THE elevator had reached the third floor. The passengers stepped off and headed for Apartment D-3. Meanwhile, down in the entry, another arrival had come into view. It was Moe Shrevnitz. The cab driver had trailed the touring car all the way.

Hawkeye had contacted Moe at a time when The Shadow was absent from the cab. Moe had headed for the poolroom; he had taken up the trail on his own. He was taking a risk—coming into the entry of this apartment building, for Moe knew that there might be spies outside. Nevertheless, Moe was a good bluffer.

He had pulled a memo book from his pocket. Consulting it, he looked along the names on the wallboard. Picking one at random, Moe faked a pressure of the button. He waited, holding the receiver of the apartment telephone. Again he pretended to press the button; this time, he dropped the little book. Apparently getting no response, Moe clanged the receiver and emitted an angry growl.

Stooping, he picked up his book and strode from the apartment house, faking the ire of a taxi driver who has been summoned to an address, only to find that the person had already gone. Moe clambered aboard his cab; the motor was still running. He drove away along the street.

As he turned the corner, Moe darted a glance back toward the apartment house. No one was on his trail. Moe grinned.

From between the pages of his little book, he drew the wadded cigarette paper. Moe had spied it on the floor. He had picked it up with the book. Unfolding the wad, Moe read the simple message, "D-3." He knew its meaning. Moe's next task was to reach a telephone and pass the word to Burbank.

UP in the apartment house, Cliff Marsland had entered Apartment D-3, to find a tall, long-faced man seated in an easy chair. Cliff knew "Dude" Cottran. The tall man came to his feet and gave him a hearty handshake. Then, turning to Bump Pannard, Dude remarked:

"Good work, Bump! I hadn't figured you could land as swell a torpedo as Marsland. Have you slipped him the lay?"

"I left that to you, Dude."

"All right." Dude turned to Cliff. "Sit down. I'll give you the inside. I've got a great racket, Marsland, if it begins to work. But I needed a couple of more men, on account of last night."

"Dude's got an outfit, Cliff," added Bump. "That's why I was going the rounds tonight. Linking up some regulars. There weren't none down at Doughboy's, Dude. Only Cliff here; I run into him by accident."

"Marsland's as good as any there," decided Dude. "We don't want lugs in this outfit. There's four of you here; two downstairs. That's enough."

Two downstairs. Cliff was ready to hazard a guess that one would be Shanty Uhving. He hoped that Dude would call the wanted thug upstairs. Dude decided upon a plan that was even more to Cliff's liking.

"Come along," ordered Dude. "We're going down to the basement."

"Want me to stay here, Dude?" queried Bump. "So's to have a lookout, just in case?"

"What's the good?" demanded Dude. "Nobody knows that this joint is mine. Come on; we'll all go down."

They left the apartment. Dude locked the door and the quintet entered the automatic elevator. Dude pressed a button marked "B"; the descent ended when they reached the basement. There,

Dude led the way toward a distant locker room. He knocked at the door.

A squint-eyed thug opened the door for them. Entering the lighted locker room, Cliff saw a door beyond.

"Hello, Herb," said Dude, to the man who had admitted them. "Where's Shanty?"

"In with the mug," returned Herb. "Waiting for you, Dude."

Dude rapped at the inner door. It opened. Cliff saw another rowdy, whom he recognized. He was the man who was a factor in the trail that Cliff had sought: Bump Pannard's pal, Shanty Uhving.

SHANTY knew Cliff. He grinned and waved a greeting. He stepped aside; Dude motioned Cliff into the inner locker room. The others followed in a group. Dude pointed to a corner, where Cliff saw a pitiful, huddled shape, bound and gagged upon the stone floor.

"Know him?" queried Dude.

Cliff shook his head. Dude stooped and raised the prisoner's head. He loosened the gag so Cliff could see the man's face. Cliff delivered another headshake.

"Didn't think you'd know him," snorted Dude. "He don't count for much. But he's a guy that we'll get plenty out of. I'll tell you who he is, Cliff. This guy's name is Culden. He's the boob that the cops think is the Gray Ghost."

Dude's henchmen joined in a raucous laugh. The guffaws pleased Cliff Marsland. Poker-faced, The Shadow's agent was covering the elation that he secretly felt. Cliff had served The Shadow well.

Thanks to keen headwork with Bump Pannard, Cliff had found the trail to Shanty Uhving. With Shanty he had discovered the man whom The Shadow sought to find ahead of the law.

Whatever Culden's part in crime, Cliff was due to learn it.

CHAPTER X
FACTS FOR THE SHADOW

"TAKE the gag off him!"

Dude Cottran gave the order. Bump and Shanty ripped the gag from Culden's mouth. Cliff saw a sallow face with lips that trembled through fear. Dude snapped a warning to the prisoner:

"No squawks out of you, mug!"

Culden was panting. He looked too scared to speak.

"Here's the dope, Marsland." Dude had turned to Cliff. "This guy Culden was working for the Gray Ghost. I got wise to it. I'll give you the lowdown. It started along about the time when the Gray Ghost first got busy.

"Culden here worked for old man Windler. Used to come into town nights and spend dough at my nightclub. He owed me money, Culden did, and a week ago he came around to tell me he was pretty near broke. Said he'd lost his job with Windler; but he'd get the dough for me later."

"I'll have the money for you!" panted Culden. "Honest, Dude, if you'll let me out of here—"

"Shut up, you double-crosser!" snarled Dude. Culden silenced. Then, to Cliff, Dude added: "I asked Culden where the cash was coming from. He let it slip that he was in with the Gray Ghost. That listened good."

Dude chuckled reminiscently.

"I saw a chance," he resumed. "A good one. The Gray Ghost was getting plenty of swag. I figured I could try his racket. So I got an outfit together and waited. I wanted to make sure that Culden wasn't passing out hokum. When Windler took the bump and the Gray Ghost grabbed Debrossler's hundred grand, I figured I'd been a palooka. I should have made Culden blab.

"I missed on the Debrossler job; but I knew there'd be others. That's why I grabbed Culden. I was the guy that went around to his boarding house and talked him into taking a ride. We brought him here; I left Bump and some other guys to cover, in case the Gray Ghost showed up to see Culden."

"And we saw him," chimed in Bump. "We went out to get him; but we run into The Shadow. That's what the fight was about, Cliff. The Shadow clipped a couple of the crew while we was making our getaway."

"Never mind that," remarked Dude. "Forget The Shadow. We've got other things to talk about.

"Listen, Cliff. I had Shanty Uhving out on Long Island, looking over the ground. Yesterday, he called in to tell me about a big house out there— an empty joint that belonged to some people named Robertson.

"When I got Culden here, I asked him about the Robertsons. He said they had dough; but that was all he knew. So I went out with a couple of fellows and we met Shanty. We got into the Robertson house, but didn't land anything worthwhile. We left it as we found it. Figured the cops would lay it on the Gray Ghost."

"And they did!"

The growled comment came from Shanty. Dude rasped an angry response.

"Did they?" he queried. "Maybe, Shanty; and maybe not. You left a trail a mile wide while you were out there. That's why I'm keeping you in here."

DUDE paused. He turned to Cliff. He stated: "We've got to make this fellow Culden talk."

Culden whined piteously.

"Honest!" he wailed. "I don't know who the Gray Ghost is! He made the deal with me by telephone. He wanted to know if there was any swag at Windler's. That's when I told him that there would be money at Debrossler's."

"Cut it!" snapped Dude. "We're wise to the way the Gray Ghost works. He wouldn't have stooges all over Long Island. He'd use one guy to hand him the lowdown on a lot of places. You're the one he used, Culden."

"Honest—"

Dude snarled an interruption. Bump put a suggestion:

"How about me and Shanty giving this mug the heat?"

"Maybe," decided Dude, "if he won't talk any other way. Look here, Culden. Give us the lowdown on the Gray Ghost. We'll get rid of him if he makes trouble. Let us in on the next jobs. You'll get your cut, as good as the Gray Ghost would give you."

"I only knew about Debrossler," panted Culden. "I only learned that by accident. How can I tell you what I don't know? I couldn't pick out the Gray Ghost if I saw him."

"Cut the stall!" growled Dude, savagely. "You heard what Bump said about the heat. He and Shanty know how to give it. If you want it, Culden, you'll have it! But remember—you asked for it."

Culden's whines were incoherent. Cliff studied the cowering man; then turned to Dude.

"Slide out to the other room," he suggested, in an undertone. "Leave Culden here alone. I've got an idea."

Dude nodded. He ordered the others to move to the outer locker room. Dude and Cliff came last; Dude shut the door and locked it.

"Spill it, Cliff."

"There's a better way to handle Culden," declared Cliff. "Maybe he knows the Gray Ghost and maybe he doesn't. In either case, he knows that the Gray Ghost can get away with plenty."

"Meaning that the Gray Ghost is more of a big shot than I am?"

"That's probably Culden's way of looking at it."

Dude grunted angrily.

"Maybe he figures the Gray Ghost is big enough to blow in here," persisted Cliff. "If Culden figures that way, he will keep on stalling."

"Not after we put the heat on him."

"Maybe not. But there's a better system. Get him to think that the Gray Ghost knows he's here."

"How are you going to do that?"

"I can swing it. He's seen the rest of you before. I'm a newcomer. Maybe Culden will fall for my bluff."

Dude nodded his approval.

"I'll go in there alone," suggested Cliff. "Leave the door open while I begin to act tough. When I motion you out, close the door. Then I can get to work."

"We'll try it."

DUDE unlocked the door. He and Cliff entered. The Shadow's agent surveyed Culden. The prisoner looked up and shifted. Cliff's glare was unpleasant. Culden was troubled at sight of this new inquisitor.

"You'll do some talking," prophesied Cliff, in a growl. "You're yellow, Culden! You won't need any heat. You squawked to the Gray Ghost about Windler and Debrossler. You'll squawk to me about the Gray Ghost."

Cliff was stooping, his face thrust forward. Culden had winced; he was compressing his lips tightly.

"Afraid of yourself, eh?" queried Cliff. "Ready to blab, aren't you?"

He motioned to Dude. The big shot stepped into the outer locker room and closed the door behind him. He nodded to his henchmen.

"Cliff's the guy to swing it," informed Dude. "We won't need the heat. Wait and see."

UPSTAIRS, another door had closed. It was the outer door of the apartment house. The Shadow had entered. From the gloom beside the door, he had easily forced the latch. In the dull light of the first-floor hall, The Shadow approached the elevator. Clad in black, he made a sinister figure.

The Shadow pressed the button that brought the elevator to the ground floor. He saw its lights come upward beyond the glass panes of the door. The Shadow entered the car and pressed the third-floor button.

On the third floor, he approached the door of Apartment D-3. Close against the door, he listened intently. There were no sounds from within. The Shadow went to the rear of the hall; he opened a window and peered out into darkness.

A dull light showed a window of Dude Cottran's apartment. The rail of a fire escape offered a starting point. Mounting the rail, The Shadow stretched along the brick wall. Suddenly, his form began to sway downward. He had passed the balance point.

The Shadow's right toe hooked beneath the rail. His left arm, swinging wide, clutched the window ledge as his falling body reached it. The stretch was a long one; but it was not too great. Poised horizontally between rail and window, The Shadow gained a higher grip with his right hand. He let his legs swing from the rail.

Swaying like a living pendulum, The Shadow hung above the solid darkness. Pressing the partly opened window sash, he forced it higher; then drew his body into an inner room of the apartment.

Swinging to his feet, The Shadow was ready for any chance lookout who might still be on hand. His fist clutched an automatic.

The weapon was not needed. Inspection told The Shadow that the apartment was empty. Herein, Cliff had gained no opportunity to tell The Shadow where his next location would be. Cliff had not been able to risk a wadded message after he had met Dude Cottran.

From reports, The Shadow had divined that Cliff had gained the confidence of Bump Pannard. That meant that he would also be acceptable to Shanty Uhving. Moe had seen Cliff with the men from the touring car. All had been friendly when they entered the apartment house.

Accepted by both Bump and Shanty, Cliff would also be well received by the big shot whom that pair served. In the apartment, The Shadow discovered a cigarette case with the initial "C"; he also found paper match packs from the nightclub that Dude Cottran owned. The Shadow easily fixed the identity of the man whom Cliff had met here.

As The Shadow finished his search, he stopped by the outer door of the apartment. In the mellow glow of floor lamps, he became a weird-shaped visitant. The wall caught the shaded shape of a hawklike silhouette. From hidden lips a whispered laugh crept eerily through the room.

The Shadow's laugh was foreboding. The Shadow could foresee trouble for Cliff, if the latter had found Culden. Cliff would be confronted with a dilemma: the task of making Culden talk without letting Dude gain the facts that Cliff wanted for The Shadow.

Though Cliff had left a message for Moe at the door of the apartment house, the process had not been repeated here. There was not a clue in Dude's apartment to guide The Shadow to Cliff's present location. Yet, wherever he might be, Cliff would find the ground dangerous. His need for aid could be urgent.

It was The Shadow's task to take up the blind trail.

CHAPTER XI
CRIME FORETOLD

THE SHADOW was right. Cliff was faced with trouble. Cliff, himself, was realizing it, as he talked to Culden. He had chosen a course that brought immediate results; but promised subsequent difficulties.

"I'm from the Gray Ghost."

Cliff spoke the words emphatically, as he crouched on the floor beside the prisoner. He added:

"I know all about your alibi. The Gray Ghost told me."

Culden looked up from the stone floor. The single light of the inner locker room showed an eager look in the prisoner's eyes. Dude Cottran had known nothing about the alibi. Culden was half convinced that Cliff was actually an emissary from the Gray Ghost.

"You brought Yenner's dog in from Holmwood," whispered Cliff. "It gave you an alibi to cover the time that the Ghost was working at Windler's and Debrossler's. I'm here to get you out of a jam, Culden."

The prisoner nodded.

"I didn't have time to find out how much you know," added Cliff. "I got the word over the telephone from the Gray Ghost. He told me to keep you from talking; but he didn't say about what."

"I've never seen the Gray Ghost," responded Culden, in a hoarse whisper. "If you know who he is, don't tell me. I—I've had a hard time holding back what I do know."

Cliff nodded. He was thinking quickly. He made a stab with his next question:

"You mean about the next job?"

A nod from Culden. Cliff took another chance.

"The one set for tonight?"

A new nod from Culden. Cliff shook his head.

"It won't matter much," he declared. "Tonight's job is off."

Culden's eyes popped.

"It's off?" he queried. "You don't mean the job at Forbel's?"

Cliff nodded.

"But it would be a setup," protested Culden. "I was out at Forbel's once; I saw his place at Narrowneck. Mr. Windler told me all about Forbel's jewels."

"I know," agreed Cliff, "but the Gray Ghost wasn't sure about you, Culden. He wanted to make sure you hadn't talked. Well, since you haven't, the job is for me to get you out of here."

"Can you work it?"

"I think so. I'll tell Dude that I'm taking you along with me. So as to get your confidence. I'll tip him off to follow us in a car. He'll give me a slow bus; and he'll be trailing in a speedy one. That will make him think it's on the level."

"But if he follows us—"

"Don't worry." Cliff was loosening Culden's bonds. "There'll be somebody else to pick up Dude's trail. Come on, Culden. Act like you're a bit squeamish; as if you didn't know whether or not to trust me."

CLIFF helped the unbound prisoner to his feet. Culden staggered, cramped. He managed to brace himself against the wall. He stretched wearily; and Cliff helped him falter toward the door. When they stopped there, Cliff waited a few moments; then opened the door and helped Culden into the outer room.

Dude and the crowd were waiting. Cliff saw Bump and Shanty spring forward, each from a different side. He waved them back and spoke to Dude.

"This fellow's all right," declared Cliff, indicating Culden. "You just had him jittery, Dude. The Windler job was all he did for the Gray Ghost. He was afraid you had him slated for the spot. I told him he was all wrong."

"Go on," suggested Dude, gruffly.

"Get me a buggy," said Cliff. "Culden and I are going out to Long Island. Maybe he'll be able to remember a few things that will help us."

Dude was nodding wisely.

"Like the dog, huh?" he questioned. "And this job that the Gray Ghost had slated for tonight? At Forbel's, huh? Out in Narrowneck?"

A gulp from Culden. Cliff tightened, and tried to preserve his calm.

"I was listening in," snarled Dude. "See those boxes? I was on top of them, with my ear to that ventilator, there at the ceiling. I heard your gab, Marsland. You're the double-crosser!"

Cliff scowled.

"You've queered it, Dude," he asserted. "I bluffed Culden; and you're dumb enough to think I was passing him the straight dope. I told you what I intended to do. You were all for it—"

"Yeah?" Dude snarled, viciously. His men had closed in about Cliff, ready with prodding revolvers. "Sure I was all for it—until I heard you pass out dope that I didn't know."

"I bluffed Culden into talking about Forbel's."

"Maybe you did. But you started the talk about that dog. Culden knew what you were talking about, as soon as you mentioned an alibi!"

There was no way out. Cliff knew that denials would be useless. Dude had listened in too early. It was plain that Cliff had known facts about Culden. Dude pictured Cliff as a henchman of the Gray Ghost. To disprove that belief, Cliff would have to announce himself as an agent of The Shadow. That would mean certain death.

Dude had yanked a revolver of his own. Six guns, in all, were covering Cliff and Culden. Dude jabbed forward, snarling an order:

"Back into that inner room!"

THERE was still a chance for life. Cliff recognized the fact, as he followed Dude's command. Dude was in a class with Culden. Dude thought that both of them knew more about the Gray Ghost. Perhaps Culden did. That was something that Cliff had hoped to uncover. But Cliff knew that his own knowledge had been practically exhausted. He knew that Harry

Vincent was covering a man named Colin Renright; but proof had not yet been gained that Renright was the Gray Ghost.

Thus Cliff had no opportunity for further bluff. In fact, he could not mention Renright, even to stall for his own life. That would be passing danger on to Harry, blocking The Shadow's further plans. Cliff eyed the ugly faces of Bump and Shanty. Torture would be their specialty. They could give the heat. But Cliff was confident that he could take it.

"Maybe we'll let you mugs live a while," announced Dude, in a tone that had become a purr. "We'll mooch in on this Forbel job ourselves. After that, we'll talk some more."

Cliff gained a hunch from Dude's smoothness. The big shot was trying to press his victims back into the inner room, by giving them a soft promise. Cliff could see a reason for Dude's policy. He wanted the victims as deep into the cellar as possible, so that the noise of gunfire would not be heard.

Culden was already cowering back into his former prison. Cliff was on the threshold. A few steps backward; then would come a surge from Dude and the crew. Murder would be done within the closed door of the inner room.

Dude had learned enough. He was ready to eliminate his victims on the strength of the one lead that he had gained. Neither bluff nor truth would suffice to keep Cliff and Culden alive.

Cliff still had his automatic in his pocket. Dude had considered it unnecessary to frisk him, because of the overweight of numbers. His shoulder against the flimsy door of the inner room, Cliff decided upon quick action. His right hand, half raised, was beside the door. The fact that the barrier opened inward was to Cliff's advantage.

With a sudden twist, Cliff grabbed the door and slammed it squarely into the faces of his captors. One man—Shanty—was quick enough to meet it with his shoulder. Yanking his gun with his right hand, Cliff hurled his weight against the door in an attempt to drive Shanty back.

Cliff failed. Shanty had wedged a revolver between the door and the frame. Others drove from the far side. The door lifted clear from its hinges. Cliff was propelled across the room, flattening beside Culden, who had cowered in a corner.

The best that Cliff could hope for was an exchange of shots, a chance to wing one or two of his adversaries while the band was shooting him down. Cliff was rising to gain aim. So were the foemen who had sprawled with the smashed door.

In that instant, there came a muffled gunshot, from the door of the outer locker room. Where a lock had been, a hole gaped; from it curled a wreath of smoke. A powerful jolt, and the outer door flung inward. Crooks had turned; Cliff was staring, transfixed.

All recognized the figure on the threshold. It was The Shadow. Arrived at the outer locker room, he had shot the lock from the door; then banged the barrier inward.

CLIFF could not guess how The Shadow had found the hideout. He had realized previously that he had made an error in leaving no clue. None, however, had been necessary. The Shadow had pieced facts, to learn where the occupants of Dude's apartment had gone.

When he had first pressed the button for the automatic elevator, The Shadow had seen through the glass elevator door as the car came up from the basement. The Shadow knew that passengers had gone below. He also knew that he had arrived soon after Cliff, for Moe's relayed call had reached him promptly.

Finding Dude's apartment empty and unguarded, The Shadow had logically assumed that the occupants were the ones who had taken the car to the basement. Descending, he had seen the closed locker rooms as the only possible hiding place. He had reached the outer door, to hear tumult from within.

Sight of The Shadow caused crooks to wheel. One alone remembered Cliff. That was Shanty, the first through the door. Shanty made a grab for Cliff, striking at him with a revolver. Cliff grappled; they floundered across the inner locker room.

Five guns had swung toward The Shadow. The crooks were belated in their aim; but they had luck. The Shadow, swinging in from the outer door, had twisted quickly to one side. He was stumbling as he struck a projecting box upon the floor. The Shadow, too, was delayed in aim.

The cloaked fighter made up for it. As he swung his automatics, he leaped forward across the short space that lay between him and his enemies. Instinctively, crooks jumped to stop him. Gun arms swung, weapons clashed. The Shadow was in the center of a mêlée.

He had an objective that the crooks did not guess. The Shadow was trying to turn the battle outward, to carry it away from the inner room, where Cliff was fighting Shanty. Guns boomed amid the fracas. It was then that The Shadow performed another action.

Grabbing the nearest of the flaying arms, he hauled one crook from the crowd. Rolling sidewise, The Shadow dropped to the floor, while revolvers fired above him. Jabbing a .45 above the shoulder of the man whom he had thrown, The Shadow spurted quick shots into the massed crew beyond. One thug wavered; another floundered, to fall as

Jabbing a .45 above the shoulder of the man whom he had thrown, The Shadow spurted quick shots into the massed crew beyond.

another shield for The Shadow.

There was an instant's lull; then a muffled shot from the inner locker room. A body thudded; Cliff Marsland came swinging toward the door between. He had managed to finish Shanty Uhving.

Dude Cottran was nearest to the outer door. He uttered a wild yell. Henchmen turned and followed him in flight. There were only two who could respond. One was Bump Pannard; the other was the squint-eyed crook called Herb. He was the one whom The Shadow had wounded; his legs, however, were still able to carry him.

Shanty Uhving lay in the inner room. Two thugs were flat upon the spot from which The Shadow arose. One was the crook whom he had first seized; the hoodlum was dead from bullets delivered by his pals. The other, too, was silent. He had taken the brunt of The Shadow's rapid fire.

BEFORE The Shadow or Cliff could aim for the scudding figures of Dude and his two followers, a wild-screaming man came rocketing from the inner room. It was Culden; the gunfire had driven him berserk. Deserting his safe corner, he was dashing close on the heels of the very men who had sought his life.

Worst of all, he came between The Shadow and the outer door. The Shadow lost a chance to drop Bump Pannard. Cliff fired; but his shot was hasty. Crooks were dashing for a stairway, Culden with them. The Shadow hissed a command to Cliff. Together, they took up the trail.

The Shadow was the first to reach the steps, which were past a projecting corner. As he reached the turn, a shot sounded. A figure came tumbling downward. It was Culden; he had been recognized by the men with whom he fled. Beyond the sprawling, lifeless body, The Shadow saw the murderer. Dude Cottran had dropped behind the others, to finish Culden.

Dude saw The Shadow. His gun already lifted, the big shot started a fusillade toward the bottom of the steps. His aim was hurried; his first shot alone came close to The Shadow.

Timed with Dude's opening came The Shadow's response. Two quick shots staggered Dude. Dude's revolver wabbled, as he tugged the trigger. The gun left his useless grip; with a coughed gasp, the murderer tottered forward and came rolling, bouncing, to twist crazily across the body of Culden. Victim and killer had found the same resting place.

Springing across the fallen bodies, The Shadow headed up the stairs, with Cliff at his heels. In the hallway, The Shadow stopped. Guns were sounding from the front street. He saw a stumbling man do a dive in the entry beyond the glass-paned front door. It was Bump Pannard. More shots told that Herb was going the same route. The last of the crooks had encountered a patrol car.

The first shot below must have been heard. A report had gone in; the police had acted with promptitude. It was too soon, however, for a cordon to have closed. The Shadow motioned Cliff to a rear exit from the hall. They reached darkness; there, as The Shadow weaved a departing course, Cliff gave the news that Culden had issued concerning coming crime at Forbel's.

SOON afterward, a coupé was speeding across the Williamsburg Bridge, en route to Narrowneck, Long Island. At the wheel was The Shadow, a shrouded, almost invisible driver. Beside him was Cliff Marsland.

Dude Cottran and his crew had been eliminated. The Gray Ghost had no rivals. One clue alone remained through which to reach the supercrook.

The Shadow was seeking the Gray Ghost.

CHAPTER XII
THE GHOST APPEARS

WHILE The Shadow was finding battle in Manhattan. Harry Vincent was stationed amid quiet surroundings. He and a dozen others were guests at the home of Thomas Forbel.

That Forbel was a millionaire, no one could doubt. The magnificence of his home displayed the fact. The place was a mansion that dominated a large stretch of ground on the very shore of Long Island Sound. The interior furnishings were elaborate and expensive.

The ground floor held at least a dozen rooms, centering upon a mammoth hallway, with a special cloakroom at the back, beyond a grand stairway. The floors were literally paved with Oriental rugs, themselves worth a small fortune. Huge pieces of antique furniture added to the amassed wealth.

Forbel's living room was the size of a small ballroom. It was used for informal gatherings only. Harry heard mention of the fact that the reception room, on the other side of the house, was twice the size of the living room.

The living room had many windows. At one side were two French windows, spaced far apart, that opened to a side veranda. The room itself was so large that the gathered guests made a very small cluster in the corner where they had assembled.

Forbel, himself, was a genial man, of small build, but energetic. He was middle-aged; his head was rotund and slightly bald. He wore large-rimmed spectacles; but his eyes were sharp. He studied each guest keenly.

Two flunkies were serving refreshments when Harry and Renright arrived. The living room was filled with cigar smoke, puffed from the heavy Havana perfectos that Forbel had provided for his guests. Forbel greeted Renright cheerily; and seemed pleased to make Harry's acquaintance. Then, counting the number of the assembled throng, the millionaire delivered an announcement.

"Make yourselves at home, gentlemen," said Forbel. "Very shortly, I shall have a treat for you. During my last trip to the Orient, I brought back a collection of rare gems. They were once the property of a spendthrift rajah; I purchased them for a New York museum.

"Some of the guests have expressed a desire to see my picture gallery. It is scarcely worth a visit, for I have donated most of my best paintings to various museums. However, there are some items that may be of interest.

"Therefore, I suggest that we visit the gallery first and make the trip a brief one. After that, I shall display the gems."

A FEW of the guests decided to accompany Forbel. Harry was undecided; he had started a conversation with a man beside him. Since that guest retained his chair, Harry did the same. The other man remarked:

"Forbel is right. Most of his best paintings are gone. It is better to wait until he comes back. The gems will be worthwhile."

"Where does he keep them?" questioned Harry.

"In this room," replied the guest. "He has a wall safe that is just about burglar proof."

Harry decided that it was best to remain in the living room. He looked about for Renright; the man was missing. He had gone along with the group to the picture gallery. Nevertheless, the information about the wall safe made Harry stick to his decision.

Watching Renright was his job—but for a specific purpose; namely, to learn if Renright happened to be the Gray Ghost. Should Renright be planning crime, his objective would be the jewels. Since they were here, this was the place to stay.

Harry continued his conversation. It was twenty minutes before Forbel returned, followed by stragglers who had evidently lost their way about while returning from the gallery. Harry saw Renright enter, nodding to another man who was saying that the house was as confusing as a maze.

Harry expected to see Forbel go to the wall safe, wherever it might be. Instead, the bespectacled millionaire proceeded with another announcement. He looked like a master of ceremonies, for while his guests had come in street clothes, Forbel, as host, had donned a tuxedo.

"GENTLEMEN," stated Forbel, "we have all heard talk of a criminal who styles himself the Gray Ghost. I have been warned that he might attempt entry here, tonight."

A buzz from the listeners. Forbel gestured for silence.

"Not a definite warning," he said, in a modifying tone. "Merely a logical assumption on the part of certain friends. Since the Gray Ghost seeks wealth, he would naturally wish my gems. It is known that I have them here.

"However, I am quite prepared for the Gray Ghost. My valet, Hembroke, is outside the house. He has three other servants at his call. All are armed with rifles. As for myself, I keep a loaded revolver in my study desk. I picked up the weapon on my way down from the gallery."

Forbel produced the weapon in question, drawing it from the pocket of his tuxedo. He smiled as he studied his guests.

"I have heard," remarked Forbel, "that quite a few residents of Long Island have obtained permits to carry guns. Perhaps some of you have come equipped for a ghost hunt. Am I right?

"Ah, Wilbersham!" He bowed to a tall, stoop-shouldered man. "And you, Greaves!"—this was to a stocky individual. "You have your revolvers with you? I should be pleased to have you act as vigilantes, along with myself."

"Greaves and I came together," returned Wilbersham. "We decided to leave our guns with our overcoats. They are in the cloakroom."

"Procure them at once," ordered Forbel. "What? Are there no others? Ah, Renright, I am glad that you are armed. I have heard that you are an excellent shot."

"I have that reputation," smiled Renright, producing his revolver from his pocket. "Furthermore, Forbel, I make it a practice to keep my gun in my own possession. I transferred this revolver to my hip pocket, when I left my overcoat in the cloakroom."

Renright aimed the gun at a lamp bracket on the other side of the room. Harry noted that he picked a spot away from any persons, the first sign of a good marksman when practicing aim. The weapon was a police positive, of .38 caliber.

"Bring on the Gray Ghost," laughed Renright, lowering the revolver and placing it in his coat pocket. "Here are Wilbersham and Greaves, back with us, Forbel."

"With their side pockets bulging," added the millionaire, putting away his own gun. "Very well. Keep posted, gentlemen. I might remind you, however"—his tone took on a mock seriousness—"that the Gray Ghost is reputed to be a spectral personage. They say that he is a living wraith; that he bears a charm over weapons. Bullets might pass through him as they would through thin air."

HEARTY laughter followed the jest. Forbel smiled himself; then went to a corner of the living room. He placed his hands upon a panel and pressed at different corners. The panel swung open, showing a safe within.

"I shall have my own revolver ready," decided Forbel, drawing the gun. "Fortunately, I can manipulate this combination with my left hand as well as with my right."

Wilbersham and Greaves produced their guns. Harry noted that the two were nervous. A tenseness had settled. Renright was smiling; with a shrug of his shoulders, he lowered his hand to his coat pocket, ready to produce his .38, if necessary.

TOM FORBEL—wealthy gem collector, who is robbed by the Gray Ghost.

Harry let his right hand slide to his hip. He had said nothing about the gun which he was carrying—partly because of Renright, also because he was a comparative stranger to the other guests. It was his turn to be ready, even though the whole thing had the semblance of a farce.

The door of the safe came open. With his left hand, Forbel removed a large jewel box and brought it toward the light. A slight creaking sound came as the millionaire approached the others. Harry attributed it to a board in the floor; he did not realize until afterward that the heavy rugs would have muffled such a sound.

It was Forbel who realized that something had happened. He was facing the others; he looked toward the group, then beyond. A horrified startlement swept the millionaire's features. Men stared in the direction of his gaze. The creak was explained.

The nearer of the French windows had opened. Just past the range of guests, stood an intruder. Tall, he was clad in garments of gray that made him appear lithe. Trousers, shirt, both were of a jersey material. Over his head extended a hood of the same dark gray. Eyes peered through slits. A snarl issued from the man's masked mouth. His hands were gloved in a fashion, by mittenlike extensions of the jersey sleeves. In one, the gray-clad man held a revolver.

The Gray Ghost had arrived!

GASPS greeted the masked marauder. Though a dozen men thronged Forbel's living room, a helplessness had seized them. The Gray Ghost stepped toward the table where Forbel stood. His hand was moving back and forth, almost carelessly. For a moment, the revolver muzzle hesitated, pointing away from Forbel.

The millionaire acted. His revolver was almost at aim. Leveling it quickly, Forbel gave a fierce cry and tugged the trigger. A *click* was his reward.

Forbel's loaded gun was empty!

The Gray Ghost laughed harshly. Forbel gaped, as the robber looked in his direction. Wilbersham and Greaves had aimed, seeing their chance to fire. Simultaneously, they pulled revolver triggers. New clicks sounded.

Somehow, the Gray Ghost had entered this house beforehand. He had found Forbel's revolver; also those of the guests. He had removed the cartridges. Such was Harry's verdict, as he saw the Gray Ghost clamp his free hand upon Forbel's jewel box.

The lid clicked open. Rare gems in curious mountings made a dazzling sight; but the glitter did not last. The Gray Ghost slammed the lid. Snarling a vicious laugh, he backed toward the door to the porch, steady with his revolver while he carried the jewels beneath his left arm.

Near the door, he paused to deliver a final harsh jeer. It was then that Renright sprang to sudden challenge.

Renright had not drawn his gun; nor had Harry. Both had been caught off guard. They were too close for comfort when the Gray Ghost had approached the table. Renright, however, had managed to shift slightly; to whip out his revolver.

Jabbing the weapon toward the Gray Ghost, Renright fired. This was no *click;* the bark of the revolver was ferocious, as flame spat from the muzzle. With each recoil of his wrist, Renright delivered another shot—four in quick succession, while the Gray Ghost watched him. Renright stopped after the fourth shot, his eyes wide in a stare.

Straight though Renright's aim had been, the Gray Ghost stood unharmed. The snarl that he uttered was one of derision. To every brain came Forbel's jest: the rumor that the Gray Ghost was immune to bullets.

The statement had been proven!

Leering toward Renright, who stood with smoking revolver motionless, the Gray Ghost snorted a contempt that made his whole body shake. Coolly, he raised the side of his jersey and thrust the flat jewel box beneath. One hand free, he tightened his

Straight though Renright's aim had been, the Gray Ghost stood unharmed. The snarl that he uttered was one of derision. To every brain came...the rumor that the Gray Ghost was immune to bullets.

hood and delivered a profound bow to those who stood within the room.

That done, the Gray Ghost stepped back, half through the French window. His spectral powers proven, the hooded marauder was prepared to make his getaway into the night.

CHAPTER XIII
FLIGHT IN THE DARK

THE Gray Ghost had played his cards well. His deliberate departure was the best of his varied strokes. It was a move that bid fair to hold men dumbfounded. Renright with his smoking revolver, stood stunned. Others, unarmed or with empty guns, did well to copy his example.

There was one, however, who still stood ready to challenge the Gray Ghost's triumph. That man was Harry Vincent, still waiting opportunity to whip forth his own gun. Harry gained the opportunity at that moment when the Gray Ghost stood framed within the window.

Shifting to the right, Harry hid his right hand; with a quick move, he wheeled to the left, uttering a shout to draw the Gray Ghost's attention. He wanted the marauder to aim for him, not for the others. With his swing, Harry was bringing his automatic squarely to aim. He had gained a quick advantage.

The Gray Ghost heard the shout. His own gun was half lowered. He saw the leveled muzzle of Harry's pistol. With a sharp cry, the Gray Ghost changed tactics. He leaped for the porch and dived for safety. He was gone before Harry could pull the trigger.

In fact, The Shadow's agent was too astonished to fire. Renright, chagrined at his previous defeat, was the man who came to action. Remembering that he had two more cartridges, Renright fired furiously. One bullet shattered a pane of the French window. The other ripped woodwork from the door frame.

As Renright's next trigger stroke clicked a dead cartridge, Harry bounded toward the window that the Gray Ghost had left. Reaching the porch, he aimed blankly into the dark and fired two shots in the direction that he thought the Gray Ghost had taken.

Already, shouts were sounding near the house. Hembroke and the other watchers had heard the gunfire and were coming up with their flashlights. Forbel had reached Harry. The millionaire shouted instructions to his men.

"It's the Gray Ghost!" howled Forbel. "He's seized the jewels! Find him—get him—"

A flashlight swung upon the lawn. It was Hembroke's. The valet gave a shout, as a jerseyed man leaped from behind a tree. Harry aimed for the Gray Ghost and fired; the range was too great to hit the leaping target. The Gray Ghost fired as he bounded—not for the porch, but toward Hembroke.

The valet's cry stifled; the flashlight hit the lawn. As the Gray Ghost dashed for the front driveway, Harry could hear Hembroke thud the lawn.

New murder had been done by the Gray Ghost.

Moreover, the killer was darting to a getaway. The path to the front was clear. Harry leaped to the lawn to take up a futile chase. Enraged men came with him, pell-mell, maddened in their desire to overtake the Gray Ghost. So far, the breaks were in the murderer's favor.

Suddenly, a glare swept in from the roadway that ran along the land side of Forbel's property. A car was swinging into the drive. Its headlights showed the Gray Ghost coming head-on. A searchlight clicked; the increased glare made the murderer stop short and reverse his course.

The arriving car was a coupé. From its interior came a challenging laugh—a cry of sardonic mockery that startled the already bewildered men at Forbel's. Those near Harry stopped, rooted by the taunt, their thoughts again reverting to the incredible.

Harry knew the arrival. The Shadow was here.

THE Gray Ghost had gained the speed of a wild rabbit. Frantically, he dived beyond the circle of the searchlight. An instant later, tongues of flame jabbed through the darkness. The Shadow had dropped from the coupé. He had fired to halt the fleeing killer. The Gray Ghost had departed an instant too soon.

Those shots brought new action from men nearer the house. A porch light came on; Harry doubled toward it, to reach the corner of the house beyond which the Gray Ghost had headed. Renright came bounding from the porch to join Harry. He was brandishing his .38, which Harry knew he must have reloaded. Harry was glad of this ally; for he had gained proof tonight that Renright was not the Gray Ghost.

Odd that Harry and the man whom he had watched should both be on the trail of the real Gray Ghost!

The thought struck Harry as he and Renright hustled ahead, shoulder to shoulder, each with a ready gun. The Gray Ghost was a fugitive; his capture seemed certain, for the lawn was alive with men. It was a freak of circumstance that changed the situation.

Off past the house, at an angle toward the Sound, was a garage. The Gray Ghost had headed somewhere in that direction. The garage had become a focal point at which pursuers from the house would join with The Shadow and Cliff Marsland, who were coming from the coupé. The Shadow had gained in the chase. He was almost to the garage when the circumstance occurred.

Someone in the garage turned on a searchlight. Mammoth rays spread over the lawn. They did not uncover the Gray Ghost. A trapped quarry, he had huddled by some shrubbery in between. But the glow revealed The Shadow.

Instantly, there was a cry from the corner of the house. Two of Forbel's servants spied the cloaked figure. They had not seen the Gray Ghost, nor had they glimpsed The Shadow when he had fired from the darkness near the coupé. Knowing only that they sought some stranger of the darkness, the servants aimed their rifles toward The Shadow.

The long guns crackled. Bullets sizzled past The Shadow, as he stood clearly outlined. Renright, too, became excited. He and Harry were close to The Shadow. Before Harry could stop him, Renright aimed to fire, blurting the name that came to his lips:

"The Gray Ghost!"

Harry sprang forward, too excited to deliver a cry. He jostled Renright as the man fired. Renright's shot went wide. Then came a blast of an automatic. The Shadow had aimed for the searchlight. There was a clatter of glass as the glow disappeared. The Shadow had scored a necessary bull's-eye.

THERE were shouts in the darkness. Flashlights played feebly toward the spot where The Shadow had been. The figure in black was gone; to avoid the congregating searchers, The Shadow was forced to travel beyond the garage.

A new searchlight came into action. This one was from the house; Forbel had run in to operate it from the second story.

The new glow revealed the real quarry. The Gray Ghost leaped from his hiding place and dashed across the lawn. He took the only opening that offered—directly down the searchlight's path, which formed a brilliant, spreading avenue toward the Sound.

New cries from the pursuers. Again the chase was on; but it had assumed its original aspect. The Gray Ghost had gained a lead that could not be overtaken. Renright was running straight after him, followed by a pack of yelling men. Harry cut away, choosing a short cut toward a tiny promontory. He soon realized his mistake.

The ground that he had chosen was cut off from a curving headland by a little cove. Harry stopped upon a rocky edge. He heard a hissed whisper close beside him. The Shadow, cutting in from the direction of the garage, had encountered the same difficulty as Harry. They could only stare across the cove, where the Gray Ghost, beyond range of pistol shot, had gained a wharf at the end.

The distant edge of the searchlight's beam showed the Gray Ghost as he leaped off the end of the wharf. He made no dive; his spring was clumsy. Floundering, he began to swim in hurried, frantic fashion, making little headway with his strokes.

Renright and others were almost to the pier.

Increasing his speed through greater effort, the Gray Ghost managed to grab the side of a motorboat, moored thirty feet from the pier.

A motor chugged. A small anchor came up as the Gray Ghost tugged a rope. The boat spurted away as Renright halted on the end of the pier. The Shadow and Harry saw Renright fire futile shots. Then the boat had disappeared into darkness, while servants barked futile bullets from their rifles.

Cliff had arrived in the darkness. He had started toward the pier too late to aid. Because of that, he had come along the shore, hoping to find Harry or The Shadow. He, too, had seen the Gray Ghost's final escape.

A quiet whisper in the darkness. The tone was addressed to Harry:

"Report!"

Amid the fading echoes of the distant motorboat, Harry told The Shadow of happenings at Forbel's, prior to The Shadow's arrival. His account was brief, but accurate in every detail. There were no faint chugs, however, when Harry had finished. The Gray Ghost had made good his flight across the night-capped waters of Long Island Sound.

RENRIGHT and others were working with a lumbering motorboat that was tied beside the pier, evidently hoping to pursue the light, speedy craft in which the Gray Ghost had escaped. They could not get the old boat started.

In the darkness of the promontory, The Shadow whispered an order. Followed by his agents, he moved across the darkened, deserted lawn. Harry entered the path of the searchlight, to head for the house. There were a few men inside: those who had carried Hembroke's body from the lawn.

Cutting close to the house, under the searchlight's beam, The Shadow and Cliff used darkness to reach their coupe. Cliff had extinguished the lights before following The Shadow. They entered the car in darkness. The Shadow coasted it along a slight slant of the driveway. The motor throbbed suddenly; the lights came on and the coupé reached the road.

Unnoticed by those who were busy elsewhere, The Shadow was making his departure. He had failed to halt the Gray Ghost tonight. Culden's tip-off to crime scheduled at Forbel's had given The Shadow an opportunity; but the Gray Ghost had made his raid too soon. Harry Vincent's cooperation had been timely; but not sufficient to delay the Gray Ghost's flight.

Luck, too, had been against The Shadow; while it had served the Gray Ghost. Cliff, solemn as he sat beside The Shadow, could still visualize the Gray Ghost floundering through the water in that mad effort to reach the moored motorboat. Cliff wished that he had been close enough to clip the rogue with a pistol shot.

While Cliff was still engaged in rueful reverie, a whispered laugh chilled him. The mirth was close beside him, delivered by The Shadow. To Cliff, the low-toned mockery had a strange significance. It carried a suppressed note of triumph.

Though he had not stopped the Gray Ghost, The Shadow had solved some mystery regarding the

The Gray Ghost ... disappeared into the darkness.

supercrook. The Shadow's laugh concerned the future. It brought new confidence to Cliff. He could guess that The Shadow and the Gray Ghost would meet again.

The depths of the Gray Ghost's schemes were plain to The Shadow. When the next encounter came, The Shadow would be prepared.

CHAPTER XIV
THE TRAP IS LAID

WHO was the Gray Ghost?

The question was everywhere. Newspapers asked it. The police sought the answer to the riddle. The matter remained unsolved. It was known only that the Gray Ghost was both a robber and a double murderer, for he had slain Hembroke as viciously as he had killed Windler.

The Gray Ghost's crimes had temporarily ceased. The last trace of the marauder had been the finding of the little speedboat on the shore of Long Island Sound, a few miles from Forbel's. The Gray Ghost had made an obscure landing and had continued his flight in some other fashion. The boat, itself, belonged to Forbel. It furnished no clues to the Gray Ghost.

Two days had passed since crime at Forbel's. Harry Vincent was back in New York, at his usual city residence, the Hotel Metrolite. Like others, he was perplexed regarding the Gray Ghost; but he could see the reason why no new raids had occurred. With Forbel's jewels, the Gray Ghost had stolen the last real swag that he could gain.

Other residents of Long Island had probably shipped their valuables to storage warehouses and safe deposit vaults. The Gray Ghost could not be stopped with guns; he could, however, be balked by lack of opportunity for theft.

This plan constituted no victory. Harry could see its weakness. It allowed the Gray Ghost to lie hidden until he chose to depart to other terrain, carrying a million dollars' worth of booty. Perhaps his depredations would begin anew, in some other section of the country. In a sense, the Gray Ghost had triumphed. He had milked Long Island; he was free to transform his ill-gained pelf into substantial cash, like the currency that he had snatched at Debrossler's.

ON this particular morning, Harry's waking thoughts concerned the Gray Ghost. When he stopped at the hotel desk to obtain his mail, he thought but little of the long envelope that the clerk delivered to him. Opening the envelope, Harry withdrew a typewritten sheet. He began to read mechanically; then suddenly gained interest.

The letter was from James Pennybrook, the lawyer. It requested that Harry call either at Pennybrook's Manhattan office or at his residence in Holmwood. It promised facts concerning the Gray Ghost. While Harry pondered over the letter, a bell boy approached to tell him that he was wanted on the telephone.

Going to a booth, Harry answered the call and heard the voice of Rutledge Mann. The investment broker delivered a drawled message. Harry was to call upon Pennybrook, immediately after breakfast.

Harry had risen late. It was nearly ten o'clock when he reached Pennybrook's office, high up in a skyscraper. Harry's thoughts had turned to The Shadow. He wondered how his chief had learned about this letter. Harry, however, had but little time for speculation after he reached Pennybrook's. He was ushered promptly into an inner office. There he found the bald-headed attorney already holding conference with other visitors.

One was Colin Renright, who greeted Harry with a warm handshake. Another was Pierce Gilden, whom Harry knew by sight only. Pennybrook introduced Harry to Gilden. There were two others: Forbel and one of his guests on the night of the robbery—Wilbersham; both remembered Harry and were cordial in their greeting.

"You have arrived just in time, Mr. Vincent," announced Pennybrook, in a dry tone. "I was about to begin a little speech. Kindly have a chair and hear what I have to say."

As Harry was seating himself, Pennybrook thumbed papers that were on his mahogany desk. He cleared his throat and began.

"Gentlemen," declared Pennybrook, solemnly, "we are all persons who hold a common desire. We wish to capture the Gray Ghost. I, for one, have an excellent reason to seek the Gray Ghost. I suffered through personal combat with the rogue. Chance alone, plus darkness, prevented him from killing me, that night at Debrossler's. All of us have warred with the Gray Ghost. Our cause is the same: We seek a new opportunity to meet him."

There were nods of agreement from all present.

"Let us consider the mystery of the Gray Ghost," resumed Pennybrook. "Culden was not the Gray Ghost. The police found him, slain in conflict with criminals, prior to the robbery at your home, Mr. Forbel. Culden, so far as we know, was merely a tool who supplied the Gray Ghost with facts.

"Who is the Gray Ghost? That, I cannot answer. I can only apply a process of elimination. Neither Martin Debrossler, nor you, Mr. Forbel, could be the Gray Ghost. Both of you were victimized by him. Nor could I be the Gray Ghost. I aided Debrossler at the time the Gray Ghost stole his money.

"We can eliminate Pierce Gilden"—Pennybrook

indicated the light-haired young man—"because he was riding into New York at the time of the robbery at Debrossler's. We have the testimony of both of the banker's daughters and Debrossler's chauffeur, Towden, to prove that neither Pierce Gilden, nor a companion—Alan Reeth—could have been concerned in the crime.

"We can eliminate three others, all present. You, Vincent; you, Renright; you, Wilbersham." As he gave each name, Pennybrook thrust a bony finger at the man whom he mentioned. "All of you were with Mr. Forbel at the time when the Gray Ghost entered. There are others, also, who can clearly be placed apart from suspicion. I expect to interview every one of them. All have received letters like you did."

PENNYBROOK referred again to his papers. He leaned across the desk and wagged his forefinger:

"The Gray Ghost is a man who knows Long Island. He is one who moves in select circles. Servants can be rejected. Some may have spied for the Gray Ghost, of course; but none are of sufficient caliber to have played his elusive part. The police have questioned servants everywhere. Gentlemen, the Gray Ghost is someone like ourselves; a man of social standing, welcomed in Long Island homes.

"Let us summarize his qualifications. We know that the Gray Ghost is tall. As to his weight, we are uncertain. Debrossler describes him as bulky; I can testify as to his strength. Mr. Forbel here, and Mr. Renright, are uncertain as to the Gray Ghost's approximate weight."

Forbel nodded; then explained:

"I wouldn't say that he was over-heavy. That gray jersey he wore looked rather paddy."

"That's possible," agreed Renright. "I'd have placed him at about my own weight, near to one hundred and ninety pounds. But he may have faked those proportions. What do you think, Vincent?"

Harry considered. He was picturing the Gray Ghost's appearance. He was unready to agree with either opinion, when Gilden asked a question.

"Tell me, Mr. Pennybrook," asked the young man—"what would you say about the matter?"

"I did not see the Gray Ghost," reminded the lawyer. "But I must admit that Debrossler's description could have fitted with this one. In other words, the Gray Ghost may have worn a padded jersey at Debrossler's, as well as at Forbel's.

"Let us say that he was tall and have it go at that. We may then add that he is agile. He escaped from Debrossler's by a second story window; he also made a swift flight across Forbel's lawn. But he is a poor swimmer. He floundered badly when he tried to gain the motorboat off the end of the pier. That, at least, is what I have heard."

Gilden inserted an objection.

"If he was overweighted, he would have been handicapped in swimming. Perhaps he is really a good swimmer."

"No." It was Renright who shook his head. "I saw him from the pier. His strokes were amateurish. A good swimmer would have used real form."

"Probably so," admitted Gilden. "Yes, under that stress, I suppose he would have exerted his best ability. I, myself, know nothing about swimming; I can hardly keep myself afloat in the water. Therefore, my opinion should be disregarded."

"SWIMMING is my specialty," stated Renright, "so I shall term myself the authority in this case. If I should have occasion to swim away from pursuers, I would display my natural ability regardless of any burdening weight. In the case of the Gray Ghost, I affirm that he instinctively swam at his best."

"Which was poor," declared Wilbersham. "I was with you on the pier, Renright. I saw how the Gray Ghost floundered."

"A good runner—a poor swimmer." Pennybrook marked down the points mentioned. "Add to this the fact that he wore a bulletproof vest."

There were startled exclamations. Pennybrook smiled:

"We know," he declared, "that the Gray Ghost must have entered your house, Mr. Forbel—to visit the cloakroom and remove cartridges from revolvers."

"Yes," agreed the millionaire. "He did the same with my gun."

"But there were two specific weapons he could not empty," continued Pennybrook, referring to his notes: "Yours, Mr. Renright; and yours, Mr. Vincent. Let me see—you fired four shots pointblank, did you not, Mr. Renright?"

Renright nodded; then added:

"I fired twice after that. I broke a windowpane and splintered the door frame. But the Gray Ghost had already dropped from sight."

"I was late with my shots," stated Harry. "I dashed out and shot from the porch."

"Bullets could not have passed through the Gray Ghost," declared Pennybrook. "He is not an actual ghost. That talk is poppycock! The Gray Ghost has proven himself human. He lost his nerve and took to flight. The bullets, therefore, must have struck him. Only a bulletproof vest could have stopped them."

"Those vests are heavy," remarked Forbel. "Maybe that accounts for the Gray Ghost's weight and bulk. He probably wears one wherever he goes."

"It is a wonder that he managed to swim at all," observed Pennybrook, tapping his desk with a pencil. Then, shrugging his shoulders: "Well, we must take all that for granted. We shall add a bulletproof vest to the Gray Ghost's equipment. The details, I must admit, are rather sketchy. Nevertheless, we have one other point to add. It concerns the Gray Ghost's activities.

"Of this we shall all be in agreement. The Gray Ghost is bold. He will make a foray anyplace where he believes wealth can be gained. He has already stolen gems—yours, Forbel; therefore, we know that he will seek such form of loot—"

New nods of agreement. There were no objectors to the lawyer's argument.

"Agreed," announced Pennybrook. "That being settled, I can come to the important point of this discussion. All of us would like to snare the Gray Ghost and settle scores with him. I have found a way in which it can be accomplished. I can provide the bait!"

EAGER exclamations indicated the interest of the listeners. Pennybrook proceeded.

"Yesterday," he declared, "a wealthy foreigner called at this office. He is a Spaniard, an exile of the old Royalist regime; but he still uses his title. He is the Count of Santurnia. Like many who left Spain, he brought away a hoard of valuable gems.

"The Count of Santurnia had arranged to occupy a large house on Long Island, beyond Narrowneck. Reading the reports of the Gray Ghost's activities, he was disturbed. He knew that his new residence would be beyond the jurisdiction of the New York City police. So he decided to visit an attorney for advice.

"He chose me because he had read my name in the newspaper accounts of the Debrossler robbery. We discussed the situation; I found the Count of Santurnia intrigued by the stories of the Gray Ghost. He stated that the rogue reminded him of the Castilian outlaws. He said that in Spain, they trap such terrorists. That fact interested me; between us, the count and I evolved a scheme."

Pennybrook smiled and picked up a sheet of typewritten paper.

"Tonight," he declared, "this story will go to the newspapers. An interview with the Count of Santurnia, telling of his heirlooms, the famous gems that he will never trust to anyone's keeping but his own. Today is Monday. On Wednesday, the count will occupy his rented mansion.

"That very night, he will hold a reception. It will resemble yours, Mr. Forbel. The Count of Santurnia will display his gems. He will welcome the arrival of the Gray Ghost."

"THIS is folly!" exclaimed Forbel. "Surely, the count will not make such a great mistake—"

"If it is a mistake," inserted Pennybrook, "it will be even greater. The count will exhibit his entire collection of rare gems."

"But half would be enough—"

"He says that the greater the outlaw, the greater the bait, if results are to be obtained. Apparently, gentlemen"—Pennybrook smiled, dryly—"this game is another old Spanish custom. The count is determined upon his course. He has asked me to invite all of you to the reception."

Astonished looks were directed toward Pennybrook. The lawyer added:

"The only guests will be those who have encountered the Gray Ghost, or who have been robbed by him. Martin Debrossler accepted the count's invitation this morning. Do any of the rest of you care to give your answer at present?"

Forbel was the first to speak.

"I'll be there," declared the millionaire. "With a loaded revolver, this time!"

A pause. Then Renright stated:

"I'll come."

Both Forbel and Renright were nodding as they looked about the group. Wilbersham joined with a nod of his own. Gilden pondered; then spoke up.

"I think you can count on me," he decided. "I'll talk it over with Mr. Debrossler. You will have my answer later, Mr. Pennybrook."

"How about you, Mr. Vincent?"

Pennybrook put the query. Harry replied:

"I think that I can make it. I'll call you later, Mr. Pennybrook."

"Good!" chuckled the lawyer. "This looks like one hundred per cent. I hope that I shall have the same results with the others, when they arrive."

After leaving Pennybrook's, Harry put in a call to Rutledge Mann. Even before he could explain matters, Mann gave the answer. Harry was to accept the invitation. That decided, Harry called Pennybrook's office and said that he would be at the Count of Santurnia's reception.

All that day, Harry pondered upon the coming event. The more he considered it, with the publicity that it would surely receive, the more he was convinced that the Gray Ghost would swallow the bait and come as an uninvited guest.

Harry could foresee another stranger who would also visit the Count of Santurnia's mansion.

That visitor would be The Shadow.

CHAPTER XV
THE SHADOW'S PRESENCE

LATE Wednesday afternoon, Harry Vincent was driving along a hillcrest above Long Island Sound. He stopped his coupé to view a toylike scene that lay below.

Pictured against greensward was a castellated mansion that clung to a slope of ground. Down from the building stretched the wide open lawn.

One corner of the area was filled with a thick grove. Trees were sparse at other spots.

A squatty pier extended into a little cove. On one side was a rocky promontory; in fact, the whole shore was stony except for one short patch of beach. Near the pier and connected with it by a broad platform was a small, square bathhouse.

There were no boats along the shore. Some fifty feet off from the wide pier was an anchored float that had a diving platform. The float was a large one, rectangular in shape.

One feature of the grounds that Harry noted was the high, spiked fence that surrounded it on three sides. The shoreline alone was unprotected. The height of the fence; the closeness of its pickets, indicated that it would be a serious barrier for anyone who might attempt an escape. The only entrance for automobiles was a wide gateway on the far sides of the ground. Harry could see that the gates stood open.

Harry's interest in the scene was definite. Those grounds below were the estate that had been rented by the Count of Santurnia. Harry had come early, so as to gain an advantage that he had not held at Forbel's. His present preview was giving him a bird's-eye picture of the premises.

A car pulled up beside Harry's, so silently that The Shadow's agent did not notice it until it stopped. The car was a coupé. Colin Renright leaned from the wheel and waved a greeting.

"Hello, Vincent! Where did you get the car with the New York license plates?"

Harry remembered that he was supposed to be a Westerner.

"Borrowed it in New York," he returned. "If I hadn't managed to get it, I would have called you, Renright."

"Too bad you didn't. I had expected to see you at Narrowneck. Say"—Renright gestured toward the water—"is this the Spaniard's place?"

Harry nodded.

"It looks pretty good from here," commented Renright. "Just the sort of place an ex-count would choose for himself. I'd like to see the Gray Ghost tackle it."

Renright chuckled then added:

"He'd have a tougher getaway than he did at Forbel's."

"If he wants a boat," remarked Harry, "he'll have to bring his own."

"That's right," agreed Renright. "Boats are conspicuously absent. That float would be no use to the Gray Ghost. It's a dandy, though, isn't it? It sets well in the water; it's large enough not to tilt if you dive from it. I'd like to take a swim off that float."

A HAZY darkness had begun to settle. Harry noted the dancing waters of the Sound; he saw the foam of waves as they splashed the rocky shore. Dusk was arriving prematurely. Renright pointed to the northern sky.

"We're due for a storm," he announced. "It will be a good evening for the Gray Ghost, Vincent."

The breeze had been heavy here on the heights. Harry could feel its increase. The clouds that Renright indicated were thick and black. From the horizon came a sheet of distant lightning.

"That won't blow over in a hurry" was Harry's comment. Then, with a laugh: "If there is a real downpour, we may have a chance to see how the Gray Ghost does on a muddy track."

"The odds will be against him, any way you figure it," predicted Renright. "I'm afraid he'll leave us holding an empty bag. Well, Vincent, we might as well get in ahead of the storm. You lead the way."

Harry started his coupé, with Renright's car following. The road curved away from the Sound; then twisted down a hill. It joined a level road and came to a corner of the fence that surrounded the count's estate. Harry reached the open gateway, a hundred yards ahead. He drove into the driveway and followed it until he reached the front of the mansion.

Liveried servants were about, awaiting the guests. Harry and Renright parked their cars and were conducted into the house. The course led them to a many-windowed conservatory, where bowing servants requested them to remain.

Lighting a cigarette, Renright strolled back and forth. He pointed out doors at each end of the conservatory. These offered additional entrances to the one from the house.

"This place is wide open" was Renright's comment. "Do you suppose that the count intends to keep the gems here?"

"He would be taking a long chance," returned Harry. "But that seems to be his policy."

"Yes. Pennybrook must have filled him with the urge to snare the Gray Ghost. I'd like to see this count chap. I suppose we landed here too early for him to receive us."

"The invitation included dinner; but that won't be until half past seven. Some of the guests will not arrive until afterward."

Both Harry and Renright had received calls from Pennybrook that day. The lawyer had mentioned that they would be welcome early. He had said that he, himself, would come directly from his office. Hence, when Harry and Renright heard footsteps, they were not surprised to see the lawyer appear.

Pennybrook shook hands and commented on the weather. The storm, it seemed, was coming closer. By the time new guests had arrived, the roar of thunder had commenced to follow lightning flashes. The patter of rain dribbled the conservatory roof.

A group of half a dozen were seated in the conservatory when Pennybrook suddenly arose and turned toward the house door. The others followed his gaze; they saw a tall figure in evening clothes. Harry noted an olive-hued visage that contrasted with the white collar beneath it. He studied a sharp-featured face, and observed white teeth that shone in welcoming smile.

"The Count of Santurnia," announced Pennybrook. "I shall introduce you, gentlemen."

THE count bowed as he stepped forward. He extended his right hand, long-fingered and as darkish as his face. Each guest received a firm grip of welcome. The count nodded as each was introduced.

Harry was impressed by the glittering decorations that formed a part of the count's attire. Gold medallions, jeweled emblems, were beneath his lapel. Across his shirtfront stretched a broad red ribbon, emblazoned with a diamond-encrusted star.

The count's distinguished manner commanded all attention. When he spoke, his tone carried but the slightest touch of foreign accent.

"Ah, *Señor* Pennybrook," declared the count, with a bow. "It is good that you have brought so many friends tonight. Are there to be more?"

"Several," replied the lawyer. "But there are four who cannot arrive until after dinner. Let me see: Forbel, Debrossler, Gilden—they are three. The other—yes, I remember him. A chap named Bixter, who was at Forbel's that night.

"All the rest of us are here, except Wilbersham. He should be here soon. Perhaps this is Wilbersham whom I hear coming with the servants."

Pennybrook was correct. Wilbersham appeared and was introduced to the count. The formality ended, the count turned to a flunky who was standing by.

"We shall dine," announced the count. "It is earlier than we intended; but since all are present who intend to dine, there is no need for delay. You may go, Pedro, and—"

The count broke off. His dark-tinted forehead showed a frown as he heard impatient voices. He turned to Pennybrook, to question:

"Who is this gentleman?"

Pennybrook saw an irate man arguing with servants, pressing himself toward the conservatory despite their protests. The lawyer exclaimed his recognition.

"Commissioner Weston!"

"HELLO, Pennybrook" was the police commissioner's response. Weston had reached the conservatory. "You are the man I want to see! What is the meaning of this ridiculous affair?"

"The meaning?" returned Pennybrook. "Simply that we intend to bait the Gray Ghost."

"Against the wishes of the law?"

"What objections can the law offer?"

"Many!" Weston's tone was a roar. "The police are on the trail of the Gray Ghost! We have the authority—"

A purred voice interrupted. The Count of Santurnia had stepped forward.

"Ah, *señor*," he asserted. "This has already been discussed. I have been told by *Señor* Pennybrook that this house is not within the limits of your city."

Weston's face purpled. The commissioner barked a demand at Pennybrook:

"Who is this man?"

"The Count of Santurnia," returned the attorney. "At present, the master of this house."

"And where are the local authorities?"

"Ah, *señor*," smiled the count, "they have been good enough to remain absent."

"At my suggestion," added Pennybrook. "Since we are outside your jurisdiction, Commissioner, I saw no need in making the same request of you."

Weston glared angrily. He turned on his heel, intending to stride from the house. The Count of Santurnia blocked him with outstretched hand.

"There should be no offense, *señor*," he insisted, suavely. "As a guest, you are much welcome. See? The night is bad. Already, the rain has become terrific. We are about to dine. Would you stay, *señor?*"

Weston smiled, apologetically.

"I was hasty," he admitted. "Very well. Since there is no other alternative, I shall remain."

Pennybrook clapped Weston on the back. An arriving servant announced dinner. The count bowed Weston and Pennybrook through the doorway. The others followed, Renright and Harry last. As Harry passed the count, a long hand gripped his arm. Harry met a keen gaze; he saw eyes look downward.

Following their direction, Harry saw the count's left hand. From it glittered a gem that the count had previously kept turned toward his palm. Harry recognized the changing hues of a magnificent fire opal, a girasol that he had seen before.

Renright had advanced. Astonished, Harry again looked squarely into the count's eyes. He caught their sudden fire. He heard whispered words from lips that scarcely moved:

"Be ready! Instructions will be given!"

Harry nodded mechanically. The hand had left his arm; the count was turning the girasol inward. Harry walked into the house, to follow Renright. The count came after him; but Harry did not turn about.

Harry had expected The Shadow to be present here tonight; but not in the guise that he had found him. He was gripped with amazement at The Shadow's craftiness. Once again, his chief had proven his mastery of disguise.

The Count of Santurnia was The Shadow.

CHAPTER XVI
THE GHOST GAMBOLS

DINNER had ended. The Shadow had led his guests back to the conservatory. All were convivial, including Weston. The police commissioner had listened to the count's persuasive discourse during dinner. He had become convinced that tonight's scheme might trap the Gray Ghost.

Not for an instant had Weston thought of any connection between the Count of Santurnia and his—Weston's—friend, Lamont Cranston. He did not suspect that either was The Shadow.

Rain was battering hard against the windows. Lightning was frequent; the rumble of thunder drowned many words of conversation. Still suave in his role of the count, The Shadow had begun to speak. At intervals, he paused, to avoid the peals of thunder.

"Si, señor," said The Shadow, to Weston. "In my country, we have the way to bait the bandits. They are greedy. They have spies. Word is taken to them in their mountain dwellings. They will always come where there is gold.

"This one you call the Gray Ghost is no different. He has no mountain abode. He does not need it. He has had a spy, as you have told me. Perhaps there are others who have served for him: Your newspapers.

"Ah, they have told that the Count of Santurnia has wealth. That he has brought many gems to this house which he has rented. It was easy that I should move here—for the furniture, it was already in place."

Weston nodded. He had recognized that the house had been rented furnished. The furniture, though serviceable, was old. The owners had themselves removed any articles of real value.

"And the Gray Ghost knew where I would be," resumed The Shadow, in his foreign accent. "That has given him opportunity, señor, to see this place beforehand. Tonight, we may expect the Gray Ghost—"

THE SHADOW broke off. A cry had sounded from Pennybrook. It came simultaneously with a vivid, prolonged flash of lightning. The lawyer was pointing toward an end door of the conservatory. With a crash, the door swung inward, striking against a heavy potted plant.

Thunder rumbled while The Shadow strolled to the opened door and closed it against the inpour of rain.

"It was nothing," he remarked, when the thunder had subsided. "The wind, señor, that was all. But it does bring to us reminder that the Gray Ghost himself may come. The bait—ah, si—it should be prepared."

From within a pocket of his evening clothes, The Shadow produced a compact chamois bag. He opened it and let brilliant jewels trickle from the pouch into his lower hand. Men exclaimed, as they stepped forward.

"Old gems," declared The Shadow. "Rich heirlooms of my ancestors. Worth hundreds of thousands of your dollars! These were from the days of Spanish conquests; none have been placed in settings, ever.

"The light here"—he looked about in disapproval —"it is bad. Very bad! The luster of the gems, it cannot show. I shall bring other lights to let you see the sparkle of emeralds; the glow of rubies; the glitter of these diamonds. Ah, Pedro!"

With his call to the servant, The Shadow looked about. His eyes narrowed; they stared toward the door that had previously swung inward. The door had opened again. This time, it was gripped by a restraining hand.

On the sill stood the Gray Ghost, exactly as he had appeared at Forbel's. His attire, however, was darker, almost blackish, for it was soaked by the torrential rain. A flash of zigzagged lightning showed him plainly; it brought a glittering reflection from the revolver that the Gray Ghost gripped.

Tonight, the Gray Ghost did not find men unprepared. Hands had gone to pockets at the instant when The Shadow had poured gems into view. Guns sped into sight.

The Gray Ghost saw the brandished weapons. With a long bound, he sprang away, slamming the door behind him.

Two revolvers spoke together. One was Renright's. The other was Commissioner Weston's. Bullets smashed glass panes of the conservatory door. The shots were futile. The Gray Ghost had fled. Harry, in fact, had whipped out his automatic as quickly as Renright and Weston had obtained their guns; but The Shadow's agent had seen no need to fire.

"After him!" bawled Pennybrook. "Get him— the Gray Ghost!"

Men surged *en masse*, all with drawn guns. Pennybrook wrenched open the door. Weston pointed to a scudding figure off between the trees. Pell-mell, the crowd took up the chase; but their opportunity was brief. It was a lightning flash that had revealed the Gray Ghost in flight. The instant that blinding light was gone, the fugitive became invisible.

Harry had joined in the dash. He saw a car come swinging through from the gate. Its headlights were feeble against the rain. Yanking a flashlight, Harry approached the car. A man within pressed a dome light; Harry saw a startled, elderly face. Then Pennybrook arrived. He recognized the newcomer in the car.

"Debrossler!" exclaimed the lawyer. "Did you see anyone pass the gate?"

"No," replied the banker. "The rain is terrific. You are drenched, Pennybrook!"

"That does not matter!" shouted the lawyer, as thunder roared with lightning. "We're after the Gray Ghost!"

There was a shout from the distance. Then shots, that sounded fizzy in the rain. Harry dashed off to investigate. A lightning flash showed Renright and Weston, heading in the same direction. Another car was standing just within the gates. The runners saw another fizz of a revolver.

As they arrived, the man who had fired came in front of the headlights. It was Pierce Gilden. Seeing the flashlights, he shouted news.

"I saw the Gray Ghost!" he cried. "I was right behind Mr. Debrossler's car! The Gray Ghost must have dodged his headlamps; but he blundered into mine! I jumped out and fired after him!"

"Which direction did he go?" demanded Weston. "Out through the gates?"

"No," replied Gilden. "Up toward the inner fence."

"Close the gates!" ordered Weston. "Bar them! Watch them!"

Another car swung into the driveway. It was a limousine, bringing the last of the arriving guests: Forbel and Bixter. The chauffeur sprang out and helped bar the gates. Weston left him on guard, with one of the servants who had arrived; then gave an order to all who had congregated about him.

"Search the grounds!" Weston was brisk. "Block off the area between the house and the high fence line! Come with me, a few of you. We must see to matters inside the house."

WHEN Commissioner Weston reached the conservatory, he was accompanied only by Harry and Gilden. Harry had taken this opportunity to get back to The Shadow; Gilden had come also, because he had a report to make concerning the Gray Ghost. Weston gaped as they entered the lighted conservatory.

The Shadow was seated in an easy chair beside a table, calmly smoking a thin cigar. On the table was the chamois bag; its strings were loose, the gems showed a glitter from within. Still playing his part as the Count of Santurnia, The Shadow was unruffled. He did not even have a gun.

"What!" exclaimed Weston. "You remained here alone? With the gems unguarded?"

"Why should I not?" returned The Shadow, suavely. "The Gray Ghost, he was in flight. He had not time to think of my jewels. It is too bad, *señor*, that he has made escape from you."

"He is inside the grounds," announced Weston. "A dozen men are searching for him. They have cornered him near the upper fence."

"Buenos, señor," approved The Shadow. "Ah, here are others. Men whose clothes have not been soaked by the rain."

He indicated Forbel and Bixter, who had found their way in from the front of the house.

"We were in our car," explained Forbel. "Debrossler is also in his machine. He will be in very shortly. None of us saw the Gray Ghost. Apparently, Debrossler arrived too soon; while I reached here too late."

"Yes," agreed Gilden. "My car was between the two. I saw the Gray Ghost dart away. I sprang out and fired after him. That gave me a soaking, like the rest of the pursuers."

Lightning flashed outside; thunder rumbled in a long roll.

"The heaviest of the storm is passing," stated Weston, "but there will still be lightning flashes. Those men along the fence should surely trap the Gray Ghost. Come, the two of you"—he indicated Harry and Gilden—"and let the dry members of our party stay with the count. But I would advise you, Count, to put away your jewels."

Debrossler's voice came before The Shadow could reply. The banker was in the front hall, trying to find his way through. Forbel and Bixter started out to meet him. The Shadow bowed to Weston.

"What you say is good, *señor,"* he declared. *"Buenos!* The bait is no longer needed. It shall be put away in safety."

The Shadow arose. He stopped before he reached the table. Again, his eyes were narrowing beyond where his companions stood, this time toward the other door of the conservatory. As lightning flashed, an evil snarl was voiced before the thunder arrived.

As the rumble started, Commissioner Weston and Harry turned about, caught completely off their guard. They stared with The Shadow.

Once more, the Gray Ghost had arrived from the rain. He was closer; he looked bulkier, more formidable in his dripping garments. His eyes were gloating through the slits of the tight, water-soaked hood. His dampened glove was tight about the handle of his revolver.

While a dozen men still searched for him, the elusive Gray Ghost had returned.

CHAPTER XVII
THE VANISHED OUTLAW

RELUCTANTLY, Commissioner Weston raised his arms. He had pocketed his revolver; hence, he had no other course. Gilden, too, had made the same mistake. His hands came up. Harry was as badly off as both. He copied their example.

The Shadow, motionless, had folded his arms. Retaining the suave character of Santurnia, he did not change his posture.

The Gray Ghost strode forward, moving his gun to cover all four persons. With his left hand he seized the chamois bag by the strings. He noted the glittering contents and gave a shake. The weight of the pouch closed it. The Gray Ghost thrust the prize up beneath the folds of his jersey shirt.

Backing to the door by which he had entered, the Gray Ghost spoke in a husky growl. His words were directed to The Shadow.

"You will die!"

On the instant, Harry realized that the Gray Ghost must have guessed the identity of the pretended count. Harry remembered The Shadow's advent at Debrossler's. The public had supposed that episode to be a return of the Gray Ghost. To the Gray Ghost, it had meant another intruder. He had known that only The Shadow could have been there.

Harry looked toward Weston and Gilden. He saw blankness on their faces. He recalled that Gilden had combated The Shadow at Debrossler's; hence Gilden could not understand the facts. He, like others, had spoken of the Gray Ghost's return.

Tonight, the Gray Ghost had suspected a trap. He had credited The Shadow with devising it. The Gray Ghost had gained a bag of jewels. But he wanted more: the death of the man whom he had robbed. Yet, despite the Gray Ghost's threat, The Shadow remained unperturbed, still retaining his part of the count.

Then Harry saw why The Shadow had chosen not to display a gun. A window of the conservatory had wedged open, unnoticed. Through its crack was projected the muzzle of a .45 automatic. The gun was directed squarely toward the Gray Ghost. Harry guessed the identity of the marksman behind it.

Cliff Marsland was here, in reserve. Outside, under the protecting ledge of the conservatory roof, Cliff had been ready for any emergency. Before the Gray Ghost would have a chance to fire, Cliff would drop him where he stood. The instant that the Gray Ghost took direct aim toward The Shadow, he would give his own death warrant.

LUCK saved the Gray Ghost. Voices sounded from the house. Forbel and Bixter had arrived with Debrossler. Forbel saw the Gray Ghost from the doorway. He shouted; he and his companions drew revolvers.

The Gray Ghost forgot The Shadow. Wheeling about, he made a dive through the end door. Forbel and the others fired wildly. Cliff's gun spurted, its roar lost in the barks of other weapons. Cliff had lost his aim. His shot, too, was futile. The Gray Ghost was away, carrying the Spanish gems.

Weston yanked his revolver and led the chase. Harry was in it, along with the others. A shouting pack, they saw the Gray Ghost by a lightning flash. Their cries brought the men who were still searching along the fence. Harry fired a shot to add attention. Gilden, running beside him, frantically dispatched two bullets.

Hard on the roar of thunder came another vivid blaze of lightning. The Gray Ghost had taken the only unguarded route. He was dashing for the Sound, his long strides carrying him farther ahead of the pursuers. Harry could remember his jest to Renright, regarding a race on a muddy track. The Gray Ghost was proving himself capable despite the slippery soil.

Rain had become a terrific deluge, with thunder and lightning delivering their last outbursts. Each flash showed the whole lawn, with the Gray Ghost making for the shore. Gilden was ahead of Harry; he slipped and skidded along the turf. A moment later, Weston took a sprawl. Harry was a dozen yards at the head of the chase. But the Gray Ghost was far in the lead.

Harry saw him reach the shore, as a final stab of lightning rocketed across the sky. Then, while thunder rumbled through the blackness, Harry stumbled upon rocks. He was near the cove. No lightning followed when he needed it. Harry pulled out his flashlight; by its glow, he managed to distinguish the little pier.

Weston was shouting orders. He was calling to others, telling them to scatter all along the fringe of the water. Soon there came new lightning that showed men everywhere; but the Gray Ghost was gone. Harry stared out from the shore; he saw no swimmer in the waves.

"He's somewhere along the shore!" called Harry. "Take a look around the pier!"

A CAR was sloshing down from the house. Forbel had come out to his limousine. The headlights were brilliant; to them, Forbel added the glare of a special searchlight which the car carried. While infrequent lightning flashes helped the watchers along the shore, the car lights threw a powerful beam upon the pilings of the squatty pier.

Weston had broken into the bathhouse. Other men were clambering beneath the pier. Harry joined Gilden just as the fellow slipped deep into the water. As he hauled Gilden on to the shore, Harry laughed.

"Guess you can't get more drenched than you are," he remarked. "Neither can I. We might as well plow right into the water."

"That suits me," returned Gilden, "provided I can keep hold of those posts. I don't want to get in too deep."

Beneath the pier, Harry used a flashlight, as did others who had come under from the far side. Waist deep in water, they scoured among the pilings,

Waist-deep in water, they scoured among the pilings to make positive that the Gray Ghost had not chosen this lurking spot.

to make positive that the Gray Ghost had not chosen this lurking spot. The water at the end of the pier was of six-feet depth. Between the central supports, Harry glared his flashlight outward, to show plainly that the space was empty.

The rain was pounding upon the boards above, with streams of water trickling through the cracks; but there was no downpour to restrict the flashlight's beam. Harry's chief difficulty lay in obtaining a good hold against the sloshing waves that splashed in from the Sound.

The search was finished. Harry heard Weston calling from above. The commissioner had received the report that the Gray Ghost was not beneath the pier. Harry emerged to find Gilden on the shore.

"We look like a couple of water rats," laughed Gilden. "So do those fellows who went out the other side. We won't mind the rain after this."

Harry nodded his agreement. He looked along the shore toward scattered spots of light. Searchers had begun to assemble at Weston's call. Hoarse, the commissioner made a final announcement.

"Half a dozen men have gone to the grove," he declared. "That's the last place the Gray Ghost could be. They can handle him if they find him. The rest of you can go indoors."

Harry welcomed the order. He went toward the house, guiding himself by a light above the front door. As he came within the glow, he joined other searchers. The front door opened. The Shadow was standing there alone.

Pennybrook had come up beside Harry. The lawyer was growling angrily. He had been outside continually since the Gray Ghost's first appearance. He had heard of the robbery after the search by the shore.

As they entered the front door, Renright arrived. He looked at Harry and laughed. His tone, however, was sour.

"I thought we were going to trap the Gray Ghost, Vincent," declared Renright. "I would have made a bet that he was under the pier. I came in from one side when you slid under from the other. But the Gray Ghost wasn't there."

"They'll find him in the grove," assured Gilden, who had also arrived. "That's the only place left where he could be."

"The count says there are dry clothes upstairs," put in Pennybrook, joining the trio. "They belong to the people who own the house. But I suppose we can use them."

THE searchers went upstairs. Soon Weston arrived with the rest of the dripping party. The grove had revealed no traces of the Gray Ghost. These late arrivals also went upstairs to find other garments.

It was a nondescript array that appeared in the conservatory half an hour later. A few were well-attired in clothes that The Shadow had provided. The rest had rummaged through old trunks and closets to find worn-out suits, overalls, and khaki trousers. All looked weary and ready for departure; they welcomed The Shadow's suggestion that they leave.

"My servants will continue the search," assured The Shadow, in his accented tones. "We have failed to capture the Gray Ghost; but we made a valiant effort. My congratulations, *señores.*"

"It is your loss that troubles us, Count," returned Pennybrook. "We were here to protect your valuables. We failed."

"The fortune of war," stated The Shadow, with a broad smile. "After all, *Señor* Debrossler was also robbed. So was *Señor* Forbel. I have no cause to protest."

"We shall capture the Gray Ghost," assured Commissioner Weston, hoarsely. "But remember, Count, I warned you against your folly."

The others were leaving. The Shadow made a slight gesture that Harry understood. He went out with Renright, following Pennybrook and Gilden. The Shadow remained alone with Commissioner Weston.

"One moment, *Señor* Commissioner," suggested The Shadow, in his suave tone. "There is something which I think will be of interest to you. One great interest, *señor!*"

Motors were throbbing outside the house. The guests were on their way. While Weston stared, The Shadow reached into a tail pocket of his dress suit and produced a chamois bag. He opened it and let gems trickle into his hand.

"The jewels!" exclaimed Weston. "How did you regain them?"

"These are the real gems," returned The Shadow. "The Gray Ghost took false stones, *señor.*"

"You never showed us the real ones?"

"You saw the genuine, *señor,* upon the first occasion. It was wise that it should be so. That the Gray Ghost could see. You recall my mention that the light was poor, *señor?* That was what you in America call a bluff. This light is excellent for the display of gems."

Weston recalled that the stones had shown a magnificent sparkle; that fact was being duplicated before his eyes. The Shadow dropped the gems back into the bag.

"While you first sought the Gray Ghost," he remarked, "I put this bag away. The one which I laid in its place—that was different, *señor.* Its contents were no gems. They were mere imitations. The Gray Ghost took but one small look at them. He was too sure of what they were."

WESTON extended his hand in congratulation. The Shadow received it with the firm grip that he had previously given. As he walked toward the front door with Weston, he carried the jewel pouch with him.

"This bag," he remarked, suavely, "is not heavy. But it would be difficult to conceal, eh, *señor?*"

"The Gray Ghost took a bag the size of it," returned Weston, speculatively. "He thrust it beneath his jersey."

"Ah, *si*. The sweater shirt that he wore. It was easy to see how it was hidden."

"Yes. It bulged plainly."

"That is grand, *señor*. Then the Gray Ghost did not carry it away. It would have been one great risk."

"But the Gray Ghost escaped us."

"That is true. Nevertheless, *señor*, it may be that we shall sometime find him. Truly, I would have gladly let him take my real gems. But it was not necessary."

Weston stared, perplexed. He wondered what had struck the Count of Santurnia. The Shadow offered no explanation. He merely bowed his good night.

"Let the newspapers believe," he reminded, in parting. "They can say that true gems were stolen."

"Of course," agreed Weston. "That is the proper policy, Count."

Stepping out into the blinding rain, the commissioner reached the small car in which he had driven from New York. After a few stalls, the motor throbbed. Weston drove away. The last of The Shadow's guests had gone.

From the smiling lips of the Count of Santurnia came a strangely whispered laugh; one that predicted a successful future. Again, the Gray Ghost had escaped. That fact did not disturb The Shadow. His laugh betokened completed plans.

The Shadow had fared well with the Gray Ghost.

CHAPTER XVIII
THE NEXT NIGHT

IT was late the next afternoon. Harry Vincent was driving into New York City from Narrowneck. He had spent the night at the club, with Colin Renright. This afternoon, in response to a call from Rutledge Mann, he had said good-bye to the husky athlete.

Presumably, Harry was going West. His vacation had ended. Actually, his work was done. So far as he was concerned, the quest for the Gray Ghost was ended. Harry knew, however, that The Shadow had not finished the game.

Harry had an idea that other agents would still be kept on duty. Certainly Cliff Marsland; probably Hawkeye; possibly Clyde Burke. In stepping from the picture, Harry was simply serving The Shadow's plans. He had reasoned the answer for himself.

Somewhere in his course of action, Harry had met the man who was actually the Gray Ghost. Of all the men whom he had encountered, Harry could not pick the right one. Nevertheless, he was positive that in his adventures he had contacted the Gray Ghost in person.

Since the Gray Ghost had guessed that The Shadow had endeavored to outwit him, it was possible that the Gray Ghost also suspected Harry of being The Shadow's aide. Harry had come into the game as a stranger. There was a chance that the Gray Ghost was watching him. The best plan, therefore, was for Harry to retire from all fields of action. That was the reason for The Shadow's order that Harry should return to New York and stay there.

Harry had always found this type of order the most difficult to follow. Through association with The Shadow, he had gained an urge for action whenever battle foreboded. His duty to The Shadow was foremost, however. Harry was obeying instructions.

To reach Manhattan, Harry had to pass through Holmwood. He remembered that he had a guest card at the Holmwood Beach Club. He decided to stop there long enough for dinner. Holmwood was actually within the city limits. This did not seem contradictory to The Shadow's orders.

In fact, the orders had a single purpose: simply to remove Harry from any likelihood of observation. Harry doubted that the Gray Ghost would be in the vicinity of Holmwood. If he happened to be there, even at the club, the sight of Harry dining alone would allay, rather than excite, the Gray Ghost's suspicions.

Long Island Sound had calmed today. A clear sky promised a moonlit night. Dusk was settling as Harry reached the driveway beside the club. He left his coupé in the parking space and strolled into the clubhouse. Immediately, he heard his name called. He looked about and saw Pierce Gilden. With the young man was Jane Debrossler.

GILDEN had a warm handshake for Harry. He introduced Harry to Jane; then began a discussion of last night's events. Jane seemed thrilled by the description of the Gray Ghost's escape. When Gilden had concluded his account of the battle, the girl made comment of her own.

"I should like to have met the Count of Santurnia," declared Jane. "He must be a jolly sport. Father said that he was not at all put out because he had lost his jewels."

"Perhaps he has millions besides," remarked Harry.

"No," declared Gilden. "Jane's father talked with him this afternoon and states that the count has been left practically penniless."

"He managed to cancel the lease on the mansion," added Jane. "He dismissed all the servants. He has gone into New York, so father says, to live at some obscure hotel. The count hopes to receive some money from friends in Buenos Aires. He may go to South America."

"Tough luck," affirmed Gilden.

"Worse than father's," agreed Jane. "Which reminds me, Pierce, that I must hurry home. You are invited for dinner, so you must come with me. We should also like to have you with us, Mr. Vincent."

Harry bowed in response to the gracious invitation.

"I am sorry, Miss Debrossler," he declared, "but I must decline. I am expecting word from a friend. It would be better for me to remain here at the club."

ONE hour later, Harry had finished dinner and was sitting in the cool of the veranda. The moon had risen; the mildness of the night made Harry loath to continue his trip to Manhattan. He decided at last that he might possibly be needed by The Shadow. If so, his hotel was the place where he should be.

Arising, Harry walked toward his car. As he neared the coupé, a local taxi wheeled up and Jane Debrossler stepped from it.

"Hello, Mr. Vincent!" greeted Jane, as soon as she had paid the driver. "Have you seen Pierce Gilden here?"

"I thought he went to your house," replied Harry.

"He did," declared the girl. "But he left right after dinner. Father went out in the big car, soon after Pierce had driven away. That left me alone, with no car. Louise my sister—was not at home for dinner. She has the small car."

"I see."

"So I was alone," continued Jane, "when my aunt called up from Northpoint. She is ill; I must go there at once. I had hoped that Pierce would be here to take me."

The girl looked about for the taxi that had brought her. The cab had driven away.

"How stupid!" exclaimed Jane. "It may take a half hour to get another taxi. The service here is horrible—"

"Suppose I drive you out to Northpoint," interposed Harry. "The trip would not require much time."

"Would you, Mr. Vincent?"

"I certainly shall. Let me see—Northpoint is only a few miles past Narrowneck, isn't it?"

"Six miles. Just a few miles this side of the house that you visited last night. The Count of Santurnia lived about four miles beyond Northpoint."

Harry ushered Jane into the coupé. They headed eastward, along the road to Narrowneck. Considering the circumstances, Harry decided that this trip would certainly eliminate him from any observation on the part of the Gray Ghost.

At Narrowneck, they passed the clubhouse where Harry had stopped the night before. Harry saw Colin Renright standing beside his coupé, chatting with some friends. Renright was turned half away; he did not observe Harry's car.

Jane Debrossler had remained silent during most of the journey. She had expressed anxiety about her aunt. Harry supposed that the girl was too worried to be talkative. But when they neared the town of Northpoint, Jane became loquacious.

"What a marvelous night!" exclaimed the girl. "Look how the shore turns. You can see the moon above the Sound. It is so different from last night."

"As I can testify," laughed Harry. "I was in the middle of all that rain, when it was at its worst!"

"Father was going to buy a cottage here at Northpoint," said Jane, "but he decided that the place was too old and too small. It was empty then and has been ever since. The best feature of the place was the boathouse. That really was a good one, and could easily have been put in fine shape.

"We turn at the next road to the left; then right when we reach the last road before the Sound. We go right by the cottage that I mentioned. I shall show it to you, Mr. Vincent. I want you to notice the boathouse in particular."

Harry made the two turns. He slowed the car as they rolled along the final stretch of road. Off to the left was a patch of jagged ground that fronted on the Sound. Next, an isolated cottage, small and much in need of paint, as the moonlight showed.

"That's the cottage," declared Jane. "In a moment we shall see the boathouse—"

She stopped short and gripped Harry's arm.

"Quick, Mr. Vincent!" pleaded Jane. "Pull over to the right, into that little road! Put out the lights!"

Harry obeyed, knowing that something important must have happened. Jane was pointing across the wheel, to a spot some distance beyond the cottage.

"Look!" she whispered, breathlessly. "See that figure going toward the boathouse? It's the Gray Ghost!"

HARRY could see the boathouse clearly in the moonlight. It was a large structure, as boathouses go; and its walls were dusky. Soon Harry saw a moving, wavering figure. Jane was right. It was the Gray Ghost!

Instantly, Harry came to action. This was an emergency—the type of situation in which quick judgment served in place of all instructions. As an agent of The Shadow, Harry had a perfect opportunity to serve his chief. This was his chance to trap the Gray Ghost.

Harry looked to the road. Shading trees hid his coupé well. A few yards more would render the camouflage perfect. Harry coasted the car farther out of view. He spoke to the girl beside him.

"Wait here," ordered Harry. "I'm going to snag the Gray Ghost!"

"Let me come also," pleaded Jane. "It would be safer. I can let you go ahead. If there is any trouble, I may be useful."

The girl was wearing a dark dress. There was little chance that she could be seen. Harry spoke his agreement. Together, they crossed the road and reached a low hedge on the other side. Harry heard cars coming from both directions. He told Jane to lie low until they had passed. The girl obeyed.

Harry looked for the Gray Ghost. At last he saw the figure again, almost motionless, against the whitish wall of the cottage. The Gray Ghost was waiting at a spot that could scarcely be seen from the road. Harry's new point of observation offset that advantage.

"He doesn't spy us," whispered Harry, to Jane. "Let's move over toward the boathouse. We can cut him off from the Sound. Be careful, though! Go slowly!"

They crept forward, close to the ground. Bush-clumped ground gave them an advantage. All the while, the Gray Ghost was visible as he paced impatiently back and forth beside the wall of the cottage. Harry and Jane reached the boathouse unnoticed.

"Wait here," whispered Harry. "I'll give him a chance to make a move."

The maneuvers had taken a full dozen minutes. Ten more passed, while the Gray Ghost still kept his position. Harry muttered grimly:

"He's waiting for something. I'd like to know what's up."

"Some new crime, probably," whispered Jane, tensely. "Look! He is moving away from the cottage. Not in this direction, though!"

"He's coming here," predicted Harry, "but he doesn't like the moonlight. That's why he is making a circuit. Come along with me. We'll move to the near corner of the boathouse. I'll be ready for him when he makes the turn."

They reached the corner. Close to the ground, Harry and Jane watched the Gray Ghost edge toward a rocky knoll no more than twenty paces distant. He was hidden from the moonlight; but there was no way in which he could leave the cluster of rocks without being seen. Harry gripped his automatic. He spoke to Jane.

"If he retreats," promised Harry, "I'm going after him. If he comes in this direction, I'll meet him. He doesn't know I'm here. The odds are all mine."

Harry crept forward, obscured from the moonlight by the shaded edge of the boathouse. His eyes were focused on the rocks where he knew the Gray Ghost must be. So intent was Harry that when Jane gave a warning gasp, he did not immediately recognize the significance.

A hiss followed. That threat made Harry swing about. He stopped, rigid, staring at the incredible. Amazingly, impossibly, the Gray Ghost had left his lurking place. The master crook had arrived beside the boathouse.

Jane Debrossler was covered by a revolver muzzle. The weapon pointed on a line straight to Harry. The gun was gripped by a jerseyed figure that stood hooded in the moonlight. Like the girl, Harry was helpless.

The Gray Ghost had trapped his trappers!

CHAPTER XIX
HARRY SEES DOUBLE

HARRY'S automatic thudded rocky soil. Covered at close range, he was stupefied by the Gray Ghost's astonishing appearance beside the boathouse. In addition, Harry knew that any antagonistic deed on his part might cost another life beside his own. Jane Debrossler was in the path of the Gray Ghost's gun.

The Gray Ghost motioned Harry toward the boathouse. Advancing with upraised arms, The Shadow's agent stopped by a padlocked double door. Using his free hand, the Gray Ghost opened the padlock. He swung the door inward; then growled:

"Move in there!"

Harry followed the order. Jane entered the boathouse behind him.

"Stop!"

Both obeyed. Flooding moonlight streaked a wooden flooring above the water's edge. The Gray Ghost had kept his prisoners from reaching inner depths, where darkness might have served them. While the captives awaited the next move, the Gray Ghost gave a low, weird wail.

Jane Debrossler gasped: "Furbison told me of that cry—"

"Sh-h-h!" warned Harry. "Say nothing!"

The Gray Ghost had entered. Moonlight faded as the door swung shut. Almost with the same move, the Gray Ghost turned a light switch. A single bulb illuminated a barren room. This was the ground floor of the boathouse. Gurgling sounds told that water lay beneath.

"Turn around!"

The prisoners obeyed their captor's orders. In the dull light, Harry gained a new view of the Gray Ghost. He was able to judge the rogue's size more accurately than before. Harry decided that the Gray Ghost had bulk, as well as height. His jersey showed no traces of padding.

Nevertheless, the crook's appearance was deceptive. There was something oddly puzzling to Harry. Mental comparisons failed him. He was trying to find the answer; when it came, it furnished a new surprise. Looking beyond the Gray Ghost, Harry saw the door move inward. For a moment, he felt elation; then an impulsive gasp escaped his lips.

Into the boathouse stepped another gray-clad figure, at first glance the twin of the one who had made the capture. As the new arrival approached, Harry sensed the difference. Both were of equal height; but the newcomer was of slender build. His garments were certainly padded.

There were two Gray Ghosts!

A deluge of explanations swept through Harry's brain. Last night's events came popping back to memory. Both Gray Ghosts had visited the mansion which The Shadow had occupied as the Count of Santurnia. The lighter man had been the first. The bulky one had made the getaway with the false gems.

Identities leaped suddenly to Harry's mind. Before his conjectures could reach his lips, the larger of the Gray Ghosts issued a snarled signal. Together, the captors pulled back their hoods. Harry saw the very men whose names were in his thoughts.

The bulkier Gray Ghost was Colin Renright. His companion was Pierce Gilden.

JANE DEBROSSLER uttered a startled cry, as she recognized Gilden. The rogue leered contemptuously. Turning about, Gilden went to the door and swung down a wooden bar that clicked into a huge, upturned hook. The barrier closed against rescuers, Gilden swung around and brandished a revolver of his own.

Harry viewed the faces of the two Gray Ghosts. He saw malice expressed on both.

"So you see the game at last," jeered Renright, facing Harry. "You meddled long enough; but you never would have guessed it. I did the job at Debrossler's, while Pierce fixed himself a perfect alibi."

"At my expense," exclaimed Jane. "That was why you went to town with us, Pierce, the night father was robbed."

"Why not?" jeered Gilden. "I had one set of friends. Colin had another. We took turns at crime, each robbing the ones whom the other mentioned."

"And Culden handed us tip-offs," growled Renright. "We took care of him, until he put himself in bad with some New York thugs. Gang methods were not in our line. Our tactics were more subtle."

"I handled Forbel's gems," asserted Gilden, proudly. "It was a tough job, particularly with that swim I had to make. Colin was better qualified."

"But I needed an alibi," smirked Renright. "So I was on good behavior that night. I helped you a bit, though, Pierce."

"By unloading the guns," ejaculated Harry, "when I thought you were upstairs in the gallery!"

"You've got it," growled Renright, "and you nearly queered the deal, yanking that gun I didn't know you had. I've had a score to settle with you, Vincent. It's too bad for you that you found your way here tonight."

"And for Jane, also," added Gilden, with a snarl. "This is the night we move the swag. No one is going to talk!"

"We'll bump them off right here, Pierce."

"That's the best way, Colin. You keep them covered while I start the boat."

Renright was firm with his gun. Harry knew the man's reputation as a sharpshooter. He realized that Gilden was dangerous also. Each had performed individual murder. Renright had slain Hiram Windler, prior to the robbery at Debrossler's. Gilden had accounted for the valet, Hembroke, that night at Forbel's.

Gilden moved past the prisoners. Harry could hear him opening a trapdoor in the floor. The sound of lapping water became more audible. It must have seemed ominous to Jane; for the girl began to gasp.

"Steady," warned Harry, quietly. "Noise won't help us."

"These men are merciless," expressed Jane. Then, steadying, she addressed Renright: "Our deaths will bring you no advantage."

"No?" Renright's tone was sarcastic. "You think that we are afraid to murder? Why do you suppose the police are already searching for the Gray Ghost?"

Jane was about to reply, when Harry broke into the talk. He spoke straight to Renright.

"Call it quits with the girl," said Harry, in a firm tone. "You bagged her father's cash. What good will it do to kill her? Rub *me* out, if you want. I wanted to get on your trail. But the girl is different. Count her out of it."

In his steady tone, Harry had done his utmost to hold Renright's attention. For while he spoke, Harry could see a motion beyond the bulky form of the larger Gray Ghost. The bar that Gilden had fastened was moving upward. Someone from outside had wedged a blade between the sections of the double door. The bar was lifting noiselessly;

but Harry wanted to cover any chance scraping that it might make.

"The girl can talk," growled Renright. "That means she is to die. Whoever you are, Vincent, doesn't matter. I thought once that you might be The Shadow. I found out differently, after I met the Count of Santurnia.

"We staged that job together, Pierce and I, so neatly that no one could have guessed our system. I studied the lay the day before. I kidded you when I met you on the road. You say you were on my trail. I suppose you were working on your own, like a lot of other dubs.

"It makes no difference. I'd have bumped you anytime I needed to. The time's here right now. It's curtains for you and the girl! I've got The Shadow's jewels here with me"—he tapped a bulge at one side of his gray jersey—"and the rest of the swag is in the boat. When Pierce comes up—"

Renright broke off. Gilden's head had popped from the trapdoor, looking in Renright's direction. Gilden saw what Harry had observed: the final lifting of the wooden bar. Half through the trapdoor, Gilden uttered a cry and shot a hand for his gun, which he had pocketed. Renright saw the move and spun about. He was too late.

The half door was swinging inward. On the threshold was The Shadow, garbed in black. His fists clutched automatics. One gun covered Renright; the other pointed straight for Gilden.

There was an instant's hesitation; then Renright's gun dropped, while Gilden's hands raised weaponless. The Shadow elbowed the door shut behind him.

THE SHADOW was unsurprised at sight of two Gray Ghosts. His manner showed that he had expected to find both rogues. As he held the crooks at bay, The Shadow spoke in sinister whisper.

"Your part was known, Renright," he pronounced. "You gave away your athletic ability by your flight from Windler's. I followed your entire trail. I had you watched."

Renright gaped. He wondered why The Shadow had left him unmolested. The answer came.

"I wanted to learn more," declared The Shadow. "When crime struck at Forbel's, you had an alibi. But you proved, despite yourself, that you were involved in crime. You did more than remove bullets from the guns of others.

"You had four blanks in your own revolver— shots which you fired at the Gray Ghost, to give credence to his supposed immunity against bullets. You kept two bullet-laden cartridges to fire afterward. Gilden, however, quailed when he saw Vincent's gun."

It was all explained to Harry. He realized how Renright had helped Gilden's bluff. The Shadow had seen through the game. He had known that a marksman of Renright's repute would not have fired wide with four straight shots. He had known also that the Gray Ghost would not have stood his ground against possible bullets. Gilden's quick flight at sight of Harry's gun was proof.

Harry understood how the game of the Gray Ghost had been spoiled. Harry himself had ruined it, unwittingly. Renright had coached Gilden to make a slow departure. Had Gilden done that, as the Gray Ghost he would have left men awed, while he effected an easy escape.

Instead, the Gray Ghost had been pursued. Rumors that he was superhuman had changed to talk of bulletproof vests. A wrong theory; but one that had sufficed to break the spell of the Gray Ghost.

"I planned a snare," announced The Shadow. "As the Count of Santurnia, I let you steal false gems. Both of you proved your parts last night. Gilden came earlier than Debrossler. He waited until Debrossler's car appeared. He showed himself as the Gray Ghost; then fled back to his own car, parked outside the gates, and drove it in the driveway."

A snarl from Renright. It was plain that he had devised the game.

"You had your alibi, Renright," resumed The Shadow. "Gilden had discarded his gray garb. You donned it, without the padding, and came for the gems. This time, Gilden had the alibi. Two Gray Ghosts were at work. But you needed a place to hide both the gems and the gray jersey.

"I had wisely provided one that I knew would suit you: the float beyond the pier—an easy underwater swim for so capable an athlete as yourself. You came back from there when the search ended. You left the discarded garb with the false gems."

"The false gems?" queried Renright, with a snarl. "What did you do? Switch them today; then wait for me to come and dive for them?"

"I changed them last night," returned The Shadow. "At no time did you hold the real gems. Your return was awaited, Renright. I was prepared to follow you—by land, or by water. You chose land. I let you reach this hiding place. I knew that here I would find Gilden also, together with your accumulated spoils."

RENRIGHT gave a shrug of resignation.

"You win," he declared, sourly. "I thought you had given up the part you played. I figured the Count of Santurnia had gone. That's why I drove out there a while ago. I wore a bathing suit when I dived under the float. I sank the old gray outfit and brought back the gems.

"The gems I thought were real. I changed to

these clothes in the bathhouse and headed here. Gilden met me, wearing an outfit of his own. We figured the Gray Ghost stuff was still good, in case we met any dubs along the line. They'd have been scared stiff.

"But you licked us." Renright dropped his left hand and tugged the chamois bag from beneath his jersey. Watersoaked, it hit the floor and spilled its imitation jewels. "Licked us from the start, last night. We'll take what's coming to us—"

Breaking off, Renright performed a sudden side leap, that came with remarkable speed. He hurled himself in back of Jane Debrossler, snatched the girl from the floor and shoved her forward as a shield, toward the gun that he had dropped.

At the same instant, Gilden swung his right hand downward. Timed with Renright's move, the man at the trapdoor whipped his own revolver into view, to aim point-blank for The Shadow.

The Gray Ghosts were in action. Each was on the move, eager to deal death to their superfoe, The Shadow.

CHAPTER XX
MID-CHANNEL

THE SHADOW needed speed. He produced it.

Two enemies had acted simultaneously. Of the pair, Renright was more formidable, though both were dangerous. Harry Vincent, had the choice been his, would have taken Renright first. The Shadow did the opposite.

The black-clad fighter fired for Gilden. He beat the lesser Gray Ghost to the shot. Gilden's gun spoke in answer; but it was tilted upward when the murderer fired. The Shadow had clipped Gilden's gun arm; the man was teetering backward as he pressed the trigger.

Gilden screeched as he plunged down through the trapdoor, missing the ladder. There was a thud; he had dropped into the motorboat beneath. The Shadow had settled Gilden for the moment; he had wheeled to deal with Renright.

Had Harry Vincent paused one moment, he would have seen his proper course. A quick dive— and he could have gained Renright's revolver. With it, Harry could have sprung below to settle Gilden, if the fellow still had fight. The Shadow would have managed Renright.

But Harry acted upon too quick an impulse. He saw Jane Debrossler in danger. Hoping to save the girl, he pounced for Renright instead of the revolver.

Renright sprawled, carrying Jane with him. He snatched up the gun and swung an upward stroke at Harry. The Shadow's agent warded off the blow and gripped Renright's arm. They floundered across the floor, Jane rolling along with them.

The Shadow, aiming steadily from the door, was at a disadvantage.

Of three persons in the scuffle, two were ones whom The Shadow must save. For the present, he had no chance to fire at Renright. The risk of hitting Harry or Jane was too great. The Shadow could only wait for a break in the fray.

From below, a motor chugged suddenly. One-handed, Gilden had managed to prepare the get-away. The Shadow could allow no further time. He sprang forward to join the mêlée on the floor. As he hit the fighters, he broke Renright's grasp on Jane. The girl crawled free of the fray.

Renright swung Harry toward The Shadow and delivered a downward stroke with his revolver. The Shadow stopped it short with an outthrust automatic. Harry sprawled sidewise; Renright gave an acrobatic heave and struck The Shadow headlong. He bowled the cloaked fighter to the floor.

The Shadow had dropped one .45; he caught his adversary with his free hand and sent Renright rolling sidewise. Twisting to hands and knees, The Shadow came up for aim. His move had given him the chance to beat Renright to the shot. That jujitsu twist had done its work; but the accomplishment proved too great.

Because of Renright's weight, The Shadow had given him a mammoth hurl. Rolling almost a dozen feet, Renright had arrived half over the opened trapdoor. Instead of aiming for The Shadow, the twin Gray Ghost shoved himself backward. As The Shadow aimed, Renright's left hand was his only target. The crook was dropping below.

The Shadow fired, just as Renright's fingers left the edge of the trap. The bullet splintered wood-work; it found no human flesh. The Shadow bounded forward; a motor roared as he reached the trapdoor. A steel speedboat shot from sight, smashing a flimsy barrier that blocked its path to the Sound.

The light showed a pathway beside the channel below. Disregarding the ladder, The Shadow made a leap. He dashed through the splintered barrier. He signaled in the path of a searchlight's beam. The Gray Ghosts had whizzed out into the Sound; the searchlight was from another boat close by. The nose of a swift motor craft sped up to the spot where The Shadow stood. The Shadow leaped aboard.

BY land or by water. The Shadow had mentioned that he had covered either path that Renright might take. He had provided a boat to trail the crook to his lair. It had not been needed in the short trip, for Renright had come by car. The motorboat, however, had followed along the shoreline.

It was contact with the craft that had delayed The Shadow in his approach. Otherwise, he would have met the Gray Ghosts earlier. The situation had changed; The Shadow's wisdom was proven. The Gray Ghosts were staging a new escape. He had the means whereby they could be overtaken.

The Shadow's boat was capable of greater speed than any other craft upon Long Island Sound.

Cliff Marsland was at the helm, Hawkeye beside him. Clyde Burke was by the motor. The swift boat carved the water. It was following the path made by the wake ahead. The Gray Ghosts had gained a long lead, heading straight across the Sound. This boat, however, could overhaul them.

The moonlight showed the chase. The Shadow, ready on the prow, had chosen a rifle as his weapon. Far ahead, Renright was stationed at the stern of his craft, armed with a rifle of his own, while Gilden managed the helm, one-handed. Marksmen were prepared for strife while the speedy boats ate the wavelets.

Rifles crackled. The battle had begun. Bullets zipped the water. At the speed with which the boats were traveling, perfect aim was impossible. Renright fired from ahead; The Shadow responded. Neither bullet found a mark.

Miles were scudding beneath the roaring speedboats. The Gray Ghosts hoped to reach the Connecticut shore before The Shadow overtook them. The space was slowly diminishing. The Shadow's boat was creeping closer to the murderers.

Dead ahead, a ghostly mass enshrouded the waters of mid-channel. It was fog, an heirloom of last night's storm; a hazy embankment that bore the semblance of a low-lying hill. Neither the Gray Ghosts nor The Shadow had expected to encounter that misty pall. It offered refuge to the Gray Ghosts.

Their boat was laden with swag, stored in water-tight lockers. Practically unsinkable, the pelf was safe. To cash it, the Gray Ghosts needed complete escape. The fog bank was their chance. It had stretched far out from the Connecticut shore; it was creeping toward Long Island. Once within it, the Gray Ghosts could accomplish the trick which they had performed before: a complete evanishment from the eyes of pursuers.

PRONE on the bow, The Shadow was ready with his rifle. He was holding fire until the Gray Ghosts reached the fog bank, thus giving Cliff a chance to close the distance. Swiftly, the roaring speedboats neared the final stretch. Wisps of mist licked toward the craft that carried the Gray Ghosts.

Renright must have guessed The Shadow's purpose. He opened a futile rapid fire from the stern of his boat. Bullets ricocheted from the water, bouncing like skimmed stones. The Shadow's rifle spoke. It delivered shots in quick succession.

A figure popped up from the boat ahead. It spun about; then settled downward in the bottom of the craft. The boat went twisting off its course. The Shadow had picked off one Gray Ghost: Pierce Gilden. Colin Renright was leaping to the helm.

Swinging wide, keeling dangerously, the boat responded as Renright managed it. The Shadow fired final shots; they were wide. No marksman could have gauged the twists of the boat ahead. One Gray Ghost had survived; alone a claimant to that title, Renright found the fog.

The Shadow's boat had gained tremendously during Renright's forced maneuvers. The pursuit was not ended. Unless Renright changed his course immediately, he would be overhauled. Driving into the fog bank, The Shadow's boat remained a menace to the lone Gray Ghost.

Swallowed by the eerie mist, the pursuing craft kept straight ahead. It struck a stretch of lifting fog. The Shadow, from the prow, caught a glimpse of Renright's boat, dead ahead. The Shadow motioned to Cliff, signaling to maintain the course.

The fog shuddered with a basso whistle, that quavered from somewhere off the starboard bow. A steamer was plowing its course through the enveloping mist. The Shadow's keen ears sensed the right direction. His hands rose in quick gesture for Cliff to throttle down the motor.

Cliff acted in response, as they struck another open patch of water—a curious oasis in the whirling fog. The Shadow caught new sight of Renright's boat ahead. He aimed his reloaded rifle then stilled his finger on the trigger.

As if governed by some magnetic hand of fate, a huge prow jammed from the cloud bank, straight in front of Renright's speedboat. The little craft seemed to leap from the water to meet the oncoming steamship. There was a crash that echoed through the fog. As Cliff swung the helm, The Shadow gazed to starboard.

Two figures had jounced wildly from the crash, tossed from the crackling shell of the shattered speedboat. One was Gilden's; the other, Renright's. Neither could be distinguished in the beam of the steamship's searchlight. Both were dead forms, folding crazily as they hit the water.

Gilden had died before Renright, dropped by a timely rifle bullet. Renright, the last Gray Ghost, had escaped a similar doom—to be shattered bodily by the steel prow that had struck through from the fog.

FOG was seething about the big steamship. Propellers were churning in reverse. Lights were barely visible through the mist. The Shadow could hear shouts from the decks. Davits were creaking; the steamer was letting down boats to search the waters.

The hulk of the water-tight speed boat had remained afloat; though the craft was riven almost in half, the air compartments were sufficient to keep it on the surface. The steamship crew would find it and search for identifying contents. Stolen swag was destined to be found. Wealth would be delivered in New York, restored to owners who had suffered loss.

But no survivors would be brought aboard the steamship. Two bodies, only, would be discovered— both garbed in jerseys of gray, with lowered hoods. The Gray Ghosts had found their doom; murderers, they had gained suitable reward.

The Shadow's boat had turned about; it was chugging toward the Long Island shore; it cleared the fog. Moonlight shone its brilliance upon The Shadow and the men who had aided him. There was something significant in the glow that had so suddenly replaced the thickness of the fog. It told of The Shadow's triumph.

The Shadow himself had ended the beclouding factors that enshrouded crime. He had brought final light upon the baffling mystery of the Gray Ghost.

THE END

INTERLUDE by Will Murray

In the summer of 1935, the pulp publishing world began to wonder if the phenomenon of the monthly magazine built around a single character had peaked. One editor claimed that these ghost-writers who toiled in obscurity behind company-owned bylines were being ruined by this type of formula writing, their vitality as writers fast running dry.

Although the hero pulp sub-genre was only four years old, already some of its demon wordsmiths—virtually chained to their typewriters in order to meet unforgiving monthly deadlines—were falling by the wayside. The originating author of the first Shadow imitation, *The Phantom Detective*, D. L. Champion, was only occasionally contributing to the series he had helped launch in 1933.

Likewise, the authors of *The Spider, Secret Agent X* and *Operator #5*, were showing signs of fatigue. Boredom, nervous breakdowns and sheer exhaustion would cause them to curtail their involvement, allowing younger, fresher writers to take their place behind the all-concealing house names.

Showing no signs of strain except other than going gray at the temples and putting on a little weight in spite of his incessant chainsmoking, the first and greatest of that hearty breed, Walter B. Gibson, continued to produce his Shadow novels every two weeks like a relentless typing machine. True, he often wore out his trusty Smith-Corona, but he simply switched to a spare until the original machine recovered its spring. And some-times the tips of his fingers would bleed from hitting the manual keys so merci-lessly. But these were the occupational hazards of the prolific pulpsters of the Great Depression. Rubber thimbles or adhesive tape were the usual cure for sore fingertips.

That Autumn, Gibson was in Orlando, Florida, where in years to come he would frequently flee the brutal Manhattan winters. And there he wrote *The Gray Ghost*, finishing it up around Halloween, appropriately enough. It was a spooky time for The Shadow's raconteur. Just a month before, he was startled to read a report of his own death in the Orlando *Sun*. The headline claimed that Maxwell Grant, author of The Shadow, had died.

In reality, radio writer Harry Charlot had passed away under mysterious cir-cumstances on September 28th. Charlot had suggested The Shadow's name, after the concept of a sinister mystery host had

been developed by producer-director Bill Sweets and Dave Chrisman of the Ruthrauff and Ryan advertising agency. Hence the confusion. No doubt reading his own death notice put Gibson in the perfect frame of mind to pen *The Gray Ghost*.

To Gibson, producing absorbing Shadow novels was the same as breathing. Despite writing almost 300 of them, he had never had one rejected. But *The Gray Ghost* stood out from the pack in its breathless, electrifying pace. Even George Rozen's striking cover promised something out of the ordinary.

First printed in the May 1, 1936 issue of *The Shadow Magazine,* it would be selected—along with the inaugural Shadow mystery, *The Living Shadow*—for inclusion in the second *Shadow Annual* in 1943, where it was cut for space reasons. It frequently showed up on top ten lists rabid Shadow fans submitted to the magazine's letter column back in those days. We are of course reprinting the original unedited text here.

The locale is a fictitious shore suburb of Long Island, which Gibson named Holmwood. It was of nostalgic significance to Walter Gibson. Based on

Howard Thurston and Walter Gibson in 1923

Walter Gibson first heard The Shadow's sibilant tones in Howard Thurston's Beechhurst mansion.

Beechhurst, Long Island where magician Howard Thurston lived, Holmwood was the setting for both *The Living Shadow* and a personal favorite, *The Grove of Doom.**

Beechhurst is a German name which refers to the groves of beech trees dominating this Long Island suburb. In German, "hurst" means grove. Readers familiar with the 1933 Shadow novel, *The Grove of Doom,* will understand the significance of the locale. Since a holm is both an islet and a European evergreen oak of the beech family, the name Holmwood is a perfect analogue of Beechhurst, Long Island.

It was at Thurston's Beechhurst mansion in late 1930 that the future Maxwell Grant first heard The Shadow's laugh emerging from the radio.

Within a few short months, Gibson would be bringing the Master of Darkness to full-blown life for Street & Smith—although at that time he never suspected it. It seemed that every time he wanted to do something out of the ordinary, Gibson set a Shadow mystery in Holmwood, which he also modeled after Swartmore, Pennsylvania. This is the third and last Holmwood mystery. And it introduced the enigmatic Count of Santurnia, who would return a year later in *Washington Crime,* one of the novels in our previous volume.

Walter Gibson and his editor, John Nanovic, took pride in producing original stories featuring the Master Avenger. Particularly, they struggled to avoid the pulp clichés that plagued rival crimefighters, making their adventures stale and repetitive.

One overused plot involved a suspect who appears guilty of various crimes, and then revealing either that it was really the work of his hitherto unknown

twin brother—or that the two were working as a team.

Knowing that Nanovic would never stand for such an obvious plot, Gibson once suggested a twist—what if the criminal twins were really triplets!

"I told John about that," Gibson once related. "But we both felt it was too gimmicky to be a Shadow story. I think somebody else [at Street & Smith] used it. I don't know what happened with it."

The Gray Ghost exploits the secret twin brother idea while avoiding the old clichés, making for one of Gibson's most arresting storylines. It features a memorable supercriminal with seemingly supernatural powers. In reality, the plot hinged on the old illusionist's "double" trick. Years later, Gibson successfully adapted *The Gray Ghost* for Street & Smith's *Shadow Comics.*

The spooky villains of *The White Skulls* may bear a superficial resemblance to *The Gray Ghost* himself, but otherwise these are two very different tales.

Published a decade later, in November 1945, *The White Skulls* is a throwback to the classic Shadow supervillains of the 1930s. Yet it invokes the Nazis, with whom the Dark Avenger rarely tangled. As a mystery character, The Shadow stayed out of the war in Europe, concentrating instead on various Fifth Columnists and saboteurs in tales like *Vengeance Bay* and *Death Has Grey Eyes.*

It's not difficult to imagine the origins of this story. It was written in May, 1945, in the immediate aftermath of the Allied victory in Europe, and Germany's unconditional surrender. Gibson no doubt thought it would be both topical and safe to employ the specter of a Nazi resurgence as plot fodder. He was probably the first writer of popular fiction to explore this fertile ground. Sixty years later, others are still following in his pioneering footsteps.

We've selected *The White Skulls* for reprinting not only because it represents a wild and memorable departure from the homefront whodunits that characterize the World War II phase of the series, but because it was the only Shadow story illustrated by Everett Raymond Kinstler, who went on to greater fame in the world of art, illustration and portraiture. His moody art was calculated to emulate the work of *Shadow Magazine* interior artist Tom Lovell, who illustrated the first six years of the series.

Both novels feature the small army of loyal Shadow agents with whom he fought crime so successfully for nearly two decades. •

The Grove of Doom, paired with *The Masked Lady,* was reprinted in *The Shadow* Volume 14.

THE WHITE SKULLS

by Maxwell Grant

A dangerous gang of men terrorizing everyone they met—their weird skeleton garb prophesying their wake of destruction. Could The Shadow identify his unknown foes—or would it be complete obliteration?

CHAPTER I

SARK'S picture glowered up from the desk and Jud Mayhew glowered down at it.

There was a difference, though, in those glowers, as Philo Brenz studied them from across the desk.

The photograph of Alban Sark wore a fixed expression. The face was dark and sinister, with a straight-lipped smile that had a creepy effect when closely scrutinized.

As for Jud Mayhew, he was going through the usual reactions that accompanied a survey of Sark's portrait. Finding the features difficult to distinguish, Jud had begun to frown, first in an annoyed fashion; then angrily.

Maybe Sark's looks had suffered from the enlargement of the photograph, which had originally been a small snapshot. The present background, a light gray, helped etch it. Sark's face belonged in shadows, had probably been lurking there when the camera had caught it. Maybe Sark had scowled because his picture was being taken, but at any rate his expression fitted him.

Chief of Sark's features were his bulging forehead; his hard, square chin. Bad lighting couldn't distort them because they were fixed features. A forward tilt of his head, habitual probably, would account for that bulging forehead. An outward shove of the lower jaw, another customary mannerism, could explain the heavy chin.

What the camera had really caught were Sark's eyes, his teeth, and a patch of nose between. From his own knowledge of photography, Jud decided that a light must have been glowing down upon Sark's face when the picture was shot. The eyes were white and glisteny, their pupils no more than black dots. The nose, projecting into the light, had caught a whiteness too. The teeth gleamed from the widened lips that formed what could be called a cold smile.

In any event, Sark's face was the sort that would be remembered from this picture. Such was Jud's opinion. He looked up from the desk and stared at the wall beyond the chair from which Philo Brenz watched placidly.

Jud's long stare at the photograph bothered his eyes. He blinked, slowly at first, then rapidly, to finish with a wide, amazed gaze.

Philo Brenz spoke quietly.

"You see it?" he queried. "The White Skull?"

There was a nod from Jud. He gave it without moving his eyes.

"I noticed it myself," remarked Brenz. "It rather startled me. An optical illusion, of course, but very appropriate."

Brenz's tone seemed distant to Jud, as remote as the submerged traffic noises of the street, half a hundred stories below. Everything was subordinated by that image on the wall, the white shape of a death's head, projected in huge size as the after-image of Jud's long look at Sark's picture.

Forehead, chin and cheeks. All the darkish features of the picture now were white, while the eyes, nose and teeth had become blackened hollows, completing the leering physiognomy of an ugly skull.

Closing his eyes, Jud brushed away the illusion, brought himself back to reality by opening his eyes again and looking straight at Brenz.

"What about Sark?" inquired Jud. "Have you ever met him, Mr. Brenz?"

"Only formally," replied Brenz. "At luncheons, conventions, and affairs of that sort."

"He looks like his photograph?"

"Exactly, except that it accentuates features that would not be noticed normally. Poor though the picture is, the camera seems to have gotten something that the eye missed."

"You mean something accurate?"

"I would say very accurate. If my suspicions are correct, it probed to Sark's heart, if he has one."

Jud sat back in his chair to listen further. It was strange to be happening in America. Jud had been accustomed to hearing reports about insidious characters while he had been trekking through the heart of Nazidom, helping to block off war criminals from flight to what they called their National Redoubt.

But right now, Jud wasn't gazing from a peak among the Bavarian mountains, where gorges and winding roads lay below. He was staring from a man-made altitude, the top floor of a New York skyscraper. In place of crags, he saw other buildings; instead of gorges, the canyons of downtown Manhattan, where there were paved streets in plenty, instead of a few dirt roads.

Yet Sark's picture, the afterimage of the White Skull, were factors that brought back the past with sudden, stark realism.

"I have told you about the construction contracts," spoke Brenz. "The ones that our companies lost to lower bidders."

Still looking from the window, Jud nodded to show that he was listening. He preferred to gaze out at the cloudy sky, rather than bothering his eyes with a repetition of that skull which still haunted the office wall, every time Jud looked at it.

"As you know," continued Brenz, "the construction of highways, factories, and the conversion of plants to wartime production was a staggering undertaking. It took a firm like Brenz, Incorporated to handle such projects at low profit, along with the necessary financing."

"Of course," agreed Jud. "I wasn't surprised when I heard you'd absorbed my old company. Tristate Engineering was an efficient outfit, but small. I might say very small."

"And you might add very good," complimented Brenz. "The records of its technical men who joined the armed services were proof of that. I hope that more men like yourself will soon be back with us, as the real assets that we acquired from the Tristate Engineering Company. I only wish that you could have returned to us sooner."

Brenz emphasized that final statement with a thud of his fist upon the desktop. Jud swung his gaze from the window to see that Brenz's broad face, usually mild, had become very grim. That fist of his was planted squarely on a sheaf of papers.

"There was something wrong with these," announced Brenz. "When a commission crowd like Universal Contractors, run by an old fossil like Townsend North, could underbid us all along the line, I simply don't understand it. How they managed it I don't know"—Brenz was leaning forward on the desk—"unless Alban Sark was the answer."

Jud's eyes opened again. He pushed Sark's picture further away, so it wouldn't start clouding him with another skull image.

"You mean Sark was in with North?"

"I don't know," returned Brenz, slowly. "It would be hard to prove, since North's jobs always went to subcontractors. With rush jobs on war plants, sudden shortages on essential materials that would allow the use of substitutes, a lot of very questionable deals could have been arranged."

Brenz's fingers were strumming the desk. His

broad face was as serious as the distant stare that had come to the gray eyes which strikingly matched his hair. In a sense, the contrast was not great between Philo Brenz and Jud Mayhew, for the younger man showed an equally sober expression.

In Jud's features, though, there was a drive that Brenz now lacked. Jud's youthful face was more than firm; it was rugged, weather-beaten. It should be, considering how he had accompanied airborne troops to accomplish engineering missions. In only a few such exciting months, Jud had gained experience that would cost another man years.

Centering on Jud, Brenz's eyes saw that fact. His ears could almost hear the unspoken word "Go" from Jud's motionless lips. Jud's steady, dark-eyed stare brought a steely flash from Brenz's gray gaze. The older man spoke with the authority that belonged to the president of Brenz, Incorporated, with the weight of millions of dollars behind it.

"It is your task, Mayhew," announced Brenz, solemnly. "As important to future progress as was the work you did abroad. Already"—Brenz gestured again to the papers—"we have received inquiries from Washington asking why our bids for postwar construction should be so high in proportion to prices established by Universal Contractors."

Jud nodded, showing he'd expected comment of that sort.

"It reflects on our integrity," added Brenz, "and if we demand an investigation of Universal, it will tip our hand to either North or Sark, more specifically the latter."

That made still more sense to Jud. He pictured Sark as a man who would be awaiting investigation and prepared for it. Folding his hands, Brenz rested his chin on them as he propped his elbows on the desk. Then:

"Sark has an uncanny faculty for spotting private detectives," Brenz declared. "He disappears like an earthworm, the moment they begin to track him. Here are some of their reports." Reaching to a desk drawer, Brenz pulled out a stack of papers bigger than the pile that lay in front of him. "Every man we have hired has failed.

"Besides, what if they did gain a look into Sark's business affairs? None of them have the technical knowledge needed to bring in a proper report. That's why I want you to take over the case, Mayhew. If you can gain access to any of Sark's records—in the right way of course—so much the better."

The idea appealed to Jud. He asked:

"Where can I find Sark now?"

"In the town of Stanwich," replied Brenz, referring to his notes. "Fortunately we have just gained another lucky lead to him. As a stranger, decidedly not of the detective type, you are not likely to arouse his suspicions."

"Where is Sark stopping?"

"At the Stanwich Arms, the one good hotel in the town. Incidentally, Stanwich is a place where North's company handled quite a variety of contracts and may be planning to do more business. The sooner you get there, the better."

Jud Mayhew thought the same. Rising from the desk, he gave a short nod to Philo Brenz. Then, emphatically, Jud reached for Sark's photograph, took another steady look at it and tossed it back among Bren's papers. With that, Jud strode from the president's office.

Eyes glittering their approval, Philo Brenz watched the technical man's departure, then gathered the photo with the papers and put them back in their proper drawer. For the work that he wanted done, Brenz could not have picked a better confidential agent than Jud Mayhew.

One thing was certain: Jud would recognize Sark once he saw him. Such at least was Brenz's impression.

It was Jud's impression too, but in a reverse way. Riding down from the fiftieth floor, Jud was staring at the blank wall of the elevator and seeing things again.

Etched before Jud's eyes was the visual reflex that looked like the negative print of Sark's photograph, enlarged to more than human size. It was a sinister visage, that thing of imagination brought to realism, the White Skull that leered an ominous welcome to this man who was seeking Alban Sark!

CHAPTER II

IT wasn't a long trip to Stanwich, but by the time Jud Mayhew arrived there, his plans were fully made. That was easy enough because the plans practically made themselves. When a stranger arrived in Stanwich, there was only one place where he would normally go and that was to the Stanwich Arms.

The question was whether he'd find a room at that hotel and the chances were about a hundred to one that he wouldn't. Nevertheless there was no harm in trying, and it fitted with Jud's role as a casual stranger in the town.

At least visitors were scarce this afternoon, as Jud learned when he took a cab from the station. There were only three cabs waiting there and this one alone had a driver; the others were shooting pool across from the depot, apparently just waiting in reserve.

The cab had a conspicuous local license bearing a facsimile picture of the driver and giving his name as Leo Trobin. So Jud tossed a few queries to Leo as they rode to the Stanwich Arms.

"What's happened to Stanwich?" queried Jud. "Looks to me as though the town were dead."

"Yup," returned Leo from a chew of tobacco. "Looks that way, only 't'aint. Stanwich is a live burg."

"You mean *was*."

"Don't fool yourself, mister. It's only the holiday that makes things look asleep."

Jud couldn't remember that today was a holiday and said so. Leo obligingly supplied the information that the holiday ruled locally in Stanwich and nowhere else.

"They're dedicating the monument to Mayor Fitzler," explained Leo the cabby. "Did a lot for Stanwich, the old mayor did. Fine monument too, and it ain't costing the town a penny."

Jud asked why.

"Public subscriptions," Leo told him. "An outfit called Universal Contractors supplied the material and labor. They're planning to do a lot of postwar building here. Got to take care of housing when Stanwich converts to peacetime industry."

Leo was darting quick looks across his shoulder to note the effect of this on Jud. The cabby's shifty eyes matched those of his picture, and Jud could guess that the fellow knew a lot that was going on in Stanwich. After all, a man who hacked visitors to and from the station ought to learn a lot, and Leo Trobin was the garrulous sort.

Just to prove that he could turn his talkative ability to smart use, the cabby suddenly inquired:

"What's your line, mister?"

"Manufacturer's representative," returned Jud promptly. "Looking for good factories that might be vacant. I heard there were some in Stanwich."

Leo chuckled.

"I'll show you just your ticket, mister. It's kind of out of the way, but we got to make a detour anyhow, considering that the main street is roped off on account of the parade."

The cab swung around through side streets that had once been pleasant but no longer were. All along these streets were old-fashioned houses that either should have been kept in their pristine state or torn down and replaced by modern homes. Instead, they had been turned into rooming houses and the owners, anxious to capitalize on the rental boom, hadn't wasted a cent on decorative improvements. Whatever paint jobs had been done were cheap, while all visible construction was in the form of wings or extensions that made the houses look grotesque.

"Used to be pretty, this neighborhood," commented Leo. "Guess maybe it will again when they get to fixing it. These streets feed right into the superhighway which will be getting a lot of traffic once there's a lot of new cars with enough gas to run them."

Swinging into the superhighway, Leo turned the cab across a broad concrete bridge that excited Jud's immediate attention. The bridge was of prewar mold and it crossed an underpass which must have been completed at the same time, for Jud could tell by the contour of the ground that the lower road had been built over a creek bed.

Further proof of the creek's existence was evidenced by an old brick building, its foundations reinforced with concrete, that jutted from a steep rise of ground close to the far end of the bridge.

"There she is," announced Leo, with a wave of his hand. "T'ain't a big factory, but it's a good one. Trucks can come in from either level and there's a railroad siding out to the back."

Jud's practiced eye was studying the structure, but more from the engineer's standpoint than that of a manufacturer's representative. However, he spoke in the latter terms.

"It hasn't been used as a factory."

"Not unless you count when it was an old paper mill," admitted Leo. "They rigged it for a war plant though, only it wasn't big enough. So it got used as a warehouse. Has a lot of confiscated enemy goods in it, they tell me, including Jap fireworks."

Jud was looking back to complete his appraisal of the brick building while he wondered if Universal had done the construction work. Then Leo was swinging the cab from the highway, down toward the lower road in order to avoid the main part of town. As they joined the other road, Jud saw where the creek emerged from a huge culvert, trickling through mushy ground that served as an automobile junkyard.

Those old graveyards had been rather depleted of late, but this one had a stock of fairly complete junkers. Probably the factory hands had run some of their old cars so ragged that they weren't good enough to repair. Then, swinging through a stretch of rocky, wooded land, the cab crossed a bridge below a bend where the creek formed a prettier stream, and pulled up at the Stanwich Arms.

Outside the hotel, Leo handed Jud a card, giving an appropriate smirk.

"If you're pulling out of town tonight, call the Apex Cab Service," suggested Leo. "There's our garage number on the card. We'll get you to your train in time."

What Leo meant was plain, when Jud went into the hotel. Though commodious in relation to a normal town the size of Stanwich, the Arms just couldn't hold its present applicants. The sizeable lobby was stacked with dozens of suitcases, their owners seated on them, awaiting their assignment to rooms.

Promptly Jud decided that he wouldn't have to stay all night. His job would be to locate Sark first.

The easiest and most impersonal way was to go to the cashier's window and make an inquiry, so Jud did. Casually Jud asked the man behind the window:

"Has Mr. Sark checked out?"

The name didn't register with the cashier.

"Mr. Alban Sark," specified Jud. "He's been here the past few days."

Apparently Sark hadn't registered either, for the cashier couldn't uncover a bit of data that concerned him. He kept repeating the name though, which didn't please Jud because other persons were crowding up to the window to pay their bills, and Jud was afraid that somebody might overhear. Jud turned away abruptly to stare across the lobby.

There was a man standing several feet away. If he had shifted, Jud would have noticed him, but the man did not budge. Close enough to hear what passed between Jud and the cashier, this witness made it his business to remain indifferent. His only reaction was to tilt his head slightly forward so that his heavy brow dominated his appearance, except for the challenging thrust of his chin.

His eyes however were sharp and whitish; his teeth gleamed from a fixed, hard smile as Jud looked his way. The man was avoiding argument, but ready for it if it came. The result was that Jud stared right past the man, conscious of his presence without defining him. Jud's gaze was focused further across the lobby, watching the people who were passing there.

Then, with a shrug, Jud stepped in another direction only to stop in his tracks.

Against the pastel shade of the blank lobby wall, Jud was seeing something too fresh to be an after-image of the past, something that cold logic told him must have come from a recent observation.

Growing uncannily, a huge, vague skull impressed itself upon that wall!

The answer flashed home. Jud remembered a man whose face he had hardly noticed in the semi-gloom along past the cashier's window. Only one face could have produced that reflex effect of a White Skull as vivid as if alive. It belonged to Alban Sark!

Acting on impulse, Jud wheeled to look for the man again. Sark was gone, and he could only have turned the corner leading to the elevators. Starting in that direction, Jud was ready to discard discretion and openly challenge Sark, except that he couldn't find the fellow.

The immediate clue to Sark's disappearance was an elevator with its dial pointing to the figure one. The door was closed but if Sark had boarded the car, there would still be a chance to overtake him. Springing forward, Jud pounded the door, hoping to add himself to the passenger list.

The door clanged open but before Jud could board the car, he realized that it had just come down. Passengers were getting off it, and the first that Jud encountered was a girl with reddish hair who was only momentarily taken aback by Jud's precipitous advent. Then, with an arm that had considerable drive, the girl brushed Jud aside.

Too intent even to mutter apologies, Jud stared into the elevator. Sark wasn't there. The girl, in her turn, paused to watch the pantomime with eyes that were as keen as they were narrowed. She was more than just aggressive, this redhead, she was smart, for she recognized the intensity of Jud's hurried manhunt.

Coolly, the girl opened a handbag that was dangling from her arm and reached within to draw out something that would have glittered in the light if she hadn't kept it artfully from view. That object was a compact revolver that the girl trained in Jud's direction.

Then Jud had wheeled around again, giving the girl no more than a passing glance. He didn't see what her eyes had noticed; the dial of another elevator stopping at the seventh floor. Instead, Jud was more interested in a door at the end of the short corridor, an exit that Sark might have used.

Abruptly, Jud headed through that door and found himself out in the street, amid the gathering dusk. The girl let the revolver drop back into the bag and turned away serenely. From somewhere in the distance came the fanfare of trumpets, announcing the assemblage of the parade that was to open this evening's events in Stanwich.

Much was due tonight and it had only just begun!

CHAPTER III

AS the crowd in the lobby thinned itself, partly because rooms had finally been assigned to prospective guests and also because people were starting out to see the parade, a young man came into sight, largely because the throng had cleared itself from around him.

He was standing beside a marble pillar, and it had given him a peculiar vantage point. A few paces in any direction not only enabled him to see all parts of the lobby; such procedure could also put him out of sight from any angle that he chose.

Not that he needed to keep out of sight. He was of a keen yet easy mannered type, the sort who could efface himself by simply minding his own business. This was quite important, considering the nature of his business.

This man was Harry Vincent, star performer in a continuous show produced by a certain person styled The Shadow. Harry was the ace among the agents who served a mysterious chief whose main purpose was to combat crime.

Lamont Cranston alias The Shadow

It wouldn't have taken a second guess to cover the fact that Harry's business here in some way concerned Sark, except that no guessers were bothering about Harry. In turn, this proved that no one knew how many others might be in town on similar business; at least no one except The Shadow and those who served him.

In watching for somebody, Harry hadn't long to wait. As an elevator reached the ground floor, Harry's expectant eye saw a tall figure step from it—that of a man in immaculate evening attire. It was as if by coincidence that both Harry and the new arrival reached the cigar stand at about the same moment. Coincidental, too, that the clerk had to leave the counter to find the particular cigars that the tall customer wanted.

That gave Harry Vincent a chance for a few quiet words with Lamont Cranston, the tall man in evening clothes.

As an important visitor to Stanwich, Cranston was to help occupy the reviewing stand when the parade went by, and later make a speech at the banquet to be held in honor of the late mayor. Cranston was a man of many parts; a noted traveler, a wealthy art collector, a New York clubman in the spare time of which he seemingly had plenty.

All that, however, was quite deceptive. Much of the time Cranston was very busy in a totally different identity—that of The Shadow.

Right now, Cranston was thinking definitely in The Shadow's terms, as his calm voice gave the order:

"Report."

"Sark went up to his room five minutes ago," stated Harry. "There was a chap looking for him."

"As Sark?"

"As Sark. He evidently didn't know that Sark is registered here as Hubert Rudland. He knows Sark by sight though, because he recognized him."

Cranston's keen eyes put a query that Harry understood, but could only answer in part. It concerned the man who had been looking for Sark.

"A young chap," expressed Harry, describing Jud Mayhew. "Looks older than he is and is probably an ex-service man. I don't know his name though."

"Neither does Sark," returned Cranston in his even tone. "He's still trying to find out."

It startled Harry for the moment; then he remembered having seen the elevator dial stop at number seven, which wasn't Cranston's floor. Quite obviously Cranston had looked in on Sark after the latter returned upstairs. In fact, right now Cranston was carrying a briefcase, probably containing testimonials to be presented at the banquet, but Harry knew from long experience that it could also hold the regalia of The Shadow.

"Sark phoned the desk and the bell captain," Cranston commented. "He asked if there had been any inquiries for him."

"By his own name?" Harry exclaimed.

"Of course," returned Cranston. "Since he is known here as Rudland, he might be looking for Sark too. But he was more interested in finding out who else was, which he didn't. I take it that Gail North didn't know the stranger either."

Mention of Gail North brought a puzzled stare from Harry. Gail was the daughter of Townsend North, the contractor, and she happened also to be the redhead who had bumped into Jud Mayhew when coming from the elevator. How Cranston already knew about that encounter was a puzzle.

Nor did Cranston's expression answer the riddle. His features merely increased the enigma as they always did. Calm, impassive, definitely masklike when a certain light struck it, Cranston's face remained constantly unchanged, except when he purposely molded it into someone else's. Among other arts, that of skillful disguise was often used by this man whose other self was The Shadow.

How Cranston could have spotted Gail and still kept tabs on Sark was the thing that baffled Harry until his chief gave the slightest of gestures.

"Look over toward the lounge," suggested Cranston, "and you will see Margo Lane doing everything but wigwag a message."

Looking, Harry saw an attractive but anxious brunette peering from just within the door of the cafe lounge. Cranston was right; it was Margo and she was trying to catch his eye.

"Gail went into the lounge," called Harry, "but I don't see her now."

"Margo does," explained Cranston. "That's what she is trying to tell us. But your report is sufficient,

Vincent. I can check with Margo later. Meanwhile, this chap you saw—"

Cranston's break-off was a cue for a quick response, so Harry gave it.

"He went out through the door past the elevators. Maybe he's still looking for Sark"—Harry paused, not quite sure—"but perhaps he just went to see the parade."

"You should certainly see the parade." Cranston's voice rose from the undertone that he had automatically adopted earlier, yet it lost none of its even tenor. "It is to be a fine affair I understand. Tanks and other military vehicles will be among the local floats. This is a great night for Stanwich. Ah!" Cranston's eyes were turning as he spoke. "My panatelas. I knew you would have my brand."

This last comment was to the cigar clerk, who had just returned without Harry realizing it. Buying himself a quota of thin cigars, Cranston turned and gave Harry a nod as if to emphasize that the parade should not be missed.

That was something with which Harry quite agreed, since it offered another chance of running into Jud, whose name Harry didn't yet know. So Harry left by the door beyond the elevators while Cranston went out through the main door, the shortest route to the reviewing stand.

One thing was certain: Alban Sark wouldn't leave the hotel unnoticed.

As he passed the lounge, Harry saw Margo relax dejectedly at her table and a glance beyond showed him Gail. Though at a distant table, the red-haired girl had a perfect view of the elevators and the stairway near them.

Finding Jud might prove difficult, but the procedure was quite definite. Harry's plan was to take a shortcut up to the broad bridge and meet the parade when it came across. By keeping ahead of it all along the route, he would stand a fair chance of discovering Jud somewhere along the way.

What Harry didn't expect were the rapid results he got. Cutting through a narrow street to the near end of the bridge, Harry picked his man right out of the crowd. The main street was brilliantly lighted, even at this end, and Jud had picked himself a rather conspicuous observation spot behind the ropes that held back the crowd.

Oddly though, Jud wasn't interested in the approach of the brass band that was marching across the bridge. He was studying a building on the other side, a red brick structure that was a white elephant. Harry knew about the old mill and its history; how plenty of money had been spent to convert it into a war plant that was never used as such.

Why it interested Jud was the question, and

Harry pushed close to see if he could guess the reason. His shoulder brushed Jud's and the young man turned suddenly only to see Harry staring blandly toward the oncoming parade. In turn, Jud forgot the brick building briefly and looked toward the bridge too.

Blaring full blast, the band came down the ramp with the feature attraction—the big army tanks—creeping along just in back of it. The rumble of the mechanized armor drowned the martial music and the bridge seemed to vibrate like the eager crowd.

Then, as though such sights were commonplace to him, Jud let his eyes rove from the roaring tanks. His gaze went back to the brick building that now served as a warehouse.

Harry kept watching Jud's expression, but not for long.

Jud's face froze suddenly. Instinctively, Harry looked for the reason, but by then, Jud was over the ropes, lunging through the marching band, flinging musicians aside as he waved his arms in wild warning to people on the far side of the street.

They must have caught Jud's meaning for they turned and looked above them; then scrambled out into the street as if their lives depended on it.

Their lives did.

Looking up, Harry Vincent found his own eyes frozen upon the thing that had launched Jud Mayhew into that frenzied warning.

Like a dying monster sagging under its own sheer weight, the massed red brick of the bulky warehouse was beginning to tumble forward as though hoping to engulf the pygmy figures that were racing madly to escape the crash of its plunging hulk!

CHAPTER IV

IN stupendous, slow-motion fashion, the toppling building literally fell apart. The crowd was running madly. Jud's timely warning was the factor. Like a music maestro he was taking over with signals that people instinctively understood, literally guiding them away from the flood of debris that was coming hard their way.

Now Harry was beyond the rope, seizing stragglers, flinging them away from harm. A few of the brightly garbed musicians were doing the same, all in those scant seconds while the cornice of the collapsing building was still descending like the crest of a mighty, crashing wave.

A sweep of Jud's arm, his own long leap away from that breaker formed of masonry, marked the last instant of safety. Then, into the fringe of the space where frantic people had stampeded moments before, came the heavy tanks, sweeping to the very curb, ready to receive the brick bombardment.

The wave smashed and the bricks hurtled everywhere, like chunks of a solidified surf. The tanks were swallowed by the flood, but they came slashing out of it undaunted. Their veteran crews had thrown them in as a buffer to protect the fleeing citizenry. A few bricks, bouncing from the steel monsters, flayed the remnants of the crowd, but few persons were badly hurt.

To Jud Mayhew belonged first credit; to the tank men next, but Harry Vincent had by no means been dilatory. The man who recognized it was Jud and rather than be congratulated as a hero at a time he wanted to remain anonymous, Jud looked around for Harry, hoping to talk that other stranger into accepting the public acclaim.

To Jud's amazement, he saw Harry breaking through the crowd more madly than some of the excited persons he had helped to rescue!

Thoughts snapped fast through Jud's brain.

Maybe this stranger just didn't want to be thanked; if so, he was taking a good way out—an excellent course for Jud to follow. On the contrary, the complete and untimely collapse of the old brick mill was something that smacked of the mysterious.

Having no notion of Harry's real purpose here, Jud was struck by its insidious aspect. An innocent bystander wouldn't have good reason to flee the scene so swiftly. Where Harry was going and why were two things that intrigued Jud, so he broke through the crowd, intent upon pursuit.

Jud Mayhew was getting himself in for more than he supposed.

What Harry had seen was a beckoning arm from above the heads of the crowd. The man who was waving the signal was at the top of some house steps, well down the street. He had a good reason to be there, for he was a reporter from New York, assigned to cover the big events in the town of Stanwich.

The reporter's name was Clyde Burke and in his spare time, of which he had plenty, he was an agent of The Shadow. What Clyde was doing right now, was calling all agents, also with good reason.

By the time Harry neared those house steps another man was shouldering through the crowd from the opposite direction. He was Cliff Marsland, also a capable member of The Shadow's corps. Together Harry and Cliff followed Clyde as he sprang from the steps and headed down the slant that led toward the old junkyard that Jud had seen that afternoon.

There, the guiding influence was a little man named Hawkeye, who hadn't been bothering about the parade. It was Hawkeye's business to spot uncouth happenings in vicinities like Stanwich and he'd been doing it. The junkyard had incited Hawkeye's suspicions because too many of its relics looked too good.

Right now, some of those old wrecked cars were coming to life. Into them were piling men who had arrived with large and weighty bundles, appearing from—of all places—that ample culvert that accommodated the old creek bed. A dozen unknown men were beginning a getaway in half as many vehicles, among them trucks, bearing a quantity of goods that represented merely the last load.

The entire shipment, whatever it was, had been rifled from the old brick building which had served as a warehouse until its very recent collapse!

Hardly had The Shadow's agents joined Hawkeye before two cars wheeled up to receive them. Each was driven by a speed king in his own right: one, Miles Crofton, formerly a member of a flying circus; the other, Chance Lebrue, whose prewar hobby had been to wreck himself, car and all, as a free attraction at county fairs.

Crofton's car took in Harry and Clyde; Lebrue's gathered up Cliff and Hawkeye. It was impolite of course, but Jud Mayhew tried to add himself to the latter crew, hoping to argue the question later. Only Jud didn't manage it, because Jericho Druke was around.

Jericho Druke was a huge African whose proportions, large though they were, gave but a slight intimation of the strength that went with them. Jericho was very amiable, even when he took Jud by the back of the neck and lifted him about four feet off the ground.

It was rather difficult for Jericho to take people by the back of the neck, because his hand was big enough to go all the way around. Therefore Jericho made it a policy to drop people very promptly and gently.

Four feet being the height of the concrete rail that lined the sloping roadway, Jericho simply dropped Jud across the rail. It was a very easy landing for Jud because the ground was soft and sandy on the other side. Of course the ground sloped downward too, so it was Jud's fault as much as Jericho's that the landing didn't mark a stopping place.

What Jud did was coast about eighty feet down into the junkyard, kicking up plenty of dust ahead of him, which helped slacken his slide. But by the time Jud arrived there, the men in the old cars were gone and The Shadow's agents were speeding to the chase along the road that led through the woods on the other side of the ravine.

Back at the reviewing stand, all this made an interesting panorama for a gentleman named Lamont Cranston, who was hemmed between a congressman and a county judge and therefore couldn't leave. Everybody was excited about the strange catastrophe that had occurred up by the concrete bridge; that was, everybody except Cranston.

With the calculating eye that was The Shadow's, Cranston was giving his agents about four miles in which to overtake the junkyard fugitives and usually The Shadow's calculations were correct.

This time they weren't.

The caravan had taken a twisty route through those oddly arranged back streets of Stanwich. The drivers knew the route by rote and were making the most of it. Apparently they expected pursuit and were acting accordingly. They had gained ground when they reached the superhighway and headed away from the town.

Those battered looking trucks and cars were anything but junkers. Their tires had no treads, but they were stout enough to stand the gaff. The caravan opened up to a speed that was really high, but it couldn't outdistance its pursuers. The Shadow's agents were riding in cars that were really geared to speed and the drivers were the sort who were inclined to bash their accelerator pedals right through the floorboards.

Only by dint of a considerable head start did the fugitive caravan manage to reach the only goal within a dozen miles, a place where the big super-highway converged with another in an elaborate cloverleaf pattern involving underpasses, ramps, circles, bridges and all the other nightmares that confront the modern motorist.

Apparently the fugitives had some artful plan of dodging all around these runways to shake off pursuers, for they went up an incline, veered the wrong direction, cut across a bridge and down the other side. Crofton and Labrue kept right after them until it became obvious that this game of hide-and-seek wasn't leading anywhere. Coming to a fork in the cloverleaf fashion, The Shadow's drivers split their paths and took different directions.

The passengers in The Shadow's cars were ready with drawn guns for the climax that seemed sure to come. Around one of these bends, perhaps down in an underpass, the caravan was going to find itself boxed. Then would come quick battle that should result in a solid mop-up.

The moment arrived. Two pairs of powerful headlights gleamed eye to eye as they swung in from the curve of an incline. One car was whipping down from a fork, the other scooting up from beneath an underpass. Then, as suddenly as they had met, the drivers gave the brakes.

Screeches accompanied swerves as two cars literally twisted alongside each other. From those two cars stepped men who eyed one another in what could only be termed stolid astonishment. Separate courses had led to a reunion of The Shadow's own agents.

The missing caravan had vanished as though its vehicles were composed of thin air. Somehow, somewhere in the maze of the elaborate cloverleaf, the fugitive cars had sped away in some fresh direction, leaving the pursuers nonplussed.

A strange singular ending to that mad chase from the town of Stanwich.

Something that even The Shadow might doubt when it was told him!

CHAPTER V

COMMOTION had quieted in Stanwich. The parade had gone its way and completed its appointed route with the ruins of the old brick warehouse far in its wake. Along with other dignitaries, Lamont Cranston had reviewed the affair and heard talk of the near catastrophe that had almost marked its progress. However, that hadn't spoiled the revelry in Stanwich.

There would be investigations and all that, but the loss of the old warehouse didn't matter, considering that its contents were all confiscated goods that might have been junked anyway. Nobody had been seriously hurt and already a theory was being voiced to explain the occurrence. It was the old business of rhythmic vibration. Probably the rumble of the tanks had been timed to the old building's sway and was therefore responsible for its crash.

They were talking about it, though, in Stanwich, after the parade was over. One man who was voluble on the subject was Leo Trobin, the cab driver who had brought Jud Mayhew from the station.

Leo was working the night shift and was therefore on hand at the Apex garage, talking to a couple of other cabbies and a few odd loungers.

"Funny thing," opined Leo. "I drove a guy up from the depot just tonight and he was talking about buying over that old building. Came here special just to look at it. Kind of funny too that there weren't any explosions after the thing caved. There was supposed to be a lot of fireworks stored there. Guess they just got smothered."

A stolid-faced foreman was answering a phone call for a cab. He turned toward the group, and Leo moved out of sight behind a pillar, beckoning a drab-faced lounger to follow him.

"Stick here, Jeff," Leo told the lounger. "I don't want Kromer to shove me out on a job—not yet. He goes off duty in about ten minutes, Kromer does. It won't matter after that."

Another cabby was anxious enough for the job that Kromer, the foreman, offered. Staring stolidly, Kromer seemed to be wondering where Leo was; then, with a shrug, he went back to his regular duties.

Watching this, Jeff gave a short nod in Leo's direction, meaning that Kromer was none the wiser. Nobody else counted with Leo and Jeff, which was why they didn't notice a little man standing nearby.

To all appearances, this fellow was just one of the local hangers-on, but he happened to be an out-of-towner. He was Hawkeye, the keen-eyed spotter who had put The Shadow's agents on the track of the cars that fled the junkyard. Having accompanied his comrades on their futile chase, Hawkeye was back in Stanwich hoping to make amends.

Hawkeye was looking for someone who might be conversant with the junkyard situation, and Jeff filled the bill. The drab-faced lounger didn't spend much of his time at the Apex Garage. Hawkeye had seen him driving to and from the junkyard in a ramshackle car, on several occasions.

This liaison between Jeff and Leo was all the more pointed, considering Leo's mention of a fare who had looked over the old brick warehouse. Having checked facts with Harry Vincent, Hawkeye had an idea that Leo's passenger was the very man who had inquired for Sark and had later encountered Jericho; namely, Jud Mayhew.

Five minutes and another cab call again found Leo lacking when Kromer gave a brief look for him. The stolid foreman was beginning to show annoyance on his chunky face; in fact, he was so annoyed that he stayed on duty after the next five minutes were gone. Then came another cab call and this time Leo promptly stepped into sight.

"Guess it's my turn, Kromer," spoke Leo, cheerily. "How come you were passing me up?"

Glowering, Kromer said gruffly:

"Didn't see you anywhere around."

"Yeah?" Leo's tone was sarcastic. "I've been here all along. Ask Jeff if I haven't."

Jeff supplied a corroborating nod.

"What's it for?" queried Jeff. "Somebody taking the last train out?"

"What else would it be?" Kromer demanded. "Hop over to the hotel right away; the guy says he's got a lot of luggage. Only the next time stay in sight. Then I can go out and eat when I'm supposed to."

Without waiting for apologies, Kromer stalked out, which was exactly what Leo wanted. Jumping to the wheel, Leo backed his cab out through a door where Jeff's jalopy was waiting. Kromer not being around to witness that procedure, Hawkeye was the only observer. Keeping neatly behind the doorway, Hawkeye saw Leo and Jeff empty the contents of a five-gallon can into the cab's gas tank.

"That's good for seventy-five miles that Kromer won't know about," chuckled Leo. "He's too dumb to know that I've rigged the meter."

"Don't forget my cut," reminded Jeff, "or there won't be any more coming from where that came from."

Piker stuff, this, but Hawkeye decided to report it to The Shadow. The fact that Jeff was bootlegging gasoline that came into the junkyard might have some slight bearing on larger matters.

More important, though, was the call that Leo was answering. Over at the Stanwich Arms, Alban Sark was standing in his seventh-floor room, staring out across the lighted town toward the blackened vacancy that marked the site of the missing warehouse.

On a table beside Sark was an ashtray filled with smoldering cigarette butts. Sark could have rigged them as an alibi, but he hadn't. The man with the heavy forehead had not been at large when the warehouse crashed. Sark had stayed in his room all evening.

Right now, Sark's face, white against the darkened windowpane, looked like a death's head in its own right. How worried Sark might be, he alone knew; but his pallor was to some degree artificial, for his lips, when they moved, simply phrased a scornful sneer. Bulging forehead, jutting chin, eyes that looked as hollow as his grin, gave Sark an expression that resembled a mask—which it was so far as any human sentiments were concerned.

When Sark's mind worked, it was in an inhuman way, as his cold, hard stare revealed. Then, suddenly those features darkened with a pained look that was partial evidence of some hidden fear, for Sark himself wheeled quickly around.

Sark didn't like the way his expression clouded. It was as if some other figure had approached behind him to block off the room lights that caused the reflection in the window.

For the moment, Sark saw blackness, like that of a fading figure. Perhaps his own eyes, with their whitish glisten, were subject to peculiar optical effects like those of persons who studied his picture too long. Sark's hand went to his pocket; the flex of his wrist muscles told that his fist was gripping a gun. But before Sark could draw the weapon and aim it toward the gloom near the doorway, the door itself flung open.

In contrast to blackness, Sark saw green, the uniform of a bellboy. Letting his hand relax, Sark drew it from his pocket and gestured toward a stack of suitcases near the door.

"Take them down to the lobby," ordered Sark, in a short-clipped tone. "Have them ready when the cab comes. Page me as soon as it arrives."

The bellboy nodded, then asked:

"What name?"

Sark's lips straightened, which was their method of forming a smile. Squarely in the light, his cold face revealed its peculiar contours. His forehead bulged as he tilted his head forward; then came the thrust of his chin, to match it.

Instead of giving the name of Hubert Rudland, this man of devious ways announced his own:

"Alban Sark."

As he pronounced the name, Sark ushered the bellhop from the room, bags and all, tucking a dollar bill into the pocket of the green uniform. Sark added a smile, free of charge, but the bellboy didn't see it. The smile was not at all a nice one.

In his turn, Sark didn't see what happened in the room behind him. From the space behind the open door emerged a figure cloaked in black, the living embodiment of the shape that Sark had half attributed to his own imagination.

That figure was The Shadow.

Silently, swiftly, The Shadow moved across the room and reached a connecting door. When Sark turned from the hallway, there wasn't a visible trace of his cloaked visitor. That didn't entirely satisfy Sark; hand to gun pocket, he closed the door to the hall, as though expecting to find someone lurking behind it.

All Sark found was vacancy, which proved the wisdom of The Shadow's opportune shift.

Satisfied that he was quite alone, Sark was in no hurry to leave. Looking at his watch, he saw that there was ample time before the cab arrived, so he took a chair beside the telephone table. Sark's eyes now were on the telephone as though he expected it to ring, which it did, quite suddenly.

Sark made a quick pounce for the instrument, but when he answered the call, his tone was steady.

"Ah, Ludar," spoke Sark, reprovingly, "you are calling a trifle late... Yes, I should have left by this time... What? You have just found out? That is singular. You should have known all along that they would do it..."

There was a pause, while Ludar's voice came earnestly across the wire, though it was heard by Sark alone. Then:

"I stayed here to watch," Sark informed, "and I saw what happened... Yes, exactly as I expected it... Of course they are fools. What else could I do but agree?"

Another pause, with Ludar doing the talking, after which Sark gave a short, hard laugh.

"You are telling me my turn is next," declared Sark. "That is funny, Ludar, very funny... Of course I guessed. Why not?... Yes, I have made the proper arrangements. I have a suitable substitute... No, Ludar, do not worry. I am safe and so are all my documents..."

Two doors were doing tricks behind Sark's back. One was the door to the connecting room, which Sark did not suspect at all. It was closing, proof that

The Shadow was leaving on some other mission. The door to the hallway, however, was doing just the opposite. Sark hadn't locked it when he closed it; now that door was coming open.

"Later, Ludar, I shall call you," Sark was saying. "Yes, when I am back in New York... Of course you can reach me if you come there at the right time... But now, time is short. Good-bye, Ludar..."

The hallway door went shut and its click was drowned by the clatter of the telephone as Sark replaced it. All that Sark gave the door was a slight glance, along with a shrug. He moved in that direction, but only to press the light switch, enveloping the room in darkness. Then Sark returned to his post beside the window.

Outside Sark's door, a figure was moving away rapidly, headed toward the elevators. But it wasn't the figure of The Shadow. This listener who had caught the closing moments of Sark's conversation with Ludar, was the trim red-haired girl who answered to the name of Gail North!

CHAPTER VI

"PAGING Mr. Sark!"

Gail North heard the call as she stepped from the elevator and immediately she was alert. When Gail went alert, she was reminiscent of a cocker spaniel of the reddish variety.

At least such was the opinion of Margo Lane, whether it was flattering or not. All evening, Margo had been watching Gail go quivery whenever anyone faintly resembling Sark appeared from the elevator. Now as before, Gail suddenly relaxed.

Of course Margo didn't know why. Since leaving his listening post at Sark's, Cranston had been quite too busy to inform Margo regarding details that he himself could handle as The Shadow. So Margo was not only puzzled, but due to be more so.

"Mr. Alban Sark!" bellowed the bellhop. "Cab is ready for Mr. Alban Sark!"

Rather than lose more time, the bellboy picked up Sark's bags and started out to the street. Gail strolled nonchalantly across the lobby and took an obscure chair, thus puzzling Margo all the further. Along with being puzzled, Margo was bothered by the fact that neither Harry nor any of The Shadow's other agents was anywhere around.

But if Harry Vincent wasn't handy, Jud Mayhew was. All nicely brushed, Jud showed no signs of the slide that Jericho had given him. Popping to his feet, he looked like any other guest at the Stanwich Arms.

Jud was thinking very swiftly, not just in terms of Sark, but of those bags that were going out.

Sark wasn't any more important than the contents of those bags, if as important. Jud was wondering just what Sark would do if those bags disappeared in their entirety. More than that, he was wondering what Sark could do, which certainly could not be very much, particularly if he missed the train on which the bags went.

So Jud strode straight out through the lobby, following the route of the bags. Finding the bellboy out front, Jud gave him an imperious gesture; then, recognizing the cab as Leo's, Jud added loudly:

"Get those bags into that cab! One of us will take the train. In any case, we want the bags to be there."

It sounded logical enough to the bellhop and spurred him into putting the bags into the cab. Jud waited on the deserted hotel steps, watch in hand, and gestured for Leo to pull further ahead, in order not to interfere with any other cabs that might arrive.

Sark's eyes now were on the telephone as though he expected it to ring ...

This was hardly necessary but it proved good showmanship. Leo responded and the bellboy went back into the hotel, thinking that Jud, whoever he was, had been invested with full authority by Alban Sark.

Immediately Jud decided to take advantage of that usurped authority. He came down the steps, intending to enter the cab. To do so, he had to stride through a plot of darkness. That was as far as Jud went.

Out of blackness came a solid figure that whisked Jud off his feet and half precipitated him through the air into the waiting clutches of a pair of men who sidled in from darkness to receive him. That pair consisted of Harry Vincent and Cliff Marsland. They rushed Jud clear across the street and into the powerful paws of Jericho who dumped him into a car that had Chance Lebrue at the wheel.

It was all so swift that Jud hardly knew what happened, while Leo in his cab knew nothing at all about it. The man who took in the most of that fast moving picture was Alban Sark.

From his seventh floor window, Sark was staring straight down to the sidewalk. He saw Jud step into the darkness beside the waiting cab; then witnessed his flying recoil, the way he was snagged by a pair who hustled him across the way to the darkness that obscured another car.

This was something that Sark had expected, for his chuckle came in a lowered basso. Leaving the window, Sark strolled from the room, out to the elevator.

Downstairs, Gail North had captured a considerable eyeload of the disaster that had overwhelmed Jud. Meddling into business that didn't entirely concern her seemed to be one of Gail's specialties, for she came full tilt from the lobby door, intent upon tracking down Jud's captors. Dashing around the corner, Gail watched the car turn a corner further down the street, but she hadn't any car of her own in which to follow.

After running a block or more, Gail turned back dejectedly, realizing how silly she had been. Whoever Jud was, he hadn't gone away with those precious bags belonging to Sark; they were still in the waiting cab outside the hotel.

Except that the cab was no longer waiting when Gail arrived back. Its driver had instructions to get to the station at a certain time and he was following those orders. All Gail saw was the side of the cab as it swung the corner. By the street lamp she read the name "Apex Cab Company" and nothing more.

It wasn't much, but it was all that Gail could use, so she made the most of it. Spying another cab that was returning from a trip, Gail saw that it bore the same name, "Apex," so she hailed it.

"Take me to your garage," Gail ordered. "I left something in a cab—something very important. I'd like to speak to the manager about it."

The Apex Garage was quite deserted when Gail arrived there. Outside was an old night watchman, who looked too lazy and decrepit to make his rounds. Gail alighted to talk to him while her cabby was putting his cab up for the night.

"I dropped a cigarette case in the cushions of a cab," Gail told the old watchman. "I don't know which cab it was. Maybe it hasn't come in for the night."

The watchman removed a corncob pipe from his lips and spoke through a trickle of smoke.

"Go inside and look, lady," he suggested. "If it ain't in one of them cabs, it will be in Leo's. He's t'only one who hadn't checked in yet."

Gail's cabby was leaving the garage, which made the situation perfect. All the girl had to do was go into the garage, fake a search among the cabs that were already there and say she couldn't find the cigarette case. That would give her an excuse to question Leo when he arrived. That way, she might learn something about those bags that Sark had sent away.

It would mean stalling for time, though, since by Gail's calculation, Leo couldn't have reached the station yet, since it was much further from the hotel than was this garage. So Gail entered the garage and started looking in the cabs.

In the very first, Gail received a startling surprise. In the rear seat, bound and gagged, was a young man whose face Gail recognized despite the way it was muffled. The prisoner was Jud Mayhew!

There was an appealing look in Jud's eyes and from the direction in which they turned, Gail saw what was in his mind. This particular cab had its keys dangling from the ignition lock, so there was nothing to stop Jud from driving away in it, except that he was bound.

That didn't apply to Gail, though, as Jud's eyes plainly told. True to the form she'd shown so far, Gail didn't hesitate. Getting into the front seat of the cab, the girl turned on the ignition, pressed the starter, and shot the cab right out through the garage door.

All that the watchman got was a whiff of gas from the exhaust as he sprang to his feet shouting after Gail. Then the cab was around the corner and Gail was speeding it off toward the superhighway.

From somewhere came a whistle blast, announcing the train that Jud wasn't going to take. Leo's cab was probably nearing the station now, but Gail was no longer worrying about Sark's bags and whatever they contained. Other people could concern themselves with that proposition. Gail's business was to get away from Stanwich with the cab she had just borrowed and then find out what Jud had to tell her.

Others definitely were concerning themselves with Leo's cab. A speedy car, cleaving in from a rough street that formed a shortcut to the station, swerved to begin a burst of speed that would enable it to overhaul that cab that Sark had summoned. This cab was piloted by Miles Crofton and in the backseat was The Shadow. His agents were giving him special service, as amends for letting the caravan slip them earlier.

Leo's cab wasn't going to do the same. Ahead were the lights of the depot and there wasn't any avenue of escape for the cab. Right now another car, driven by Chance Lebrue, was coming in to block off any trick stuff if Leo tried it. Quick work on Chance's part, swinging around by the Apex Garage, so that Jud could be deposited there; then he continued on to the station to help round up Leo's cab.

Perhaps it was Chance's sudden appearance in the picture that caused The Shadow to intone an order to Crofton, an order which called for slackened speed. Logical enough, that since both The Shadow's cars were present, they should converge at once. Again, it might be that The Shadow wanted Leo to unload at the station before the cars closed in.

There could be still another reason, fantastic though it seemed. In a vicinity where solid buildings could crumple at a moment's notice, where an entire caravan of cars and trucks could disappear within a dozen seconds, anything might happen.

Possibly The Shadow just wanted to convince himself regarding the status of Leo's cab and any tricks it might perform. If so, he called the proper turn.

The thing happened as the cab came to a stop at a traffic light just outside the parking plaza beside the station. It was Leo's first stop since leaving the hotel and also his last. Fortunately, The Shadow's cars were far enough away to have the vantage point of witnesses, not of victims. For Leo's cab vanished itself in a style far more spectacular than anything previous.

There was just a sudden cough, a burst of flame as brilliant as a magnesium light. The air snapped together with an explosive "Pow!" that sounded like four tires blowing simultaneously. With that flash, there wasn't a fragment left of the cab nor any of its contents.

The great searchlight of the Midnight Limited, drilling from the locomotive that was veering from a switch, showed charred and blackened cobblestones at the entrance to the parking yard.

That was all!

CHAPTER VII

NOON in Manhattan.

In a quiet side-street cafe in the Greenwich Village area, Jud Mayhew and Gail North were reading over the newspaper accounts that related but a fragment of their adventures.

"It looks like I'm two people," commented Jud. "The unknown hero who warned the crowd about the warehouse collapse, and the unidentified man who left the hotel to take a fatal cab ride. Luckily they haven't linked one with the other yet—or should I say luckily?"

Gail shook her head. She didn't know. Then, brushing back some of her stray red tresses, Gail faced Jud seriously.

"I'm the one who ought to worry," Gail argued. "If they find out I was the mystery girl who stole that cab out of the Apex Garage, what will happen next?"

"Nothing," returned Jud. "I'll take the blame for it."

"Then we'll both be arrested."

"Hardly." Jud tapped the newspaper. "There is still some doubt as to which cab exploded. It might have been ours, not Leo's."

"But when they don't find Leo?"

"Then they may think he scampered on his own. Things are very mixed up in Stanwich. For one thing, that half-blind watchman at the garage didn't know you had red hair."

Gail's eyes widened.

"He didn't?"

"Nope." Jud exhibited the newspaper as proof. "I wonder why he didn't. I should think it was something always to be remembered, that lovely hair of yours."

It was lovely, all right, as Jud now viewed it, but the watchman hadn't had the benefit of the noon-time sunlight that gave the scintillating burnish to Gail's present hairdo. As for Jud's reaction, Gail preferred to keep matters on a strictly business basis.

"This is no time for sentiment, if that's what you call it," rebuked Gail, across the table. A frown rose above her snub nose as she avoided Jud's eyes by studying the newspaper. Then, laughing in spite of herself, Gail passed the paper back to Jud, as she added, "Read that!"

Jud read it and laughed too. It was the garage watchman's testimony given in detail. He described Gail as having dark hair and dark eyes, which certainly didn't fit with either auburn or blue.

"I'll tell you who it does describe," stated Gail. "It fits that catty creature who was watching me at the hotel. I hope they found out her name was

Margo Lane. If they do, she'll have to explain what she was doing in Stanwich."

Never having heard of Margo Lane by name or otherwise, Jud's expression became quizzical.

"She's a friend of Lamont Cranston," explained Gail, "but Margo doesn't know that I'd seen her around town."

"Around Stanwich?"

"Of course not," returned Gail. "Around New York. She belongs here, too."

"And Cranston?"

"He's a New Yorker, too. He was up in Stanwich with the other bigwigs who were reviewing the parade."

"What would Cranston know about Sark?"

As Jud put that question, Gail's face became troubled. Its sudden flush gave her complexion a color resembling her hair, despite the way Gail's lips tightened as she bit them. Then, in a low tone, the girl declared:

"I don't believe that Cranston is concerned with Sark. I am afraid he was thinking in terms of my father."

Gail put it so frankly that Jud was forced to nod. That cleared the situation considerably. Without the slightest reserve, Gail inquired:

"You are thinking in terms of my father, too?"

"To some degree," admitted Jud. "You see, I work for Philo Brenz."

If Jud expected Gail to denounce him as a cad, or anything like it, he was happily disappointed. There was nothing of the ogre about Brenz, where Gail was concerned.

"Brenz has a right to doubt my father," conceded Gail in her same frank tone. "After all, his company lost some very good contracts which my father not only admitted, but wished, had gone his way. Was that why Brenz sent you to Stanwich?"

"He sent me there to check on Sark."

"Of course," nodded Gail, "because Sark was the man who arranged those contracts through smaller companies. That's just the trouble, Jud."

Until now it had been "Mr. Mayhew," whenever Gail addressed Jud. But now the girl was leaning forward, her hand appealingly clutching Jud's arm. That Gail was more than serious, Jud could tell from the way her fingers trembled.

"The accounts are all wrong, Jud," Gail undertoned. "It isn't just a case of checking on some of those little companies. He can't even prove that the companies existed. Where some of the materials came from is a mystery; there were supposed to be priorities, but all the evidence is missing."

Jud's teeth gave a grit.

"In Sark's suitcases, I'll bet! That's why he got rid of them and himself along with them!"

Gail shook her head.

"I'm not so sure about either," she declared. "Sark may just be trying to make us think that he disappeared in a puff of smoke, taking those documents with him."

"At least he tried to coax me into being the fall guy," conceded Jud, "but I still don't see why he would keep evidence against himself."

"The evidence points to my father," explained Gail. "That's why Sark wanted to preserve it. Besides, Sark has enemies of his own."

That truth came right home to Jud as he remembered how he had been snatched from what would otherwise have become a fatal cab ride. Who Jud's brief captors might have been, he couldn't even guess, and the perplexity that registered on his face made itself understood to Gail.

"If I tell you more," said Gail, "you'll keep it to yourself, won't you? I mean you won't give facts away—not even to Brenz—until I say you can?"

"Not if you tell me something I don't already know."

"All right then." Gail drew a deep breath of relief. "Did you ever hear of a man called Tanjor Zune?"

"No," admitted Jud. "In fact, I never heard a name like it."

"Does the name Ludar mean anything to you?"

"Another blank."

"Very well, then," decided Gail. "Since you're not to mention either, I'll tell you what little more I know about them. Zune is Sark's chief enemy; Ludar is the go-between."

"You mean just sort of a mutual emissary?"

"No. I mean that Ludar works for Zune but tells Sark whatever happens. But I'm not sure that Ludar doesn't tell it all right back to Zune."

"What gives you that idea?"

"Listening in on Sark's telephone chats with Ludar. Somehow it seems like a double cross all around."

"What sort of people are Zune and Ludar?"

"I've never seen them," admitted Gail. "I've only heard Sark talk to Ludar about Zune. But you won't mention this to anybody."

Jud smiled at Gail's tone, which carried command more than request. That explained itself by what followed.

"Because if you do mention it," stated Gail quite positively, "I won't show you where Sark lived. If I don't do that, we won't be able to go into the place together and find Sark's papers, if they still are there."

"An excellent proposal," returned Jud, "except that it would amount to burglary."

"Why not?" queried Gail. "We stole a cab last night, didn't we? By the way, Jud"—Gail put mock toughness in her tone—"where did you stash the hack?"

"In one of Brenz's garages," replied Jud with a smile. "Nobody is going to find it, stuck in back of a lot of concrete mixers, unless—"

Gail's hand interrupted with a warning clutch. At the same moment, Jud was conscious that somebody had just come in the door. Then Gail eased her grip.

"It's all right," she confided. "I thought for the moment it was that Lane job wandering on my trail. I recognized the blue ensemble. It comes from Fifth Avenue in the Fifties. Margo doesn't have a monopoly on those styles though. This one has a blonde in it."

Jud was smiling at the comment, when Gail added:

"Don't look now, but I know that blonde, too. She has an odd name: Ilga Vyx." Gail pronounced the "y" like "i" and then continued: "I don't think she's a friend of Margo's. At least she won't be, if each sees the other copying her patterns. Suppose I run along; then you can watch Miss Vyx and make sure she isn't too interested."

That suited Jud, so Gail left. Paying the lunch check gave Jud ample time to stall and finally, when it was his turn to leave, he gained his first look at Ilga Vyx. She was rather a startling blonde and of a definitely foreign type, with eyes that moved dreamily and became blank when they fixed on anything such as Jud.

What impressed Jud chiefly about Ilga's getup was the broad, circular hat she wore, tilted well back on her head. Full front, the hat accentuated her blonde hair, but when Jud looked back from the door, he saw that the hat completely concealed the blonde evidence, which explained why Gail, sighting Ilga from the back, had mistaken her for Margo.

If Ilga Vyx had some connection with this case, it wouldn't surprise Jud Mayhew at all. With a redhead and a brunette already mixed in it, there was certainly room for a blonde. But that had nothing to do with Jud's next mission, which was to turn in a report to Philo Brenz.

Taking a cab to Brenz's building, Jud went directly to his employer's private office. The president of Brenz, Incorporated received his star investigator with a warm hand-clasp, then turned to introduce him to a calm-faced visitor who was seated beside the desk.

"A friend of mine," announced Brenz, "who is very anxious to hear your report on what happened in Stanwich last night. Jud, I want you to meet Lamont Cranston."

CHAPTER VIII

THERE was nothing for Jud to do but give an honest report, something which he had planned to deliver anyway. But any temptation to let slip with names such as Zune or Ludar was immediately ruled out.

That Gail North was sincere was something Jud Mayhew did not question. Maybe she was blind in her loyalty to her father, Townsend North, whose peculiar practices had played hob with Brenz's contracting business, but that could be determined later.

Right now, Jud felt that he could concentrate on Alban Sark and the various happenings that Jud himself had witnessed in Stanwich, without committing himself too far.

So Jud began it very simply. He stated:

"I located Alban Sark."

"Excellent!" exclaimed Brenz, rubbing his hands warmly. Then, his tone turning troubled: "But did he suspect that you were looking for him?"

"I'm afraid he did." As he replied, Jud looked straight at Cranston who met him with an impassive gaze. "I may have made a mistake in asking for Sark. He was registered under another name."

"What name?" interrupted Brenz.

"I don't know," replied Jud. "I ran into him by accident."

"The other name was Hubert Rudland," put in Cranston, placidly. "The room number was 720."

Wrenching his eyes from Cranston's somewhat hypnotic stare, Jud looked to Brenz for an explanation and was rewarded with a beaming smile.

"Cranston has been looking into those North contracts," Brenz explained. "That was one reason why he was in Stanwich. When he found out that North had gained them through unusually low bids, he naturally wanted to tally with other companies. That is why he is here."

"And meanwhile," put in Cranston in an even tone, "I was interested in learning more about Alban Sark. He is something of a mystery in his own right, this man Sark; but the mystery that concerns us more is the collapse of the warehouse in Stanwich." Cranston's eyes were steadying on Jud, as he added: "Perhaps you can tell us more about it."

Jud could and did. In fact he was eager to cover that question rather than others.

"I saw the warehouse fold," asserted Jud, "and the present theory is all wrong."

"You mean it wasn't due to the vibration?" queried Brenz in surprise. "Why, the experts said—"

"The experts weren't there," interrupted Jud, "unless you count me as one; I saw the Remagen Bridge collapse after our army had used it to cross the Rhine. It wasn't vibration that did it. The bridge was weakened."

" ... Jud, I want you to
meet Lamont Cranston."

Brenz lifted his gray eyebrows.

"You think the Stanwich warehouse was structurally weak?" he queried. Then, turning to Cranston, Brenz answered his own question. "That would account for one of North's cheap contracts. Poor materials, insufficient labor, perhaps other contributing causes. Still, the experts may be right"—slowly, Brenz shook his head, as though to banish Jud's claim—"because the warehouse did collapse just as the parade went by."

"*Before* the parade went by," corrected Jud. "The tanks were still on the concrete bridge when the crash came. That's the key to the whole situation, if people would only see it. If anything had cracked from the vibration, it would have been the bridge."

"But the bridge was concrete," argued Brenz. "I recall the contract for that superhighway, even though it was North who handled it."

"The warehouse had concrete foundations too," returned Jud, "and if North had skimped on one job, he would have done the same with the other. But you're missing the main point, Mr. Brenz. Any sway from those vibrations would have been confined to the bridge itself. They couldn't have carried to the solid ground and then to the warehouse. In my opinion, the collapse of the warehouse, occurring at the time it did, was purely a coincidence."

Cranston's tone came evenly, repeating those very words:

"Purely a coincidence?"

"Unless somebody framed it," Jud declared, "which is quite possible. It would have been a smart stunt, even though they did beat the gun."

Brenz was keenly interested.

"What makes you think that?" he inquired. "It would have been suicide for men to enter that building and bring it down upon themselves."

"Not while they had an outlet," explained Jud, "and they had one. I think that building was sabotaged and the men who did it escaped through a culvert leading to an old junkyard. A batch of cars and trucks pulled out from there."

"You saw them?"

"Yes, but I couldn't stop them. What's more, somebody stopped me first. The same thing happened over again when I tried to take Sark's cab and find out what was in his bags."

Strumming the desk in his reflective style, Brenz decided that Jud had rendered a report both thorough and satisfactory. He ended the interview by making an appointment for the next day, which pleased Jud doubly.

Going down in the elevator, Jud was glad that he hadn't needed to go into details involving Gail North. He was sure that by tomorrow he would have more facts for Philo Brenz. The prospect of raiding Sark's own preserves, wherever they might be, rather appealed to Jud right now.

Except that there was now an unknown factor: Lamont Cranston.

How heavily Cranston figured, Jud couldn't guess, but he was forced to the conclusion that Cranston's path at least ran parallel to his own. Maybe Cranston knew a lot more than he had told; he was the sort who probably would. So it behooved Jud for the present to look closer into the Cranston situation.

Jud was determined on that policy by the time he completed the elevator ride. Out on the street, Jud began to study the possibilities of obtaining a cab, if he needed one in a hurry. This being Manhattan, not Stanwich, Jud preferred a more conservative method than borrowing a cab outright.

Across the way, Jud saw a likely opportunity. A cab was parked at a little lunch room and in the window was a cab driver specializing in coffee and doughnuts. So Jud crossed the street, tapped the window, and gestured to the cab with one hand while brandishing a batch of dollar bills with the other.

The cab driver was a peak-faced character who gave Jud a shrewd and pointed stare. At last he nodded as though he understood. Jud wanted to hire his cab on a continuous basis, which was a rather attractive idea.

But it wasn't just Jud's offer that brought the cabby's nod. Behind Jud's back, a little, stoop-shouldered man had sidled from the shelter of a newsstand and was poking his wizened face past Jud's shoulder. The nod that the little man gave in passing, was the thing that brought a similar response from the cab driver in the window.

Jud didn't even have a chance to see the little passer-by, let alone recognize him. The man in question was Hawkeye, the able spotter who had served The Shadow in Stanwich.

As for the cab driver in the lunch room, he was another of The Shadow's agents, Shrevvy by name. Not having met Jud, Shrevvy couldn't identify him and was therefore dependent upon Hawkeye. And now, Shrevvy, about to gulp his coffee, received another tip that Jud was the right man.

The tip came from Jud himself. He gestured for Shrevvy to take his time. Lighting a cigarette, Jud idled by the window, looking across the street; then, when he saw Cranston emerge from Brenz's building, Jud turned and gave Shrevvy an impatient gesture.

By the time a big limousine was rolling up to take Cranston on board, Shrevvy appeared from the lunch room and took the helm of his own cab, with Jud as a passenger. When Shrevvy asked, "Where to, mister?" Jud wasn't tactless enough to say

"Follow that limousine" and no more. Instead, Jud took Shrevvy into his confidence. This being in the Wall Street area, Jud had a take that sounded good.

"See that limousine?" queried Jud. "There's a customer in it and I'm a customer's man. In case you don't know, that means I work for a stockbroker and try to keep his clients in line. So tag after that limousine for me."

Shrevvy nodded and obeyed, spurred by a few dollars on account which Jud thrust through the front window. Up ahead, Lamont Cranston looked back from his limousine and gave the slightest of smiles.

Giving Jud Mayhew a chance to run up an expense account with Brenz, Incorporated was quite to Cranston's liking, since it was just another thing that Jud would somehow have to explain. Cranston was interested in Jud's explanations—or lack of 'em.

Of course, Cranston's interest was The Shadow's; but there were others who held similar notions, as events were soon to prove.

CHAPTER IX

MARGO LANE blew a cloud of cigarette smoke that made her look like Ilga Vyx. Which meant that the smoke simply curled up and around her face, obscuring the dark hair that formed a foreground to her halo hat. Margo was wearing her favorite blue outfit, quite oblivious to the fact that Ilga was at present sporting a duplicate array.

It was early evening and despite herself, Margo was a trifle piqued at the way she and Lamont weren't getting anywhere. They had just drifted from one place to another and were at present in a little cafe having coffee, with no plans as yet for dinner or further functions. But if anybody deserved blame, it was Jud Mayhew.

Having trailed along from one spot to another, Jud was at present playing ostrich behind an evening newspaper at the far side of the little restaurant.

"What's he doing?" Margo asked Cranston. "Still trying to find out how much the newspaper didn't find out about what went on in Stanwich?"

"Probably," agreed Cranston, "but he's stalling, too. Those occasional phone calls that he's made aren't just reports to somebody. They've been too short. I'd say that he's been calling a number without getting an answer."

"And the number is Gail North," asserted Margo. Then, abruptly, she queried: "What did go on in Stanwich? I still don't know the half of it."

"Nor do I," conceded Cranston. "It was rather uncanny the way that caravan disappeared from the superhighway. Quite as amazing as the collapse of the warehouse."

Margo smiled at Cranston's use of the words "uncanny" and "amazing," two adjectives which were usually applicable to his own activities. Then the very thought sobered her, for when Lamont became confronted with the impossible, it must mean that singular things were stirring.

"Vincent covered the terrain today," Cranston resumed, "and couldn't find a trace. He learned, though, that some trucks resembling those from Stanwich had gone through a couple of small hamlets, several miles away from where the caravan vanished."

"And from there?"

"No trace," replied Cranston. "We are right back where we started, if that far. Unless we count the deduction that I made from what Marsland learned at the Apex Garage today."

Immediately, Margo was agog, for the garage angle, with the subsequent obliteration of Leo's cab, was important in itself.

"Marsland traced a chap named Jeff," explained Cranston. "This Jeff had been bootlegging gasoline that was left at the junkyard, and Leo was one of his customers. Oddly, Jeff couldn't provide a single clue, even under pressure."

Realizing that Cliff Marsland was the dynamic sort who knew the meaning of applying pressure, Margo thought the matter closed. But she hadn't heard Cranston's deduction yet.

"The fact still stands," analyzed Cranston, "that Leo's cab was supplied with fuel brought from the junkyard that the warehouse raiders had left. Since we know that they carried a large load, those raiders, we may assume that Leo's gasoline was part of it."

Margo's eyes opened wide.

"You mean some super-explosive!"

"Exactly," nodded Cranston. "Self-acting under certain conditions, after a given time interval."

"And the stuff was in the warehouse!"

"Yes, until the raiders took it. Undoubtedly they used some of it to destroy the foundations of the building, which were probably already weak. Therefore I would class the stuff as a powerful disintegrating fluid, explosive under certain conditions."

Margo sat fully awed.

"Leo didn't go to pick up Sark by accident," continued Cranston. "Somebody arranged it and since Jeff didn't, the blame hinges on the last man that anyone would normally suspect. He was the garage foreman, Kromer by name."

"Did Marsland talk to him?"

"No. Kromer has disappeared, too. He had an excellent record and was due for a vacation, which they think he has taken. By an odd coincidence, Kromer used to work for a construction company, now defunct—"

Cranston paused long enough only to watch a question start to form on Margo's lips. Then:

"And that company," Cranston added, "supplied the materials used to convert the old brick mill into a factory. It was just another of those puzzling sub-contracts let out by Townsend North, as head of Universal Contractors."

"Then Sark must have known all about it?"

"Naturally, since he was the chief instigator. But matters went beyond Sark, as we learned last night."

"Yes, his friends were certainly out to get him."

"And Sark knew it," reminded Cranston. "That's why he tried to decoy Jud Mayhew into the cab. Fortunately, we intervened."

Margo began to speculate.

"If Sark saw what happened to Jud," she said, "he might have taken that cab himself. Unfortunately I didn't see whether he went out or not. I was trying to trace Gail. Besides"—Margo pursed her forehead—"I didn't get a good look at Sark in the first place, so maybe I wouldn't have recognized him."

For answer, Cranston placed a photograph upon the table. It showed the darkish face of Alban Sark, with all the insidious glitter of eyes and teeth that went with that insidious countenance.

"That is Alban Sark," declared Cranston. "Philo Brenz gave me the photograph today. Study that face closely, because you will be seeing it again; perhaps this very evening."

Margo's eyes were startled as she raised them. That Sark might still be alive was bad enough; that he might be seeking Margo, was something strictly horrible.

"Don't worry," soothed Cranston. "Sark won't be looking for you. I want you to go and find him."

Instead of calming, Margo's eyes fairly bulged with terror. She was staring straight past Lamont toward the wall, and her hands shook so badly that the photograph fluttered from her fingers to the floor. Stooping to regain the picture, Cranston allowed Margo a better view of what she thought she saw.

"Don't let that White Skull bother you," spoke Cranston. "It's just a symbol. It comes as an after-effect of looking at Sark's picture. I have an idea that the photograph was specially posed."

From across the cafe, Jud was watching everything; his own experience was an index that told him what Margo's horror was all about. Jud saw Cranston replace the photo on the table and lean forward to talk to Margo, who answered with understanding nods. That was about all that Jud needed to conjecture that one or the other—or perhaps both—were thinking in immediate terms of Alban Sark. Edging from his chair, Jud went to the pay telephone to put in another phone call to Gail North.

Jud's guess was right.

"Sark is now a hunted man," Cranston was telling Margo. "Don't ask me all the details, because they're what I'm trying to learn and theories are too plentiful to keep adding more. But being hunted, Sark will not be dangerous if approached innocently or mildly.

"Sark's chief enemy is a man named Tanjor Zune, who uses an intermediary named Ludar to reach Sark. Just where Ludar stands is a question; the phone calls that I overheard between him and Sark still leave the issue in doubt. We now know that Kromer is also in the game, definitely on Zune's side. You can mention these facts as seems fit."

Margo began to stammer.

"But how—but—but why—"

"How are you going to see Sark?" queried Cranston. "Simply enough, by calling on him at this address." Cranston placed a card in Margo's hand. "Why should you go to see him? Because you are suspicious of Gail North. She's working for her father, so you think, to help him cover up a lot of shady business which he intends to blame on people who trusted him—like myself."

Margo was nodding now and with assurance. A man as canny and mysterious as Sark would doubtless know that Gail was checking on him and that in turn Cranston had been watching Gail. What was more logical than that Cranston's girlfriend, Margo Lane, would move into a picture where another woman was involved?

From his phone booth, Jud was watching Cranston and Margo leave the cafe. He was talking to Gail now, for she had finally arrived home. Any doubts that Jud had so far cherished about visiting Sark's premises were herewith vanished.

"Get into your hat and hurry," Jud was telling Gail. "I'll be around in the cab right away... No, not the one you stole, this is a local job I hired for the evening... Yes, we're going to Sark's, that's why I need you—to show the way... Of course we'll crack into the place. We want to be there when somebody else arrives..."

Leaving Gail to worry over that one, Jud hurried from the restaurant, took a look to make sure that Cranston and Margo were really gone, then climbed into Shrevvy's waiting cab.

Jud Mayhew thought that he was stealing a march on everyone tonight, including The Shadow!

CHAPTER X

SARK'S house looked like a skull in its own right. Yawning from a row of forgotten brownstone residences, it was one of those architectural monstrosities that had characterized Manhattan at the turn of the century.

Built to stay, the building had, and it was unquestionably the best in an otherwise dilapidated block. It's skull effect was due to the grilled windows on the ground floor, their bars giving the effect of leering teeth; while the hollow nose was a second floor balcony; the eyes, tall, gloomy windows belonging to the higher stories.

The commodious limousine that rolled past Sark's paused only slightly, as though its chauffeur were taking precautions against bad paving in this ancient block. That slackening speed however marked the advent of The Shadow, creature of blackness who preferred such shrouded surroundings.

From the moment that he reached the darkened sidewalk, The Shadow was literally swallowed by the night.

Next, The Shadow was moving up the building wall, the grillwork serving him as a ladder. Another climber might have been noticed; but not The Shadow. Even the men who were moving into the block in the wake of the departed limousine were unable to discern him. They of all people should have, for they were the agents who formed The Shadow's own clan.

Reaching the jutting balcony, The Shadow paused there; then, continuing higher, he skirted the dim windows that might have barely revealed him. His goal was the roof, on the chance that it afforded a trapdoor entry. If not, The Shadow could return to one of the tall windows and make an entrance there.

This night's business was hazardous, risking not only The Shadow's life but those of his agents, by a margin which might exist only in The Shadow's imagination.

If The Shadow was right, all was right. If wrong, this expedition could mean complete obliteration.

As a mass proposition, the issue lay between The Shadow and an unknown foe named Tanjor Zune. Just as The Shadow had his crew of competent agents, so did Zune, whoever he might be. Mystery shrouded The Shadow, but the same was true of Zune. When it came to action, The Shadow's agents, though capable against great odds, were faced with an opposition that even their chief could not outweigh.

If Tanjor Zune unleashed the forces that he had used in Stanwich, this entire block might crumble or explode, eliminating everybody in it. But in calculating that fact, The Shadow had come to the conclusion that the residence of Alban Sark was free of such danger.

To liquidate Sark in his own home, or to wreck the place itself, would give away Zune's game.

Zune wanted to be rid of Sark, but he could only try it in settings such as Stanwich. Zune might attempt to capture Sark, should the latter still be alive, in these premises that were Sark's own. But Zune wouldn't unleash total destruction—or at least so The Shadow hoped.

Five minutes after the passing limousine had disgorged the fleeting figure of The Shadow, a cab pulled into the block and dropped two passengers. That done, the cab went around the corner to remain on call. It was Shrevvy's cab and the persons from it were Jud Mayhew and Gail North.

Jud and Gail hadn't stopped at Sark's front door for a very good reason. They didn't intend to use that door. In fact, one look at the place decided Jud that they wouldn't be able to enter at all, but Gail drew him into a little passage that formed a blind alley beside the brownstone house. There Gail whispered:

"Look!"

Jud looked back toward the street, and didn't like what he saw. There were lurking places in the form of house steps across the way and Jud thought he saw figures shifting there, as though prowlers were getting a vantage spot to watch what happened in the blind alley.

"Not out there, silly!" undertoned Gail. "Here, above this brick wall. The little window. I think we can squeeze through it, don't you?"

Staring upward, Jud saw the window that Gail meant. It was directly above the six-foot wall that blocked off the alley and it wasn't barred. It looked like a stairway window, which had been classed as inaccessible, because someone had forgotten about the brick wall being just below it.

Feeling that retreat to the street had been blocked off, Jud decided that the window was a good bet. Cupping his hands, he extended them to Gail and decided:

"Let's try it! Up!"

Inserting her foot in the step that Jud provided, Gail reached the top of the wall with her other knee. Standing up, she couldn't quite reach the little window, but she was able to give Jud a helping hand that sped his own progress to the wall top. In his turn, Jud reached the window, worked it open, and hauled himself up through. Within he found a stairway landing, and reaching out, he prepared to help Gail follow.

Right then, Gail gave a warning whisper.

Sudden alarm filled Jud, not for himself, but for Gail. As she stood there, the girl formed a tense, rigid target, had anyone started shooting from the street. True, Gail was wearing a dark-gray dress, which reduced visibility, but her red hair wasn't fully concealed by her tam-o-shanter hat, while her trim legs, encased in suntan stockings, might have been seen from a distance. Besides, Gail's face showed very white in the darkness.

Then, the reason for her strain became evident. Jud felt relieved as Gail expressed it.

"It's a car!" the girl told Jud. "Stopping in front of the house!"

"All the more reason to hurry," returned Jud, gripping Gail's elbows to hoist her upward. "It's probably just Sark."

"But I'm sure Sark is dead—"

"And I'm sure he isn't. Not that fox. He knew they were after him—say, look out! You'll be breaking your neck if you aren't careful!"

Jud added this as Gail came headlong through the little window. Her dress catching on a hook, Gail tried to wrench it free and as a result peeled her shoulders right out of it. Her arms entangling in sleeves, Gail couldn't ward her fall with her hands and she went sprawling backward, her head aimed for the steps.

Fortunately, the steps went downward, otherwise Gail would have bashed her head at floor level. Jud was able to catch her shoulders and turn her sprawl into a half somersault which finally ended when Gail's flying feet hooked the banister posts. There was plenty of clatter in all this, but it was drowned by the dull clangor of the front doorbell, ringing long and impatiently.

"That's a break," declared Jud. "Sit down and catch your breath."

Shaking back her ruffled hair, Gail sat on the steps and fished the torn back of her dress up to her neck, where she pinned it with a brooch that she was wearing.

Her arms entangled in sleeves, Gail couldn't ward her fall with her hands and she went sprawling backward ...

"Lucky I wore this brooch," decided Gail, "but don't worry about the noise we made, Jud. There's nobody home."

The bell lulled at that moment, and from below, Jud heard the slow tread of footsteps. He looked at Gail and said:

"No?"

In the dull gloom of that stairway, Gail turned very pale. In her daylight trips past this house, she had come to the conclusion that Sark lived alone here. Since last night, Gail had felt equally sure that Alban Sark was dead. Now, the sound of those footsteps, slow, ominous with their drag, made her think of something ghostly.

"It can't be Sark," whispered Jud, without understanding Gail's pallor. "It's probably just some old servant who works for him. But that may be Sark at the door. Let's sneak down and take a look."

A dim light appeared in the hallway below and dispelled most of Gail's ghost theory; therefore, she was willing to accept Jud's plan, particularly as he motioned for her to be cautious as they descended the stairs.

In fact, the appearance of the light was better received by Gail than it was by another young lady who had been ringing the doorbell. Out on the front steps, Margo Lane had been hoping her ring wouldn't be answered.

Now the drawing of big bolts was a worrisome sound, and Margo looked hopelessly toward the street. Cranston's limousine hadn't waited after bringing her here on its second trip, and Margo felt very much deserted. Maybe that was good psychology, for it caused her to face the door as it opened.

Inside stood an old, tired-faced servant, who bowed quite scrapingly.

"Good evening, ma'am," he said, in quavery style. "I am sorry, but no one is at home."

Margo became emphatic.

"But I want to see Mr. Sark."

"Sorry, he isn't here, miss—"

The servant changed from one title to another because he could see Margo more clearly now, and she looked younger in the light. The reason she was in the light was because she was pressing her way into the hallway. To the servant, Margo said boldly:

"And who are you, to tell me Mr. Sark isn't in when I'm so sure he is?"

"My name is Tobias, miss," the servant explained. "I wouldn't be here if Mr. Sark was, because I'm just a hired caretaker. I'm only here when Mr. Sark is away."

Margo was looking toward the stairs, thinking she saw motion there. If she had seen such, it withdrew from the light before she could identify it. Thinking in terms of The Shadow, Margo was

a trifle worried, knowing that he wouldn't have shown himself unless purposely.

"Mr. Sark won't like it," began Tobias. "To have people coming in unannounced is something he wouldn't approve—"

"Are you sure?"

The question came in a short, clipped tone that made Tobias wheel. There, standing at the lighted door of what was evidently a study, was Alban Sark. Head bowed toward the light, his chin thrust forward in its challenging style, the man's features matched his photograph to the dot.

Margo had never seen a face so frozen, so artificial in expression. If Cranston's face had often impressed her as masklike, Sark's could be described as having no mask at all, not even a human one.

Sark lifted his head and his face caught some light, but its cold, gray resemblance to a skull worried Margo all the more. Then, dismissing Tobias with a wave, Sark gestured Margo across the threshold of the study. Timidly, the girl advanced; once inside, she waited, ready to run out through the door again if Sark started to close it.

Hand on the door, Sark closed it, but only part way. Through his teeth, which seemed to smile only because his lips were spread like an oval around them, Sark gritted a laugh. Yet the laugh itself was not unpleasant. Sark's character, like his picture and its afterimage, seemed to run in positive and negative.

Bowing the girl to a chair, Sark turned to a corner of the old-fashioned but well-furnished room. Riveted, Margo sat there, her eyes glued to the figure that reminded her of some monstrous raven—a logical simile, because Alban Sark was unquestionably a creature of prey.

So strained was Margo Lane that she didn't hear the slight creaks from the hallway, announcing interlopers who intended to view her meeting with Alban Sark.

Jud Mayhew and Gail North too had their interest in the affairs of the strange man who lived in this strange house!

CHAPTER XI

IF Alban Sark had any virtue, it was patience. The reason he had stepped to the corner was to open a large, old-fashioned safe that stood there. Apparently the safe was balky, as was often the case with old worn combinations, for Sark had to begin over half a dozen times. Yet Margo, in her turn, felt that this might simply be a stall.

Perhaps Sark was expecting someone else!

That thought turned Margo's attention to the hall and she was briefly conscious of the creaks, which ceased immediately. The door was opened in Margo's direction, hence she couldn't see beyond it, but she gained an increasing impression that someone was peering in from the hall.

Then the safe clattered open and Sark, rising from beside it, brought a stack of documents that he laid on the desk near Margo.

"Mr. Cranston would like these," announced Sark, in his choppy tone. "You will take them to him, Miss Lane."

Margo stared, quite amazed.

"You will tell him that I am in danger," continued Sark. "There was a plot against my life in Stanwich. Fortunately I foiled it."

Again, Margo nodded, but now it was dawning on her that Sark was merely coming up to expectations. If able to cope with such enemies as the mysterious Tanjor Zune and the band which served him, Alban Sark should certainly be capable of checking on others who moved into his affairs.

"I shall remain here," declared Sark, bluntly, "but I want no further visitors. Things might happen to them for which I could not be held responsible. Now you must leave, Miss Lane."

As he spoke, Sark rolled the papers and affixed a rubber band around them. Politely, he stepped toward the door, as if to open it further for Margo's departure. His stride at that moment was exceptionally silent and swift, for a reason which evidenced itself a moment later.

So rapidly that Margo blinked, Sark whipped the door wide, wheeled around it, and snapped a revolver from his pocket. An instant later he was covering two startled people who stood flat-footed on the threshold: Jud Mayhew and Gail North.

That forced grin of Sark's evidenced itself and with it his face clouded. Recognizing the intruders, his eyes held an ugly glisten that boded no good for them. Sark's gun made a quick, impatient beckon, and Jud nudged Gail into the room, since he could think of no better course.

Most persons would have classed this a time when quick thinking was needed, but not Jud Mayhew. Sark held an option on rapidity; the only antidote was to be cool and deliberate. Even to play sluggish would be good, as Jud knew from experience. There had been a time when Jud had dodged loose from a whole squad of krauts, over beyond the Rhine, just by playing dull until the right moment. He could do the same with Sark.

But there was something else to consider, the safety of the two girls. Jud wasn't just including Gail, for he counted Margo on his side too. The fact that Sark had given her papers to take to Cranston didn't incriminate Margo, nor Cranston for that matter. It smacked more of some deal that Sark

was planning. Apparently Sark considered those documents a security against Tanjor Zune, to date his one great enemy; but it followed that he wouldn't want them to fall into the hands of Gail North.

Right now, Jud's cool calculation told him that he must, at all costs, keep Sark from gaining the false notion that Margo's visit had been just a blind for Jud and Gail to enter. Along with this, Jud hoped that Margo would be smart enough to play the right part.

At the moment, real distress was showing on Margo's countenance, and Jud knew that she was concerned for him and Gail. Fortunately, Gail didn't get it; in her turn, she was throwing dagger looks Margo's way. Sark was taking all this in as he turned his head back and forth. Profiting while Sark's glance was swinging the other way, Jud gave a quick headshake that Margo caught. Then, Jud was staring stolidly again, when Sark looked back at him.

Relaxing, Margo forced a laugh which at least sounded as genuine as those in which Sark specialized.

"I thought you were springing a little surprise on me," Margo told Sark. "Bringing these people in at the wrong moment rather gave me a jolt. They've been meddling in too many things lately."

Sark's eyes rested momentarily on Margo; then returned to Jud and Gail. It was good policy for Jud to look surly, so he did; as for Gail, she needed no prompting for she believed that Margo meant the things she said.

"Some contracts go to the lowest bidder," remarked Margo, significantly. "That was the way Townsend North did business. But there are other people who sell to the highest bidder. Mr. Cranston works that way, so I know he'll listen when he hears your terms, Mr. Sark. After all, keeping papers in a nice safe place is a very simple matter, isn't it?"

Gail really glared. She would have stormed a few accusing statements if Jud hadn't nudged her to be silent. He faked that, while stepping in front of Gail as if to shield her, a move which brought a snarl and a gun gesture from Sark.

It was small wonder that Gail fumed. She thought that Margo intended to walk out scot-free, taking along the evidence that Jud and Gail themselves had come here to obtain. Nor did Margo seem at all worried any longer about what might happen to her rivals.

Jud's interpretation was different. From the way Margo had taken his cue, Jud was sure that she intended to contact Cranston and arrange a rescue. To do that, she would have to get out of this house; therefore, she was playing the best possible game.

There, standing at the lighted door of what was evidently a study, was Alban Stark.

If Jud had known that Cranston in his other life was The Shadow, he would have counted this game in the bag. Even now, it looked sure enough when Sark stated crisply:

"Very well, Miss Lane. You may leave. But remind our friend Cranston that he is not to come here. I have other guests"—Sark turned a smile that was really a scowl upon Jud and Gail—"and I prefer them. Documents are dangerous to keep, but hostages are excellent. Ludar will have something to tell Tanjor Zune when I inform him that I am holding these prisoners."

With that, Sark turned his back on Margo and used his gun to motion Jud and Gail to the corner near the safe. It was the logical corner, for it formed a perfect pocket. At the other deep corner was a door which Jud had been eyeing enviously as a possible outlet in emergency. But Sark wasn't giving his prisoners—or hostages as he preferred to call them—anything that might resemble a break or a chance for it.

In turning, Sark remained fairly close to the main door of the room, which was Margo's exit to the hall. Bundling the rolled papers under her arm, Margo started toward the hallway, feeling that she had begun a death march. What was to prevent Sark, that master of the double cross, from wheeling about and making her a target?

The very thought was terrorizing; it made Margo turn her head and throw a quick look in Sark's direction, only to see that he was still facing Jud and Gail. Beyond Sark, Margo saw Jud, his face very grim, but telling a story by its very grimness. His expression meant just this: that if Sark swung to aim at Margo, he would have Jud to deal with. From the tense pose that Jud showed, Margo knew such dealings would be swift indeed.

It was better to go through with this; better for Margo to get clear and come back with aid as soon as she could bring it. Yet somehow Margo felt uncertain, as though the very atmosphere of this old musty house had all the characteristics of a morgue. It was like a death factory in miniature, giving Margo doubts as to whether Jud and Gail would still be alive, once she was beyond the outer door.

Nevertheless, Jud wanted her to chance it, so Margo turned toward the hall. She was in the doorway when she stopped, halted by a new fright that momentarily seemed silly. It was the death's head again, that afterimage produced by a long look at Sark's face and Margo had taken too long a look for comfort.

There it was, a shifting, grinning skull, against the gloomy background of the hall. Margo blinked to shake off the illusion, only to realize that it wasn't the same that she had gained before. This skull wasn't a big one, leering from the far wall in two dimensional form. It was human in size and alive!

Nor was it a single skull. Margo was seeing three of them, all in a cluster, and they weren't bodiless. They were white skulls painted on black hoods that encased human heads. For Margo could see the bodies that belonged to them, bodies garbed in tight-fitting black costumes that were painted with the white ribs of skeletons!

New intruders these, and below each leering painted face was a hand that clutched a gun. Behind the sinister trio was Tobias, the old caretaker, standing at an open door that led up from the cellar, gesturing the three invaders toward Sark's study!

Though Margo stood riveted for a mere moment, that moment seemed forever. The hooded men with the painted skulls seemed to mock the horror that showed so plainly on Margo's chalk-white face, against the background of her dark hair and the circle of her halo hat. Compared to such creatures as these, even Sark seemed preferable, unless he had summoned them as a grim jest, to cut off Margo's escape.

But Margo didn't think of that. Her thoughts were a couple of jumps behind. All she could do was turn and fling herself back into the study, shrieking incoherently of the danger that had menaced her from the hall. Simultaneously, the skeleton men sprang forward, thrusting their guns ahead of them. Even uglier was Sark's face as he wheeled about and Margo's brain reeled with the thought that this was the end of everything.

It would have been the end, if Sark hadn't shown that same rapid ability which he had exhibited before. Spinning, Sark hooked Margo with his gun hand and flung her toward the corner by the safe, bowling Jud from his feet as he lunged forward. With the same move, Sark's other hand flicked the light switch, darkening the room. The driving skeleton men saw him bound toward the other deep corner of the study, but by the time they arrived from the hallway, a slam of the connecting door announced that Sark had reached another room.

They went halfway after him; then turned. Darkness had swallowed them; now it disgorged them as they started back into the hall, thinking that they could use it to cut off Sark's escape. Sprawled over near the safe, with Jud on hands and knees beside her and Gail huddled further in the corner, Margo saw what happened next.

It was like another illusion, that mass of solid blackness that loomed from somewhere to cut off the skeleton trio. At least it seemed an illusion until it voiced a shivering, challenging laugh that no other fighter could begin to imitate.

That fierce mirth stood for rescue. It was the laugh of The Shadow!

CHAPTER XII

HOW The Shadow had arrived so suddenly seemed quite explainable to Margo. He had a habit of appearing at a crucial moment; hence this was his usual form. What Margo couldn't understand was why The Shadow hadn't arrived sooner. It wasn't his normal way to leave emergency situations in the hands of doubtful characters like Alban Sark.

Even now, The Shadow was handicapped by his own delay. He didn't have time to open fire with an automatic and scatter the men in skeleton costumes. They were upon him all at once, swinging their guns instead of firing them, trying to beat down this adversary who had shown himself too boldly.

On his feet, Jud was charging out into the hallway, hoping to aid The Shadow. Jud had a gun that he had been unable to draw until now, but here was his chance to use it. Pulling the gun, Jud surged into the black-garbed whirl that was mixed with the kaleidoscopic effect of skeleton ribs and skull-faces, all in white.

Then something struck, like a living tidal wave. It was another crew of hooded men, coming up from the cellar. Reeling away from hard swung blows, Jud saw The Shadow detach himself from one cluster and wheel back toward the study. Cutting across the path of The Shadow's attackers, Jud was hurled ahead and pitched headlong through the open doorway, just as The Shadow beat back another drive of half-groggy foemen.

In all that fray, not a single shot had been fired. Always, the members of the death's head corps had been too close, too clustered, to risk shots without hitting each other. In his turn, The Shadow had preferred that close-up fighting as a means of beating down the opposition without wasting bullets. Now, in a lull which was hardly more than an instant, The Shadow gestured his gun hand across the study and gave the quick order:

"That way!"

Margo understood. They were to take Sark's way out. Grabbing Jud by the arm, Margo dragged him along; and Gail, rather than be left behind, hurried after both of them. By the time Margo reached the corner door that Sark had slammed earlier, Gail was gripping Jud, telling him not to trust Margo too far.

It seemed that Gail couldn't quite understand.

Out in the hallway, the lights were blinking off. The men in the skeleton costumes wanted complete darkness. Now they were dashing back down into the cellar, The Shadow after them. For the first time, shots were heard, but they were muffled, so deep below the house that their reports could not have carried to the street where The Shadow's agents waited.

Margo heard them, however, as she found her way through a dimly lighted kitchen. Satisfied that The Shadow had put his enemies to rout, Margo decided that the best way was out. In all this turmoil, she hadn't lost her sense of direction and ahead she saw a door which she knew must lead to the back of the house.

Beckoning to Jud, Margo brought him along despite Gail's protests, which only resulted in Jud dragging Gail along too. The precious papers tucked under her arm, Margo went through a swinging door that led into a pantry, then through another into a dining room.

Here, a pair of lighted candles were glowing on a large table as though in preparation for some gruesome feast. By the dim light, Margo saw two doors and she picked the one which she was sure must lead out to the back. Her guess wasn't entirely right; she'd missed the back door, but what she found was a side door at the end of a little hallway. It was bolted, but in the dim light, Margo coolly unbolted it and gave another beckon to draw Jud and Gail along.

Then, Margo was in the fresh air of a narrow alley that led to the front street. She went that direction, only to drop back startled, as figures rose to meet her. Then, Margo was laughing lightly, happily, when she realized that these were The Shadow's agents, waiting on call.

Margo's laugh became half hysterical as she tried to control it. She was turning, telling Jud and Gail that everything was all right now, except that neither Jud nor Gail was standing there. About her, Margo saw doubtful faces, particularly those of Clyde Burke and Cliff Marsland.

So silent had been the slugging struggle in the thick-walled mansion that none of these watchers had heard a sound. They were wondering if Margo's talk of other people could be a product of her own imagination. Then, Harry Vincent decided to test the question; he went to the door from which Margo had emerged and tried to open it.

That door was now locked from the inside, indicating the impossible; namely, that Margo must have come out through a solid barrier!

There was only one way to disprove that unreality; the way was to pry open the door and go into the house itself. So Harry and the others began that process, finding it difficult, considering the strength of the door. Meanwhile Margo stood by in complete disbelief, unable to understand why Jud and Gail hadn't followed her outdoors.

The answer was more astounding than the question. Jud and Gail were still following Margo inside the house—at least so they thought. In the dining room, they'd seen her beckon, not from the rear door but the front. Thinking that Margo knew her way around, they had gone in that direction.

Now they were back in the large hall and finding it totally deserted, though its lights had been turned on again. Totally deserted, that was, except for Margo, until Jud and Gail learned that they were wrong on that supposition too. For when the girl in blue turned about, she wasn't Margo Lane.

Blonde hair now showed against the halo hat; cold, steel-gray eyes accompanied the hard smile that belonged to Ilga Vyx. Equally steely was the gun muzzle that covered the former prisoners of Alban Sark, prisoners who had escaped one captor to fall into the hands of another clan.

From corners of the hall arrived two leftovers of the skeleton contingent, men who took immediate charge of Jud and Gail, starting them down by the cellar route, with Ilga bringing up the rear. All during that march, Ilga dealt in hard-toned gibes.

"So Sark thought he would keep you as hostages," declared Ilga. "It's just the other way about. Zune will hold you and make Sark come to terms. Those papers of his mean very little; they don't tell the real story.

"The only thing that matters is if Sark talks. He won't talk now, because he needs your evidence. Besides, he will soon know that we could frame him, now that we have the right people to serve as victims. Ludar will tell Sark that."

They reached the cellar during Ilga's harangue, and there Jud saw a sight that he could hardly believe. In the cellar wall was a humpy archway that looked as though some mighty force had compressed the stone up into itself. Nor did the arch stop there. It led in the shape of a long narrow tunnel, in a direction which could only be under the rear street.

"Don't think The Shadow will help you," sneered Ilga, as the skeleton-clad men thrust Jud and Gail through the tunnel. "Our men led him on a wild-goose chase through the connecting cellars of the other houses. They were scheduled to shake off the trail at the end of the block. By the time The Shadow is back, we shall be gone."

They were gone as Ilga declared it. Through the tunnel, they had emerged into the cellar of an old house in the rear block, which was one place that neither The Shadow nor his agents would look for them. Jud was just about to ask how Ilga intended to cover up the evidence, when she proved how easily it could be done.

There was a peculiar machine in this old cellar, with wires leading from it to the wall. Ilga pressed a lever, the machine began to quiver. Like misshapen cardboard, the jammed wall began to regain its shape, under the powerful vibration. Stonework settled down in place, all through the tunnel, marking the end of the pressure that had arched it. The whole effect was silent, uncanny in its action.

With Ilga covering the astonished prisoners, the skeleton men packed up their equipment and led the way further through the cellar, where others met them to aid in controlling the captives.

Back in Sark's house, The Shadow's agents had just begun to work the door loose when it opened. A whispered tone ordered silence, then told them to enter. Margo followed the others, still gripping those papers that Sark had given her, until in the hallway The Shadow took the bundle from her and spoke one word:

"Report."

Taking it for granted that The Shadow knew the first part of the story, Margo mentioned the matter of the double disappearance staged by Jud and Gail. The Shadow sent his agents off to search the house; then, deciding that the cellar required further inspection, he went down there.

At the very rear of the cellar, The Shadow studied the stonework. It looked solid enough, but it bore peculiar traces. It looked as if it had been pounded with sledgehammers, pulverizing some of its surface. Near the bottom, some of the masonry was loose, the component stones twisted a trifle askew.

Yet when The Shadow tested those stones, he found that he couldn't budge any of them. Nothing short of an earthquake shock or the force of some terrific explosive could have caused that result. This was something that even a scientific mind would doubt, or perhaps attribute it to some peculiar tremor due to a flaw in the ground stratum. The Shadow had a scientific mind, but he was gifted with imagination too.

Instead of doubting, The Shadow laughed. His tone was grim, mirthless, as it echoed its strange whispers through the low-roofed cellar.

Things from the past were explaining themselves by the present, and from them, The Shadow was gauging the future. What that future held for Jud Mayhew and Gail North was a very doubtful question.

Nevertheless, The Shadow had a way to solve it. That way was to play two strange and singular personalities each against the other: Alban Sark versus Tanjor Zune.

The Shadow knew!

CHAPTER XIII

PHILO BRENZ strummed his big desk and studied Lamont Cranston very speculatively. His gray eyes were troubled, and Brenz was showing the broad, grim expression that went with a worried mood.

"I don't like it, Cranston," Brenz insisted. "Young Mayhew wouldn't have forgotten his appointment today. Something has happened to him."

Cranston shrugged as though the matter were unimportant. That brought a sudden outburst from Brenz.

"You were the last person to see him," reminded Brenz in a half-accusing tone. "To some degree the responsibility is yours, Cranston."

"No more than yours," returned Cranston, calmly. "I was still here when Mayhew left."

Thinking a moment, Brenz nodded.

"So you were," he recalled. Then, his mood becoming hopeless, he added: "What could have happened to Jud? Do you think"—a sparkle came suddenly to Brenz's eyes—"could that North girl have had anything to do with Jud's disappearance?"

"Very possibly," declared Cranston. "It might be a good idea to question her."

That brought a snort from Brenz.

"Try to find her first!" he asserted. "Here, Cranston, look at these reports!"

The reports were from various private detective agencies and they covered not only Gail North but Alban Sark. The word "covered" was hardly correct, however, because the facts that the reports gave were too slim to be of much account.

Gail had been tabbed chiefly when she went to visit her father, Townsend North, who was at present in a private sanitarium recuperating from a nervous breakdown. Sark had been checked only on those rare occasions when he showed himself in towns like Stanwich or appeared openly but briefly in New York.

None of the private operatives hired by Brenz had begun to penetrate to the question of Tanjor Zune. As for Sark's residence, scene of last night's fantastic combat and another disappearance of the principals concerned, Brenz's investigators hadn't even learned that such a place existed.

Their reports dealt with the same old matter of contracts, a subject on which Brenz knew more than they did. There wasn't a single fact pointing to anything deeper, unless the general ignorance of the reports could be so interpreted.

"Phone me later this afternoon," suggested Brenz, as Cranston prepared to leave. "Perhaps we may have learned something by then."

"Why say 'we' when Mayhew will report to you?"

"Because Jud is covering every angle of the case," explained Brenz, "and you are one of the angles, Cranston."

"I suppose I am," conceded Cranston with a slight smile. "I just hadn't looked at it that way. Among other things, I was in Stanwich when things fell apart there."

"Exactly. You are a bit of a mystery man in your own right, Cranston. Now that I've put the case in Jud's hands, he may think that by checking on someone like yourself, he may gain a lead to Sark if the fellow should still be alive. Anyway, phone me, Cranston."

Brenz shook hands and Cranston left. Though he went from the Wall Street section, his next stop was a place that had some relation to it. Lamont Cranston called at the uptown office of an investment broker named Rutledge Mann.

Of all the serious-minded persons that Cranston knew, Mann rated tops. That was why Mann rated as an agent of The Shadow. Publicly, Mann was just a roundish-faced gentleman whose chubby expression was that of a sleepy owl and whose idea of a huge adventure was a good, rousing chess game. Privately, however, Mann's methodical mind, his meticulous way of winnowing everything down to the last grain and then winnowing the chaff, made him invaluable to The Shadow where research was concerned.

Mann was also a contact agent, through whom The Shadow's active workers reported. Right now Mann had a visitor who was going over papers with him when Cranston arrived. The visitor was Margo Lane; the papers were those that once belonged to Alban Sark.

"It's all a hodgepodge, Lamont," expressed Margo, gesturing to the pile of papers. "With all the fuss Sark made about this evidence, you'd think some of it would be important."

Cranston was writing a list of names which he handed to Mann. Then:

"Call these private detective agencies," Cranston told Mann. "Find out why they bogged down on the investigations they made for Brenz."

That took care of Mann for a while. Cranston let Margo show him through the papers.

"Maybe Sark thought the papers were more important than they are," argued Margo. "He couldn't have opened that safe for a long time, because he had a lot of trouble with the combination. Maybe he was nervous, but he didn't show it, except that he acted awfully fast when he got started.

"Why, the way Sark turned out those lights was even speedier than when he trapped Jud and Gail. When those skeleton men chased him across the study, he was through the other door before they had time to fire at him.

"It was while they were trying to find Sark that they ran into The Shadow." Margo paused to gaze at Cranston as though expecting him to admit that he knew all about it, but he simply kept on looking through the papers. "So Sark really helped us," Margo said, "though probably all he wanted was to get away, which he did."

Sorting the various papers into piles, Cranston gestured for Margo to do the same. The process wasn't very helpful, considering that the letters, memos and all that, were definitely incomplete and anything but incriminating. In fact, the contents of Sark's safe contained a lot of immaterial things, such as racing sheets, theater programs, and receipted bills from nightclubs.

It was these last that specially interested Cranston. One batch of receipts was stamped with dates that showed them to be a week apart. Working along that line, Cranston found the same true of some ticket stubs that came from a large movie house.

Next, Cranston was examining Pullman receipts which were some indication of Sark's travel habits. Like a link to all these was a little daybook, its pages blank, except for a few printed pages that included such things as postal rates and a calendar. The one page that was fairly well thumbed was the one that bore the calendar.

"Rather a methodical chap," commented Cranston. "Or I might say that Sark had regular habits. He seemed to know where he was going to be at certain times. I wonder who else knew."

That speculation still remained unanswered, except possibly in The Shadow's own mind, when Mann returned with a report on his phone calls. They were very much of a pattern.

"All the detective agencies say the same," declared Mann. "Brenz became impatient with them too soon for them to get results. If an operative didn't produce a good report on Sark, Brenz said the job was poorly handled. If one good report wasn't followed by another, Brenz decided that Sark must have found out that he was being watched."

Cranston gave no comment, but Margo did.

"Brenz was right," declared Margo. "Sark proved last night that he knows what is going on. He had me tagged as Lamont's friend, and he was expecting Jud and Gail. I wonder"—Margo gave Cranston an anxious look—"what did become of those two last night!"

"Of course, the detective agencies may have been giving me their usual talk," continued Mann. "Actually, I don't think they could be very competent. Those I called had a very poor credit rating in Dunn and Bradstreet."

"Those you called?" queried Cranston. "I thought you were going to call all of them."

"I couldn't," returned Mann, "because some of them are out of business. Apparently they were nothing more than fly-by-night concerns. I suppose Brenz wanted cheap service; if so, he got it. You might tell him that it doesn't pay to patronize cut-rate companies."

That brought a smile from Cranston, since if anyone should have preached that lesson, the man was Philo Brenz. In fact, Brenz's greatest criticism of the enterprises managed by Townsend North had been their practice of underbidding. Mann's statement, however, was a reminder that Cranston was to phone Brenz and learn if he had gained any further leads to Sark.

It was now after five, so Brenz would be home by this time. Cranston promptly put in a call, only to find that the line was busy. This proved to be the case with three repeats that Cranston made, but finally he managed to get Brenz on the wire.

When Cranston informed Brenz that he was hard to reach, Brenz had a prompt answer.

"I've been calling lawyers," Brenz explained. "All the lawyers who had anything to do with those North contracts. I've insisted that they look into the details, and they're doing it right now. But meanwhile, I have found something important. Come right over, Cranston; I'd like to have an hour with you. It may do a lot to clear the question of Sark."

Liking that promise, Cranston agreed to visit Brenz. Telling Mann what Brenz had said, Cranston remarked:

"You may phone those same lawyers, Mann, and see what you can find out for me. Phone me at Brenz's in about an hour. Any other questions?"

While Mann was shaking his head, Margo put one.

"We have a dinner date," she said to Cranston, "or don't we?"

"I don't recall one," replied Cranston.

"Of course, it's a trifle late," admitted Margo. "Just a matter of twenty-four hours. We never did meet up in time to eat after I left Sark's last night."

"I'll call you later," promised Cranston, as he was going out the door. "Just be patient, Margo."

"How much later?"

"An hour or so."

"If you mean an hour multiplied by twenty-four," rejoined Margo, "maybe I'll dine with someone else."

"Who else, for instance?"

"For one instance," retorted Margo, "I might have dinner with Alban Sark. Or wouldn't he do?"

"He might if you can find him," decided Cranston. "Good hunting, Margo."

The door closed, and Margo gave it an angry glare which Mann didn't notice because he was busy looking up lawyers in the red book. Then, with a sudden dawn of an idea, Margo turned to the papers on the desk, remembering that they might furnish some clues to dining habits.

When it came to dining, Margo was seldom forgetful, though Cranston often was. At present, Cranston wasn't thinking of dinner, at least not in specific terms. What Cranston was considering was the present plight of Jud Mayhew and Gail North.

After all, the plight of hostages was not apt to be too pleasant, though Cranston doubted that it would become too difficult within a single day. At least he could spare an hour with Brenz, who might furnish some real information, before embarking on the one course that might aid two helpless prisoners.

It happened that Lamont Cranston was embarking on a lot more than he realized, even as The Shadow!

CHAPTER XIV

DUSK was deepening over the Hudson River when Lamont Cranston turned from the window and watched Philo Brenz lay down the telephone with a final shrug of disappointment. In his turn, Cranston laid down the drink that Brenz had furnished him.

"At least the visit has been enjoyable, Brenz," said Cranston. "You have a nice outlook here, along Riverside Drive. It's probably worth the rent it costs you."

Despite himself, Brenz laughed. He waited until a stolid servant had removed the tray with its glasses. Then Brenz said:

"The rent is nothing. What matters about this place is the number of the servants I need to keep it up."

"So I noticed," nodded Cranston. "You must have close to a dozen."

"Too close to a dozen," admitted Brenz. "But let's forget the servant question. That phone call was from the last of the lawyers. I've kept them working overtime in their offices, and they've found out—"

Pausing, Brenz waited for Cranston to supply the word and Cranston did. The word was:

"Nothing."

"Exactly nothing," agreed Brenz. He picked up a paper that lay on a side table. "But still, this may mean something—"

"Just a moment," interrupted Cranston, picking up the telephone. "This is the first chance I've had to call my broker and find out how we made out today."

Cranston's phone call was brief. He looked worried as he laid the phone aside. Brenz in his turn appeared puzzled.

"Why call your broker so late?" queried Brenz. "The Exchange closed hours ago. Surely, he would have known about the market long before this."

"It wasn't the market," said Cranston. "It was a couple of horses. We were both playing the same daily double."

"And?"

"Exactly nothing," replied Cranston. "Funny, he called a lot of places without even getting an answer. But getting back to Sark. What about this message he sent you? What does it prove?"

Brenz passed the paper to Cranston. It bore a roughly typed message, as though done in a hurry, by someone who knew as little about using a typewriter as repairing it, for the imprint was out of line.

The message read:

I am in danger. I must see you. I can give you information, the very kind you want. Come alone to Thorneau Place at seven o'clock this evening.

If you think that prying into my affairs can help you in any way, you are welcome to try. I prefer to state my case in full to anyone who is prepared to listen. Are you?

It was indeed a curious message, but the thing that gave it weight was the signature "Alban Sark" that was scrawled boldly beneath. Cranston had seen that signature often enough, both on actual contracts and in the letters that Margo had delivered, to know that it was genuine.

The simplicity of Sark's signature was its validity. Though ragged, the man's writing of his own name was blunt. It was the hardest kind of signature to forge, and Cranston was sure that this one wasn't.

Looking at Brenz, Cranston asked:

"Are you going there?"

In reply, Brenz gave a smile that was a cross between mild and grim. He asked a question in return:

"Would you?"

Cranston shook his head.

"Then add that to your collection," said Brenz, meaning the badly typed paper. "At least it is the only thing of any consequence that I am able to give you."

Pocketing the paper, Cranston started to the door. Politely, Brenz showed him the way out from the elaborate apartment. With all the servants in his household, Brenz found none available when he needed them and grumbled over the fact.

"These servants have their dinner while I wait for mine," complained Brenz. "Half of them always seem to be taking an evening off. I have chauffeurs enough for three cars but only enough gasoline to run one. When my lease is up, I'm going to give up this apartment and move to my club."

Cranston agreed that it would be the best thing to do. But as he spoke, his manner was reflective. Brenz's servant problem was a minor matter, compared to Cranston's speculations. Realizing that Cranston's mind was on the message, Brenz said in parting:

"At least we know that Sark is still alive. A dangerous man, Sark—too dangerous to tackle. It is obvious now that he must have framed that cab explosion himself, probably by planting a high explosive charge in his own luggage. Personally I intend to ignore the message, but if I can find Matthew, I might have Hugo drive him down there to see if anyone is around."

Matthew was Brenz's butler, Hugo one of his chauffeurs. Cranston had seen both of them among the various servants who had been in and out during Cranston's brief visit at the apartment. But Cranston's own personal opinion was that the business at Thorneau Place, if important at all, would prove too important to be investigated merely in passing fashion by someone's butler and chauffeur.

This was proven not only by the fact that Cranston's own limousine headed directly for Thorneau Place with himself as passenger, but by the fact that his trail was picked up by other cars, among them Shrevvy's cab. Cranston had a system with his limousine, which even its driver, Stanley by name, did not recognize, Stanley not rating as one of The Shadow's agents.

By ordering changes in route which meant odd stops or turns; by telling Stanley to increase or slacken speed, Cranston was able to signal when he wanted his agents to follow and how far. Thus when the limousine neared Thorneau Place and Cranston stopped it, ordered it further on, then alighted and finally dismissed the big car, half a dozen of The Shadow's staunch henchmen knew where he had gone although they did not see him go.

Merely stepping into sheltering darkness, Cranston enveloped himself in a cloak that he had been carrying over his arm. Clapping a slouch hat to his head, he became his favorite character, The Shadow. From then on he might have been a patch of night moving of its own volition.

In that brief interval before he became The Shadow, Cranston's figure was hidden by his own departing car. Even if a chance observer had glimpsed the tall form, he could not have sighted Cranston's face. It might have been anybody who stepped into that darkness and very shortly the gloom contained nobody.

The Shadow had gone to keep an appointment which belonged to Alban Sark and Philo Brenz, though the latter wanted no part of it. Now, even Lamont Cranston, self-appointed as a substitute for Brenz, had effaced himself from the scene.

Small wonder, for entering Thorneau Place was like going into a trap. The Place was shaped like a collar button and the interior, where it widened, was mostly a matter of solid walls. Warehouses and other homely structures had replaced the old-fashioned residences surrounding this courtyard which was in effect a blind alley.

Brenz had only dimly recalled hearing of Thorneau Place, but Cranston had known all about it, though he hadn't expressed himself too volubly on the subject. A cul-de-sac of this variety was just the sort of locale that The Shadow considered in his plans. Someday—or more specifically some night— The Shadow had anticipated that he might be in Thorneau Place under trying circumstances.

Tonight was the night.

As silent as he was invisible in the gloom, The Shadow passed through the portals formed by two hulking walls. Here again, he was chancing that the whole surroundings might collapse, but he doubted that such would be arranged on this occasion. The Shadow was certain, however, that Thorneau Place had been turned into a trap.

Perhaps The Shadow could see in the dark; maybe he possessed that uncanny sense common to certain creatures, of distinguishing obstacles that sight could not discover. Whichever the case—or possibly just by some hunch—The Shadow paused at just the proper moment. Extending his gloved hands, he felt a waist-high object that he identified a sizeable ash can, its cover tilted loose.

The ash can was heavy, but only because it was of sturdy metal construction. It was empty, as The Shadow ascertained by tilting it, very slightly, upon the cobbles that formed the paving of Thorneau Place. This obstacle had been set here just so someone would blunder into it and send it rolling together with its clattery top.

Half a minute passed, with sounds so subdued that no listening ear could have caught them. Apparently The Shadow was making up his mind whether to test this trap or not; all the while he seemed to be on the point of trying it.

Then The Shadow did it.

Over went the big ash can with a clanging thump, a roll that brought echoes from the cobbles. Instantly there was a response from low rooftops and high walls surrounding the court. Powerful flashlights hurled their beams, sweeping inward from the entrance to the courtyard, as though to comb in anyone who might have started out that way.

With the sweeping rays came spasmodic shots at clumps of darkness, probing those spots with bullets rather than await gunfire from them. At least half a dozen marksmen were surrounding Thorneau Place, intent upon eradicating the foolhardy intruder who had defied their snare!

Men of murder were acting like marionette manipulators, their gunfire the strings with which they were staging a dance of death, in which The Shadow was scheduled to play the puppet!

CHAPTER XV

SWEEPING lights, blazing guns, both had their play but briefly. The lights certainly weren't uncovering The Shadow; therefore, it seemed logical that the gunfire had found him. All this was happening while the overturned ash can was completing its roll to the wall from which it slowly recoiled, its metallic echoes drowned by the louder fury of the guns.

And then, as suddenly as the attack had opened, the counterattack arrived.

Other guns spurted valiantly from the alley entrance, the spot that killers had immediately ignored. Whining bullets skimmed the edges of the roofs and bashed against the tops of walls. Flashlights went flying from hands of owners who realized that they were making themselves targets.

The Shadow's agents had arrived promptly in the wake of their chief and were giving the opposition plenty.

Lurking murderers hadn't bargained for such a response from an unexpected quarter. They took to flight and wisely, for The Shadow's fighting crew didn't stop at walls, or for that matter, roofs. They scaled the walls as the first step in reaching the roofs, and during the process, they seemed to draw themselves up by their own gunfire. Though lacking time to chop down the routed opposition, they reduced it to an amateur status. Aces all, The Shadow's fighters took over the rooftops in no time, only to find that the enemy had scattered.

There still was the question of The Shadow's fate, for in this rapid fray he hadn't fired a single shot, which was something more than unusual. Anxiously, the agents gathered abandoned flashlights and turned them down into the courtyard, hoping to find some sign of their chief.

The Shadow was gone, as totally as if the cobblestones had swallowed him!

All that remained as evidence of the cloaked invader's brief adventure was the overturned ash can lying empty with its lid beside it.

That happened to be the answer to the riddle. The ash can hadn't lost its lid until after the counterattack. The Shadow had turned that crude device to his own use.

All he had done was ease himself into the big container, drawing down the lid before overturning it from within. The Shadow, encased in a cylinder of metal, had been rolling across Thorneau Place while his enemies were raking it with shots that were directed at every spot but the right one, which in turn was the one invulnerable item on the scene of battle!

Now that his agents had taken over, The Shadow was departing by the very route that he had entered, hoping if possible to handle other phases of this peculiar situation.

Only a block from Thorneau Place, a big car skirted nervously as its front-seat occupants went into a sudden huddle. This car belonged to Brenz; its driver was Hugo; his companion, Matthew. Chauffeur and butler couldn't understand the prolonged outburst from the depths of Thorneau Place. As they veered around the block, Matthew hoarsely urged Hugo to avoid the path of a car that came racing from the next street.

That car was followed by another, both making their getaway while distant police sirens gave evidence that the gunfire had been reported. Hugo turned the big car in the opposite direction, determined not to be linked with the fugitives that had just sped past. Matthew started to commend the choice, only to interrupt himself as he heard the car door slam.

Then a crisp voice was delivering orders, for between the shoulders of Matthew and Hugo peered a face that both recognized under the passing street lamps.

It was the face of a man who had visited Philo Brenz, but not recently. If the face had belonged to Lamont Cranston, Brenz's men might have accepted him as something of a friend. But the face was one that bulged, with eyes that glistened from their hollows like the teeth that formed an ugly smile.

The unexpected passenger was Alban Sark!

Not only did Sark give orders; he backed them with a gun that moved from one man's neck to the other. Hugo took those orders and Matthew approved them, though silently. This car really had a backseat driver, for Sark deserved the term, considering how his mere gestures guided their course.

Uncannily, this skull-faced man directed Hugo away from the paths of converging police cars, until they were riding entirely in the clear. Then, Sark stated exactly where he expected to be taken.

Reaching a neighborhood far removed from Thorneau Place, Brenz's car disgorged Sark and then scooted off like a boy finishing his last day of school. Unlike Cranston, Sark didn't step into sheltering darkness, instead he stood conspicuously on the curb. His eyes, though, probed the gloom around him, inviting any lurkers to come out and fight, but none put in an appearance. Then, pocketing his glittering revolver with a defiant, jerky motion, Sark shifted a squarish package under his arm and stalked along the street and around a corner.

There, Sark walked into a little restaurant that bore the sign:

CAFE UNICORN

Above the door was a sign bearing a picture of the heraldic creature from which the cafe was titled, but Sark paid no attention to it; likewise, he ignored the hatcheck girl who smiled and reached for his odd package. Continuing to the rear of the cafe, which was modeled somewhat in the shape of Thorneau Place, Sark took a table for four and placed his package very carefully upon one of the vacant chairs.

A waiter came over, nodded, and tendered a bill of fare, which Sark gestured away as something unnecessary. Nodding again, the waiter decided that Sark wanted his usual order. Relaxing, Sark simply waited for something to happen. It did.

From a corner of the cafe came a girl in blue, whose blonde hair showed conspicuously against the high circle of her halo hat. She stopped at Sark's table and faced him boldly, covering a certain trend toward apprehension with a wise, steady stare. Receiving no invitation to sit down, the girl reached to a chair.

"Not that one!" spoke Sark, quickly. "Around here. I have a package on that chair."

The girl saw that there was a package and gave the chair a wide berth. Noting a quick change of her expression, Sark gave a short laugh.

"Worried, Ilga?" queried Sark, soothingly. "You needn't be—at least not yet."

Ilga Vyx set her lips firmly; then became quite casual, even to the gesture that her pliant fingers made in the direction of the package.

"Since when have you been carrying your own, Alban?"

"Only recently," returned Sark. "The idea came to me as in a dream."

Ilga's dumb stare was a pretense.

"A nightmare," specified Sark. "I saw that cab blow up in Stanwich, clear from my hotel window. I took a room on the seventh floor just because of the view."

Placing a cigarette in a holder, Ilga poised so Sark could provide a light. When he had, the blonde said:

"You were very lucky, Alban."

"More so than I realized," stated Sark. "Some people had the notion that one of my suitcases contained the explosive that obliterated that cab. It gave me the notion."

"And that is why the package?"

"That is why the package. Two can play with dynamite as well as one, except that Zune uses something more than dynamite."

Ilga was raising one hand warningly.

"Maybe that package contains something more than dynamite," confided Sark. "Perhaps I know more than Zune realizes, or has he thought of that?"

"I wouldn't know."

"At least you came here to watch for me," expressed Sark. "Of course, it's Wednesday, my usual night at the Unicorn. But I might have changed my habits after what happened in Stanwich."

"Yes, you might have."

"I would have," assured Sark, "if I hadn't brought along that package. Go tell that to Zune."

Ilga gave a rather hopeless shrug.

"Don't accuse me, Alban." Ilga failed badly when it came to faking a pleading tone. "You know I never see Zune."

"I may have thought you didn't," retorted Sark, "or I may have made you think I thought you didn't. But after what happened at Stanwich—"

"Quit harping about Stanwich!" gritted out Ilga, savagely. "What would I know about what happened there?"

"Enough to keep you from taking a ride in the wrong sort of taxicab," declared Sark, reducing his tone to a purr. "Being alive ends your bluff, Ilga."

Momentarily disgruntled, Ilga finally managed a disparaging shrug.

"All right," she admitted, "I did see Zune. But I'm like Ludar. I'm trying to help you."

"Ludar?" queried Sark. "The name does sound familiar—"

"Ludar sent me here tonight," interrupted Ilga. "I told him I'd phone him if you were here, so he could talk to you."

"Why didn't he just phone for himself?"

"Because he didn't want to ask for you if you weren't around. If you'll only believe me, Alban—"

"All right, call Ludar."

Ilga went to a phone booth in a corner of the cafe. When she returned, she merely paused at Sark's table.

"Ludar is on the phone," undertoned Ilga. "I'll see you later, Alban."

Sark carried his precious package with him to the phone booth, while Ilga hurried out the nearest door, not anxious to remain in the proximity of such a bundle. Over the phone, Sark laughed when Ludar, speaking in a stolid tone, expressed the wish to meet Sark somewhere.

"Very well, Ludar," said Sark, at length. "Come around for me, but be sure you stay in the car. We can chat while we ride, but I'll have the package that Ilga probably told you about. If I decide to blow myself up, I intend to have company."

Back at his table, Sark had less than a ten minute wait before the doorman entered to tell him that a car was waiting for him outside. Having canceled his dinner order, Sark was ready to leave, but he was careful to take his package with him. The car proved to be a sizeable sedan, with two men in the front. A third occupant, Ludar, was in back, beckoning through the open door.

Stepping into the car, Sark sat down, all the while handling his package very carefully, without tipping it more than a few inches. Ludar reached around him and across, showing a blunt, darkish face that did not reflect the apprehension which he must have felt. Hand on the door, Ludar paused.

"All right, Ilga," he said, "come along if you want."

Before Sark could turn, the girl had stepped into the car and was sitting down beside him, turning her head to adjust her overlarge hat while she closed the door with her other hand. It took quite a dip to get a hat like that through the door in the first place, which was why Ludar hadn't noticed something that became apparent when this new passenger turned her face toward the men beside her.

Ilga had more than a new hairdo; she had a hair dye. At least it looked as though the blonde had converted herself into a brunette, until Sark and Ludar saw her face. Then they realized that she wasn't Ilga at all.

The girl was Margo Lane, smiling grimly above the muzzle of a compact automatic that she had drawn from her purse. All Margo had to say was one word:

"Surprised?"

CHAPTER XVI

THEY weren't surprised, exactly.

The big surprise was past; the fact that Ilga Vyx had decided to take this ride voluntarily. Ludar had credited Ilga with a sudden show of bravado, which Sark had apparently shared; but it now seemed more logical that Margo Lane should be in the car, since she didn't know about the package.

Neither man spoke, so Margo smiled. She felt quite confident over the fact that she had found a trail and followed it before The Shadow.

"I was looking over some of your odd papers," Margo told Sark. "Somehow they seemed to fit with your calendar. You liked to see movies every Monday night, always at the same theater. Tuesday, you just loved to see the races. Wednesday, you always dined at the Unicorn and kept the receipts from the waiter's check."

Ludar grunted something that didn't sound complimentary to Sark, but Margo interpreted it differently.

"If you're worrying about Ilga," remarked Margo, across her gun, "she's all right—or will be when she gets back from the cleaners."

That seemed to call for further explanation, so Margo gave it.

"I saw her coming out the side door," Margo continued, "so I stopped her—like this." To emphasize the method, Margo gestured her gun at the faces which were turned toward her. "I didn't mind ruining that blue dress of hers, because it really isn't a blonde's type, you know.

"Anyway, I needed chunks of it so I could tie her up and gag her. The laundry wagon was waiting there, so handily, all loaded with nice bundles. I just stacked them all around Ilga, so that if the lot goes down a chute, she won't get hurt.

"Ilga ought to have a nice time, since she likes playing hide-and-seek. Or maybe it was follow-the-leader. Anyway"—Margo's eyes moved from Sark to Ludar—"now I know why a couple of people didn't go out the door I tried to show them—that door in your house, Sark. Ilga must have crossed their path and coaxed them her way."

There wasn't a sign of a response from either Sark or Ludar. The reason dawned rapidly on Margo.

"It wasn't your work, then," she said emphatically to Sark. "I suppose you were gone before it happened, Sark. As for you"—her eyes traveled on to Ludar—"you probably don't want to admit that you knew what happened."

Ludar's blunt face showed a scowl that made it into a darkish blur.

"You must be Ludar," decided Margo. "No wonder you don't want to show your cards to Sark. He might guess that you've been double-crossing him with Zune."

It was just a shot in the dark, but it took. It wasn't the mention of the double cross, however, that enraged Ludar, for Sark had already expressed suspicions on that point. What angered Ludar was that Margo was acquainted with the existence of Tanjor Zune.

He must be a mighty personage, Zune, to hold the control his mere name indicated. A snarl issuing from his faceless visage, Ludar came half to his feet, as though to rocket across the car and lay his hands about Margo's neck. He didn't care any longer whether Sark knew the two-way game. All Ludar wanted was to choke Margo, so that she could never again reveal the name of Zune.

Perhaps it was fortunate that Margo wasn't quick-triggered. If she had shot Ludar, he would have jarred Sark, which might have proved very serious. Sark himself indicated that prospect by a thrust of his square package; the moment that nudged Ludar, the fellow recoiled back to his corner of the car.

"Look out!" panted Ludar. "That box is loaded with explosives! If Sark drops it, we are finished!"

"I do not have to drop it." Leveling the box, Sark tilted his ear toward it. "Too much of a slant would be sufficient. But I do not hear the clockwork."

Margo's gun was wobbling in her hand.

"You mean it's going to explode?"

"Not yet," reassured Sark. "This is different from most infernal machines. They have clockwork that goes tick-tick and tells people what they are. Have no worry while this one is silent. It works in reverse."

"But if the clockwork starts, you would hear it?"

"Yes, but not for long. Now tell me"—Sark supplied one of his obnoxious grins—"does this make any difference in your plans?"

"It means I'm stopping the car and getting out," Margo decided. "The rest are coming along with me, but you are staying in this car, Sark, until I send the police to get you."

With that, Margo threw a glance from the rear window just on the hunch she wouldn't have to wait for the police. If Cranston had gone through Sark's papers as thoroughly as Margo hoped he had, he logically would have watched the Cafe Unicorn too. Probably he wouldn't have entered there as Cranston; maybe he had been delayed as The Shadow.

But there were others, a string of agents whose names were lining up in Margo's mind, who might have been deputed individually or collectively to check on Sark's usual Wednesday habits. How Margo wished for a sight of Shrevvy's cab, back through that window!

Occasional headlights were distinguishable along the darkened street, but Margo had no way of telling if any belonged to Shrevvy's cab. Then, as if realizing that Margo wouldn't be looking for a police car, and therefore must be thinking of some quicker aid, Sark said crisply:

"We do not intend to stop."

"Sorry," began Margo, thrusting her gun firmly, "but we do."

For answer, Sark let his own hands ease from the box, which tilted precariously upon his knees. Margo recoiled as Ludar had. Then, finding her voice again:

"You'd be a fool, Sark, to let Ludar take you to Zune!" exclaimed Margo. "Don't you realize that he intends to do just that?"

"Quite," returned Sark, straightening the box. "I should like to see Zune."

"But he tried to kill you once—"

"And would probably try again, should occasion warrant. Am I right, Ludar?"

Ludar grunted something that sounded affirmative.

"Sulking, Ludar?" sneered Sark. "You shouldn't be, considering that I am letting this ride continue. Suppose you tell Miss Lane just how I stand with Zune."

A snarl meant that Ludar wouldn't, but when Sark let the box swing about until it rested on only one corner, the blunt-faced man capitulated.

"Sark is with the White Skulls," asserted Ludar, "but he is not our leader. He is only the custodian."

Margo stared at Sark and asked:

"Custodian of what?"

"Let Ludar tell you," returned Sark, leaning back and drawing the box toward him. "Only put away that gun. It makes me nervous, and it isn't right that I should be nervous."

Margo decided that Sark shouldn't be nervous and therefore put away the gun, though reluctantly. Sark nodded for Ludar to proceed.

"Custodian of the treasure," stated Ludar. "After all, if you know so much, why should you not know more? Sark came to this country before the war began, to guard the treasures which we knew that we would send him."

By "we" Margo knew that Ludar must mean the bigwigs of the Nazi swarm that had spread all over Europe like a locust plague. Only why they should send treasures to America, Margo didn't understand until Ludar explained further.

"Some fools thought they saved their treasures," sneered Ludar, "but we had the facts in every case. Our agents not only posed as refugees; they encouraged others to put whatever they still owned in places where we wanted them.

"It was Sark who had charge of all that, and it was his business to arrange everything for our convenience when we arrived as we did in other countries, using the white skull as our secret symbol."

The full light broke on Margo. It was the game of the Wooden Horse as played in Norway and other countries. In terming Tanjor Zune the leader, Ludar must mean that Zune had come as the head of the secret tribe of invaders.

Suddenly, Margo became defiant.

"But it didn't work here," she asserted. "You were stranded, all of you. There's nobody home in Nazi-land to receive the goods that you can't even ship. You'll only give yourself away if you try to steal those treasures."

Instead of taking that to heart, Ludar responded with a snarl:

"So Sark said!"

Those big hands of Ludar's were itchy, this time for a grip on Sark's throat. Toying with the box as a reminder that Ludar shouldn't try, Sark said bluntly:

"After all, I am the custodian."

"But Zune is the leader!" stormed Ludar. "He said we would proceed despite you, and we did! Our first victory gave us what we needed to gain the treasures that are really ours!"

"And Zune did well," complimented Sark. "I shall tell him so. If I had known how perfectly all would work, I would not have obstructed matters."

Ludar relaxed with an ugly laugh that fairly teemed with confidence.

"Try to make Zune believe that now."

"I shall," assured Sark, "because I know the one thing that Zune needs. He wants a hostage."

That made Ludar laugh again.

"Zune already has two hostages," said Ludar.

"He brought them from your house, Sark."

"Those two?" Sark gritted a hard chuckle. "They were scarcely more than strangers where The Shadow is concerned. To influence The Shadow, you must hold a hostage that he values. I am bringing one as a peace offering to Zune."

Finishing his cold laugh, Sark stared straight at Margo Lane. Under the frigid glare of those glistening white eyes, the girl felt a chill that seemed to creep to every fiber. Alban Sark was right. His was the master stroke. In Margo Lane he had produced a human weapon that Tanjor Zune would welcome as a threat against The Shadow!

CHAPTER XVII

ALONG with the chill that swept her, Margo felt a sinking, sickening sensation that she thought was mental, like the blackness that came with it. Then, with a last despairing glance through the back window, she saw the reason.

This car had reached its destination, somewhere in Manhattan, but it was entering a sort of place that Margo hadn't believed existed. Here, in an alleyway that squeezed between two old buildings, the car was being swallowed by the ground itself!

The street had dipped down like a hinged contrivance, and looking back, Margo saw the whole thing springing up again. There was a last sight of streetlights, but no sign of a pursuing cab among them; then the view was blotted.

Blackness in back and not the blackness that represented The Shadow, who somehow must have been diverted from the trail. If Margo had known of that recent fray in Thorneau Place, she might have had an explanation of The Shadow's absence. But as it was, explanations didn't matter. The Shadow wasn't here; that was all.

Dipping deep into this subterranean domain, the descending car came to a lighted area where the ramp leveled toward a blocking wall. Now more amazed than frightened, Margo saw the great wall split and spread like two parting curtains, its steel halves sliding into buttresses of concrete. Next the car rolled through a rough-hewn tunnel to a second door, which opened like the first, the tunnel serving as an anteroom between.

Stocky men approached, and Margo heard voices speaking in a peculiar language which was probably of an international variety. She could guess why it was used, as she alighted from the car along with the other passengers. The men who occupied this underground realm looked like the renegades of a dozen nations, hence they required a special language to talk among themselves.

Here was firsthand evidence of pre-invasion methods that the Nazis had used and which still existed in this relic of their vast plans. Under Sark's direction, a vest-pocket city had been hollowed deep beneath New York itself, the workmen being these renegades who passed as citizens of threatened countries, not of the menacing German nation, or its satellites.

This beginning, of course, must have dated back to the pre-war period and Sark, the future treasure custodian, had arranged it. Even now, some of the underground dwellers showed respect toward him, and Margo noted that Sark was listening to catch and analyze the words of the jargon that they uttered.

Other doors, smaller doors, were sliding open, producing a deeper route into this strange domain. Ushered along as though she were an invited guest, Margo kept watching Sark and Ludar as they accompanied her. All the while, Sark was carrying that precious box of his with a nonchalance that was maddening to anyone informed as to its contents.

While most of the underground inhabitants accepted Sark's presence, there were occasional men who sprang forward angrily, ready to challenge the skull-faced visitor. Ludar always gestured these back, firmly and swiftly, with explanatory words in that tongue which Margo was now beginning to understand. One word for instance that Ludar repeated was "mordo," which Margo guessed meant "death."

It applied to the contents of Sark's box, of course, and was sufficient to force bold men back. But when Margo looked over her shoulder to watch the reactions of such individuals, she saw each one leer behind Sark's back.

Maybe that term "mordo" would apply in reverse after Sark met Zune. For these men who flashed that antagonism toward Sark, appeared to be those who were strictly in the know. Margo heard Ludar address one as Kromer and remembered that such was the name of the man who had been planted at the Apex Garage in Stanwich.

From the grim smile that Kromer furnished, Margo was sure that Sark had escaped one death warrant only to invite another. Still, final decision would rest with Zune.

Unless there was other intervention!

Margo held no brief for Sark.

The man deserved to die as much, if not more, than any of the dwellers in this invisible realm, Zune included. But as the target of fellow criminals, Sark was a threatened person, who should be protected just as a way of frustrating the plans of murderers.

The Shadow would therefore prefer to keep Sark alive, in fact had already demonstrated that preference. That to Margo meant that The Shadow would reach this realm if possible, and as soon as he could manage it.

But did The Shadow know that such a place existed?

Something important must have engaged The Shadow this evening; otherwise he would have been at the Cafe Unicorn. Perhaps as the result of some run-in with roving foemen, The Shadow had traced them here!

Looking back a few times more, Margo saw that blackness kept constantly closing in behind her, in the form of dropping curtains and sliding doors, which respectively seemed like the falling of shrouds or the clamping of coffin lids. If only The Shadow were part of that following blackness!

Then, what seemed to be a death parade came to its conclusion, as curtains parted to admit the small procession to a room hung in purple. There, in contrast to the regal surroundings and the gilded furniture, a plain desk was at the far wall.

Behind that desk sat a man who seemed to grow in proportions as he arose and stood with his fists doubled on his hips. Across his heavy, bloated face played a venomous expression that beggared any efforts at imagination.

This visage from a nightmare belonged to Tanjor Zune. It was little wonder that the man who owned it stayed deep in the concrete molehill which he ruled, and let others handle public relations for him. Nobody who saw Zune once would ever forget him.

Peculiarly, Zune seemed glad to see that Sark was still alive. When Ludar pointed anxiously to the square box and began to speak in terms of "mordo" and other appropriate words, Zune glowered, but not at Sark.

Zune's glare was of the silencing variety and it cowed Ludar. Then, letting his features writhe into a less ugly contour, Zune furrowed his thick eyebrows and inquired in English:

"Who is this?"

The hand that gestured from Zune's elbow indicated Margo.

"A hostage from The Shadow," explained Sark, in his crisp tone. "Better than those you already hold. They did not come to my house at The Shadow's bidding; they were intruders there."

Zune's hands performed a peculiar cross-slap that furnished a sharp sound like that of a beaver's tail smacking the water. Instantly curtains parted, and two of Zune's bitter-faced henchmen introduced Jud Mayhew and Gail North to the scene.

No fakery was needed on the part of those prisoners. The challenging contempt that Jud showed toward Sark; the dagger looks that Gail tossed at Margo convinced Zune that there has been no prearrangement where this meeting was concerned.

Turning, Zune parted a pair of curtains behind his desk and drew down a huge roller map. The guards were about to remove Jud and Gail, while Ludar was drawing a gun to cover Margo. Only Sark stood unmolested, by virtue of the package he carried. Swinging about, Zune spoke imperiously:

"Let them stay!"

Eyeing Sark steadily, Zune questioned:

"You are prepared to collaborate as before, now that I have demonstrated what can be done?"

"*Cooperate* is the correct word," returned Sark, crisply. "I am ready."

"And you are right," Zune acknowledged. "We need no Quislings any longer. They would handicap, not help us. We shall be masters of our own underworld."

Sark supplied a bow t;o that.

"I shall show you my plans," stated Zune. "In return I expect you to prepare a full report, covering the information in the documents you destroyed."

Again Sark bowed. Remembering the paucity of evidence in the papers Sark had sent to Cranston, Margo realized that Sark must have disposed of anything and everything important.

Satisfied, Zune turned to the big map and used a long ruler as a pointer to indicate its details. Here was the time so long awaited, when the inner machinations of stupendous crime were to be disclosed.

All that was needed was one all-important witness for whom Margo Lane looked in vain.

The Shadow!

CHAPTER XVIII

ZUNE'S large-scale map showed a network of highways some miles outside of New York. The roads were marked in various colors, some stretches being mere segments; hence the map was very unusual, but Zune did not comment on that fact.

Conspicuous on the map was the town of Stanwich. Zune tapped that point with his ruler.

"Our first stroke was there," asserted Zune. "It was essential in order to obtain the valuable supplies that you had planted in the warehouse."

This was spoken to Sark, who nodded.

"You did well, Sark," complimented Zune. "I was truly sorry that it seemed necessary to liquidate you later. When I first arrived in New York, I wondered why these quarters were so cramped." Zune gestured about him as he spoke. "Considering the quantity of the disintegrating fluid that we sent you, I had expected something like the huge hidden city that lay beneath Berlin.

"When you explained your other uses of our Formula Four Hundred, I was greatly pleased." Though facing Sark, Zune gestured toward the map. "Even better was your plan of saving a surplus to

Behind that desk sat a man who seemed to grow in proportions as he arose and stood with his fists doubled on his hips.

store in Stanwich with the neutralizer. We have enough of the N-Five to cover up all we may do with Formula Four Hundred. I salute you, Sark!"

Clicking his heels, Zune was about to hoist an arm in Nazi style when he remembered Sark's package and desisted before Sark could start to copy the salute. Then, with a happy leer, Zune gestured to the package:

"We can add that to our store, Sark, when you no longer need it—or think you need it."

Reverting to the map, Zune wangled a ruler cross-country until he came to the area of a town marked Hartfield, some twenty miles from Stanwich.

"The treasures are there," announced Zune. "Art treasures worth millions, enough to finance our future indefinitely. Or should I say *definitely?*"

As Zune leered from the map, he saw that Jud was drinking in all these details, something which Zune could ignore. It was Sark upon whom Zune concentrated.

"Your objection sounded solid, Sark," stated Zune. "Why should we reveal our hand?" Zune shook his head. "By using Formula Four Hundred and N-Five in combination, we would not reveal it."

This made much sense to Jud. He remembered the vaulted tunnel that Zune had literally pried into

Sark's cellar, only to close later by another process. Zune was talking about it now.

"The treasures are in the old Crabtree Museum," reminded Zune, as though Sark didn't know. "In and out—and we shall have them, leaving only death and mystery on the premises. That should please you, my friend of the White Skull."

Eyes narrowed, Zune was staring at Sark as though trying to produce the optical illusion that Sark's face supplied, but the light was wrong for it.

"I have learned, however," continued Zune, "that the treasures may soon be removed; in fact, that plans were already made for it. Was that your idea, Sark?"

Sark did not answer, but he did not flinch his face in the strong light which Zune had purposely directed on it.

"Or could it be," demanded Zune, "that you were conforming to the plan of somebody else? Of somebody we no longer need, for the reason we both have stated?"

Trying to think who might be meant by "somebody," Margo lingered on the name of The Shadow, but she wasn't too certain. Then came an interruption, a sharp cracking sound, but this time it wasn't the cross-clap of Zune's hands. It was the sudden rolling of the map as Zune released it.

"We shall keep all the hostages," decided Zune. "I agree with you, Sark, that she is best"—Zune pointed to Margo, then gestured toward Jud and Gail—"but these others may be valuable. As for yourself, I have this."

Scrawling something on a slip of paper, Zune handed it to Sark, and added:

"A pass for yourself, so that you can leave these premises. But I am sure you will prefer to wait until my full plans are made, as I would like to discuss them with you. However—"

Finishing with a shrug, Zune beckoned to one of his stolid retainers:

"Show our friend Sark to his own apartment."

There was a reason why Zune did not first send away the hostages. Zune was the type who preferred an appreciative audience whenever he revealed himself as a master of the double cross. As soon as Sark had been ushered out, Zune turned to Ludar and Kromer.

"We start for Hartfield within the hour," announced Zune. "If Sark tries to leave his quarters, eradicate him. After we have gone—myself and the men with me—use your own discretion. For Sark—*mordo!*"

Ludar and Kromer nodded their pleased agreement.

"At your own convenience," added Zune, "and with due discretion. That box Sark has with him, we need its contents for ourselves. Remember, too, that Sark still has a few friends among us. Therefore, it is better that only you two should know."

Clapping his hands, Zune produced other servitors who marched Margo away with Jud and Gail. They arrived at a cell block, which did not look too uncomfortable, except for its barred doors. There they were stowed in separate cells to await their fate.

This wasn't to be a long wait.

Elsewhere in this honeycombed domain, Ludar and Kromer had taken over watch outside of a fancily curtained doorway that represented the apartment which Alban Sark, as the famed White Skull, had provided for himself. Having dismissed the other guard, Ludar and Kromer buzzed between themselves.

"It would be *komika,*" stated Ludar, "yes, funny, if Sark should try to use that pass with us!"

"He may try," rejoined Kromer, "since he does not know that we are here."

"But how soon would he try?"

"Perhaps very soon."

There was a pause; then Ludar's faceless visage twisted uglily.

"Maybe too soon, Kromer!"

"Too soon?"

"Yes. Perhaps already, while the other guard was here!"

At Ludar's notion, Kromer's face distorted in its own right. Then:

"We are friends of Sark," reminded Kromer, "or we can pretend to be. We enter and address him as *amiko,* saying that Zune has sent us to ask if he has any further request. Then we shall see if he is still there."

"And the box!" added Ludar, warming to Kromer's suggestion. "Perhaps—"

The two sidled through the curtains and past another door beyond. There they reached a small but comfortable living room, with the half-opened door of a bedroom just beyond. Near that far door was a table, on it Sark's precious package. Lying on the package was the pass that Zune had provided.

So eager were Ludar and Kromer that they didn't think of the gloomy anteroom through which they had just passed; in fact, they hadn't paused there and certainly would not do so now. That was why they failed utterly to see the stir of the anteroom curtains.

Out of those drapes came blackness, living blackness, which stole swiftly up behind the interloping pair. It was the cloaked form of The Shadow, and his gloved hands shot forward from the end of piston arms just as Ludar and Kromer were about to grip that all-important box which lay upon Sark's table.

Simultaneously The Shadow's gloved hands took two necks and brought their accompanying heads together with a crack as resounding as Zune's beaver clap. The Shadow had to catch Ludar and Kromer by their collars and give them slight flings at opposite angles, to keep them from landing on the table and overturning it, box and all.

Neatly done, that job—a fitting sequel to The Shadow's mysterious and unsuspected arrival in this realm. But there was more to follow.

Outside the cell block, a short while later, a patrolling guard paused to look contemptuously at the hostages who peered from their cells like creatures in cages. A moment after, the guard wilted, his face much pained.

It looked as though a pair of black tarantulas had crawled around his neck to press his throat from either side. But when the choked guard sagged, those black grippers revealed themselves as gloved hands belonging to a cloaked owner.

Margo Lane gasped the name spontaneously:

"The Shadow!"

A whispered laugh as The Shadow stooped to pick up the guard's keys. Then the cells were open, but as Jud Mayhew emerged, The Shadow clapped a hand on his shoulder and turned him into the light. As Jud paused, wondering, The Shadow brought a gauze mask from beneath his cloak.

Next, he was placing that object on Jud's face, molding it there. Though thin, the mask had structure and could be shaped. It took The Shadow only a few minutes to smooth back the edges and tighten them with their gummed borders. Jud felt his lips drawn apart by the tight gauze; he could feel a pressure, like that of hollows, around his eyes.

In fact, Jud felt like a grinning ape and thought that Margo and Gail ought to be laughing instead of giving the amazed gasps that they did. Then, The Shadow turned Jud toward a mirror at the end of the corridor, and Jud gulped too, as well as he could.

The face that leered at Jud Mayhew from the mirror was a perfect replica of the skullish countenance of Alban Sark!

Next, Jud was pocketing an envelope that The Shadow gave him, speaking brief, whispered instructions that went with it. Then, in Jud's hand, The Shadow placed the pass that would take him to the outer world.

Jud nodded. Then:

"It's a sure bet," he said, "provided I don't meet Ludar or Kromer—"

"Which you will not," interposed The Shadow. "From then on, follow the instructions in the envelope."

Nodding again, Jud gave an anxious glance toward Margo and Gail only to see that they weren't worried, at least not for themselves. In the company of The Shadow, they were safe; their only concern was for Jud's future.

Maybe that future still boded strange events. For as Jud Mayhew turned to leave as The Shadow's messenger to the outside world, he heard a weird, whispered laugh that seemed to warn him to guard his actions well.

Strange, that laugh of The Shadow!

CHAPTER XIX

ONE hour later, the invasion of Zune's underground citadel came as swift and as short as the explosion of a blockbuster, with about the same result, except that there was no explosion. These preserves, which Sark had planned as something impregnable, proved to be anything but that.

It happened right after a string of automobiles bearing Zune and his followers had emerged from their secret alley. The paving locked behind them, but it didn't stay that way. Deep underground, two guards that Zune had left behind suddenly found themselves confronted by guns. Margo and Gail were taking over, backed by The Shadow.

There was a third man present, another of Zune's henchmen. He was at the switchboard that controlled the automatic doors. The Shadow was handling him personally, again using that gloved neck grip that had the effect of velvet-plated steel. Tossing the limp man aside, The Shadow operated the switches, then drew a pair of automatics and relieved Gail and Margo of the job of covering the two prisoners.

Soon, cars arrived from the ramp, three of them, headed by Shrevvy's cab. From them came The Shadow's agents, to learn their chief's next plans. The Shadow unrolled the big map from Zune's room and showed them the route along which he intended to travel with them, in pursuit of Zune.

Except that Margo and Gail weren't going. They were steered right into the cab, and next thing, Shrevvy was whizzing them up the ramp to the outside world. Reaching the street, Shrevvy drove a few blocks; then stopped at a cigar store to make a phone call.

Good friends now, Margo and Gail could discuss the turn of events that had put them in the discard. It was Gail who brought that up by asking:

"Who is the cabby calling?"

"The police, probably," replied Margo. "He's tipping them off to Zune's setup so they can take over while Zune is away. I only hope they don't forget to look through a few laundries and gather Ilga Vyx for a bonus."

"Tanjor Zune will have a big surprise waiting for him," decided Gail, "when he gets back from Hartfield."

"*If* he gets back," corrected Margo. "Meanwhile, I'm wondering what became of Alban Sark. I mean the real one."

"That's right!" exclaimed Gail. "Sark must have gotten away! I only hope nobody mistakes Jud for him, now that it's no longer necessary."

By that time, Shrevvy had returned, and Gail, to ease her worries over Jud, put a hopeful question to the cabby.

"You didn't happen to meet a friend of mine, did you?" queried Gail. "His name is Jud Mayhew, and he's the person who gave the word about that underground city where you found us."

It was Shrevvy's policy to play ignorant, at least to the degree where he seemed merely a chance cab driver who had been commandeered by The Shadow's agents without knowing who they were.

"Don't know anything about it, miss," rejoined Shrevvy. "But there was a passenger I took up to Riverside Drive. He was going to see somebody named Brenz, I think it was."

That meant Jud. Calling on Brenz was part of his business. It meant too that he was out of the disguise The Shadow had fixed for him. Gail couldn't drop around and see Brenz, but she had another idea of how to while away the time during the next few hours.

"Riding in a cab reminds me of something," Gail told Margo. "I ought to take a certain cab back where it belongs, so people will stop saying it was stolen instead of just borrowed. I know where it is, so let's go and get it."

The idea appealed to Margo. She knew the cab Gail meant; the one that belonged in Stanwich. If they took it there, they would be closer to Hartfield than they were at present. Therefore, they might get news of The Shadow's expedition sooner. At Margo's nod, Gail told Shrevvy where to drive them.

Meanwhile, Jud Mayhew was finishing an important interview with Philo Brenz. His hand strumming the table, Brenz's face showed an expression which carried a considerable quota of amazement.

"Incredible, these things you tell me," expressed Brenz. "But if they are true, Jud, we should do something about them."

"About everything has been done," asserted Jud. "All we can do is sit back and wait."

"Not quite." Brenz shook his head. "Wait here a few minutes, while I see if Hugo is around. He is the chauffeur who works for me on Wednesdays."

When he returned, Brenz was shaking his head.

"No Hugo," he declared. "In fact all the servants are either out for the evening or gone home. Well, we can use my coupé to drive to Hartfield. Suppose we phone the Crabtree Museum first and warn them."

Brenz tried the call, only to learn that the museum phone had been disconnected.

"The place is probably closed," decided Brenz, "and they are getting ready to move the art treasures, I suppose. We'd better drive out there right away."

How Brenz and Jud were to fare in the general race for Hartfield was a question, considering the head start that others had gained. But there was a factor in their favor that did not disclose itself as they sped along in Brenz's fast-geared car, which really clipped the miles as soon as they were free of the New York environs.

The persons who were to learn that factor were Gail North and Margo Lane. They discovered it because Gail insisted on trying a short route to Stanwich. Coming over a hill, Gail halted the taxicab that belonged to the Apex Cab Company. This cab had a double seat in front, being of the small-town variety. Seated beside Gail, Margo also saw the moonlit panorama that lay before them.

Down the slope was the superhighway, dominating a small network of roads. The question was which of two forks to take, here on the hill, in order to reach the best spot on the superhighway. What confused the issue was the fact that this was near the elaborate cloverleaf pattern of bridges and underpasses that formed a feature of the highway system near Stanwich.

Only from this spot could the girls have observed the singular thing that occurred amid the rolling valley.

Like little scooters, a row of cars whipped into sight along the superhighway and suddenly spread apart to take different routes among the cloverleaf ramps. They seemed to be playing a game, those cars, until three others came into view, pursuing them.

... A string of automobiles had emerged from their secret alley.

**There was a third man present, another of Zane's henchmen. He was
at the switchboard that controlled the automatic doors.**

"Zune's caravan!" exclaimed Margo. "And there
are The Shadow's cars catching up to them!"

"But they ought to be over by Hartfield!"
expressed Gail. "What made them head for
Stanwich instead?"

"It must have been something on that map,"
decided Margo. "Let's see what happens next."

They saw, and promptly. One by one, Zune's
cars began to disappear. It happened each time one
swung down into the deepest underpass, a spot to
which they all purposely converged. At the sharp
bend each car veered and a portion of a concrete
buttress swung back from a framework of steel
girders, swallowing the arriving cars, which came

caravan, since it was the easiest to overtake. That was the way The Shadow's agents had tried it, the night they had made a chase from Stanwich. But on this occasion, the first pursuing car took the route that the leader of the fleeing caravan had used.

Margo and Gail saw the result. Having taken the shortest course in this blind game, The Shadow's car, first of the pursuit party, was gaining its objective at the expense of the last car in Zune's group. Just at the last car made that fancy veer, The Shadow's car sighted it.

There was time for Zune's last car to scoot from sight; time, too, for the concrete portal to slide shut. But The Shadow had cracked the system. His car duplicated that wide swing over toward the buttress; the barrier opened and The Shadow stayed on the trail.

So did the rest of The Shadow's cars. Coming by the various routes, in the same order that Zune's cars had used, the pursuers saw exactly what awaited them and copied The Shadow's system to the dot.

Gail drew a long breath and said:

"Just try to imagine that!"

"I can't," rejoined Margo. "Not even after seeing it happen!"

"Well, we did see it happen," Gail declared, "and there's nothing to stop us from trying it ourselves."

Try it they did when they reached the cloverleaf and when the concrete opened magically in front of them, the girls found their car burrowing right through a tunnel beneath the superhighway.

Something struck home to Gail.

"This was one of those contracts let out by Sark!" Gail exclaimed. "We never could understand what happened to some of the materials. We were sure they were delivered, because the highway was completed, but it seemed just tons and tons short of concrete!"

"It came from here, then," returned Margo, "or rather this is where it didn't go. I have an idea where it is though."

"So have I," declared Gail with a nod. "Bolstering that underground citadel that Sark built for Zune to occupy!"

"Somehow Sark strikes me as the real genius," mused Margo aloud, "and therefore the more dangerous. This highway would have been good for ten years before it began to cave, and by then its purpose would be served."

"There must be a dozen others like it," said Gail, unhappily, "all places where that White Skull crowd could vanish and disappear. My father had all these contracts and Sark figured in every job."

Coming out through a camouflaged exit that lifted like a portcullis, the car swung into a narrow byroad that Gail recognized as one leading to Hartfield. The tunnel had carried them off through

in such quick succession that the great door hadn't time to close before the next car reached it.

The clever feature of the system was the divergence of the original routes. This made differences in the distances traveled to the focal point; hence the cars arrived at intervals and disappeared as neatly as by clockwork.

There was another tricky point to the system. The lead car of The Shadow's pursuit party should logically have followed the tail car of Zune's a hill, away from the superhighway. Then Gail remembered something else.

"There's another of those cloverleafs near Hartfield," Gail told Margo. "I suppose we'll find the same thing there. If we do, I can guess where it will lead."

"Under the old museum?"

"Either that or pretty close to it."

"If we do," decided Margo, "we'd better drive into the tunnel. There's nothing we can do to hurt, and there might be some way we could help."

There was good reason for the confidence in Margo's tone. She felt sure that The Shadow's plans—like those of others—were coming to a climax.

When that happened, bets were best laid on The Shadow.

CHAPTER XX

WHIPPING into the outskirts of Hartfield, a speedy coupé took the hill leading up to the Crabtree Museum. Coming around a final turn, the car gave quick toots of its horn, and a big gate swung open.

Next the coupé rolled into an inside court where men were loading quantities of crates and bulky frames into some waiting trucks. The coupé stopped and Jud Mayhew stepped from one door; Philo Brenz from the other.

Promptly, Brenz convinced the truckers that he had a right to be here. He was ushered into the museum itself to find some attendants helping pack the art treasures. The hired help at the museum had been expecting the trucks almost any day and were glad that they had arrived so soon.

So was Jud Mayhew.

Jud's only wish was that the truckers might have arrived sooner. Still, there was time for them to get everything out before Tanjor Zune arrived. At least Brenz thought so, for he stepped right into the position of supervisor and began to make things move.

Apparently taking it for granted that the more important treasures had been stored away from public eye, Brenz asked where the vaults were and was shown there. Jud went along and the truckmen followed, down to a great arched cellar where goods were already packed.

Hardly had the truckers and attendants started to remove the massive crates from the cellar before the dreaded stroke arrived. The whole building seemed to quiver as it absorbed the vibrations of a peculiar explosion that had a flowing effect, as though spreading itself up through the foundations of the museum.

The floor heaved itself apart as men recoiled from its upward thrust. Then, from what seemed a self-splitting molehill of gigantic size, invaders appeared, wearing the black costumes that bore the painted skeleton ribs and hooded death's heads of the White Skull.

The truckmen must have sensed such danger while it was still on the way. As they fell back to the corners of the great cellar, they drew revolvers to offset the guns that the invaders displayed. Philo Brenz did the same; stepping forward, gun in hand, he was about to call for combat when Tanjor Zune appeared from the slanted gap in the cellar floor.

Zune barked an order and his men spread to vantage spots. Gun for gun, Zune faced Brenz while the truckmen, Jud among them, dodged for shelter of their own. Both groups seemed to cancel themselves in pairs, leaving the field to Brenz and Zune.

The thing became an immediate stalemate. All around the cellar were pillars, supporting its vaulted roof. Those pillars served as the shelter that both fractions needed. Each group seemed dubious about starting battle, fearing to heap reprisal on itself.

And Jud, finding himself an ex-officio member of the trucking crew, decided that he'd better stay right where he was, until something broke this spell.

Face to face, Zune and Brenz were eyeing each other like creatures from another world. Then Zune spoke, in that harsh, fierce tone of his.

"I should have known you would be here," declared Zune. "Whoever you are, whatever your name, you had too much at stake to stay away."

"The mistake was yours," retorted Brenz, abruptly. "You were a fool not to know when you had lost—as I did."

Staring, Jud could hardly believe what he heard.

"I have not lost," sneered Zune. "I am proceeding with a duty. I am here to take the treasures."

"Which proves you are a fool," specified Brenz. "The thing at Stanwich is still a mystery, but if the contents of this museum are stolen, it will be no riddle."

Zune eyed Brenz sharply. Then:

"Speaking of riddles," queried Zune, "why are you here to steal the treasures?"

"Only because you are" was Brenz's cool reply. "When I learned you were on the way, I had no other choice."

"You forget one thing." Zune's tone was rising, angrily. "I was the man appointed to take all this in charge!"

"I had more than an appointment," stormed Brenz. "I was promised full control once the work was done!"

Zune's anger suddenly changed to contempt.

"Everywhere there must be a leader," he declared proudly. "But to be successful in a country not yet conquered, that leader must depend upon some person there. A person who, to the world, is called a traitor—such as you."

"The greatest traitor," retorted Brenz, "is the man who hires one."

Knowing that the epithet was meant for him, Zune snarled back a single word that applied to Brenz.

That word, singularly suited to the term of perfidy, carried a contemptuous sound. The name that Zune had for Brenz was:

"Quisling!"

That utterance cleared Jud's brain.

It meant just this, and simply. Zune was the leader of a criminal band, come to America and stranded here, no longer able to serve the purposes of the defunct Nazi regime. But to prepare for his arrival, Zune had needed the services of a man ready to betray his own country.

Such a man was Philo Brenz.

Brenz had been approached; he had done more than listen. It was Brenz who had supplied the ways and means of underbidding his own contracts and attributing the crooked work to Townsend North. Of all persons, Brenz was best equipped to stage such underhanded action, while North was equally eligible as his dupe.

But there was one man who had arranged both angles, a man who was the perfect go-between: Alban Sark.

Jud's mere thought of the name produced the man in question.

As Zune and Brenz stood glaring at each other, a harsh laugh intervened. There, emerged from the hole that Zune had hewn with Formula Four Hundred, stood Sark. How he had come along with Zune's own crew was a slight mystery in itself. For the present, the important thing was the fact that Alban Sark had arrived.

The grin from Sark's skullish face was more livid than ever. He seemed to relish this scene.

"Allow me to introduce you," spoke Sark. "Tanjor Zune, leader of the White Skulls, intended as the shock troops of an occupation force. Philo Brenz, the man appointed to be America's Quisling. Both disappointments to themselves—as well as to each other."

For the first time, Zune and Brenz found themselves in agreement. That agreement was their hostility toward Sark.

"I am no disappointment," argued Zune. "I am here to take wealth as my own, that is all!"

"I have been trying to keep what I gained," declared Brenz. "I landed plenty of contracts, and high-priced ones. Why should I sacrifice my profits for a title that no longer counts, or for treasures I could not keep?"

Zune wheeled toward Brenz.

"You were after the treasures here—"

"To keep them from you," interrupted Brenz, "as I told you. I hoped to get them safely away and let you take the blame for a raid that failed. Perhaps they would never have found you, Zune, but they never would have even suspected me."

Zune's only answer was a glare. It was Sark who spoke, and mockingly.

"Brenz is right, Zune," argued Sark. "You failed to learn who the Quisling was—"

"Because you never told me," interposed Zune, fiercely. "You said it was your business—not mine. Now I know why!"

"And why?"

"Because you made a deal with Brenz. You were to share his profits. Am I right?"

"Quite right." It was Brenz who gave the answer. "I made a deal with Sark. I was too clever to try to kill him, even if I had wanted."

That thrust deflated Zune. Brusquely, he tried to throw it off. With a wave toward the men who waited behind pillars on Brenz's side of the cellar, Zune demanded:

"These men? Who are they?"

Sark eyed the faces that were half-poked in sight and answered:

"Brenz's servants. I have seen them before."

Brenz nodded that Sark was right. More than once, Sark had been a secret visitor to Brenz's apartment. Then:

"I needed you again tonight, Sark," stated Brenz. "I tried to dispose of The Shadow, but it did not work. Remember that note you sent me once, saying to meet you at Thorneau Place? I added a threatening paragraph at the front of it, on that old typewriter that used to be yours."

Sark gave a grinning smile, as though he appreciated the ruse even though it had failed. Then, Sark's drawn lips stiffened. He turned to Zune.

"I prefer men who do not fail," announced Sark. "Perhaps you have better claim to that, Zune. Of course"—Sark swung to Brenz—"I am open for conviction. Since all these treasures are at stake"— Sark was sweeping the well-stocked cellar with his glistening gaze—"what is the use to wait?"

Cold words, but they raised the rivalry between Zune and Brenz to a white-hot pitch. Neither waited for the other; both wheeled and bellowed for the attack to begin. Like unleashed hound packs, Zune's fighters surged to meet Brenz's servants, who launched themselves with equal fury.

One man wasn't in that fray.

That man was Jud, who no longer belonged on Brenz's side and wouldn't fight on Zune's. As his target, Jud took a neutral who in Jud's estimate was the real menace in this case. All Jud wanted was to settle scores with Alban Sark, otherwise White Skull.

Sark's face seemed to loom gigantically as Jud drove forward, opening fire with his gun. Only it wasn't Sark at all, it was that old illusion, that of a white skull coming as an optical reflex after staring at a darkish face with grinning teeth and glistening eyes.

It seemed to float ahead of Jud, that thing that wasn't there, until Jud found himself actually tripping into the pit that represented the newly hewn tunnel. There, Jud was caught by a rising figure that emerged as suddenly as Sark had disappeared.

The Shadow!

A strident laugh sounded above the rattle of the gunfire with which Zune's men and Brenz's were chopping each other down. Reeling fighters turned to see The Shadow brushing Jud aside with a sweep of cloaked arms that brought two huge automatics into a pair of gloved fists.

From amid their faltering followers, Zune and Brenz wheeled apart, each intent upon being the first to deliver a concluding treatment to The Shadow.

Both were too late. The Shadow's shots came first. Flame-tonguing automatics drilled the rivals who had tried to salvage all they could from a ruined scheme, but who had each wanted all for his own and therefore had lost.

As they sprawled, Tanjor Zune and Philo Brenz looked up with glazing eyes and saw the face that was beneath The Shadow's slouch hat, which he had purposely tilted back.

It was the face of Alban Sark!

Jud Mayhew saw it too and couldn't believe it, until The Shadow cloaked a gun and used his hand to wipe that face away. On the floor he flung a gauze mask of that same molded pattern that he had given Jud for a temporary disguise. A tug of The Shadow's hat brim and his own face, that of Cranston, was obscured.

Zune's voice croaked from the floor.

"So we did blast Sark—that night in Stanwich—"

"But you couldn't believe your luck," coughed Brenz. "When Sark showed up again, you didn't guess he was The Shadow."

"It was in the gasoline—the formula—it blew up the taxicab—"

"And Sark was in that cab—The Shadow knew—only you weren't sure—"

That was all. Zune's say was done and he hadn't heard the words that Brenz added for him. Nor could Brenz add more than those few phrases. Like Zune

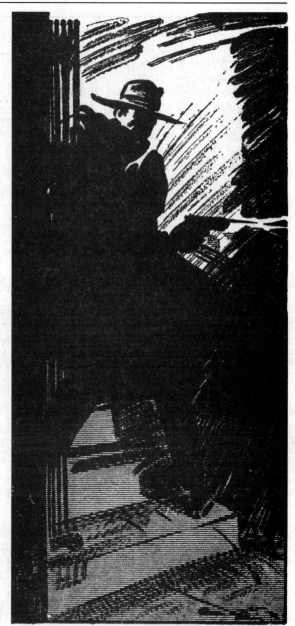

Flame-tonguing automatics drilled

he had sagged completely. Like the living link who had once been their connection, namely Alban Sark, both Tanjor Zune and Philo Brenz were dead.

They, the successors of White Skull, could no longer hope to profit from the schemes that his evil genius had founded.

As for the followers of Zune and Brenz, those that remained had likewise completed their own undoing. Having whittled each other down to pitiful remnants of their original numbers, the few survivors were firing stupidly and wildly at a surge of new fighters who were literally overwhelming them with a climactic gunfire.

the rivals who had tried to salvage all they could from a ruined scheme ...

The newcomers were The Shadow's agents, sprung from the great gap in the floor, through which they had followed Zune's tribe to await The Shadow's call, which he had finally given.

Behind them came two others to witness the mop-up. Margo Lane and Gail North had followed the same route, but they didn't care to linger. Margo was beckoning Gail back through the gap when Jud Mayhew glimpsed the girl whose cause he had helped to vindicate.

"Gail!"

With that call, Jud disappeared into the tunnel where Gail was turning to meet him. As he went,

Jud heard a strange, triumphant laugh that came upon the last echoes of the gunfire that conquered crime.

It could have been a knell for Zune and his men who had left their impregnable lair, or possibly that tone of parting mirth was in recollection of Alban Sark, the notorious White Skull whose death had enabled The Shadow to adopt his ways and thereby put an end to his evil successors, Tanjor Zune and Philo Brenz.

Only The Shadow knew!

THE END

Spotlight on The Shadow:
BILL JOHNSTONE
by Anthony Tollin

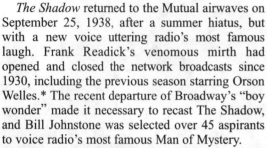

The Shadow returned to the Mutual airwaves on September 25, 1938, after a summer hiatus, but with a new voice uttering radio's most famous laugh. Frank Readick's venomous mirth had opened and closed the network broadcasts since 1930, including the previous season starring Orson Welles.* The recent departure of Broadway's "boy wonder" made it necessary to recast The Shadow, and Bill Johnstone was selected over 45 aspirants to voice radio's most famous Man of Mystery.

A decade earlier, Johnstone had begun his acting career by accident while returning home from New York's McBurney School: "I was standing around on West 51st Street in New York, where I lived at the time, watching the workmen complete the new Guild Theatre. Before I knew it, someone yelled at me: 'Stop gazing and get in line with the others.'" The teenager obeyed and ended up carrying a spear in the Theatre Guild's production of *Caesar and Cleopatra* starring Helen Hayes. Better roles followed as Johnstone performed in Rodgers and Hart's *Garrick Gaieties of 1926* and enacted the title role in E. E. Cummings' *Him* at the Provincetown Playhouse.

The Brooklyn-born actor moved onto the airwaves in the early 1930s when his friend Allyn Joslyn recommended him to play roles in the mystery adaptations he was scripting. Within a few years, Johnstone was regularly heard in the top New York radio shows including *The March of Time* and *The Cavalcade of America. Radio Guide* recognized him as one of the "Scene Stealers of Radio."

Having played supporting roles opposite Frank Readick, James LaCurto and Welles, Johnstone was familiar with both of The Shadow's radio incarnations. "The Shadow was originally the voice of conscience and it was through the fear which he aroused in the minds of criminals that they exposed their own villainy or destroyed themselves," he told the *New York Times* in 1941. "Ten years ago, when the show was first presented, The Shadow was only a sound effect, a nasty, snarly voice that would burst in with a blood-curdling laugh, and sneer, 'The Shadow knows.' Now the part has been expanded into that of a dual personality—Cranston, the educated, society man, and The Shadow, the

name he affects when employing his unusual talents to a good cause."

Johnstone brought a mature sophistication to the role of Lamont Cranston and a commanding authority as The Shadow that quickly eclipsed Welles' portrayal. With difficulty, he mastered the trademark laugh that had eluded his mercurial predecessor. "Bill Johnstone had an awful time perfecting that Shadow laugh," recalled his lifelong friend Kenny Delmar. "I felt so badly for him, because the trick is not to laugh but to have an audible sneer... it has to be free to flow. Poor Bill suffered every time he had to do the laugh."

During Johnstone's five seasons as The Shadow, the program progressed from a curious novelty to become an American institution. In 1942, C. E. Hooper reported that "since they first began rating daytime shows in February 1938, no other daytime commercial program has ever attained as high a rating." By March of 1942, *The Shadow* owned the Sunday afternoon airwaves, commanding a Hooper rating of 17.2 and a 55.6% share of the listening audience, "the highest daytime rating of the entire week." *The Shadow*'s audience was double that of his highest-rated daytime rival, *Kate Smith Speaks,* which achieved a rating of only 8.9.

Bill Johnstone left *The Shadow* in the spring of 1943 to follow *The Cavalcade of America* to the West Coast. "I was making about $150 a show when I left," he recalled. "I was very happy with it, because it seemed that everybody who ever listened to the radio had heard *The Shadow.*"

However, he was drafted almost immediately after arriving in California. Entering the Army as a Signal Corps private, he later produced shows for Special Services and was eventually placed in charge of a WAC recruiting group.

Returning to civilian life in January 1946, Bill became a fixture on *Suspense* and *The Lux Radio Theatre* and later starred in Blake Edward's *The Lineup.* During the summer of 1948, he enacted the title role in CBS' "intercontinental" production of *The Whistler,* voicing an opening inspired by *The Shadow*'s famous signature: "I am The Whistler, and I know many things for I walk by night. I know many strange tales hidden in the hearts of men and women who have stepped into the shadows. Yes, I know the nameless terrors of which they dare not speak!"

---

*Orson Welles was never able to master The Shadow's laugh, so recordings of Readick's opening and closing signatures were heard on all the 1937-38 broadcasts.

In Hollywood, Johnstone appeared onscreen with Barbara Stanwyck in *Titanic* (portraying John Astor opposite Edgar Bergen's wife Frances) and with Loretta Young in *Half Angel* and Broderick Crawford in *Down Three Dark Streets*. In 1951, he played a G-Man in *My Favorite Spy*, performing alongside Bob Hope and radio Shadow John Archer.

The veteran radio actor moved back to New York in 1954 and the following year began a 23-year run as Judge Lowell on television's *As the World Turns*.

Bill Johnstone starred as The Shadow for five seasons. However, four decades later he could only recall a single episode: "The Red Room," the opening broadcast of the 1942-43 season. "I'll never forget the sound of the killer ants eating their victims," Johnstone related in 1983. "It was horrifying, and I can still clearly hear it in my mind."

We're proud to present the long-lost episode by Sidney Slon that left such a haunting memory on the man with The Shadow's voice. •

Bill Johnstone intones The Shadow's laugh.

THE SHADOW
"THE RED ROOM"
by Sidney Slon
originally broadcast September 27, 1942

(MUSIC: "SPINNING WHEEL"...FADE UNDER)

SHADOW: Who knows what evil lurks in the hearts of men? The SHADOW knows! (LAUGHS)

(MUSIC UP...SEGUE BRIGHT THEME)

ANNR: Once again your neighborhood 'blue coal' dealer brings you the thrilling adventures of The SHADOW...the hard relentless fight of one man against the forces of evil. Every week at this time we bring you a new episode in this fight for the triumph of justice. These drama-tizations are designed to demonstrate forcibly to old and young alike that crime des not pay!

(MUSIC UP...SEGUE INTO NEUTRAL THEME)
(OPENING COMMERCIAL)
(INTRODUCTION BEFORE START OF SHADOW STORY)

ANNR: The Shadow, mysterious character who aids the forces of law and order, is, in reality, Lamont Cranston, wealthy young man-about-town. Several years ago, in the Orient, Cranston learned a strange and mysterious secret...the hypnotic power to cloud men's minds so they cannot see him. Cranston's friend and companion, the lovely Margo Lane, is the only person who knows to whom the voice of the invisible SHADOW belongs. Today's drama... "The Red Room."

(MUSIC UP AND THEN UNDER)

SHADOW: I have known many men who have killed without mercy, cruelly and savagely. But of them all, there was none so mad with greed and blood...as the human devil whose diseased brain hatched...The Red Room!

(MUSIC UP FOR A MOMENT THEN FADE OUT. DOOR OPENS AND CLOSES)

NIXIE: Well, Chief...here's the guy you wanted snatched!

MIKE: Yeah. It was easy. Me and Nixie waited outside the bank, like you said. He walked right into our hands!

NORCROSS: Good work, boys. Excellent. (OILY, UNCTUOUS) Ah! Good evening, Mr. Rankin!

RANKIN: Who are you? Why have I been kidnapped...blindfolded...and brought here?

NORCROSS: You were brought here because you have some information I need.

RANKIN: Information? What information?

NORCROSS: Why—that's easy to answer—Mr. Rankin...as chief pay teller of the Seaboard Trust Bank...you have intimate knowledge of the inner and outer vault combinations. You also know where the burglar alarms are...and how to operate them.

RANKIN: You're wrong. I don't know anything about them.

NORCROSS: (INGRATIATING) Come, come, Mr. Rankin. I have made inquiries. Knowing these facts...is part of your job.

RANKIN: (DESPERATELY) I tell you, I know nothing.

NIXIE: Say, Boss...this guy is stalling!

MIKE: Yeah. Shall I bust him one in the mouth? Maybe that'll open it!

NORCROSS: (CHIDING) No, no...Mike. That would be...shall I say...too crude? Now, Rankin, for the last time...

RANKIN: (STUBBORNLY) I tell you I don't know a thing!

NORCROSS: (SIGHS REGRETFULLY) Very well. We have another way to make you talk…

MIKE: You mean…the Red Room, Chief?

NORCROSS: Yes…the Red Room. Remove the blindfold from Rankin's eyes, Nixie…

NIXIE: Okay.

             (SLIGHT PAUSE)

NORCROSS: (OILILY) Mr. Rankin…you have been very unpleasant…very stubborn about this whole thing. But I think you're going to change your mind. Nixie…remove the floor carpet!

NIXIE: Right.

             (SLIGHT SWISHING SOUND OF CARPET DRAGGED ALONG FLOOR)

NORCROSS: And now, my friend…look down through that glass trapdoor in the floor…and tell me what you see…

RANKIN: (SLOWLY) Why…there's a room down there…it's colored deep red. (VOICE BREAKS IN HORROR, THEN HOARSELY) Why…why…that color comes from ants…millions of giant red ants! The room's full of them! They're crawling an inch thick…on the floor…on the walls!

NORCROSS: (SINISTER) Yes, my friend. Those beautiful blood-colored creatures are flesh-eating, legionary ants…sometimes called "the Red Demons of the Jungles"…and well deserving their name, as you shall see!

RANKIN: (HOARSELY, FRIGHTENED) I don't understand…

NORCROSS: (EVILLY) You will, Rankin…you will! I have a microphone down there in the Red Room. It's connected to this dial, here in the wall. Listen…as I turn it!
             (FADE IN: AN INHUMAN, SINGING INCESSANT SOUND, STEADY SUSTAINED. SOMEWHAT HIGHER THAN THE SOUND OF A HUGE SWARM OF BEES, PERHAPS LIKE THE SINGING SOUND OF MILLIONS OF MOSQUITOS. HOLD THROUGH FOLLOWING.)

NORCROSS: (MACABRE) Listen, Rankin. My little half-inch pets down there are singing for their supper… singing the music… of death! Do you understand?

RANKIN: (HOARSELY) I tell you…I don't know anything…Nothing at all!

NORCROSS: Still being stubborn, eh, my friend? Still playing the fool! What a pity? What a pity, indeed! Mike!

MIKE: Yeah, Chief?

NORCROSS: Mr. Rankin needs further proof. We'll give him an…er…exhibition. There's a slab of beef over there…in the corner.

MIKE: I get you…

NORCROSS: Watch closely, my friend. You'll find this very interesting. All right, Mike… open the trapdoor and drop the meat in…

MIKE: Okay…

             (SOUND OF TRAPDOOR OPENING. SLIGHT PAUSE, THEN DULL HEAVY THUD.)

NORCROSS: Watch…and…listen!

             (THE STEADY SONG OF THE ANTS RISES IN INTENSITY. IT KEEPS RISING UNTIL IT HITS A CRESCENDO, AS THEY DEVOUR MEAT. HOLD CRESCENDO STEADY.)

NORCROSS: (DRUNK AT THE SIGHT) See…Rankin…how my carnivorous red beauties devour that flesh! See how they crawl over that carcass…millions of them…see how they gorge themselves! Ah! Listen to them, my friend! Listen to them sing!

RANKIN: (IN HORROR) You…fiend! You…evil fiend!

NORCROSS: (NOT HEARING) Yes…yes…they're hungry…very hungry indeed! There's white showing through the red already! Look, Rankin…it's bone! Clean white bone…

NIXIE: (IN AWE) It's terrific…terrific!

MIKE: Get a load of that! There ain't anymore meat left!

NORCROSS: Nothing now…but bones! My little pets have feasted well!

(SONG OF ANTS BEGINS TO DROP GRADUALLY FROM CRESCENDO. FINALLY SETTLES INTO STEADY HUMMING SOUND, SUBDUED IN COMPARISON.)

NORCROSS: (SMOOTHLY) Well, my friend? Are you willing to talk now? Or shall I have these gentlemen drop you into the Red Room?

RANKIN: (FRIGHTENED, NERVE IS BROKEN) No! No! I'll talk! I'll talk! I'll tell you everything…everything! Only don't throw me down there. Please—please—I'll do whatever you say—only don't throw me in there.

NORCROSS: I knew you'd see it my way, Rankin!

(SHORT MUSIC BRIDGE, MUSIC DOWN UNDER FOLLOWING)
(TRAFFIC IN B.G.) ·

NEWSBOY: Extra! Extra! Read all about it! Robbery at Seaboard Trust! Half a million dollars in cash and securities taken in haul! Police comb city for missing pay teller! Extra! (FADING) Read all about it!

(MUSIC UP FOR A MOMENT AND THEN FADE…DOOR OPENS AND CLOSES)

NORCROSS: (HEARTILY) Well! Hello, Lamont…hello Miss Lane! This is a surprise!

CRANSTON: (FADING IN) I told her that there wouldn't be anything exciting in this interview, Norcross. But she insisted on coming along!

NORCROSS: I'm glad she did. Miss Lane…to use the old, but descriptive expression… you're a sight for sore eyes!

MARGOT: Why, that's very gallant of you, Mr. Norcross. By the way, Lamont tells me you've just come back from South America.

NORCROSS: That's right.

MARGOT: I suppose you were hunting a few rare butterflies for that perfectly marvelous collection of yours …

NORCROSS: (REGRETFULLY) No. I don't have time for hobbies anymore. This was strictly business… arranging loans to some Brazilian banks. And speaking of business, Lamont, that's why I phoned you to drop in.

CRANSTON: Yes?

NORCROSS: As your financial adviser… I have bad news for you. You had a large block of negotiable securities at the Seaboard bank…and the thief got most of them last night…

CRANSTON: I see. That *is* bad news!

Bill Johnstone and Marjorie Anderson starred as Lamont Cranston and Margot Lane in "The Red Room."

NORCROSS: Oh, well…it may be just for the time being, Lamont. Of course, the police may catch Rankin, the missing pay teller, and recover your securities. But if they don't, I think the bank will ultimately have to make good on their cash value…

CRANSTON: You know, Norcross…I can't believe that Tom Rankin robbed that bank.

MARGOT: Nether can I. You see, Mr. Norcross, both Lamont and I have known Tom for years. He *couldn't* be a thief!

NORCROSS: (DRYLY) Well…I've never met the man, but I'm afraid everything points to it, Miss Lane. I dropped in at Seaboard this morning. They tell me it was a perfect inside job…

CRANSTON: (PUZZLED) I'll admit it looks bad…especially Tom's disappearing the next day.

NORCROSS: There's no question about his guilt in my mind. But getting away from the subject, Lamont…I'll list the securities you lost, and keep you posted of any progress I make…

CRANSTON: Thanks, Norcross. I'll leave the whole matter in your hands. Come on. Margot.

MARGOT: Where to?

CRANSTON: Police headquarters. I want to find out what Commissioner Weston has to say about all this!

(MUSIC BRIDGE)

NORCROSS: (UNCTUOUSLY) My congratulations on the accuracy of your information, Mr. Rankin. That affair at the bank came off…without a hitch!

NIXIE: Yeah. It was a pip!

MIKE: A cinch…all around.

RANKIN: Well…you got want you wanted. Now…let me go!

NORCROSS: (OILILY) Let you go? Surely, Mr. Rankin…you don't think me *that* stupid?

RANKIN: What do you mean?

NORCROSS: Just what I said, my friend. Wouldn't it be foolish of me to release you…so that you could go straight to the police!

RANKIN: I don't understand. What…what are you going to do with me?

NORCROSS: There's only one thing *to* do with you, Rankin. All right, boys!

(SOUND OF STRUGGLE, AD LIB: "COME ON, RANKIN!")

RANKIN: (OVER SOUND OF STRUGGLING) Take your hands off me! What…

MIKE: It's no use putting up a scrap, buddy. You're cooked…and I mean…cooked!

NIXIE: Yeah. It'll be quick and easy, Rankin…you'll never know what bit you! (LAUGHS COARSELY)

MIKE: All right, Nixie. I'll open the trapdoor. You shove him down…

RANKIN: (SCREAMS) No! No! Don't! Don't throw me down there! Don't throw me to those ants!

(SOUND OF TRAP DOOR OPENING. FADE IN: HUMMING SOUND OF ANTS)

MIKE: In you go, sucker!

RANKIN: (SCREAMING) NO! No!… (SCREAMS AGAIN)

(THEN DULL THUD OF BODY ON FLOOR BELOW. SCREAMING, AGONIZED, SOMEWHAT OFF MIKE. SONG OF ANTS RISES TO CRESCENDO, OVER AGONIZED SCREAMING)

(SCREAMING BELOW BECOMES WEAKER AND DIES UNDER HUNGRY CRESCENDO OF FEASTING ANTS)

NORCROSS: (CRUELLY) Interesting spectacle, isn't it, gentlemen?…Watching ants eat a man's flesh away to nothing but bone and gristle! In a few moments, our stubborn friend down below will be nothing but a clean skeleton. And skeletons…like dead men…tell no tales.

(SONG OF ANTS BLENDS INTO MUSIC TRANSITION)

CRANSTON: You know, Weston, this Seaboard job takes me back several years to the bank robberies Little Joe Brenza used to pull…that is, before you caught up with him.

MARGOT: Now *there* was a genius! If this Seaboard thing had happened five years ago…I'd say Brenza was behind it.

WESTON: Well, Brenza served his time and went out West…several years ago. He's been an honest citizen…ever since.

MARGOT: The straight and narrow must be pretty dull for a man of Little Joe's talents…

WESTON: Maybe. Anyway…this is an open and shut case if I ever saw one. It's obvious that Rankin did it.

CRANSTON: You're pretty sure about it, are you, Weston?

WESTON: (EXPLOSIVELY) Of course I'm sure! I can add two and two, Lamont! That pay teller pulled a smart inside job and took it on the lam. But not for long!

CRANSTON: No?

WESTON: (EMPHATICALLY) No! We expect to pick him up within forty-eight hours. I've got men at every airport, railroad terminal, bus station…

CRANSTON: (AMUSED) Can I quote you on that in my newspaper, Commissioner?

WESTON: (ABSENTLY) Of course. Furthermore, we expect… (STOPS SUDDENLY THEN ANGRILY) … All right…all right … Lamont! That isn't funny at all. Sometimes you can be an infernal nuisance!

MARGOT: (SWEETLY) Does that apply to me, too, Commissioner?

WESTON: Yes, that goes double. But now…I've got work to do. (SARCASTIC) If you'll excuse me…

CRANSTON: Tell me, Weston…I still don't see…

WESTON: (IRRITATED) Now look here, Lamont. I've heard enough. You're just trying to twist a simply criminal case into a pretzel. Now I'm a busy man and…(DOOR OPENS)

CARDONA: Say, Commissioner…

WESTON: (IMPATIENTLY) What is it, Cardona?

CARDONA: I've just come from the river…We've been dragging the bottom for the body of that escaped lunatic…

WESTON: I know. You've been on that job for three days! Did you have any luck?

CARDONA: Well…we didn't find the body. But we pulled up something else on our grappling irons…a pile of bones.

WESTON: A pile of bones? Where?

CARDONA: Just off the Eighth Street docks. They were large bones…from some big animal.

WESTON: Well…why bother me about it, Cardona? There's probably a slaughterhouse in the vicinity…

CARDONA: No, sir. The nearest slaughterhouse is way over on the North Side. And that isn't all…

WESTON: (IRRITABLY) What else is there?

CARDONA: Among that pile of animal bones, we found a human skeleton…the complete skeleton of a man.

WESTON: What!

CARDONA: Yes sir. The bones were as clean as a whistle…not an ounce of flesh on 'em…

WESTON: That just doesn't make sense…

CRANSTON: I should say it doesn't, Weston. A drowned corpse would float on top of the water. And even if it became waterlogged and finally sank…there'd still be flesh on the bones…

WESTON: Cardona…

CARDONA: Yes, Commissioner?

WESTON: Have the boys pick up those bones and bring them to the Laboratory for identification…at once!

(MUSIC TRANSITION)

NORCROSS: (FADING IN) Now, Goodrich, head pay teller at the Boulevard Bank, will be working late tonight. About nine o'clock, he'll come through the side door of the bank…and walk across Central Square to the Fourth Street subway entrance. I want you boys to pick him up before he gets to that station…and bring him here. The Red Room will take care of the rest. Is that clear?

MIKE: Yeah, Chief.

NIXIE: It ought to be a cinch.

NORCROSS: (CHUCKLES) Two or three of these little jobs…and we'll be able to retire for life on our *savings*…eh, boys?

(HE BEGINS TO LAUGH EVILLY, THEY JOIN IN. AD LIB.
"ON OUR SAVINGS, YEAH!" "THAT'S A HOT ONE, BOSS!")
(MUSIC MONTAGE)

NEWSBOY: (YELLING) Extra! Extra! Second mysterious Bark Robbery. Boulevard Bank Cleaned Out in Inside Job! Strange Resemblance to Seaboard Robbers as Police Hunt Martin Goodrich, Second Missing Pay Teller.

(FADE) Extra! Read All About It!
(MUSIC UP AT THEN FADE OUT)

CRANSTON: It's amazing…amazing. Both the Seaboard and Boulevard Banks were broken into in exactly the same way.

MARGOT: Like two peas in a pod…right down to the last detail

CRANSTON: What do you make of it, Weston?

WESTON: I think it's pretty obvious, Lamont. This fellow Marshall saw how Tom Rankin got away with that haul at Seaboard …and tried it himself.

CRANSTON: Well…I suppose that's the obvious deduction.

WESTON: (POSITIVE) It's the *only* deduction!

MARGOT: You'll pardon me if I change the subject, Commissioner. But what about those bones they found in the river?

WESTON: Well, Miss Lane, the laboratory identified the animal bones as those of parts of a cow…beef bones, you might say…

CRANSTON: (THOUGHTFULLY) Beef bones, eh? And what about the human skeleton?

WESTON: We're checking that for identification now. Here…look at this photograph…

CRANSTON: Hmmm. Interesting…

MARGOT: Why…it's a picture of teeth…teeth in the mouth of a human skull…

WESTON: Yes…We photographed the teeth of the skeleton. You can see for yourself that the deceased had some pretty complicated bridge and crown work done…

CRANSTON: Any idea who it is?

WESTON: Not at the moment. But we're sending a copy of this photo to every dentist in town in the hope that one of them might identify it…

Kenny Delmar voices Weston opposite Marjorie Anderson as Margot Lane.

CRANSTON: That's a very clever idea, Weston.

WESTON: (DRYLY) Thanks, Lamont. Coming from you…that *is* a compliment!

           (PHONE RINGS) (CLICK)

           Hello. Commissioner Weston talking…

EDWARDS: (FILTER) Commissioner…this is Dr. Harvey Edwards calling. I'm a dentist up on the North Side…

WESTON: Yes?

EDWARDS: (FILTER) I just got a copy of that photograph you sent out.

WESTON: (ALERT) Yes, Dr. Edwards?

EDWARDS: (FILTER) The bridgework done is rather unusual…and it corresponds exactly to some work I did on one of my patients.

WESTON: (GETTING EXCITED) Now were getting somewhere! Who was that patient, Doctor?

EDWARDS: (FILTER) Thomas Rankin. The bank employee you're looking for!

           (MUSIC TRANSITION)
           (MIDDLE COMMERCIAL)
           (MUSIC FADE INTO CAR ENGINE NOISE)

The 1940s Shadow cast (clockwise from top left): Keenan Wynn, announcer Ken Roberts, organist Elsie Thompson, director Wilson Tuttle, Arthur Vinton, Marjorie Anderson and Bill Johnstone

MARGOT: (SIGHS) You know, Lamont, this searching for a man who makes frequent purchases of beef sides…is like looking for a needle in a haystack. *We've* been to every meat-packing house in town! Their only customers…are butchers.

CRANSTON: I know, Margot. But we've got to keep looking. Those beef bones are our only real lead. We'll try the super meat markets next…

MARGOT: (SUDDENLY) Oh, Lamont…by the way…I almost forgot to tell you.

CRANSTON: Yes?

MARGOT: Mr. Norcross called you…but you were out. He phoned and left a message with me…

CRANSTON: What is it, Margot?

MARGOT: The Seaboard bank has promised to make good your securities…in cash…

CRANSTON: Well…I'm glad to hear that. (CAR BEGINS TO SLOW DOWN) Now, let's see…Margot. There's a big meat market over there on the corner. Let's start by inquiring there…

MARGOT: (SIGHS) Lead on, MacDuff. We'll find that beef buyer if it takes us to doomsday!

            (MONTAGE MUSIC)

BUTCHER I: Help you, sir?

CRANSTON: Yes—could you sell me a side of beef?

BUTCHER I: A whole side of beef?

CRANSTON: Yes…

BUTCHER I: Well, I can get it for you—but I'd have to call the warehouse. I haven't had an order for a whole side of beef since I've been in business.

CRANSTON: Well, don't bother—thank you just the same— Come on Margot—

            (MUSIC UP FADE DOWN HOLD UNDER)

MARGOT: Here's another one, Lamont—shall we try here?

CRANSTON: Might just as well— Come on—

            (DOOR OPEN—BELL TINKLES)

BUTCHER II:(GERMAN) Can I help you?

MARGOT: Yes, you can— Could you tell us if you have a customer who buys a side of beef regularly?

BUTCHER II:(LAUGHING) A side of beef? He must have a big family, yah— Who would buy a side of beef? Nobody in this neighborhood has that many kids.

MARGOT: Thank you— No luck here, Lamont—

CRANSTON: We'll keep on trying, Margot— Come on—

            (MUSIC UP FADE DOWN HOLD UNDER)
            (DOOR CLOSES—STREET TRAFFIC UNDER)

CRANSTON: Well—at least he didn't laugh at us—

MARGOT: No—but he didn't help us any either—

CRANSTON: Look, Margot, there's another butcher shop across the street—let's try that—

MARGOT: You know, Lamont—with all the butchers there are around here, I'd say the competition in the meat business must be pretty keen…

            (MUSIC UP FADE DOWN AND OUT)

            (SOUNDS OF MEAT MARKET. CHOPPING OF MEAT. SAWING OF BONE, ETC. OCCASIONAL CLANG OF CASH REGISTER. SLIGHT BUZZ OF VOICES) (CONTINUOUS THROUGH SCENE)

MARGOT: Well…We've been to five of these markets already. I wonder how crazy *this* butcher will think we are!

CRANSTON: I'll admit we're asking for some unusual information. It isn't everyone that buys half a cow just like that. Still...we've got to keep *trying* and (STOPS SUDDENLY) Say...Margot!

MARGOT: What is it, Lamont?

CRANSTON: I just caught a glimpse of someone in that office...in the rear of the market...as a clerk opened and closed the door...

MARGOT: Well?

CRANSTON: The man who is sitting at the desk...there happens to be an old friend of ours.

MARGOT: An old friend? Who?

CRANSTON: Little Joe Brenza...

MARGOT: (ASTONISHED) Little Joe!...Lamont...are you sure?

CRANSTON: Positive.

MARGOT: But...how could that be? Brenza's supposed to be out West. And the proprietor of this market is a Mr. Powell...

CRANSTON: He could have come east again...and he could have changed his name

**Bill Johnstone
as The Shadow**

MARGOT: What on earth is Little Joe Brenza doing...running a meat market?

CRANSTON: I don't know, Margot. But you stay here. Mr. Brenza is going to receive a visit...from The *Shadow!*

(MUSIC BRIDGE SHORT)
(DOOR OPENS AND CLOSES SOFTLY. PHONE RINGS. RECEIVER CLICK)

BRENZA: Hello. Yeah...this is Powell. Oh...hello, Nixie. Another side of *beef?* Say...this is getting to be a regular thing. Big doings tonight, eh? Well...good luck. Where do you want it delivered? Same address? Okay. I'll send a truck out with it right away.

(CLICK OF RECEIVER)

SHADOW: (LAUGHS)

BRENZA: (FRIGHTENED) What was that? Who's laughin'!

SHADOW: The voice you hear...is the voice of The Shadow!

BRENZA: The Shadow? What are you tryin' to do...kid me? There ain't any such thing...

SHADOW: (LAUGHS AGAIN) Those who break the laws of society know The Shadow...to their sorrow.

BRENZA: But where are you. I can't see you!

SHADOW: No one has ever seen me. I have the power to cloud your mind, Brenza...

BRENZA: (FEARFULLY) You...you got me wrong, Shadow. My name isn't Brenza. It's Powell!

SHADOW: (STERNLY) Don't lie to me, Little Joe. I knew you in the old days!

BRENZA: (SCARED) What do you want?

SHADOW: Who pulled the robberies at the Seaboard and Boulevard Banks?

BRENZA: (TERRIFIED) I don't know! Honest, Shadow...I don't know!

SHADOW: (INEXORABLY) It could be *you,* couldn't it, Brenza?

BRENZA: (DESPERATELY) No! No! Look, Shadow...I'm on the level, so help me! I changed my name and bought this business. I've gone straight ever since I got out of the pen. Give me a break, will you? I haven't done anything...

SHADOW: That remains to be seen. But there's one more thing. Brenza…a moment ago you received a phone call for a side of beef. Where are you going to deliver that beef?

BRENZA: (CONFUSED, FRIGHTENED) I…I…I can't tell you, Shadow!

SHADOW: Tell me the address, Brenza!

BRENZA: (PANICKY) I…I can't …!

SHADOW: (INEXORABLY) I'll give you one more chance, my friend!

BRENZA: (TERRIFIED) All right! All right! I'll tell you. It's Number four, River Street…corner of Eighth.

SHADOW: Thank you, Little Joe. You've been very helpful. But I warn you…if you have lied to me…you shall pay. Remember…The Shadow is watching you! (LAUGHS)

(MUSIC TRANSITION…INTO STEADY SINGING SOUND OF ANTS COMING FROM RED ROOM)

GOODRICH: (HOARSELY) Let me out of here! Let…me…out…of here! Those red devils…just listening to them…they're driving me insane!

MIKE: You ain't heard anything yet, Goodrich!

NIXIE: I'll say you ain't, buddy. Wait'll the Chief gets Here. You'll hear some *real* music then…

(SOUND OF DOOR OPENING AND CLOSING)

MIKE: Here he is, now.

NORCROSS: (OILILY) Good evening, Mr. Goodrich!

GOODRICH: Let me out of here…whoever you are! I've told you everything!

NORCROSS: My compliments on the accuracy of your information, Goodrich…and the forethought of your bank in keeping so much cash on hand. You have served me well!

GOODRICH: You can't do this! No!…No!…You'll pay for this.

NORCROSS: No, my friend. You will. You see…I have no further need of your services. Therefore…I must dispense with you!

GOODRICH: (HOARSELY) What do you mean?

Sidney Slon, scriptwriter of "The Red Room"

NORCROSS: (INCAUTIOUSLY) Simply this. I am going to retire you…to the Red Room! All right, boys…

GOODRICH: (AGONIZED) No! No! You're not gong to throw me to those…those…devils! You're not…

SHADOW: (LAUGHS)

MIKE: Hey! What was that?

NIXIE: (FEARFULLY) A voice. Somebody laughin'…

NORCROSS: But that's impossible. There's no one else in this room!

SHADOW: You're wrong, Norcross. The *Shadow*…is here!…Beside you!

NORCROSS: (ALMOST A WHISPER) The…Shadow? I can't see you!

SHADOW: No, Norcross, no one can see me. I've cast a hypnotic mist over your eyes.

MIKE: (FRIGHTENED) I don't get it. I can't see a thing…but I can hear him talkin'…

NIXIE: (FRANTIC) Come on, Mike. Let's get out of here!

SHADOW: Stay where you are…both of you! You'll never be able to run away…from your crimes!

(HARSHLY) *Stand where you are!*

NIXIE: (BADLY FRIGHTENED) Okay, Shadow…okay.

MIKE: (FRIGHTENED) We ain't movin', Shadow…

NORCROSS: (SNARLS) You don't think you're going to get away with this, do you, my invisible friend? (SOUND OF SHOT…THEN ANOTHER AND ANOTHER, QUICK SUCCESSION)

NORCROSS: (LAUGHS) These'll go through a*ny* ghost… (MOMENT OF SILENCE) Well, Shadow? Why don't you say something, now? Why don't you talk, eh? Why don't you talk? You can't anymore, can you? Because…*you're dead!*

SHADOW: (LAUGHS)

NIXIE: (AWED) He's still here!

MIKE: (AWED) Yeah…

SHADOW: You are a fool, Norcross. I am the one thing you cannot kill…as you have killed the others!

NORCROSS: (BREAKING, LOSING NERVE) No! No! I…it can't be...

SHADOW: It was clever of you, Norcross, to bring these ants up from Brazil and breed them here…for murder. As an amateur zoologist…you knew how deadly they were. Your greed for money, alone, was not enough to satisfy the devil in your soul.

NORCROSS: (FRIGHTENED) You can't prove a thing…not a thing!

SHADOW: Tom Rankin's body has already been identified, Norcross. And Martin Goodrich's testimony here…will send you and your henchmen…to the electric chair!

GOODRICH: Just get out me of here! I'll talk… plenty!

NORCROSS: (PASSIONATELY) They'll never get me! (VOICE MOVES OFF SLIGHTLY) They'll never take me…alive!

MIKE: Hey! The Chief's makin' a break for it!

NIXIE: (YELLS) Look out, Boss! The trapdoor to the Red Room! Look out!

(SOUND OF TRAPDOOR FLAPPING DOWN…AGONIZED SCREAM. THEN A DULL HEAVY THUD. THEN CONTINUOUS SCREAMING)

MIKE: He went right through the trapdoor! Forgot to step over it!

NIXIE: Yeah. Look! Those red devils are swarmin' all over him now!

(SOUND OF ANTS QUICKLY RISING TO CRESCEDO AND HOLD STEADY AGONIZED SCREAMS BECOME WEAKER THEN DIE)

SHADOW: Though justice moves slowly, it is as sure as life…as certain as death! (THEN SOUND OF POUNDING ON DOOR. WESTON'S VOICE OFF. "OPEN UP! OPEN UP!" "THIS IS THE POLICE!")

SHADOW: And now, gentlemen…

MIKE AND NIXIE: Yes, Shadow.

SHADOW: Goodbye. I'll leave you to the tender mercy of Commissioner Weston…and the Law! (LAUGHS)

(THERE IS THE SOUND OF SPLINTERING CRASH AS DOOR BREAKS THROUGH. LAUGHTER OF SHADOW FADES OFF)

(MUSIC TRANSITION)

CRANSTON: Lawrence Norcross was heavily in debt, Weston. He had gambled away huge sums of his client's money…and he had to make good.

MARGOT: He almost did. What about the loot, Commissioner?

WESTON: (SQUIRMING EFFECT IN DIALOGUE) We…found…it…right…on…the…premises… Not…a…dime…was missing. As for Little Joe Brenza and the others…they're going to live at the expense of the state for a long, long time. (GRUNTS)

CRANSTON So Brenza was in it up to his ears?

WESTON: Yes. Nixie Marroni's confession implicated him. That meat market was only a front. (GRUNTS) Norcross was the brains…Little Joe furnished the bank-busting technique. (GRUNTS)

CRANSTON: (HALF TO HIMSELF) So he *did* lie to me!

WESTON: What was that you said, Lamont? (GRUNTS)

CRANSTON: Oh…nothing, Weston…nothing…Just talking to myself.

MARGOT: For heaven's sake, Commissioner…what are you squirming about?

WESTON: It's those red ants, Miss Lane. We've just exterminated them with gas fumes…and I think a few of the little devils got under my skin. Anyway… I've… been… itching… all…over…for…an…hour! (GRUNTS)

CRANSTON: Well…how about having dinner with us, Weston? Maybe some good food will make you forget your troubles...

WESTON: No thanks, Lamont. I think I'll skip it…in favor of a Turkish bath!

(MUSIC UP TO FINISH)

(STANDARD CLOSING)

Announcer Ken Roberts

ANNR: The Shadow program is based on a story copyrighted by Street & Smith Publications. The characters, names, places and plot are fictitious. Any similarity to persons living or dead is purely coincidental. Next week, same time, same station, the SHADOW again will demonstrate that…

SHADOW: (FILTER) The weed of crime bears bitter fruit. Crime does not pay. The Shadow knows…(LAUGH)

(MUSIC)

ANNR: These programs are brought to you by your friendly 'blue coal' dealer. He is listed in the yellow section of your classified phone book. Help him serve you and your neighbors well this winter by sharing coal deliveries. In that way, you'll "keep the home fires burning" with 'blue coal.' This story was produced by the D.L. & W. coal company, distributors of 'blue coal.'

(MUSIC UP . . . SYSTEM CUE)

MAN OF MAGIC AND MYSTERY

Walter Brown Gibson (1897-1985) came to the Shadow freighted with a deep background in magical lore, which he poured into his Shadow novels. From his life-long friend, Thurston the Magician, Gibson gleaned deep knowledge of misdirection and the art of illusion. From Houdini, he learned breathtaking escape techniques. Dunninger taught him mentalism. Gibson also had an enduring interest in the weird and the occult, which flavored "Maxwell Grant's" mysterioso approach to things uncanny.

When Street & Smith gave him the task of bringing the sinister-voiced radio narrator to life, Gibson began with a blank slate.

"They told me to cook up a weird character to fit their idea, write a 60,000-worder and, if they liked it, they'd give me an order for three more." Amazingly, he produced nearly 300 Shadows.

Gibson's first magical pass was to turn a mere radio voice into a pulp magazine phenomenon.

"For that," he once explained, "I needed an outstanding character and I had been thinking of one who would be a mystery in himself, moving into the affairs of lesser folk, much to their amazement. By combining Houdini's penchant for escapes with the hypnotic power of Tibetan mystics plus the knowledge shared by Thurston and Blackstone in the creation of illusions, such a character would give unlimited scope when confronted by surprise situations, yet all could be brought within the range of credibility."

A master mysteryman who wore a sweeping black cloak over classic evening clothes, The Shadow developed into a sinister version of a stage illusionist who brandished twin .45 automatics instead of a magician's wand and employed Ninja stealth techniques. To this nebulous character, Gibson added certain signature elements—the penetrating deductive powers of Sherlock Holmes and a frightening presence borrowed from Count Dracula.

"The Shadow when placed in your hands was a laugh, nothing else," Doc Savage writer Lester Dent once reminded him.

In another clever feat of legerdemain, Gibson concocted his mysterious byline, Maxwell Grant, from the names of two dealers in shadow-themed magic

tricks—Maxwell Holden and U. F. Grant.

"He had the newspaperman's knack of giving you enough facts so that you wanted to read on to the next paragraph," praised Shadow editor John L. Nanovic, "and enough of the magician's flare to flash things before you long enough to intrigue you, but not give the point away."

Gibson developed his own style of pulp prestidigitation.

"Once I got the tempo of the pulps," he revealed, "I would suddenly get a new idea, like getting a new trick. If an idea came up in the course of a story, I'd lay it aside for another story."

While writing The Shadow, Gibson encountered other pulp writers—many of whom shared his lifelong love of mystification.

Richard Wormser, who graduated from writing short stories in the back of *The Shadow Magazine* to penning the exploits of Nick Carter, remarked, "Walt had a few eccentricities. For one, he never blinked; you could talk to him for hours, and his eyelids never closed.... Also, he didn't have too much faith in his new career as a novelist, and wanted to keep in shape in case he had to go back to the vaudeville stage. So, as he chatted, various things appeared and disappeared in his hands: rubber balls, knives, forks, playing cards, red roses, glasses of water colored to look like wine. He never deigned to look at these props; he just stared at you, unblinking."

"Walter's pockets were always bulging with magic paraphernalia," remembered Street & Smith mystery writer Frank Gruber. "I once kidded him into emptying his pockets and among the other items he produced eight packs of playing cards."

Gruber liked to tell the story of the day Gibson took a long subway, train and taxi trip out to his Scarsdale home during rush hour.

"Shortly after his arrival he performed a new magic trick he had just learned. The climax was changing a roll of toilet tissue into an egg, which he broke into a glass. In order to do the trick he had to bring his 'tools' with him, and I still chuckle thinking of Walter bringing that tissue and egg concealed on his person during the long trek to our place.... How he kept that egg from being smashed in his pocket, I don't know!"

Another writer who graduated from the back pages to the front was Theodore Tinsley, who shared the "Maxwell Grant" byline with Gibson. For years, Tinsley ghosted four Shadow novels a year.

"I remember him very pleasantly, mostly at parties, where after a few drinks he would snatch lighted cigarettes out of the air (with no sign of a concealed lighter) or he'd move balled-up newspapers from one hat to another in a big-hat group on the floor, to the plaudits of one and all, including me.... He loved magic so much you almost couldn't get him to quit."

"All the pulp writers knew and enjoyed Walt's magic prowess," Nanovic once said. "If discussions ever got dull at Gately's Bar and Grille, out would come the cards, the coins, the little balls; and Walt would lighten up everything."

The number of pulp writers who also dabbled in sleight-of-hand was remarkable. One was Kendall Foster Crossen. As "Richard Foster," he created one of the more intriguing Shadow imitations, the Green Lama.

"Walter Gibson and I were very good friends until we were separated by the entire country," he said in 1975. "It's difficult to do magic at that distance. But we used to meet fairly often. I don't think we ever talked about The Shadow or the Green Lama. Walter (writer and magician), Bruce Elliott (writer, editor and magician), Clayton Rawson (writer and magician), sometimes Ted Annemann (magician) and I spent many an evening together. If any of the leading magicians were playing within fifty miles of New York City, we would go at least once during the engagement. And after the show we'd all go out and find an all night cafeteria and stay there, drinking coffee and doing magic until daylight. I doubt if any of our wives appreciated it, but we did."

As "Stuart Towne," Clayton Rawson created the

Walter Gibson performs the "Hindu wands" illusion.

famed magician-sleuth Don Diavolo, aka the Scarlet Wizard. Rawson also performed professionally, Bruce Elliott was another "Maxwell Grant." He wrote The Shadow while Gibson was touring with Blackstone the Magician in 1946-47.

"I met so many nice people in the work," Gibson once remarked. "I would land in New York. And Nanovic would say, 'Gee, it's great you came in! Can you stay a couple of days? Les Dent is coming in from Missouri. Gruber's in from the Coast.' And so forth. We'd all go down to Chinatown, or a party. Or try one of those restaurants. We were all a very happy crowd because we were all selling and working up to capacity. We were all exchanging ideas, helping each other with stories."

Why did so many mystery writers dabble in sleight-of-hand?

"Magic and Mystery," Gibson once noted, "are so closely interwoven that it is hard to tell where one leaves off and the other begins."

Ken Crossen put it best, "It's just like

Theodore Tinsley and Kendall Foster Crossen

writing whodunits. You have to love to fool people."

For his many contributions to magical lore, Gibson was awarded the Master's Fellowship of the Academy of Magical Arts and Sciences in 1979. It was an honor rarely accorded to a magic historian. But it was richly deserved.

As Frank Gruber wrote in 1970, "Walter was and is, first of all, a magician, and sort of backed into writing as a profession.... Although he does not perform professionally, Walter is as good a magician as any I have ever seen on the stage. After the demise of The Shadow, Walter was at loose ends for a time, then became associated with the Great Blackstone. They came out to Hollywood, and Walter and Blackstone visited me at the studio where I was employed at the time, and, of course, both began performing tricks in my office, and we soon had a considerable audience. Blackstone was great at 'Spectaculars' on the stage but I thought Walter was much better at close-hand sleight-of-hand tricks."

"Remarkable guy," concurred Doc Savage ghostwriter Ryerson Johnson. "He wrote two a month when the other boys were doing one. A fine guy and a terrific magician. Good enough to be a professional."

Everyone who knew him seemed to recall The Shadow's raconteur as if enveloped in a mystical aura.

"Walter Gibson was a highly nervous man—who wouldn't be, turning out 100,000 words a month!" observed Gruber. "He smoked about four packs of cigarettes per day, frequently lighting one from the butt of another. But he had a tremendous amount of physical energy and was a brilliant story plotter. His talent for excellent narrative writing was equally great."

"I remember Walter as this little elf almost completely obscured by a haze of his own cigarette smoke," said Jean Francis Webb, another veteran of The Shadow's back pages, who also recalled

Harry Blackstone examines *The Bunco Book* **as publisher Sid Radner and author Walter Gibson look on.**

that Gibson's lap was usually piled high with gray ashes from the numerous cigarettes he chain-smoked—and juggled—in those storied Depression days.

Tall and lean, Gibson was not an elf except perhaps in spirit. But some, looking back on his heyday, seemed to see it through some ultra-nostalgic haze.

It was Ted Tinsley who later reminisced, "Pulpland seems a strange, purple-clouded island, in a warm sea somewhere far off, where some of the damndest elfs and goblins I ever met used to say and do the strangest things, especially when drunk."

Magic and mystery forever permeated the pages of The Shadow—thanks to the greatest magician of the pulps, Walter B. Gibson.   —Will Murray

From left: Walter Gibson and magic friends George Karger, Mrs. Gibson, Bill Neff, Mr. and Mrs. Joe Karson, Mrs. Ross, Miss Margaret Gibson and Jerry Ross.